The ancient wisdom of astrology and the magic of modern technology merge in a suspense-filled novel of political intrigue. Set in the year 2006, *The President's Astrologer* takes its readers from the power-filled corridors of Washington, D.C. to the sun-bleached mesas of New Mexico, as its astrologer-heroine uncovers the shocking secret behind the vice president's mysterious birth certificate.

ABOUT THE AUTHOR

Barbara Shafferman is a writer who discovered astrology in 1972 and embarked on what she calls "a lifetime study." She has taught astrology in adult education classes, currently lectures at libraries and high schools, and has written more than forty articles for *American Astrology* and *Horoscope* magazines. Her short stories have appeared in magazines as varied as *Potpourri, Mystery Time* and *Grand Times,* and in the anthology *Reader's Break.*

TO WRITE TO THE AUTHOR

If you wish to contact the author or would like more information about this book, please write to the author in care of Llewellyn Worldwide, and we will forward your request. Both the author and publisher appreciate hearing from you and learning of your enjoyment of this book and how it has helped you. Llewellyn Worldwide cannot guarantee that every letter written to the author will be answered, but all will be forwarded. Please write to:

Barbara Shafferman
Llewellyn Worldwide Ltd.
P.O. Box 64383, Dept. K674–2, St. Paul, MN 55164-0383, U.S.A.

Please enclose a self-addressed, stamped envelope for reply, or $1.00 to cover costs.
If outside U.S.A., enclose international postal reply coupon.

BARBARA SHAFFERMAN

THE
PRESIDENT'S
ASTROLOGER

1998
Llewellyn Publications
St. Paul, Minnesota, 55164-0383, U.S.A.

FIRST EDITION
First Printing, 1998

Cover design by Lisa Novak
Cover photo: Digital Stock, Washington, D.C. collection
Editing and interior design by Connie Hill

Library of Congress Cataloging-in-Publication Data
Shafferman, Barbara, 1928–
    The president's astrologer / Barbara Shafferman. — 1st ed.
    p.   cm.

    ISBN 1–56718–674–2 (trade paper)
    1. Title.
PS3569.H3116P74   1998
813'.54—dc21   98-42517
                                                    CIP

The President's Astrologer is a work of fiction. Any resemblance to events or persons living or dead is purely coincidental.

Llewellyn Publications
A Division of Llewellyn Worldwide, Ltd.
St. Paul, Minnesota 55164-0383, U.S.A.

Printed in the U.S.A.

To my parents,
in memory of their unconditional
love and support.

For your enlightenment, astrological charts of the president and vice president are featured on page 375. If you would like to know more about this fascinating subject please refer to pages 376–378 for information about books and other products or services dealing with astrology.

CHAPTER ONE

On a rainy April morning in the year 2006, life came stalking Addie Pryce. She had kept it at a safe distance for so long that she hardly recognized it.

Washington, D.C. was the perfect city for a thirty-seven-year-old astrologer to hide from life. People were too mesmerized by their own egos and preoccupied with their own careers to bother with those who preferred to remain aloof. That suited Addie fine. Twelve-hour days dealing with other people's troubles wrapped her in a cocoon of work that insulated her from her own problems.

Until today. Addie walked over to the window and stared outside. Through sheets of driving rain, she watched the two men who had just left her apartment hurry into a waiting limousine. She had never seen them before today. Now it seemed she had known them forever.

Addie had been studying the chart of a prosperous businessman in preparation for his eleven o'clock appointment, when the telephone interrupted her. She frowned and picked it up. It was Peter Samson, her 11:00. Her frown deepened. He must be calling to cancel.

"Sorry to give you such short notice," he said. "I won't be coming today."

"I wish you'd called earlier. I could have given your time to another client." She tried to keep the annoyance out of her voice.

"No, you couldn't have. Someone else is coming."

"I can't discuss your chart with anyone but you. You know that."

"It's not about me at all. Some friends want to see you, and I let them have my time."

"Peter, you can't do that—make appointments for me." She clutched the phone tightly. "I won't have strangers just wandering in off the street."

"Look Addie, this is important. These people will be at your place around eleven. I'll call you later to reschedule."

A sharp click ended the call. Addie replaced Samson's chart in its folder and slammed it on the desk. How dare he do a thing like that! He was a prestigious client, but that gave him no right to play games with her. How typical of a certain type of Aquarius: a mind so fixed on its own agenda that he ignored other people's feelings. She'd make Peter Samson squirm before he got another appointment.

Addie closed her eyes. Although ten years had passed, she could feel the old pain sweeping over her. She knew she was smart and resourceful. Look how quickly she had become one of the top astrologers in Washington. She knew men found her desirable with her classic features, thick black hair, and luminous, startlingly blue eyes. She had caught some of her clients' furtive, sidelong glances. Yet whenever something like Samson's stunt happened, something that made her feel weak and powerless, all her hard-won self-assurance vanished. The old Addie of ten years ago would surface: a trembling, twenty-seven-year-old, betrayed wife who had vowed *never* to let any man take advantage of her again.

She looked at the flashing numerals on her lucite desk clock and sighed. Too late to do anything but wait for the mysterious callers.

The downstairs buzzer sounded at 10:55, five minutes early. Addie hesitated for a moment, then hit the security button. Two faces appeared on the screen embedded in the door. One looked vaguely familiar: a high, domed forehead above earnest, thoughtful eyes and a generously rounded chin. She didn't recognize the other man's face at all, with its mass of unruly brown hair and boyish good looks.

Addie pressed the door release and crossed the room quickly to her computer. "15 April 2006, 10:55 A.M., Washington, D.C." she said into the microphone. Instantly, a chart, mapping the positions of the planets, appeared on the screen. Before she could study it, the entry sensor beeped in response to approaching footsteps. "Print," she said, and the printer whirred quietly into action.

Addie hit one of the buttons embedded in the frame of a Monet landscape print that hung near her desk, and the door opened slowly. Two men stood there, one almost a head taller than the other. The taller man walked in first and extended his hand.

"I apologize for the surprise," he said. "Peter Samson was kind enough to give us his appointment. I'd better introduce us. I'm Walter Turner, and this is Jonah Stern."

Now Addie knew who he was. She had seen his picture often in the newspapers, some sort of political adviser, one of D.C.'s very important people. She ignored his outstretched hand.

"I don't like surprises," she said.

"Sometimes they can be very nice," the other man, Stern, said. "May we come in and sit down?"

He smiled, but looked at Addie as though his alert, hazel eyes were examining some strange specimen. She smoothed her hair and felt loose strands already escaping from the band that held it in place. With a shrug, she led them into the living room.

Turner looked around, surveying the room. He stopped before a glass-enclosed cabinet and peered inside at Addie's collection of pewter, china, and crystal unicorns.

"Very unusual," he said, "Very attractive. How did you manage to find so many?"

"Wherever I go, I seem to meet unicorns looking for a home."

Turner smiled. "Looks like they've found a good one here."

"I hope so." Addie gestured toward the couch. "Please sit down—Mr. Turner, Mr. Stern."

Turner pushed aside a pillow and settled his long frame on the floral-print sofa. Stern sank down beside him, and Addie perched on the edge of a straight-backed chair across from them.

"This is a very personal matter," Turner said, "so I think we should get on a first name basis right away. We're Walter and Jonah. I hope you don't mind if we call you Addie."

"I suppose not Mr.—umm—Walter. I'm not much of a mystery fan. Exactly what is this all about?"

"Let's see." Turner pressed his fingertips together. "Where do I start?"

"The beginning is usually a good place."

"Ah, but that's not so clear here. I think we'd better just jump into the heart of the matter."

"By all means." Addie picked up a pencil and pad from the long wooden table between the sofa and chair.

"I'm representing a friend," Turner said, "A very good friend—a very important friend—who'd like to engage your services."

"I told you, I don't like mysteries. And I don't have much time for new clients right now."

"Would you refuse the president?"

The pencil made a hollow clunk as it fell from Addie's limp fingers onto the table.

"The president! You mean the President of the United States?"

Turner nodded.

"But why would he—I mean, what does he—?"

"There are a lot of people out there who don't exactly have the president's interests at heart. He wants to find out whom he can trust, the best times to take action—things like that. He thinks astrology can help him."

"That's a big responsibility. I don't know if I want to take on something like that."

Turner leaned forward and gazed at her searchingly. "Look, Addie, there's top security involved here. Before we go any further, I have to know if you would consider working for the president?"

"How can I give you a quick yes or no answer? I have to think about it. Besides, I'm not sure I want to know any secret information. What makes you think I'm such a great security risk?"

"Oh, we did a complete check on you. You might be interested to know that you passed with flying colors."

"Yes," Jonah Stern said. "In spite of your—umm—exotic profession, your life is amazingly routine."

Addie wheeled around to face Stern; she had almost forgotten he was there. His voice had a light, amused tone that annoyed her.

"What did you expect? Secret meetings with aliens from outer space?"

"No offense intended." Stern cleared his throat. "You have to admit your work's a little unusual, and I thought you'd be—"

"You thought I'd be wearing flowing robes and a pointy hat. How disappointing to see my working outfit—just slacks and a shirt. You know, your views are a little out of date."

"I think I'd better apologize for Jonah," Turner said. "He's a deputy press secretary for the president, but he used to be a science writer for the *New York Times*. I'm afraid he's spent too much time among the data hunters and too little time developing his spiritual side."

"And you?" Addie looked at Turner.

"Oh, I've lived long enough to know that anything's possible. I'm totally ambivalent on the subject." He stretched his long legs under the table. "My wife's the expert, as a matter of fact. She's interested in the whole esoteric scene. You may know of her—Janice Durand?"

"The novelist?"

Turner nodded.

"Of course. I love her books. They have a beautiful spiritual quality. I didn't know—"

"She writes under her maiden name. Says it helps her maintain her identity. So I'm familiar with these ideas by osmosis. I don't know anything about astrology, but I do know it's gaining a lot of supporters."

"Yes, it's more respectable these days—certainly more than when I started, back in the nineties. Though we still have a lot of skeptics." Addie looked at Stern. "Obviously, President Wycliff doesn't share *your* opinion."

"No," Stern said, "I guess not. And that brings us back to why we're here. What do you say, Addie. Is it a 'go'?" An infectious grin spread over his face. Addie forced herself not to smile back.

"I've got to know more before I can give any answer. I've got lots of questions."

"Fire away."

She looked at Turner. "How do you figure in all this, Walter—officially I mean?"

He smoothed the sleeve of his charcoal pinstriped suit. "Officially, I'm a minister without portfolio. I don't have any title. I'm the president's personal attorney, old friend, trusted adviser. Let's just call me the guy who knows where all the bodies are buried."

"Why does President Wycliff want me?"

Turner nodded. "He's heard a lot about you and he's eager to have you come aboard. Astrology interests him. You know, it's not public knowledge, but he consulted an astrologer occasionally when he was governor of Maryland."

"Why doesn't he use her?"

"Him—it's a him. The guy moved to Utah, and this wouldn't work long distance."

"No, I guess not. Exactly what would be expected of me?"

Turner stood up and walked to the window. He looked out for a moment, then turned back. "That's the hard part. You'd have to put your practice on hold and devote yourself entirely to the president. He wants you on call at all times. You'd be paid well, of course."

"Hmmm. Well, it would be prestigious." Addie said. "I guess that might make up for lost clients."

Turner frowned and his thoughtful brown eyes showed concern. "The thing is—this whole business has to be kept secret. Look, we know you're a solid citizen, Addie. But we can't have the country aware that the president is using astrology. It would make him seem weak, irresolute—even, I'm afraid, somewhat unstable."

"If you remember," Turner continued, "back in the eighties, it came out that President Reagan was using an astrologer. He took a lot of flak for that."

"He developed Alzheimer's, didn't he? Maybe that was the first sign." Stern looked at Addie and winked. "Sorry. I couldn't resist that."

Addie glared at him. "As I recall, it was his wife who consulted the astrologer. And she had possession of all her faculties."

"But look at the picnic the press had ten years ago, when President Clinton's wife started taking advice from dead people."

"For your information, Jonah, astrology doesn't deal with spirits. We look at the positions of the planets, precisely calculated." She pointed to her computer. "Then we make our judgments."

"Judgments! See, that's what I mean."

"Jonah, be quiet. You're not here to voice your opinion." Turner looked at Addie. "I only mentioned Reagan to show you the public's attitude—why we have to keep you secret."

"I see," Addie said. "I'm supposed to give up everything I've worked for all these years—lurk in the shadows, like some backstreet quack. I've worked hard to build a reputation and a clientele. I can't chuck it all, just like that."

"But think of what you'd be doing, working with a world leader. And when his term is over, there'd be no need for secrecy. You could write books, lecture—whatever."

"Exactly how do you plan to keep me secret?"

"See, that's where I come in," Stern said. "I'm an expert at keeping things out of the public eye. You know, people think press aides spend all their time getting people into the papers. The truth is I spend most of my time keeping the president out of the papers. That's why I'm here. I've gotta know what's happening." He laughed. "Or not happening, if you catch my drift."

"Hmm—I guess you're a necessary evil," Addie said.

"Necessary, yes. Only moderately evil."

Addie smiled faintly. "Well, I think I've got a pretty good picture now."

"And how do you feel?" Turner asked.

"Oh, part of me is flattered. No, it's more than flattered—thrilled—that the president of the United States wants *my* services. Then a part of me is sickened by the feeling of being used, of being turned into some kind of shadow."

She leaned forward, hugging herself. "But there's something else—I'm scared. There's so much going on that I don't know about. And—I don't know—somehow I think what you're asking me to do is dangerous. I'm not the heroine type."

"You've been watching too many movies," Stern said. "You'll simply be a staff member—an adviser, without a title."

"I've got to have time to think about it."

"I was hoping I could take your answer to the president today," Turner said. "But, I understand. How about if I call you Monday morning—day after tomorrow. Would that give you enough time?"

Addie nodded and stood up, anxious to end the meeting.

Turner shook her hand firmly. "One more thing," he said. "You understand the need for secrecy. We—and the president—would appreciate your not mentioning this meeting to anyone."

"I understand."

"All right, then. I'll be in touch on Monday. I hope you'll have a 'yes' for us then." He turned and headed for the door.

Stern rose and joined him. He was just a little taller than Addie, and his gray jacket seemed too big at the shoulders and too long at the wrists, giving him the look of an overgrown boy wearing his big brother's clothes. At the door, he turned back to her, grinning. "No hard feelings, I hope."

"No," Addie had said, smiling in spite of herself, "No hard feelings."

Addie stood at the window, staring out at the rain, long after the limousine sped away. An adviser, Stern had said...an adviser to the president of the United States. But without a title. Oh, I'd have a title, all right, Addie thought. I'd be the president's astrologer.

CHAPTER TWO

Addie rubbed her eyes and watched the sun streaming through the blinds form patterns on the wall. Damn, she must have overslept. She sat up and saw her bedside clock flashing 10:07.

Luckily it was Sunday, and she had no appointments.

The shower's stinging needles jolted Addie awake. She pulled on a pair of blue pants and a white shirt with blue and purple embroidered flowers. Her thick black hair, damp from the shower, fell in a straight cascade to her shoulders. She tied it back with a purple ribbon.

In the kitchen she heated coffee, put a slightly stale bun in the microwave, and swallowed two energy-enhancer pills. No wonder she'd overslept. All afternoon and evening she had buried herself in work, but thoughts of that morning meeting with Turner and Stern kept crowding into her mind. It had been difficult to concentrate and then impossible to sleep. At 5 A.M. she had finally slipped into a coma-like slumber.

Addie turned on the radio, sipped her coffee, and listened to the news. President Wycliff was meeting with Premier D'Arbenois, the newly elected head of the Eurotrade Organization. To think she might play a part in this, no matter how small! But would the changes in her life be worth it?

She finished her coffee, wiped up some stray crumbs, and walked over to the work area in the living room. The chart she had done yesterday for the time of the meeting lay on her desk, already worn from handling. Addie picked it up and frowned. She was too involved to be objective. In spite of the need for secrecy, she had to have another opinion. As always, whenever she was confused or troubled, she called Livonia Matthews.

Livonia had been Addie's salvation when she arrived in Washington ten years ago, weighed down with the debris of her broken marriage. She had sought out Livonia, one of Washington's top astrologers, for a reading. She left that reading determined to learn all she could about astrology. Her relationship with Livonia had blossomed from client to student to close friend.

After a year and a half of study, Livonia had pushed Addie out of the nest, declaring her ready to practice on her own. Five years later, when Livonia retired at the age of eighty, she transferred the bulk of her clients to Addie. She missed her work, however, and welcomed Addie's frequent calls for advice.

Addie picked up her old-fashioned voice phone and punched in Livonia's number. People wondered why she didn't own a video phone. It was one of her idiosyncrasies. Addie preferred to see her clients' charts before she saw their faces. Livonia answered at the first ring, and Addie pictured her old mentor, head thrown back and gray eyes twinkling with excitement as she listened to Addie's story. They made arrangements to meet at Livonia's apartment that afternoon.

The Yoshino cherry trees in the little park near Addie's building were blooming. On her way to the station she paused to admire them, savoring the pale pink blossoms. Just in front of her a white car pulled into a parking space. Strange, she had noticed one exactly like it, with the same three narrow red stripes along its side, parked in front of her building.

Addie continued walking. As she crossed the street to enter the station, she saw the same white car double-parked in back of her. Could someone be following her?

At the ticket machine, she looked suspiciously at the people waiting in line. They seemed a harmless bunch. Jonah Stern was right; she had been watching too many movies. She climbed the stairs and boarded the new high-speed monorail train that connected her neighborhood with downtown Washington. When she left the station, she looked both ways. No white car with red stripes in sight.

Livonia lived in the Watergate, an apartment complex that had once symbolized the height of luxury and power, but had begun to show a slight seediness that belied its elegant past. Addie crossed the beige-tiled lobby, walked over to the security desk and gave her name. The concierge scanned a list in front of him. With a bored look, he announced her.

Whenever Addie entered Livonia's apartment, she experienced a feeling of security, savoring its clutter and warmth. Livonia, a Taurus, possessed that sign's insatiable appetite for collecting.

Tables covered with fringed shawls displayed a wealth of eclectic objects. Statues mingled with giant chunks of crystal;

a silver samovar presided over an ivory chess set; lamps with colorful shades illuminated clusters of artfully carved animals.

And everywhere, there were books. Shelves sagged under the weight of them; they ranged from astrology to philosophy to popular fiction. Magazines were stacked in racks and on low shelves.

Livonia, elegant as always, wore a long brocaded skirt and chiffon blouse. Her hair formed a silver sculpture around her face. She took Addie's hands in hers and gazed at her, head cocked to one side.

"Well, Addie. I see you're casual as usual."

Addie glanced down at her slacks and shirt. She smiled, slipping easily into the role of dowdy student deferring to an elegant teacher.

"I've got more important things on my mind than clothes, Livonia."

"Sit down and let's take a look at that chart of yours." Livonia waved her to the couch, sweeping a stuffed lioness and her three cubs to one side.

"Here's the chart," Addie said. "It's cast for the moment they came to my apartment. I know I can't be objective about it. I need your advice."

"That's what I'm here for," Livonia said with a smile.

"You know, I shouldn't even be here." Addie chewed her lip and frowned. "It's supposed to be a secret. I broke the rules already, just by telling you."

"You know your secret is safe with me. The confidences I've heard over the years—none of them have ever left this room."

Livonia picked up the chart of the meeting and studied it. Only the ticking of her three antique clocks broke the silence. When she looked up, she smiled at Addie.

"I think the Moon tells the story, don't you? It rules the ascendant and it's so favorably placed, so close to Jupiter and trine Venus. I think you would benefit from it, Addie. I really do."

"I thought so, too. But I can't trust my judgment here."

"You know—that Moon in the fifth house. Someone's going to have a romantic encounter."

Addie laughed. "Not me. I don't think I'm the president's type."

Livonia shook her head. "Well, I don't know. That Moon—it's beautiful—except for that square it makes to Neptune. There's something deceptive there."

"Yes, I worried about that. Maybe it shows all this secrecy."

"That might be. How about that Saturn in the second house? It looks like some kind of financial loss."

"That describes it perfectly." Addie tapped that part of the chart with her finger. "They said I have to give up all my clients. They'll be paying me. But it will never match what I'm making now."

"Well, I think there'd be a benefit from all this that outweighs the money. The one thing that really troubles me is that twelfth house Mars. And it opposes Pluto. There's something going on behind the scenes. Some kind of violence brewing."

"I don't like that Mars either. It frightens me." Addie shivered. "It's in its fall. And it's working against everything else in the chart. I wonder what—or who—it symbolizes."

Livonia shrugged. "That's the trouble with the twelfth house. It's the hidden part of the chart, and all our guessing won't help."

Addie sat back and looked at Livonia. "So, what do you think?"

"I think there may be some uncomfortable times, but it should be fascinating."

"Then you think I should do it?"

"Nobody can tell you that. I'm only interpreting the chart. You have to make that decision yourself. Whatever you decide, I'm proud of you. Just think—the president of the United States wants to hire you. I guess I was a pretty good teacher."

Livonia closed her eyes and leaned her head back against the couch. Addie had never seen her look so tired. She always had so much energy.

"Are you feeling all right?" she asked.

"Just a little weary. I'm afraid my age is starting to show."

Addie frowned. A world without Livonia could not even be contemplated. "Nonsense, Livonia," she said. "You're ageless. But I have to be getting back anyway, so I'll leave you in peace. Thanks for your wisdom."

"Come on, Addie. I didn't tell you anything you didn't already know."

"But you confirmed it. You know, things always sound more authentic when you say it."

Livonia smiled with delight. "What would I do without you to bolster my ego. Now go on home and make your decision."

Addie hated to leave the warm security of Livonia's apartment. On the ride home, her fingers beat a tattoo on the window as she watched the setting sun cast long shadows over the buildings. Just before the train reached her station, a calmness, together with a feeling of inevitability, swept over her. Addie closed her eyes and smiled to herself. Deep down, she had known what her answer would be from the very beginning. She would do it.

Turner called as promised, early the next morning. After she gave him her answer, things happened quickly. Within an hour, three Secret Service agents arrived at her apartment. They walked through all the rooms, taking notes. Then they unpacked long rods that glowed faintly at the tips and swept the apartment, opening drawers and poking in closets, searching for listening devices. They spent extra time going over the phone, the fax, and even her computer.

"Everything's clean," announced the man in charge, a no-nonsense type whose broad shoulders made his body seem top-heavy. He walked over to Addie and handed her a watch on a leather strap.

"Here's your radiophone," he said. "It's embedded under the watch face. The White House can reach you at any time. It's just to make contact though—not for long conversations—too easy for people to monitor them."

Addie strapped it on her wrist. She'd heard about this, but had never seen one. As she stared at it, it began to beep.

"We're testing it," the agent said. "Sam's calling from the other room. Push this little knob."

Addie did as he said, and a man's voice came through the tiny speaker with amazing clarity.

"Answer, please," the voice said. Addie spoke into the watch and was rewarded with "I read you loud and clear."

The agent nodded with satisfaction. "Good. It's working fine. Better keep it on whenever you leave your place. Oh—and here's your White House pass. It's a computerized I.D. that will get you past the guard. Hope you don't mind—we used your license photo. It's not very flattering."

He looked around the apartment. "That does it then. We'll be off." They left as quickly as they had come.

Addie picked up her list of clients and sat down at the phone. Turner had suggested that she tell them she was taking a sabbatical from her practice to work on a book. She had just finished her third call, when the radiophone on her wrist began to beep. She pressed the knob, and heard Jonah Stern's voice.

"Hi, Addie. I'm testing out your new toy. Am I coming through all right?"

"Yes. Can you hear me?"

"Clear as a bell. Listen, you're due at the White House tomorrow at 10:00. Okay?"

"That soon? Where do I go?"

"To the North Portico. Someone will meet you there. Don't forget to bring your pass. You'll need it to get through the gate."

He was gone. Just like that. And tomorrow *she* was going to the White House.

CHAPTER THREE

H ello, Mr. Stern."
Jonah smiled at the pretty young data processor. She'd been putting herself in his way a lot lately. He turned and watched her figure disappear down the hall, admiring how her ass wiggled. Maybe he'd give her a try.

Jonah hurried down the West Wing corridor. He had counted on being first at the meeting. He liked the subtle advantage it always gave him, but a phone call had delayed him, and now he was late. Jonah turned to the right into a narrow corridor and opened a door at the end.

Walter Turner and the astrologer, Addie Pryce, were already seated on a couch at the far end of the room, deep in conversation.

Walter stood up when he saw him."Jonah, what happened to you? I was just telling Addie how punctual you are."

"I was on the phone with Brewster from the *Post*. Do you know him?"

"Sure, I know him. What's he after?"

"A fishing expedition. He's sniffing around for dirt on the roboplane business."

"Let him sniff, the damn buzzard. Always circling wherever he smells some carrion. Anyway, no harm done. The president's going to be a little late, so we've got plenty of time."

They exchanged glances. Jonah knew what "a little late" meant: Wycliff was having a last-minute meeting with the bottle.

Walter turned to Addie. "Please excuse me. Now that Jonah is here, he can fill you in. I have things to do before the president gets here."

Jonah stared at Addie. She looked different than he remembered. She was wearing a powder blue suit that accentuated her large, extraordinary sapphire eyes. Funny he hadn't noticed them before. Her black hair hung loosely to her shoulders, making her look younger—a lot younger than her thirty-seven years. And her short skirt revealed legs that should never be hidden under pants. She cradled a large gray briefcase on her lap.

Jonah smiled at her. "I guess I'll sub for Walter. Actually, it's good we have this time to talk. We'll be working together and I want us to be on the same wavelength."

Addie's eyes swept over the small room, resting on the table and chairs squeezed into one corner and the prints of Washington scenes on the far wall.

"Somehow I didn't picture anything this—umm—cozy."

"Well, this is one of the rooms we keep tucked away for small, private meetings."

"I see. You know, I didn't expect to be meeting in the oval office, but this..." Addie gestured around the room. "It doesn't seem very presidential."

Jonah found himself apologizing. "Don't feel that you're being swept into a corner, Addie. We wanted to keep this meeting as intimate as we could and—"

"And as far away from everyone else as possible, right?"

Jonah smiled. He liked the way she cut right through the crap. Her directness was a refreshing change from the usual Washington games.

"We did tell you that secrecy was top priority, remember."

"I know. But I wish it could be different."

Addie frowned, and little lines crept across her forehead. There was something about those worry lines that made Jonah want to smooth them away. She seemed vulnerable suddenly, as though a swath had been cut through her prickly defenses.

"It's gonna be fine," he said. He touched her shoulder lightly and sat down beside her on the couch, handing her a black notebook.

"Here's some stuff I pulled together for you. Basically, it's a working list of some of the main players around the president—the people he deals with every day. There's a photo and a little bio on each one, and a description of what they do. An inside slant on life at the White House."

Addie opened the notebook, and he moved closer. "Here, let me go over it with you while we wait."

Addie looked at the first page, at the photograph of a handsome man with chiseled features and a charismatic smile.

"Oh, that's Simon Furst," she said.

"Yes, our estimable vice president. You won't see much of him. The president doesn't like to have him around."

Jonah flipped a few pages. "Here's someone you probably won't recognize: Senator Andrew Granit from New Mexico. The vice president is his boy. Doesn't make a move without

Granit's blessing. And here's my boss, the president's press secretary, Martin Shaw."

Addie closed the notebook and looked at Jonah. "Very interesting, but I need a lot more."

He winked. "Ask and it shall be yours."

"Walter just told me that the president wants me to make up astrological charts for everyone he considers important—the people he wants to know about. Walter's going to go over the list with you. I'm going to need birth information for all these people as soon as possible. And I mean exact information: date, time, place. It has to be straight from the birth records. I'm sure with your resourcefulness, you won't have any trouble getting it."

"You really need all that?"

"Look, if I'm going to do this job, I have to do it right. And I'll need the same information for you and Walter too."

"You're going to keep tabs on us?"

Addie smiled. "Especially on you."

Jonah walked over to the window and looked out through the half-opened blinds. He watched two pigeons pecking on the ground, their heads bobbing in concerted rhythm.

"You know Addie," he said, "You don't want to go overboard on this."

"Exactly what do you mean?" He could feel her defenses springing up around her again like thick hedges.

"Well, it's just...see, getting all those birth records might start someone wondering, and we don't want anything about this to leak out."

She stared at him. "I don't think that's all that's bothering you."

"No, you're right. I think this whole thing is getting out of hand." He clenched his fists.

"I don't understand."

"Look, the president is on shaky ground right now. A lot of people are on his case, and he needs all the support he can get. Well, if he wants a little help from the stars, that's fine with me. Build up his confidence—tell him everything's going to turn out fine, But I don't think you should start drawing up astrological dossiers on everyone in sight."

"Do you think that's what this is all about?" Addie jumped up, her body shaking. "Did you really think I was giving up all my work—everything I consider important—just to hold the president's hand and invent things to make him feel better?"

"Isn't that what you people really do?" Jonah's words fell like hard little marbles between them.

"I don't think I'll be able to work with you, Mr. Stern." Addie's voice dripped icicles. "You may be a genius at information and misinformation. But you don't have the faintest idea of what I'm about."

"Come on, Addie. Don't be so sensitive. We're gonna *have* to work together, so—"

There was a knock on the door and it swung open. Walter entered, followed by the President of the United States.

Henry Ambrose Wycliff, forty-fourth President of the United States, stood in the doorway, surveying the room before he entered.

Addie's heart pounded at her first sight of the president. Parts of her hasty research flashed through her mind. A moderate Republican...political science professor at Johns Hopkins...twice elected Governor of Maryland...three published books on the social problems of early twentieth-century America...brilliant mind...able to communicate easily on any level.

Wycliff was followed into the room by a tall man in a blue, double-breasted suit and striped tie. The man walked over to the window and leaned against the wall. Addie guessed he was Secret Service.

The president crossed the room to Addie and shook her hand. "I've been looking forward to meeting you."

"Thank you, sir," Addie said.

In person, Wycliff did not appear very presidential. He was shorter than Addie, no more than five-feet-six, and looked older than his sixty-one years. His gray-flecked hair was combed carefully straight across the top of his head to cover the bald spot underneath. A patterned red sweater, worn over an open-necked shirt, concealed wide hips and a thickening waist. Narrow shoulders and rimless bifocals completed the impression of a man more at home in a library than embroiled in political combat.

When Addie had cast Wycliff's chart, she sensed some of his problems. He was a Gemini, with that sign's quick wit and sharp intellect. Mercury, the planet of communication, dominated the chart and its influence was evident in his masterful speeches.

His eloquent inaugural address was still being quoted. But there were few indications of the toughness and strength needed by a president. The driving ambition was there, but the chart was somehow unfocused, lacking much of the strength and leadership Addie had anticipated. She worried most about Neptune's difficult placement, which hinted at unrealistic ideas and possible addictions.

"Let's sit down and talk." Wycliff led Addie to the couch and sat down beside her. "I'm sure you have a lot of questions."

"I—I don't quite know where to begin," Addie said. "I guess the most important thing is—umm—exactly what do you want me to do? Just what is it that you're looking for in astrology?"

"Well, of course I want to learn more about myself—like everyone else, I guess. I want to know precisely what my chart shows about me."

"We'll need a private session for that."

"Why, is it that bad?"

Addie smiled. "Not at all. But I don't want to be inhibited in what I say, and neither do you." She glanced at the Secret Service man standing in the corner.

"Addie, this is Bruce Hanover," Walter said. "He'll be the only person on duty whenever you see the president. Bruce is the soul of rectitude and a specialist in keeping his ears closed and his eyes open."

Hanover smiled and nodded to Addie. Then he turned back to the window, seemingly absorbed in something outside.

"I guess that will be acceptable," Addie said.

"I also need descriptions of the people around me," the president continued. "I want to know what you, as an astrologer, see about them. What they're really like. I have a lot of friends, but I also have a lot of enemies."

Addie nodded.

"You'll get a list of everyone I want you to research. We'll rely on Jonah to get you their correct birth data and anything else you need."

Addie glanced at Jonah, her lips curving upward in a small smile of triumph. He returned her gaze and shrugged his shoulders.

"Most importantly," Wycliff continued, "I want you to work out some kind of timetable for me. I've got so many meetings to attend, so many things to do. Sometimes it can be over-whelming. I plan to give you a list and I want you to come up with the best times. I can't promise I'll always follow your timetable, but I need to have it."

"I understand," Addie said. "The biggest problem I can see is that as I'm working, a lot of questions may come up. What kind of access will I have?"

"Jonah is your immediate line of communication. Call him on his direct line at the White House with any questions, and he'll get the answer back to you as soon as he can. Right Jonah?"

Jonah nodded.

"If you can't reach him," Wycliff continued, "call Walter. He'll be able to answer all your questions. And he can contact me, if necessary."

"That should be fine," Addie said. "I think I understand exactly what you want, Mr. President. But there is one thing. I wonder why you decided to—I mean it's unusual for someone in your position..."

"You want to know exactly why I decided to consult an astrologer, correct?"

Addie nodded.

"I've always felt there are matters beyond our temporal knowledge. Hidden behind a veil, if you will, but waiting to be discovered. I want that knowledge. I'm hoping astrology can provide some of it. The pressures around me..." he closed his eyes, "I need all the help I can get."

"I'll try to do all I can," Addie said.

"All right then." Wycliff leaned forward and took Addie's hand in his. "I believe this will be very rewarding. I'm sure of it."

He stood up, then turned back. "Oh, one more thing. I hope you understand the need for discretion. Not everyone feels the way I do about astrology. Our relationship would give my enemies, who at this point seem legion, one more weapon to use against me."

Addie frowned. "But will you really be able to keep it secret? There'll have to be a lot of contact…"

"I have every confidence in Jonah to accomplish that."

"We're gonna give you some sort of title after all, Addie," Jonah said. "I haven't decided what it'll be, but something to get you access without causing suspicion."

Wycliff looked at his watch and patted his stomach. "I'm late for a luncheon appointment, so I'll have to say goodbye. Come along and keep me company, Walter. There are some things I want to discuss with you." He looked at Addie. "How long will it take you to prepare for that private session?"

"A day or two."

"Good. Walter will arrange something. Goodbye, then."

Walter and the Secret Service man followed President Wycliff from the room. Addie and Jonah were alone again.

"Well," Addie said, "the president doesn't seem to share *your* cavalier attitude toward astrology. He wants you to get the birth data for charts on everyone—which, if you recall, was exactly what I told you I would need."

Jonah gave her a placating look. "Addie, I'm sorry if I hurt your feelings before. You have to understand…."

"I don't think we have anything to discuss. You said what you thought."

Jonah shrugged. "All right, madam. Tell me what you need. I'm at your service."

"I'm going to have to work quickly. I'll need exact birth data on everyone—date, time, and location—as soon as the president gives us his list. And that includes the first lady. I know the vice president isn't married. Is there a significant other who has an influence on him?"

"The most eligible bachelor in Washington appears to be totally unattached." Jonah grinned. "I'd sure like to know what you see about him."

"Oh, really? If astrology is such a fraud, why would you be interested in anything I see?"

"Look Addie—we've gotta work together whether we like it or not. You're not making it easy. Jeez—right now we're at opposite ends of the universe."

Addie put her pad and pencil into her briefcase and stood up. Her hands were shaking, but her voice remained firm. "I think this meeting is officially over. Goodbye, Mr. Stern. I'll wait to hear from you."

Jonah shrugged. "Right. I'll be in touch in a day or so. If you have any questions, call me. Here's my direct number."

Addie stuffed the paper into her jacket pocket and started towards the door. Jonah put his hand on her arm.

"Wait. I'll show you the way out. They don't like people wandering around here."

Addie pulled her arm away. "Thank you," she said coldly and followed him down the long hallway to the exit, keeping two steps behind all the way.

CHAPTER FOUR

President Wycliff and Walter Turner strolled down the corridor, with Hanover following a few steps behind.

"I thought it went very well," Wycliff said. "What do you think, Walter?"

"You know what I think. I'm not comfortable with the whole idea. I've got nothing against astrology, but it's a bad time to start something like this. What if the media gets hold of it. You're just asking for trouble."

"You worry too much. I find the whole subject fascinating."

Walter pressed his lips together. The president was like a child with a new toy. Walter had seen him this way many times, throwing caution to the wind when something stimulated him intellectually.

"Actually," Wycliff continued, "I stretched the the truth a little in there. I'm not really late. I wanted some time to relax before my luncheon appointment with the Future Poultry Growers of America."

He looked at Walter and grimaced. "To think I sold my soul for the joy of meeting with a bunch of adolescent chicken farmers. I need time to fortify myself. Come upstairs with me for a few minutes. I want to discuss some things with you."

Walter nodded, and the three men walked to the elevator that would take them from the ground floor offices to the president's private living quarters on the second floor. They were silent, each engrossed in his own thoughts, until they entered a small room that had been transformed into an inviting den. Paneled in a light tan knotty pine, one wall was lined with bookshelves. A beige tweed couch stood against another wall, flanked by two turquoise chairs. Turner eased his lanky frame into one of the chairs. Hanover remained in the doorway, leaning against the wall.

Wycliff headed for the small bar near the window, picked up a bottle of Chivas Regal and poured some into a glass, adding ice and water.

"I'll need this before I take on the Future Poultry Growers. Care for something, Walter?"

Turner shook his head. "Too early for me." He tried to keep the disapproval out of his voice.

The president took a large swallow, smacked his lips, and sank down onto the couch.

"Now—give me the benefit of your excellent counsel," he said, "although I warn you I won't take your advice about the astrologer. I am sorry you feel that way, though. I just went through a hair-raising session with Ellen about it this morning. She thinks the whole thing will either send me down the highway to damnation or the road to public ridicule. You know how she can get."

Turner nodded. He had seen Ellen Wycliff change from gracious Southern belle to screeching shrew many times during his long friendship with the president. Now that she wore the title of first lady, however, she was more discreet about her rages.

"I'm sure I'd get some support from your wife," Wycliff said.

"Well, Janice has always been receptive to anything that smacks of New Age. She's working on a new novel—something to do with reincarnation."

"We'll have to get Janice, Ellen, and Addie together and watch the sparks fly." Wycliff chuckled at the picture.

"Henry, I don't think you brought me up here to discuss a social gathering for our ladies. What's on your mind?"

Wycliff leaned forward. "Well, for starters, my esteemed secretary of the interior has been pressuring me to meet with that gang from PEP on the Three Rivers project. I keep putting him off, but he never lets up."

"You're going to have to meet with them, Henry. People for Environmental Protection is too powerful to ignore."

"I know." Wycliff shook his head. "Nothing will satisfy that bunch, short of turning the country back into a wilderness. Well, I tell you, I'm going to get that dam built—and PEP be damned."

Walter grimaced at the unintentional pun. "You're going to have to meet with them," he repeated.

"I'll do it—but when I'm good and ready. I'll have Addie set a time for the meeting. They'll have Mother Nature on their side. I'll have the stars on my side."

"Just be sure you have Sidney Snyder there. If anyone can handle those people, he can. Don't count on the stars."

Wycliff nodded. "Then there are the deficit figures that came out today. The Democrats will use them to push for their tax increase. Stop in at Debbie's office and she'll give you a copy. I'd like you to take a look at them."

"I'm no economist, Henry."

"I don't want an analysis of the figures. I have Debbie for that. I want to know what you think about them. We have some options here, and I'm not sure which way to go."

"I'll take a look."

"Fine. Oh, one more thing—" Wycliff cleared his throat elaborately.

Here we go, Turner thought. This is really what he wants to talk about.

"Those damn rumors about my health and this—" He lifted his glass, swirled the amber liquid, and drained the glass. "They're starting again."

"How do you know?"

"Marty Shaw got the word from a few of his newspaper buddies. I tell you, even if Shaw wasn't such a damn good press secretary, he'd earn his keep from the feedback we get from his old cronies."

"Do you know where the rumors are coming from?"

"I suspect—no, I'm positive—it's that fucking Andrew Granit."

"What makes you so sure?"

"Because he's out to get me, that's why. You know Granit. He has this master plan to topple me and put his fair-haired boy on the throne. He's starting to tighten the screws."

"Henry, I think you're reading too much into this."

"Am I? I think not. Granit is starting to leak tidbits about his goddamned committee hearing on the roboplanes." Wycliff slammed his fist into the cushion. "Shit. We've got a hundred senators. Why does Andrew Granit have to be Chairman of the Armed Services Committee?"

Walter's face grew pensive. "You know, Jonah did just get a call from the *Post*. They're trying to sniff out something about the roboplanes."

"Goddammit! See, I told you. Granit's flunkies are out spreading the word that there'll be fireworks at that hearing."

"Do they have a date set yet?"

Wycliff shook his head. "Last I heard, it would be sometime near the beginning of summer."

Walter stared at him. "Level with me, Henry. What have they got?"

"Dynamite, that's what."

"What's the fuse?"

"The fuse is my goddamn Secretary of Defense, may he rot in Hell."

"Seabright? All the way up to him?"

"All the way up to him!" The president walked over to the bar and poured himself another glass of scotch. "He's had his hand in the cookie jar once too often."

Wycliff turned to face Walter. "The air force just got seven new unmanned aerial vehicles with digital relay systems so fucked up they can't find their way off the ground. Those god-damn UAVs were supposed to be the most sophisticated ever made—so smart no radar could touch them. Instead they can't even find the sky."

"I knew there was trouble with the new roboplanes, but that bad?"

"Even worse. And Granit's revving up his committee to find out just why. Except he knows why already. There's a paper trail leading right up to Seabright and his sweetheart deal with Aerotech Systems."

Walter rubbed his forehead. He could feel the tension spreading into a band of pain. "How long have you known about Seabright?"

"About a week."

"Are you sure about this?"

"Positive. And Granit knows all about it, but he doesn't want to show his hand yet. That's not his game plan. He's going to keep the story alive in the press until his goddamm hearings. Then, when the whole country's watching, he'll drop the ax on Seabright and everyone around him."

"Sounds like him. I think you're right, Henry."

Wycliff began to pace back and forth. "And it's all to get me. Granit wouldn't give a damn if the whole air force collapsed. All he wants to do is show a corrupt department of defense and a president who's so weak he can't control anything. Now he's starting those damn rumors about me again. By the time the hearings begin, the people will think I'm a drunken incompetent who can't—"

"All right, Henry. Calm down." Walter walked over and put his arm around the president's shoulders. "I think I know how we can cut him off at the pass. But it means throwing Seabright to the wolves."

"Walter, I can't do that."

"You'll have to. Look—Granit wants to build this up, little by little, till you're in a box. We'll let him drop his hints for the next few weeks, while we get all the evidence together. Then you go nationwide with a speech that spells it all out. Your shock and dismay. Seabright's resignation. Criminal charges against him and whoever else is tied in with this. And *you're* the man of action who did it all."

"I don't know if I can."

A thought hit Walter like a blow to the gut. "Henry, are you connected to this in any way?"

"Good God, no. I give you my word."

"Then that's it. You don't owe Seabright any loyalty. There's no other way to go. You'll come out a hero, and Andrew Granit will be left holding an empty bag—no rumors, no hearings."

"You really think this speech will work?"

"Your speeches always work. In the meantime—why don't you kind of ease up on the sauce. Don't give them any more ammunition."

"This?" Wycliff said, holding up the glass. "This is not a problem. Look at what I have to deal with. Future Poultry Growers, PEP—my God, allow me this little pleasure."

Walter pressed his lips together. "Okay, old buddy. You go meet with your chicken farmers. I have to get back to my office. I still have a law practice to run."

He walked away and turned in the doorway. "By the way, Henry. Maybe I'm wrong about your astrologer. I'm beginning to think it'll do you good to talk to her." The president would never see a psychologist, and if anyone ever needed a sympathetic ear it was him. Walter rubbed his aching head as he walked down the hall toward the elevator.

CHAPTER FIVE

Addie took a folder out of her briefcase and spread out the papers from her first session with President Wycliff. She could organize everything later. For now, she would just sort through her notes and rerun the meeting in her mind.

Addie had arrived at the North Portico entrance at 8:55. While she was admiring the rose petals carved in the stone on top of the massive columns, Bruce Hanover came out to greet her. The Secret Service agent took her to the book-lined den on the second floor, where the president was waiting.

"Hello Addie, it's good to see you again." The president took her hand and led her to the couch.

"I hope this will be adequate." He pointed to the square maple table in front of the couch. "I don't know how much space you need."

"Not much. Just room for some charts and my tape recorder."

"A tape recorder?" The president looked concerned.

"I usually tape my sessions. Then afterward my clients can listen to the tape and jot down any questions they might not think of at the moment."

"I hadn't counted on recording anything. I'm sure things will come up that I won't want…"

"Oh, I always turn the tape recorder off when anything really personal comes up," Addie said. "And, of course, you keep the tape, so no one else can hear it."

"We'll try it and see how it goes." The president sat down next to Addie, peering over her shoulder, as she took a chart and some notes out of her briefcase. Addie glanced at Bruce Hanover. He sat on a folding chair near the door, his head buried in a paperback book. Soon she forgot he was there at all.

"Start with the basics," Wycliff said. "I know a little about astrology, but refresh my memory."

"Well, here's your natal chart. It's a flat, one-dimensional view of the sky at the exact moment of your birth." Addie moved her finger around the chart. "We divide it into twelve segments that we call houses. Each house represents a different part of life. For instance, the second house shows finances, the seventh house shows partners, the tenth house shows career. You get the idea?"

The president nodded.

"The lines that divide the houses are called cusps. The most important cusp is the first house cusp." Addie pointed to it. "That's your ascendant, the face you show to the world. You have a Virgo ascendant, which helps you project an intellectual image, a person who relies on his mental strengths."

Wycliff laughed. "I'm glad that's what the chart says, because I've always been a washout on the athletic field."

"Your chart is extremely intellectual. You've got the Sun in Gemini, the most mental of all the signs, and Mercury, Venus, Saturn and Uranus are in Gemini too. That's a tremendous emphasis. See, there they are, together in the ninth house. That's the house of the higher mind, just to emphasize your mentality even more. But I don't have to tell you how brilliant you are. You know that already."

"Tell me anyway, Addie."

Addie laughed. She felt relaxed and confident, speaking the language she knew best. She wished Livonia could see her now, with the president hanging on every word.

"This is the chart of a class valedictorian, a mental prodigy," she said, "That is if he doesn't waste his talents through lack of focus."

"Ah, yes. That's always a problem, isn't it?"

"Not for everyone. For you, it's a danger. Remember how important the ascendant is?"

Wycliff nodded.

"Well, a planet very close to the ascendant becomes one of the major influences in the chart. You have Neptune, the planet of illusion, there. That can be very positive or very negative. For instance, Neptune connects very favorably to Mercury, the planet that symbolizes communication. You can weave spells with your words."

"All right, that's very positive. What's the negative side of Neptune?"

"For one thing, it can create a lack of focus—just what we were talking about. Neptune tends to diffuse things. Also, there can be problems with reality. But there's something else."

"Go on."

"Well, you have a Pisces Moon. That's a very idealistic place-ment—we call it the Don Quixote Moon. It's also very emotional, which doesn't quite fit in with the rest of your chart."

"You mean with all that cool intellectualism?"

Addie nodded. "But there's more. See, Neptune influences Pisces strongly—we say it rules Pisces. With your prominent Neptune and the Pisces Moon in the sixth house of health, you'd be very susceptible to any—umm—mind-altering sub-stances. Like alcohol, drugs, you know. You have to be very careful—"

The president slammed his fist on the table. "Goddammit. Who's been talking to you? Walter? Of course. *He* told you to say that."

Addie looked at him wide-eyed. She stopped the tape recorder. "Nobody tells me to say anything. If you don't want me to tell you the truth, then you're wasting your time—and mine." She stood up.

"Sit down, Addie. We're not through with the session. We could use a break, though." Wycliff walked over to the bar near the window. "You must be thirsty after all that talking. Can I fix you something?"

She stared at him and shook her head.

"Well, I can use a drink." He poured some scotch over ice and returned to the couch. He held the glass high. "To Nep-tune," he said and took a large swallow.

"Oh, don't look so solemn, Addie. I may like liquor a bit more than most people, but it's not a problem. It just relaxes me."

It did seem to relax him, and the outburst had swept away any stiffness between them. The rest of the session went well, and Addie sensed that the president was as sorry to see it end as she was. Addie had left the White House feeling an elation that still persisted.

The telephone rang, jolting Addie back to the present. She decided to let her answering machine handle it. But it might be the president with a question. At the last minute, she picked it up.

"Hello Addie—I'm glad you're home." She recognized Jonah Stern's voice immediately.

"I'm working on the president's chart," she said in a tone that dismissed all small talk.

"I know. You saw him this morning. Listen, I've got most of the information you need. I'll bring it over in about an hour or so. Is that okay?"

"I guess so. But I don't have much time. I've got so much to do…"

"Don't worry. I won't stay any longer than I have to. You know, I'm kind of busy myself."

Before she could say goodbye, he had hung up. The phone spit out a dial tone, and she replaced the receiver. Addie frowned. This feuding with Jonah was becoming uncomfortable. She would try to be more pleasant.

Addie swept the papers into their folder and glanced at her watch. She just had time to eat and straighten up the apartment. She found some leftover chicken salad in the refrigerator, and as she washed it down with a glass of diet cola, Addie stared out the window. A man stood across the street, leaning against the building. He smoked constantly, stamping out one cigarette as he lit another. Occasionally, he glanced up in the direction of her window.

Suddenly, Addie remembered him. This morning, when she had left for the White House, he had been standing on the corner, watching and smoking. She was sure it was the same man. Could they have the Secret Service spying on her?

Addie moved around the living room, plumping pillows and replacing stray books on the shelves. She even took out the vacuum cleaner and ran it across the carpet. This was ridiculous, cleaning her apartment for Jonah Stern. But she had seen how his eyes moved around a room, alert and observant. He might regard her as some kind of freak, but at least her apartment would be neat and ordinary—as if his opinion of her mattered.

Still, she was determined to get them off on a better footing. Addie wondered if she should offer Jonah a drink, but decided against it. This was, after all, not a social call.

Jonah Stern smoothed the wrinkles in his jacket as he waited for Addie to open the door. He straightened his tie and shrugged. No matter how carefully he dressed, his clothes always had a rumpled look. Not that it mattered here. The main thing was to get past Addie's prickly hedges and build a better working relationship.

The door opened. "Hi Addie," he said, trying for his most engaging grin.

She smiled. One hand played with her hair, as if searching for loose strands. He had noticed her doing that before, some kind of nervous habit. Good. She felt as ill at ease as he did.

He glanced around the living room, surprised again at its simplicity. The first time he had seen it, he had expected some sort of exotic clutter, everything overstuffed and crowded together. Instead, he had found a large, tastefully decorated room, divided into sitting and work areas. A mix of subdued grays and greens provided a soothing atmosphere. The only exotic touch was the large terra cotta vase filled with brightly colored peacock feathers, standing on the floor in one corner of the room.

"Where will we work?" he asked.

"Here." Addie pointed to a large walnut desk positioned against one wall, with a multi-level table for a computer and printer on one side and a wooden filing cabinet on the other. She sat down in the swivel chair in front of the desk and he settled into the contour chair beside it.

Jonah took two bulging folders out of his attaché case and placed them on the desk. "Before we start," he said, "I better tell you who you are."

"Oh, that's one thing I thought I knew."

"No, you've got a new identity now. You're officially a part-time speechwriter for President Wycliff."

"I've never written a speech in my—"

"I know. You won't have to. It's just to explain your comings and goings at the White House. And it'll also explain our meetings. You see, I coordinate the president's speeches. In a manner of speaking, I'm sort of your boss now."

"Oh." Addie smiled. "Do I have to be properly respectful?"

"Well, let's see. You can still call me Jonah, not Master or My Lord or anything like that. Oh yes, and we can eliminate all the usual nonsense like bowing in my presence or throwing rose petals in my path."

Addie looked thoughtful. "Actually, I like the title. I enjoy being called a writer—any kind of writer."

"I made a good guess, didn't I? I checked out your background to see what kind of job we could give you. You used to teach English in Boston, right?"

Addie nodded. "Is there anything about me you don't know?"

"Oh, lots. But I expect to find all that out in time. I'm a very curious sort of fellow."

Addie smiled again. "We'll see about that. In the meantime, I'd like to know what's in there." She pointed to the folders on the desk.

"Exactly what you asked for. All the birth data for the people around the president. And I've added some new bios to the ones I already gave you—including ones for Walter and myself."

"Do you have the president's wife too?"

Jonah nodded. "I divided everything into two folders, 'friends' and 'foes'. Though I must admit, I didn't know which one to put our estimable first lady into."

Addie seemed shocked. "I knew his seventh house was difficult, but I..." She stopped and began smoothing her hair. "Sorry. I made a vow that I wasn't going to mention anything astrological to you."

"Look, Addie. Let's get this out on the table right now. I can't help feeling the way I do and I'm not gonna pretend. I've been involved with science one way or another most of my life. Believe it or not, I wanted to be a doctor. Then, halfway through college I realized I couldn't stand being around sick people. So I switched to journalism." He laughed. "And I've been around sick people ever since."

"I started out writing science articles," he continued. "Sometimes I still think of myself as a scientist who happened to wander into communications. I can't help thinking like a scientist. Do you understand?" Jonah was surprised at how much he wanted her to understand.

Addie nodded. "I guess so. I just wonder why you scientists are so positive and close-minded."

"We're not so positive. We don't claim to know everything. See, we know there's a natural order governing everything. We snoop around the fringes, finding bits and pieces. It's like a giant jigsaw puzzle. Every once in a while, someone completes a section, and he gets a Nobel prize."

Addie leaned forward. "But that's exactly it. Say there's a natural order—think of it not on a physical plane, but on a metaphysical plane. And say we've discovered how to decipher one tiny corner of that order by learning the language of the stars. This tiny fragment gives us a clue and we can begin to understand the nature of the whole."

"That all depends on whether the language is accurate or not."

"Exactly. But how can you say it isn't, without ever learning it?"

"Got me there, Addie. Like I said, I'm a curious fellow. I'll listen to you with as much of an open mind as I can."

"I'll see just how open-minded you are when I look at your chart."

Jonah squirmed. It was all nonsense, but somehow he didn't want her to have that advantage—to be snooping around his psyche. He stretched and leaned back in the chair.

"So, now that we have that cleared away—what was all that about a seventh house?"

"Well, that's the area in the chart that tells us about relationships, especially marriage. It's pretty afflicted in the president's chart, but I didn't relate that to his wife. I thought it showed his open enemies."

"You mean the same area covers spouses and also enemies?"

Addie nodded.

"That's pretty complicated," Jonah said. "How do you tell the difference?"

"Sometimes there isn't any difference. They turn out to be one and the same person." Addie's voice broke and she looked away.

"You sound like you've been there," Jonah said softly.

"You should know all about it. You know everything about me, don't you?"

"I know you've been married and divorced—that's all. I didn't mean to pry."

"No, that's all right. It's very dull, really. The most common story in the world. Lawyer husband meets pretty paralegal at office. Decides he has more in common with her than with dull school-teacher wife, who worked to put him through law school. Off the two lovers go into the sunset, and wife is left alone with her students, which is definitely not enough."

"Is that when you moved to Washington?"

Addie nodded. "I wanted to get away from Boston. And I wasn't about to crawl back to my family in Cincinnati."

"But why Washington?"

"Why not?" She shrugged. "It seemed like a good place to get lost. Besides, I found a teaching job here right away."

"Yeah, everything's transient here, including our teachers."

"But I found much more in Washington." Addie's eyes glowed. "I stumbled onto astrology and the best teacher in the world, Livonia Matthews. I learned all I could and things began to fall into place. I found answers that..." She gazed past Jonah. "I'm still learning and discovering things every day."

"So you decided to go into it full time?"

Addie nodded. "I gave up my teaching job, as soon as I had enough clients to support myself. I love astrology, but it's very demanding. It's a twenty four hour a day occupation."

"So, your life's all work and studying. Don't you feel there's more to—"

"Now you *are* prying." She picked up one of the folders and began leafing through it. Jonah felt a door snap shut. He peered over Addie's shoulder at the papers and sniffed a spicy floral aroma. Astrologers wear perfume, he thought.

He pointed to one of the pages. "That's a photocopy of Ellen Wycliff's birth certificate. Her official bio makes her three years younger. She'd kill me if she knew I had this."

Addie closed the folder and stood up. "You don't have to go over all this with me. I prefer to look at it by myself. If I have any questions, I'll call you."

"I offended you, didn't I?"

"No. It's just—I don't like talking about myself." She attempted a weak smile. "You know, Jonah—you look tired. Would you like a cup of coffee or something?"

"Now that you mention it, I haven't had a chance to eat since breakfast."

"I think I can scare up a sandwich for you."

"Great." Jonah followed Addie into the kitchen, perched on a stool in front of the counter, and watched her as she sliced a tomato and added lettuce and thick slices of cheese to a club roll.

"Mayo all right?" she asked.

Jonah nodded. He liked sitting in the shiny blue and white kitchen, watching Addie move around. The room reflected her personality. The Dutch-figured tiles gleamed, and the white countertops were clean and uncluttered. The smell of fresh coffee began to fill the room.

Addie put the sandwich and coffee in front of him and poured a cup for herself. She took a sip, cleared her throat, and then in a hesitant voice said, "How about you, Jonah? How has your seventh house been?"

"I'd better tell you the truth, right? You'll know all about it when you look at my chart, won't you?"

Addie smiled, but didn't answer.

"I've never been married myself. Got close a couple of times, but chickened out at the last minute. Forever is a word I don't take kindly to."

"A fear of forever is no reason not to get married—not in this day and age. I'm a living example of that."

"I suppose so. All I know is when I get close to the edge, I refuse to jump. Also, I start getting bored, and that's one thing I can't stand." Jonah shrugged. "So here I am. A year away from forty and light years away from marriage."

He got up and walked over to Addie, empty coffee cup in hand. "Mind if I have a refill?"

Addie started to get up.

He put a hand on her shoulder. "No—I'll help myself." But instead, he put down his cup and let his hand move slowly from her shoulder to her hair. It twined softly around his fingers. He caressed her neck lightly with his fingertips, cupped her chin in his other hand and leaned forward.

Addie jumped up. "I've got to get back to work. We've wasted too much time already—"

"Sure." Jonah stretched elaborately to hide his discomfort. "I've got to get back anyway." He looked up at the clock on the wall. Christ, it had zodiac signs instead of numbers. He'd be glad to get out of this place.

Addie twisted her hands together. "I'm sorry, Jonah. I didn't mean—"

"No problem. Forget about it." He picked up his attaché case and started towards the door.

Addie raised one hand. "Oh—I almost forgot. Why do you have to have a Secret Service man watching me? You know all about me already."

"What?" Jonah was startled. "What are you talking about? We don't have anyone watching you."

Addie bristled. "You don't have to lie about it. I just don't like the idea of anyone spying on me."

"Look, Addie—I'm not a liar. The Secret Service isn't spying on you. At least not that I know about. And I'm sure I'd know about it."

"Why don't I believe you? Here—take a look for yourself." Addie pointed to the window. "Across the street. He's been out there all morning."

Jonah looked out the window, his eyes sweeping both sides of the street, corner to corner. A man walking his dog, two women carrying bundles, a kid skipping beside them—that's all he saw. Besides being slightly loopy, she was paranoid. He turned back to Addie, shaking his head.

"There's nothing out there. Take my advice. Stick to your charts and stay away from windows. That way you won't see mysterious strangers lurking behind every tree."

"I'll try to remember," she snapped. "And if I see any strangers, don't worry. I won't bother telling you about them."

"Good, 'cause they've got nothing to do with me. Thanks for the sandwich."

CHAPTER SIX

A ddie switched on the TV. Figures emerged from the screen, so real they appeared to be standing in the room. Her holographic video set was new. She had purchased it a few months ago and still marveled at the three-dimensional images it produced. Addie didn't understand the technology—something to do with splitting a laser beam in two and a complicated juggling of mirrors and lenses—but she enjoyed the results enormously.

She still had fifteen minutes to wait: the president's speech was scheduled for 7:40. Addie had stressed the importance of starting exactly on time. This was her first important assignment, and she had worked hard to find just the right moment.

At their second session, the president had told her about the speech. The subject was top secret, so he could only give her the details she needed for timing. It had to do with the Air Force and a special FBI investigation. The speech would shock the nation, and the response to it might affect the future of his administration.

Addie had to choose a time during the evening, starting two weeks after the session. She worked for hours and changed her mind several times before arriving at the proper moment. Then she checked with Livonia to confirm it. Now, as the time approached, Addie began to doubt her judgment. She paced back and forth in front of the TV set, wishing she had someone to talk to.

The announcer's voice interrupted an ongoing discussion, and Addie's heart pounded as she heard, "We take you to the Oval Office of the White House."

The cameras zoomed in on President Wycliff, who looked poised and confident, seated behind an enormous desk. His holographic image rose slowly, and Addie looked at her watch. Perfect—right on time.

"Good evening, fellow Americans," he began. "Tonight, as your president, I am faced with a very difficult task—to expose the transgressions of people I trusted with the country's welfare. In the final analysis, I have no choice. My loyalty must be first and foremost to our nation, not to the individuals who falsely swore to serve it."

Addie watched in fascination. As President Wycliff spoke, he became transformed. All the eloquence and charisma revealed in his chart shone through. He was spellbinding as he told of the Secretary of Defense's actions and the consequences on the safety of the country. He became an avenging angel, sent to strike down criminals undermining the country's unmanned aerial vehicle program. His three-dimensional figure stood in Addie's living room, shaking his fist and demanding justice.

When the speech ended, she was stunned. It was hard to believe that she, Addie Pryce, had played any part in it, however small. She felt herself standing on the threshold of history.

The telephone rang, and Livonia Matthew's familiar voice brought her back to earth.

"Addie—the speech was wonderful. The people will rally around him, make him the hero of the moment." She chuckled. "Nobody will think of saying, 'But this happened on your watch.' The timing was perfect. Every ounce of his charisma came through."

"Oh, Livonia—I hope you're right. I was so worried about this."

"Of course you were. If you weren't worried, then I'd start worrying. When will they know how the speech went over?"

"I understand the pollsters start in right away. They even have focus groups flipping dials while he's still speaking. And then they start working the phones. I guess I'll find out tomorrow morning."

"Well, there's nothing you can do now. Take a good, stiff drink, go to bed, and try to get some sleep."

"You're right, Livonia, but I'm so keyed up. I'll try."

When she hung up the phone, Addie watched television for a while. The pundits were busy at work, dissecting the president's speech. Addie smiled. They seemed positive, even the ones who were usually hostile. All agreed that the president had acted courageously to expose corruption eroding the country's defense. The real test, however, would be how the public reacted.

Addie rose early the next morning, after a restless night. She had her usual breakfast—coffee, a roll, and vitamin pills—and tried to bury herself in work. She began glancing at the telephone, willing it to ring, but it remained silent. It was almost 10:00. Surely they must have some idea of the speech's impact by now.

Finally, Addie decided to telephone Jonah. She wished there was someone else to call. She had only spoken to him a few times since that day at her home, and each time he had been cold and distant. If only that incident hadn't happened. How could Addie explain that it had nothing to do with him personally—that romantic moments had no place in her life.

Her husband's betrayal had cut through her psyche like a surgeon's scalpel, eviscerating all capacity to love and trust. They had been a team all through college. She had always put his welfare first and had expected him to do the same. Her blindness and stupidity still rankled. Addie had vowed never to let anyone hurt her that way again.

She thought of Jonah and his fear of forever. How many women had he hurt with his boyish grin and casual affections? For someone like Jonah, making a pass was a reflex action, as natural as eating or breathing, without any thought of the consequences.

She pictured Jonah's chart: his seventh house. Saturn, the planet of restriction, was there, and Addie understood why he felt frightened and hemmed in at the thought of commitment. But Saturn also symbolizes permanency, and eventually Jonah would find that special person who could erase his fear of forever.

Addie wished he had already found her. Then the incident in her apartment would never have happened, and Jonah might have been her friend. She needed one. Being the president's astrologer was lonelier than she had ever imagined. All her clients were gone, everything was cloaked in secrecy and she had no one to talk to but Livonia. And she was breaking the rules to do that. Addie sighed, picked up the phone and hit Jonah's direct line number.

"Jonah Stern, here." She was lucky—he was at his desk.

"Hi, this is Addie."

"Yes?" He wasn't making it easy.

"I—umm—I wondered if you've gotten any poll results yet."

"You mean about the speech?"

"Well of course I mean about the speech. What else would I be calling about?"

"I have no idea. You might be calling about spooks shadowing you."

She took a deep breath. "Jonah, I'd appreciate it if you'd let me know when you hear anything about the reaction to the speech."

"I can let you know right now, Addie. The speech went over big. Public response is overwhelming. You're the fair-haired girl around here right now. The president's convinced it was your timing that did it."

"And of course, you don't—"

"No, I don't. It was a damn good speech. And the old man was in rare form. It wouldn't have mattered when he made it. That speech would have sold the public anything."

"Thanks, Jonah. You managed to spoil a really good moment for me." Addie slammed down the phone. She pictured Jonah staring at the suddenly dead instrument: his eyes wide, his mocking smile erased. She hoped she had made him feel a little guilty.

A wave of triumph swept over her. She had done it. Sure it was a good speech. But she had selected that special moment in time when it came to life. No one could take that away from her.

She could hardly wait to share her success with Livonia. Just then the phone rang. It must be Livonia, reading her mind.

"Addie Pryce here," she sang into the phone.

"Hello Addie. This is Walter Turner. You sound happy. You must have heard the good news."

"Oh...yes I have."

"Well, the president is ecstatic. He thinks he's found a lucky charm and can do no wrong. I hope he's right."

"Walter, I think you ought to—umm—explain to him that I can't always find such a good time. Everything was perfect last night."

"Sure—but if he feels this confident, what's the harm. Anyway, he's going to call you later himself, but he wanted me to touch base now. And to let you know about the party."

"Party?"

"There's going to be a cocktail reception at the White House Monday night. It's ostensibly to celebrate our formal entry into the Eurotrade Organization, but it's really a good excuse for all the movers and shakers to get together. The president wants you to come."

"Me. What would I do there?"

"Have a good time, I hope."

"Walter, I—I don't like parties much. Especially something like this. I don't think I can—"

"Addie, you don't understand. The president wants you to come. You can't refuse. Think of it this way—it's part of your job. You can observe all the people whose charts you're doing. Really see them in action."

"I've never been to anything like this. What should I wear?"

"Something pretty. People get all dressed up for receptions at the White House."

"But I won't know anyone. I'll—"

"My wife will be there, Addie. She knows all about your work with the president and she's anxious to meet you."

"What time is it?"

"You'll get an official invitation. You have to have one to get in."

Addie swallowed hard. "All right, Walter. I'll be there." Monday was only five days away. She dreaded it.

Walter Turner leaned back on the couch in the White House den and watched the president pace back and forth. It was the day after the speech, and he still hadn't come down to earth. Wycliff jabbed one fist into the air, as he often did when he wanted to emphasize a point.

"I tell you, Walter, I'm really on a roll now. I can feel the power of the people behind me. It's like right after the election. Remember? When it seemed I could walk on water?"

Walter nodded. Those early days had made all the grinding effort worthwhile. This last year, when everything had turned sour, seemed an eternity.

"I feel like everything's starting to turn around," Wycliff continued. Those bastards in the Senate can come after me all they want. If the people are behind me, they can't touch me." He laughed. "I'd love to see Andrew Granit's face this morning."

"Forget about Andrew. He had the wind knocked out of him on this one. He'll have to do some fancy footwork, when the reporters start asking him about the hearings."

"I can't wait to read about it." The president rubbed his hands together in delight. "I can just picture what…"

A rap on the door interrupted him. It swung open and Ellen Wycliff entered the room. Her blond hair looked carved, each strand lacquered to perfection. A string of creamy, graduated pearls set off her orange wool dress, which swirled gracefully as she walked. She sat down on the couch next to Walter, gazing up at him.

"Well, Walter. How nice that you're here. I swear I haven't seen you in a month of Sundays."

"It's good to see you too, Ellen." We're in Southern belle mode today, Walter thought.

She smiled, and glanced at Wycliff.

"Darlin'," she said, patting the seat on the other side of her. "Come, sit down here by me. We've got some important things to talk about."

"Then I'd better be going," Walter said, starting to rise.

"No, no—please stay." She placed her hand over his and gave it a conspiratorial squeeze. "We do rely on you so, Walter. For your old-fashioned common sense."

He smiled and sank back into the sofa. Common sense, as defined by Ellen Wycliff, meant agreeing with her gospel.

The president walked over to the bar, dropped a few ice cubes into a glass, and poured some whiskey over them. He took a large swallow before seating himself next to his wife on the couch.

"So—what's on the agenda?" he said, his eyes fixed on the liquid in his glass.

"We have to discuss the cocktail party on Monday. Sally and I have been going over the list and found that some names have been added."

"Where is Sally? Don't you think she should be in on this?"

"Now darlin'—this is a private conversation. Sally doesn't have to hear everything we say, does she? She's only my social secretary. Not a friend, like Walter here."

She smiled and turned to face Walter, so he would know the smile was exclusively for him. He grinned back weakly. Ellen must really want his support badly to waste so much charm on him.

"Like I was saying, we're going over the guest list, and we found a couple of names..." Her voice drifted off as she opened a small pink notebook with gilt-edged corners. "Here we are. Who's this Nathan Connors?"

"I don't know every name on the list, Ellen. He's probably some contributor who wants his payoff in political jollies. I don't have the time to personally screen all our guests. Go downstairs and check with Harry Paterno if you want to do a person by person countdown."

"Well—here's a name I'm sure you'll know." Her voice took on a sharp, hard-edged tone. Now we're at the heart of the matter, Walter thought.

"Adelaide Pryce. Don't tell me *she's* one of your contributors."

"You know very well who she is, Ellen."

"I surely do. What I don't know is what this Pryce person is doing on the invitation list."

Wycliff drained his glass. "I want her there—that's what she's doing on the list."

"I think you're losing your mind, I surely do. Do you want to make a public announcement: 'Ladies and gentlemen, meet the president's personal astrologer.' Do you?"

"She's a part-time speechwriter. That's all anyone needs to know and that's all they're going to be told—if anyone's interested enough to even ask, which I doubt."

Ellen Wycliff jumped up, rigid with fury. "Someone is bound to recognize her. Out of all those people, there are bound to be some fools who know her. Do you want everyone to know you are so weak-minded you can't even make a decision without checking some nonsense going on in the sky?"

"Now we're down to insults. Well, it won't work, Ellen. I want her there."

"Walter, I'm appealing to you." Ellen held out her hands to him. "Talk some sense into him. You know I'm right. If the papers ever get hold of this story, they will have a field day. With all the rumors floating around as it is, we can't be too careful."

"She's got a point, Henry. I said the same thing, when you first mentioned Addie being there, remember." Walter cleared his throat. "Though I think I worded it a little differently."

"I want her there," Wycliff said. "It's important to me that she see these people—gather impressions, absorb vibrations. So what if anyone recognizes her. The only connection she has with me is writing speeches. I can't control what else she does, can I?"

"You're a fool," Ellen hissed.

"Your opinion of me holds very little weight these days. So now, angel, if you're finished with the matter at hand, Walter and I have some things to discuss that would only bore you." Wycliff stood up, made a courtly bow and gestured toward the door.

"You can't dismiss me like one of your flunkies."

"I think I already have. Oh—and one more thing. If I hear of any surreptitious phone calls to Addie, I shall not be amused."

Ellen stormed out. The slamming door reverberated in the silence between the two men.

"Sorry I had to see all that," Walter said.

The president walked over to the bar and poured himself another drink. "Can't be helped," he said. "It's the norm around here lately."

"Bad as all that?"

"You know things haven't been good between Ellen and me for a long time. But she's always been able to spread her good old Southern veneer over all the cracked places. Lately that veneer is a little thin."

"It must be hard to handle—especially when you've been in a pressure cooker all day."

"It's not easy." Wycliff removed his glasses and massaged the bridge of his nose. "You know, if things were different, Ellen would have left me years ago. But she's as ambitious as I am— maybe more so. She'll stay with someone she despises if it improves her social position."

"Come on now. You're being a little hard on yourself, don't you think?"

"No, it's true." Wycliff swallowed the last of his drink. "Ellen always felt she married down—no one's good enough for the Madigans of Maryland, you know. Maybe I became president just to convince her that she didn't." He sighed and closed his eyes.

Walter stared at the president and shook his head. Poor bastard—he's still in love with her.

CHAPTER SEVEN

Addie leaned against the wall near the entrance to the Green Room watching the people swirling past. They milled around, greeting each other with squeals of delight, forming tight little groups, and finally moving on into the larger East Room.

Addie had staked out this spot when she arrived and felt rooted there for eternity. She fingered the neckline of her new lavender silk dress. It was lowcut, and she hoped her bra straps weren't showing.

"Taking in the scenery, Miss Pryce?"

"It's Addie," she said, smiling gratefully at Bruce Hanover's familiar face. Though she and the Secret Service man had been together often, they had exchanged very few words.

"Your work never ends, does it?" Addie said.

"Actually, I'm not on duty tonight. I've got an open invitation to these things. They're glad to have an extra body around just in case—" Hanover's voice trailed off as he took a practiced glance around the room.

"Especially when it doesn't cost them anything," he continued. "This is my only salary tonight." He beckoned to a waiter passing by and took a glass of champagne for Addie and one for himself from the tray.

Addie took a sip from the fluted crystal goblet. It wasn't very good champagne and she pursed her lips.

Hanover laughed. "Now you know that I'm not really here for the White House champagne."

"Why are you here, then?"

He looked embarrassed, and Addie regretted asking. "It's none of my business," she said.

"No—umm—it really is your business. See, I came here because I knew you were coming, and I figured I'd have a chance to talk to you personally. I can't while I'm on duty."

"Me!" Addie was stunned. "That's a lot of trouble just to talk to me. Why not just call me?"

"This is a personal matter. I'm not sure about the integrity of your telephone."

"You mean you people are tapping my phone? It's bad enough following me, but listening to my phone conversations..."

"We're not following you, not that I know of. Funny, Jonah Stern was asking me about that a few weeks ago."

"He was?" Addie felt a surge of pleasure that he had taken her seriously after all. "Well, if you didn't follow me, who did?"

"There was nobody following you, Addie. After Jonah asked me about it we had two guys check it out thoroughly. They didn't spot anyone."

"Someone was following me. I saw him. I'm not crazy."

Hanover smiled reassuringly. "Nobody thinks you're crazy. When you get involved in government intrigue that you're not used to, you start looking over your shoulder and imagining all sorts of cloak and dagger things. Happens to everyone."

"You think that's it?" Addie looked at him thoughtfully. "I haven't seen anyone lately, but I was so sure—"

"Put it out of your mind. And about your phone—I'm afraid I've been in this business too long. The techies said your phone was clean, but I can't be sure what the top brass is doing."

Addie frowned. "I hate the thought of anyone spying on me."

"They're probably not, Addie. But I'm such a suspicious guy, I didn't feel comfortable calling you."

A sudden surge of excitement rippled through the room. Someone near Addie began humming "Hail to the Chief" under his breath, and the people with him laughed. Everyone's eyes turned toward the entrance.

The president and first lady stood framed in the doorway. He seemed plain and unassuming in a dark blue suit and jacquard patterned tie. She was several inches shorter and very thin, exuding a Dresden doll-like fragility. The wide-skirted, gold brocade dress emphasized her tiny waist. Her hair, done in an elaborate French knot, was a similar shade of gold.

They stood together for a moment and then separated. Flanked by Secret Service men, they formed two distinct phalanxes as they moved wedgelike through the room, greeting people and smiling at special friends.

Addie watched their seasoned motion, almost like an elaborate dance step, as they passed through and disappeared into the East Room. She turned back to Bruce Hanover.

"That went smoothly, didn't it?"

"When you've done it a hundred times, it looks easy."

"Tell me," Addie said, "What exactly did you want to talk to me about? You've gotten my curiosity going."

"Nothing very earthshaking, really." Hanover glanced around to see if anyone was within earshot. "See, I've always been sorta interested in astrology. Nothing serious. Mostly glancing at my horoscope in the paper now and then."

Addie grimaced.

"Yeah, I know that stuff in the paper is nonsense," he continued. "But it's funny how right on it is when something important happens."

"Oh, then you were probably born around dawn."

"That's right—6:02 A.M. How'd you know?"

"It's a little technical. The Sun would be rising then, and your timed houses would be similar to your solar houses. They write those newspaper predictions for the solar houses, but it's the timed houses that tell the real story."

Hanover nodded. "I've done a little reading about astrology in the last couple of years, so I follow what you're saying. See, I've got a confession to make. I requested this particular assignment. I wanted to hear what you were telling the president. See if it made any sense to me."

"You mean all the time you had your nose buried in a book, you were really listening?"

"Sure. But you know those three monkeys—I'm all of them, rolled up into one. Have to be in this business."

Addie laughed as the Secret Service man screwed his eyes shut, clapped one hand over his mouth, and held the champagne glass against one ear.

"The thing is, I've got some decisions to make—some important stuff's coming up in my life—and I'd really like you to do my chart."

Addie hesitated. "I'll pay you, of course," he added quickly.

"It's not that. I'm so busy with the president's work, I've had to give up all my private clients."

"I wouldn't expect much time—if you could just squeeze me in. My wife would appreciate it too. See, these decisions affect her just as much. She's been after me to make up my mind."

"Bruce, you understand I can't make decisions for you."

"I know, I know. I just want to ask some questions and see what you have to say."

Addie wanted to have this solid, dependable man on her side. The loneliness was getting so strong. It felt good, knowing he was her friend in this court of strangers.

She nodded. "All right, I'll manage somehow."

He grinned. "I just happen to have my birth data with me." He handed her a paper, which she slipped quickly into her purse.

"After I do the chart, I'll set up an appointment with you," she said. "It will feel funny, seeing you without the president there."

He chuckled. "I won't bring my book along either. We'll just concentrate on me. Oh, and Addie—I'd appreciate keeping this just between us. I'm not supposed to—"

"Ah, Hanover—keeping an eye on our girl?"

Walter Turner stood in front of them, with a woman on his arm who had to be the novelist Janice Durand. Addie recognized her from her book jacket photograph, though she looked quite different from the tall, windblown figure in pants and turtleneck shirt on the back cover. She wore a handsome black cocktail dress with a large diamond pin near the neck. Matching diamond earrings glistened against her thick chestnut hair.

Addie felt incredibly dowdy in her lavender dress. She had chosen it because it brought out an interesting shade of purple in her eyes. How she wished she had picked the black dress that the salesperson recommended.

"Addie, I'd like you to meet my wife, Janice," Walter said

Janice clasped Addie's hand in hers. "I've wanted to meet you, ever since this business started," she said. "I've heard such nice things about you."

"You're very kind," Addie murmured.

Janice laughed. "No I'm not—at least, sometimes I'm not. If you've read any of my books, you know what I mean."

"Oh, but I have. I've read all your books. I loved *A Farther Dawn*. I couldn't put it down." Addie knew she was babbling, but couldn't seem to stop.

"Now you're the one who's being kind," Janice said.

Bruce Hanover shifted from one foot to the other. "I've got to be running along now," he said, turning to Addie. "I enjoyed our talk."

Walter narrowed his eyes and watched as Hanover disappeared into the crowd. "What was that all about, Addie?"

"Bruce just—umm—wanted to ask me something."

"Walter, why don't you go and do your political thing. I'll show Addie some of the local scenery," Janice said. Before he could answer, she had linked her arm through Addie's and propelled her into the East Room.

Giant crystal chandeliers hung from the ceiling of the cavernous East Room. Heavily draped floor to ceiling windows lined the walls. As Janice and Addie walked through the crowded room, a tiny man with darting eyes and a bristling black beard called out to Janice. She waved to him, but moved on quickly.

"That's Gregory Harmon," she told Addie. "Be sure you stay away from him. He writes the 'Front Page Rumors' column for the *Sentinel* and he's got the nastiest pen in the business. He knows how to pry secrets loose. You talk to him for five minutes and you find yourself telling him everything. Next day it's in his column."

Addie looked back at the gnomish, bearded man to freeze his face in memory. "I'll keep far away," she promised. "Oh, look. Isn't that Vice President Furst?"

Janice nodded, and Addie stared at the tall, broad-shouldered man, surrounded by women. He was strikingly handsome, with thick, brown hair, combed back from his high forehead, a small, straight nose, and a mouth that turned up charmingly at the corners. But there was something about his eyes: a remoteness that seemed to separate him from the people around him.

"Would you like to meet him?" Janice asked.

"I don't think so. Not now. Not with all those women around him. He certainly attracts them, doesn't he?"

"I know what you mean. He is stunning, isn't he? But there isn't too much up there." Janice tapped the side of her head.

Addie laughed. "I know. Funny, his chart seems too intelligent for some of the things he says. How did he ever get this far?"

"That's how." Janice pointed to a man who was engaged in a heated discussion in a corner of the room near a huge grand piano. "There's his mentor, father confessor, and general protector, Andrew Granit."

"So that's the famous Senator Granit," Addie said. "You know, I did his chart first, because the president seemed so concerned about him. He's a Scorpio. And I have to tell you, his chart is the most interesting one in the bunch."

"More interesting than Walter's?"

Addie shrugged. "Granit's a very complicated man."

"Amen to that. Let's get ourselves a drink and I'll tell you all about Andrew Granit. Then you can meet him face to face."

Janice wrinkled her finely chiseled nose and pointed in the direction of the champagne-toting waiters. "None of that White House garbage for us. You wait here and I'll get us something decent. Armagnac all right?"

Addie nodded and watched Janice walk toward the bar set up against the wall. She passed a small group of people, and Addie recognized Jonah among them. He looked up at that moment, and their eyes met. Jonah looked away, put his arm around the girl next to him and whispered something in her ear. She threw back her head and laughed, then tapped him lightly across the cheek.

Addie swallowed hard and turned away, fastening her eyes on a woman whose strapless gown looked like it was fighting a losing battle with gravity. A paste-on tattoo above one breast called attention to the battle.

"Here I am Addie—and just in time. You look so sad." Janice stood in front of her, holding two glasses.

"Oh no. It's just...I guess I'm not used to this kind of party. I'm overwhelmed."

"Well, don't be. It's really just a lot of show and tell. Now, let's see, what were we going to—oh yes, I was going to tell you about Andrew Granit."

"The president gets tense whenever he mentions him."

Janice sipped her drink. "They have a history. Andrew Granit has been the senator from New Mexico forever. When the president was a freshman congressman from Maryland, they had some kind of falling out. I don't know the details.

But I do know that Granit kept Wycliff from getting on the appropriations committee, and they've been bitter enemies ever since."

"And that's it?" Addie asked.

"Oh no, there's much more. When Wycliff was elected to his first term as Governor of Maryland, a buddy of Granit's, Harold Merriday, ran as an Independent. He siphoned off so many votes that our guy just squeaked in. Wycliff was livid. He accused Merriday of being Granit's puppet and worse. He bad-mouthed him so that Merriday filed a libel suit. It was squashed by cooler heads, but..." Janice shrugged. "The enmity lingers on."

"How does the vice president fit into all this?"

"Oh, that's the worst of all. Simon Furst was a minister in Santa Fe. He started building up a big TV following, and Granit was quite taken with him—saw him as the future junior senator from New Mexico. And he got his boy in there. But as it turned out, he had bigger plans for him. Oh, much bigger."

"The vice presidency?"

Janice nodded. "Wycliff had the presidential nomination dangling in front of him by a thread. And guess who held that thread?"

"Andrew Granit."

"Exactly. He had the votes Wycliff needed, but Furst went along with those votes. Wycliff went crazy. He really felt there should be a first class person a heartbeat away from the presidency, not a posturing preacher. That's his pet phrase for Furst. But he wanted that nomination."

"So he caved in to Granit?"

"Yes. Of course, he tried to rationalize it. He decided that Furst was really necessary to the ticket. He had the good looks and sex appeal that would help carry it. God knows, Henry Wycliff's not too strong in that department."

Janice set her unfinished drink down on a table. "But it's been eating away at him ever since. I don't think he even dislikes Furst that much. It's Andrew Granit all over again, with another power base. The president's convinced he's sniping away at him from there. He's practically paranoid on the subject."

"It's too bad. The president has enough to worry about."

"What do you mean?" Janice asked.

"Oh, I don't know—stuff any president would worry about."

Addie couldn't tell Janice about the storm clouds she saw gathering in the president's chart, even though she felt strangely comfortable with her, as though she had known her for a long time.

They began to stroll toward Andrew Granit, when Janice pressed Addie's arm, her dark eyes twinkling mischievously.

"Fasten your seat belt, Addie," she said. "I can't resist this."

Ahead of them, in the center of a small knot of people, stood the first lady. She was a shimmering, golden vision, holding court among adoring subjects.

"Janice, darlin'," she exclaimed as she caught sight of them. She presented an upturned face, and the two ladies brushed cheeks lightly.

"You look ravishing tonight," Janice said. "As always."

"Why, aren't you a sweetheart."

"I don't think you've met my friend, Addie Pryce. She's been working on the president's speeches. In fact, I think she had a lot to do with the one last week."

Ellen Wycliff stiffened, but the smile remained frozen on her face. She gazed at Addie, as though she were some strange specimen to be examined and discarded.

"How very nice," she said at last. "We are most appreciative of your work."

She turned to the man on her left. "David, darlin'—do you think it would be too tiresome if we paid our respects to old Sam Hodgkins? At his age, I don't know how many more parties he'll get to." She looked around at the others. "Please do excuse us."

Ellen took the man's arm, and they walked away.

"The art of the gracious exit," Janice murmured. "The first lady has it patented." Janice and Addie turned and moved on, leaving the group staring after them.

"Why do I get the feeling she hates me?" Addie said.

"It's not you. It's everything you represent. Ellen Wycliff dislikes anything that can't be reduced to its material essence. It's the only thing she's comfortable with."

"Then she's against my working for the president?"

"Oh, that's putting it mildly. I heard she had quite a fit about it the other day. I shouldn't have brought you over to her, but I just couldn't stop myself. Walter's going to kill me when he hears about it. And believe me, he'll hear about it."

Janice began to laugh—a hearty, infectious chortle that engulfed Addie in its merriment. She began to laugh also. They were both still smiling as they made their way toward Andrew Granit.

He was standing alone, a very tall, lean figure, gazing around the room. Granit's face was filled with the lines that age deposits judiciously, each bearing a tale of some mission fulfilled. His wiry hair had once been red; now only a few dulling auburn strands remained among the grey. But his thick eyebrows had retained their color, bristling above deepset, piercing eyes. He gave Janice a thin-lipped smile as they approached.

"Janice, my dear. How nice to see you."

Janice extended her hand and Andrew Granit clasped it in his.

"And your friend—I don't believe I know her." Strange. Addie had sensed a flicker of recognition in his eyes.

"This is Addie Pryce, Andrew. She just joined the president's speech-writing staff. Addie, meet Senator Granit."

"A pleasure." Granit released Janice's hand and clasped Addie's in a firm grip.

Addie gazed up at him. "I'm delighted to meet you, Senator."

Their eyes locked. Addie was the first to look away. She sensed a cold flame burning within the man that attracted and frightened her at the same time.

He turned to Janice. "I just finished your latest book, *Cry of the Hunted*. I think it's your best."

"Why thank you, Andrew. The critics didn't agree, but it's the readers that count after all."

"Perhaps they didn't understand its subtleties. Especially the mysticism."

"And do *you* appreciate mysticism, Andrew? I wasn't aware of that side of you."

"I appreciate every facet of the human existence. I am open to experience, wherever it exists."

"And you, Miss Pryce," He turned to Addie. "Do you share Janice's interest in the occult?"

Addie cleared her throat. He was probing, she was sure. "Umm—I guess so. If you define the occult as the unknown, then I think everyone is interested to some extent. We're all searching for answers of some kind."

"Yes," Granit nodded, "The unknown does hold a special fascination. Most of us are wanderers in the wilderness, but there seem to be a special few who try to pierce the veil and retrieve a message for the rest of us. Are you—"

"Which brings us back to my book," Janice said quickly. "Did you find its message timely?"

"As always, Janice, you're right on target. I thought—" He stopped as someone approached in back of them. "Ah, Stern, I've just met your delightful new—ahh—speechwriter."

Addie whirled around. Jonah stood there with a fixed smile on his face.

"Senator, I must apologize," Jonah said. "I've got to collect these two ladies."

"My loss," Granit said. "I hope we repeat our brief encounter soon, Miss Pryce." He turned to Janice. "Do give my regards to Walter."

"He is rather charming, isn't he," Addie said, as Jonah hurried them along out of the crowded East Room into the now nearly deserted Green Room.

"Like a hooded cobra," Jonah muttered and leaned against the wall. "I don't know what you were thinking of, Janice, taking Addie over to meet Granit. Luckily, I happened to look over and see the two of you."

"We managed very well without you," Addie said. "Your rescue was quite unnecessary."

"This isn't a game, Addie—it's real life. You're such a pathetic innocent. You're a sitting duck for someone like Granit."

"Really, and who do you fancy yourself—Machiavelli or Sir Galahad?"

Janice narrowed her eyes and looked at the two of them speculatively. "Now, now children," she said. "No squabbling among the troops."

"Actually," she continued, "It's good that we spoke to Andrew. I found out something valuable for you. He knows all about Addie. I'm sure of it."

"What makes you think that?" Addie said. "Did I say anything that…"

"No, no—you were fine. But did you notice his expression when he asked you about the occult? You did stammer a bit, but you recovered nicely. Anyway it didn't matter. He knew—and he was enjoying himself, playing cat and mouse."

Jonah shook his head. "Damn it. Do you think he's sure? Maybe he was just on a fishing mission."

"He's sure. But I don't think it's important to him right now. You know Andrew Granit. He always has a master plan and he never makes a move until every piece is in place."

"Anyway," Janice continued, "I don't see how you can keep it a secret in this town. I told Walter that at the beginning. And I don't see why you have to, if it's handled right."

Jonah shrugged. "I'm only following orders."

"And so am I," Janice said. "You know, Addie, Walter told me to be your chaperone tonight. And I enjoyed every minute of it. But we didn't really have a chance to talk, did we? I'd like to have you come over for dinner soon—how about it?"

"I'd love to. But only if it's your own idea—not part of your orders."

Janice laughed. "No, this is strictly on my own. But I warn you, I'm going to pick your brains."

"I'm flattered."

"Good. I'll call you when I've got my calendar in front of me." She looked at Addie, and then at Jonah, her eyes twinkling with the same mischievous glint Addie had seen before. "And Jonah—if you behave yourself, you might get an invitation too."

Chapter Eight

A ddie was glad she had agreed to take on Bruce Hanover as a client. Their first consultation had gone well and she looked forward to their meeting today. Addie picked up his chart and smiled. It was all there—the qualities she had recognized instinctively. The solid reliability, the forthright honesty, the pleasant optimism. She studied the chart, checking her ephemeris every now and then to see the current positions of the planets.

Hanover's wife had been pressing him for some time to leave the Secret Service, to find something safer and less demanding. An opportunity had come up to join his brother-in-law as part owner of a resort hotel in Colorado. He liked the idea: the outdoors, the social atmosphere, the slower-paced life.

Addie shook her head. The timing didn't seem right. There were difficult aspects to his chart that could cause problems. It wasn't a good time to make a change. Maybe in six months.

Strange—the president's chart showed similar problems. Yet the charts weren't at all alike. Was there some connection?

Addie thought back to her meeting with the president two days ago. By now the procedure had become routine: meeting Bruce Hanover at the entrance, the quick elevator trip to the second floor den, then settling back on the couch to wait for the president.

This time the president had been more abrupt than usual. With a quick nod in her direction, he had tossed some papers onto the table in front of the couch, walked to the bar and poured his usual drink. He plunged in without any small talk.

"Addie, I'm disappointed. The astrological portraits you've worked up for some of the people aren't helping me at all. They're too general."

"I thought that's what you wanted. I tried to give an overview of what—"

"Maybe I wasn't clear enough." The president frowned. "I know what these people are like. God knows, I'm around them all day. What I want to know is how to deal with them. I guess I'm thinking along the lines of hidden weaknesses, soft spots, you know."

He sat down next to her and began rummaging through the papers on the table. Addie looked over at Bruce Hanover, who was sitting in his folding chair near the door, head buried in a book. She stifled a smile; the book was upside down. At that moment he looked up at her and winked.

"Here, this is what I mean." The president pulled out a chart clipped to some papers. "This stuff about Granit. That's exactly what I mean."

Andrew Granit—she should have known. With the president's obsession about him, Addie could have ignored everyone else and concentrated only on him. She would have saved herself days of work.

He pointed to a page. "I don't need to know that he's a man of strong convictions and weak moral standards. I don't need to know that he has an obsessive need to control everything around him. I don't need to know that he manipulates the truth to feed his enormous power drive. I know all that already."

He put down the papers and looked at her. "I want to know about the bastard's soft underbelly. I want to know where the chinks are—the times that he's weakest—that kind of thing."

Addie twisted her hands together "I don't think I—I mean—that's such a negative way to use astrology."

"Well, it's the way I want to use it. Don't you see, Addie, you'll be giving me an edge—I need that edge to do my job." His tone had changed subtly from annoyance to entreaty.

Addie shrugged her shoulders. "Do you want this for everyone?"

"Let's just start with Granit and Furst. We'll take it from there." He sat back with a satisfied smile. "Now let's concentrate on me."

She opened her briefcase and gave the president a list of times for the next two weeks when it would be wise not to schedule appointments. She had also found two good dates a few months from now for his upcoming Asian trip.

He drained what was left in his glass and cleared his throat. "Now, I'd like to get onto something more personal—remember last time we were talking about connections between charts. You said you'd work up some details about my wife and me."

"Well—umm—" Addie leafed through her papers until she found her notes. "Some really stressful contacts between the two of you are being triggered right now, but that's only temporary."

"I hope so." He shook his head. "Stressful is a very mild way of describing it."

Addie looked at him. "You know, there are difficult adjustments shown between the two charts. You're two very different people with very different needs. But there are also strong indications of permanence. One of the most favorable connections between charts is when the Sun in one links closely to the Moon in the other. It brings a friendship and understanding that can withstand a lot of buffeting. And your Gemini Sun is only two degrees away from her Gemini Moon. Your Saturn is involved in this as well, and though it may cause her to feel somewhat restricted, it's a planet that brings responsibility and permanence."

She went on to tell him in the most diplomatic terms that he and Ellen Wycliff were two people enmeshed in a web of attraction and repulsion that neither one could break. He had seemed pleased with her explanation, nodding in accord from time to time.

Addie stood up, annoyed that her thoughts had wandered. Forget about the president for once, she told herself. Bruce Hanover would be here at any moment.

The telephone rang. She picked it up, smiling when she heard the voice at the other end.

"Hi Addie. It's Janice—Janice Turner. I bet you thought I'd forgotten all about you."

"No—no. I've been so busy, I haven't had time to think."

"Well, I didn't forget. I promised you a dinner, and you're going to get one. And you're in luck. We have a new housekeeper and she's a wonderful cook."

"Oh, in that case, I accept."

"Good. I knew if I dangled Sophie's cooking in front of you, I'd get you. How does this Friday look?"

"Fine. But Janice—I don't even know where you live. How will I—"

"Walter will pick you up on his way home. And we'll see that you get back safely. Can you be ready by six?"

"Sure. That will be fine." The downstairs buzzer sounded. Bruce Hanover was right on time.

"I have to get off now," Addie said. "I'm expecting someone, and he's buzzing me now. Thanks again for the invitation."

"You're welcome, love. Oh, by the way, we're very informal. Be sure to dress comfortably. See you on Friday."

Addie hung up, pressed the security button, walked over to her desk and picked up her calendar. She turned to Friday— only four days away—and penciled in the appointment. As if she had to write it down; but she did like the way it looked, "dinner at the Turners, 6:00 P.M."

While she waited for Bruce Hanover, she thought about Janice. How considerate of her to tell Addie how to dress. While the Turners would have been relaxed, Addie would have been stiff and formal in something she thought appropriate for a Friday night dinner. Now she could wear her good black slacks and blue silk blouse. With her studded silver belt, it would make a flattering outfit.

The entry sensor detected footsteps, and Addie pressed the button to open the door. Bruce Hanover walked in, grinning. Any awkwardness between them had vanished, replaced with an easy rapport. He handed a small, gaily wrapped package to Addie.

"Here's a little something for you."

Addie took the package and tore off the wrapping. It was a carved rosewood statue of three monkeys, with their paws covering their eyes, ears, or mouth. Engraved on the base was the inscription, "See No Evil, Hear No Evil, Speak No Evil."

"It's exquisite." Addie smiled. "And the monkeys are so comical."

"We were talking about them at the party, remember? I think it's our theme, don't you? We're both in businesses where we're exposed to everything, but have to be blind, deaf, and mute."

Addie nodded. "It's going right on my desk, where I'll always see it and get the message. I love it. Thank you."

"Glad you like it."

"Now, let's get to work." Addie sat down at her desk, opened Hanover's folder, and spread out some charts. He settled into the chair beside her.

"So, what do you think?" he asked. "My wife's really been pressuring me about this. She wants to go back to Colorado. She's got family there. And she's fed up to the teeth with the Secret Service. She worries all the time about my getting hurt, or worse. And she's lonely. I'm gone so much, and she's home alone with the kids. She wants me doing something where I'm around all the time, though I can't understand why she'd want that."

If I were married to Bruce Hanover, I'd want him around all the time too, Addie thought. She laughed, "I can't understand it either."

"So, what do you think?" he repeated.

"You know Bruce, I can't make decisions for you. But here's what I see. For starters, you're a Libra, the most people-oriented sign in the zodiac. With your social Leo ascendant and your gregarious Aquarius Moon, you'd be very well-suited for resort management. You're friendly and outgoing. You genuinely like people. You have a strong streak of optimism and with that Mars in Aries you're a bit of a risk taker. I think all that's important for that kind of business."

"So, it looks good."

"It does. On the whole, I think the change would be a good move. In fact, I think you're better suited for the resort business than for what you're doing now. You're extremely loyal, that's true, but you're a very open person. It must be hard for you to work in such a secretive atmosphere."

Hanover laughed. "An unsecretive person in the Secret Service. How typical!"

"No, I'm serious. It must be hard for you—always having to be so tight lipped."

"Yeah, you're right. Especially at home. I don't like to keep secrets from my wife. So then, in your opinion it looks good."

"I'm just telling you what I see. I'm not making any judgments."

Hanover smiled. "Don't worry, Addie, you're not making any decision for me. I think I made the decision already. I just wanted it confirmed. So—what do the planets say about when I should make my move?"

Addie leaned forward. "See, that's the thing. Right now you've got some difficult aspects to your chart. Now, that could indicate potential problems with the deal. Or, it could show something else going on in your life. I don't know. But in a few months those aspects will be over, so it might be wise to wait."

"Sounds good. I've got some loose ends to tie up anyway." He tapped the side of his head. "Hey, I almost forgot. I wanted to ask you about something. Does the name 'Karl Salazar' mean anything to you?"

Addie shook her head. "I've never heard it."

"I just got a tip about something from my brother-in-law in Colorado. It's so weird and way out that I haven't told anyone in the Service about it, not until I track it down a little further. I thought you might recognize the name."

Addie smiled. "You mean 'anything weird, just ask Addie about it.'"

"Come on. I didn't mean anything. This guy Salazar—he seems to be tied in with New Age stuff. It's a small world, so I just thought, you know..."

"Sure, I know." Addie wrote the name down on a piece of paper. "I'll mention Salazar to a few weird people, and if I hear anything, I'll let you know. What's it all about anyway?"

"My brother-in-law met this Salazar guy in a bar. A real nut case. Crazy look in his eyes, nervous tics—but very smart, my brother-in-law said. He starts talking about the spirit world and past lives. Like I said, New Age things. All of a sudden he switches to politics. Starts rambling on about how corrupt everything is, not to trust anyone—the usual stuff. Then he says the president's in danger. Some kind of plot, and he's in the middle of it."

"Then, while everyone's gaping at this Salazar guy, a couple of tough looking creeps who seem to know him come into the bar. The next thing my brother-in-law knows, they all disappeared."

"Do you think there's anything to it?" Addie asked.

Hanover shrugged. "Probably not. We get dozens like this all the time. But I figured as long as it was dumped in my lap, I'd check it out before I bother anyone else with it. Matter of fact, I've got one interesting lead that I'm going to follow up."

"What is it?"

"Sorry. I can't tell you any more. I wouldn't have mentioned it at all, but I thought you might have heard about this guy. See, now I'm back to my uncharacteristic secret self."

Addie smiled. "The chart only shows your potential. If you want to go against it, that's up to you."

Hanover stood up and stretched. "Well, I guess we're finished. Can I come see you next week, same time?"

"Sure. I'll try to work out some timing for the resort deal. See what we can come up with."

"Great." Hanover took a check from his wallet, placed it on the desk and headed for the door. As he opened it, he turned around. "You made a lot of sense, Addie. See you next week."

After he left, Addie remained seated at her desk. She gazed at the little statue for a long time. She would miss Bruce Hanover when he moved to Colorado.

CHAPTER NINE

Walter Turner veered off onto the side road that wound through the Virginia countryside to his home in McLean. His spirits lifted. He felt the tension beginning to ease, as he neared the safe haven he had carved out for himself. While storms raged around him, his home had become his sanctuary.

It had not always been this way. His thoughts drifted back to what seemed another lifetime: to a twenty-year-old Walter, already so careful and thoughtful, so conscious of right and wrong, so ready to give advice to others. When the time came to face his own problems, he hadn't hesitated. His girlfriend, Doris, was pregnant. The only honorable option was to marry her.

The baby, Victoria, had not disrupted their lives very much. They were both at the University of Maryland and had simply exchanged dormitory rooms for an off-campus apartment. They arranged their schedules to take turns baby sitting. Walter's love for his daughter more than compensated for his loss of freedom, and if he and Doris were not madly in love, they had at least achieved a comfortable accommodation.

Memories bombarded him: final exams and diapers, law school and kindergarten, the small house in Arlington, filled with Victoria's presence. She had been an exceptional child, combining Walter's gravity and intelligence with Doris' blonde beauty and sweet nature. Nothing ruffled her. When Walter's growing prominence dictated a move to Georgetown, she adapted instantly.

Even the tortures visited on her during her last year of life failed to sour her outlook. At thirteen, on the threshold of adolescence when she should have been enjoying friends and parties, Vicky faced hospital corridors and chemotherapy. A year later the fevers and aches of leukemia had taken their toll, and an emaciated Victoria gave Walter a final smile.

With a bleeding of the soul that rivaled his daughter's brutal hemorrhaging, Walter tried to stay strong. Doris sought solace in religion. As her fundamentalism deepened, the gulf between them widened. She became convinced that the cause of their punishment lay in the sin of Victoria's conception and could not bear to have Walter touch her.

The loneliness of their two years together after Vicky's death became a heavy hand crushing them both. Walter's work hours grew longer and longer. His life centered around friends like Henry Wycliff—anything to keep him away from his own home. The final separation and divorce provided relief as life giving as oxygen.

During the decade of determined bachelorhood that followed, Walter became a popular figure around Washington: the nice-looking, well-connected extra man who was such an invaluable commodity at dinner parties. He developed an amused tolerance for his hostesses' matchmaking and relished the privacy of his small apartment.

Everything had changed from the first moment he saw Janice at the Stanton gallery show almost fifteen years ago. He still remembered the feeling. She had been at the center of a small group, and her bright crimson dress had been eclipsed by the brilliance of her smile. When she looked at him, Walter felt a jolt of electricity surge through him. He asked around and discovered who she was: Janice Durand, the novelist. He had never heard of her, but decided to use that to his advantage. He smiled to himself, remembering his opening line after they were introduced.

"Miss Durand, I'm afraid I've never read any of your books, but I intend to stop at the bookstore tomorrow morning and buy them all."

"Oh—why is that?" she had asked.

"So we'll have something to talk about when I take you to dinner this Saturday."

It had worked, but it had not been an easy courtship. Walter knew from the start that he wanted to be with her forever. Marriage, however, was not on Janice's agenda, and with characteristic honesty, she let Walter know that right away. Janice prized her freedom above all else; she wanted no permanent entanglements. Slowly, doggedly, Walter had won her over, and their love had grown into something so tangible, it seemed to have a separate existence all its own. He could not imagine life without it.

Walter turned off the road onto the long, poplar-lined driveway leading to his home. He steered the car into the garage and hurried into the house, inhaling on his way the aroma of roses and honeysuckle.

"Janice, I'm home," he called as he opened the door.

She appeared on the landing. Even in what she called her writing garb, stretch jeans and an oversized shirt, she looked stunning. Her chestnut hair swirled about her face in a mass of ringlets and her large brown eyes gazed directly at him, as she came down the stairs.

"Were you working this late?" he asked.

"Just polishing up a few chapters. I didn't realize the time." She brushed her lips across his. "Do you want a drink?"

He shook his head. "I just want to sit down and relax for a minute."

He sank into an armchair in the living room, and Janice stood, leaning against the arched doorway, watching him.

"I've decided what I'm having tomorrow night for the dinner," she announced, "breast of duck. Sophie says she does it with burgundy cherries."

Walter grimaced. "All this fuss over having Addie for dinner. I don't understand it."

"And Jonah—don't forget Jonah. I spoke to him today and told him he'd have to take Addie home, that the guest who had promised to do that disappointed me." She winked. "Somehow he thinks there will be other people here besides Addie and him. I wonder where he got that idea."

"Janice—Janice—these aren't characters in one of your novels, to be moved around at your pleasure. You can't manipulate people that way."

"I'm not manipulating anybody. I'm simply taking two nice people, who happen to be extremely available, and putting them in a very pleasant setting. And then watching what happens."

Walter shrugged. "If that's your pleasure, enjoy yourself. I really don't care."

He put one hand on his forehead and began massaging his temple, where a dull ache had started. "You know, I think I'll take that drink after all. It's been a very rough day."

Janice walked over to a small bar tucked in one corner of the room. Walter leaned back and closed his eyes.

"Here," she handed him a glass. "I decided it was a scotch on the rocks night."

"You're psychic as well as beautiful."

"I know. Tell me about the day." She settled onto the arm of his chair.

"Oh, the usual stuff. Henry gets more paranoid every day. He sees enemies behind every speech—and leaks behind every news item. And the booze. It's getting worse and worse."

Walter frowned. "And we had another bad mess today. A Secret Service agent committed suicide, and we had to keep it out of the papers."

"Can you do that?"

"It wasn't easy, but I think we pulled it off. You know, a thing like that gets out, and the whole Service looks bad. The public has to think it's the Rock of Gibraltar."

"Who was it? Anyone I know?"

"Bruce Hanover. I don't think you ever met him. Wait a minute," Walter frowned. "Come to think of it, he was the fellow Addie was talking to at the White House cocktail party."

"What a shame. What happened?"

"He shot himself—in the head. Right in his own backyard, too. His wife found him. She's still pretty hysterical."

"God, that's terrible." Janice shivered and hugged herself. "Do they have any children?"

"Two. Luckily they were at school—one's in preschool and one's in first grade, I think. Lousy if they'd seen it."

"But why? Did he leave a note or anything?"

Walter shook his head. "Nothing. He just went out in the backyard about nine o'clock, pulled out his gun and shot himself. Apparently his wife didn't hear anything. She came looking for him a little later and found him, lying there in a puddle of blood, with half his brains splattered around."

"Excuse me, Mrs. Turner." Sophie was standing in the doorway, looking uneasy about intruding. Her wide face wore a sober expression and she flashed an apologetic half smile.

"What time would you like dinner, Mrs. Turner?"

"Oh, I think in about half an hour, Sophie. All right, Walter?"

Walter nodded, and Sophie headed back toward the kitchen.

"I can see why you needed that drink," Janice said. She smoothed his thinning hair with her fingers. "Poor Walter."

"Yeah, it was awful. You've no idea what strings we had to pull to keep it out of the papers."

Janice jumped up and stared at Walter. "I don't believe what I'm hearing. A young man died. There's a widow and two kids. And you're saying the worst part is that you had to work hard to keep it out of the papers! You're getting as bad as the rest of them."

"Come on, Janice. You know what I meant."

"I'm afraid I do. And I don't like it—not one bit."

Walter's face hardened. "I don't need this. Not on top of everything else."

"I think you do need this and you're going to hear it. This has been a long time coming, Walter, but it's going to be said."

Janice took a deep breath. "Ever since the election I've watched you change. At first I figured it was the rarefied air up there at the top, and once you got used to it, you'd be back to yourself. But things have gotten worse. Why, I've seen you—"

"You don't know what it's like. One crisis after another. And I'm the only cool head that Henry turns to. Goddammit, Janice—he's president of the United States."

"And what are you, Walter? Exactly what are you? Answer me that."

"Right now I feel like I'm everybody's fall guy." Walter's shoulders sagged and he buried his face in his hands. Janice looked at him thoughtfully.

"I know what you are. You're a background person."

He looked up. "A what?"

"You know—when you plot a novel, you have the main characters and then you've got the background people."

Walter shook his head. "Fine. Now I've got my wife telling me I'm a nonentity."

"I didn't say 'nonentity.' I said 'background character.' In a novel, they're only there to serve the purpose of the main characters. And that's exactly what you're doing—pushing your whole life to one side, just to serve Henry."

"What would you suggest I do?"

"Get out. While you still have a life left."

"What am I supposed to say? 'So long, Henry. I know you're one of my oldest friends. And I know you've got the toughest job a man can have. And I know there's no one else around you can trust. But my wife says I've gotta move out of the background. So, it's been nice, fella, but—'"

"Oh, you're as good with words as I am, Walter. You can twist it around so it sounds all wrong. But you know I'm right. You're a senior partner in a good law practice, but you hardly ever go there. You've got a beautiful home that you grace with your presence for a few hours every night, too tired and tense to enjoy it. You never have a day to yourself. There's always a meeting, a function, a strategy session. I don't think we've spent a whole weekend together since Henry got elected."

Janice turned away and rubbed her eyes. "I'm sorry," she said in a choked voice. "I'm trying to keep me and my feelings out of it."

"No," he said. He got up and put his arms around her. "Your feelings are more important to me than anything else in the world. What do you want me to do?"

"I want you to turn back into the man I married. I want you to get away from Henry and the whole damn presidency. Oh, not all at once, maybe—but I want you to reclaim your life. You're sixty-one years old, Walter. You've always wanted to travel. You've always wanted to paint. If not now, when?"

He stared at her. She really cared about what happened to him. Not the power, not the prestige, not the money—only him. He leaned forward and kissed her. Burying his face in her hair, he murmured, "I love you so much Janice. I'll think about it. I swear I will."

CHAPTER TEN

Jonah steered his new Toyota carefully along the Turner's driveway. It was one of those new electric cars with gasoline backup, and the handling was tricky. He gazed at the empty parking circle near the house. As he expected, there were no other cars there. Janice had been so transparent about this dinner party. Jonah knew he was being served up as a burnt offering to Addie, her latest pet. He hated playing puppet, no matter who pulled the strings, especially where it involved Addie. The memory of that morning in her apartment rankled. Still, this was the only way he would ever get an invitation to dinner at Walter Turner's, and he wasn't about to let the opportunity pass. Jonah smiled. He could do his share of manipulating too.

The house was large and impressive, with marble columns framing the entrance. Jonah pressed the bell and was surprised when Walter opened the door himself.

Walter took his coat, and the two men stood awkwardly in the high ceilinged entrance hall, smiling at each other. Jonah thrust the bottle of wine he was carrying into Walter's hands and followed him into the living room.

Janice and Addie were seated on the couch, heads bent over a Siamese cat cuddled between them. Addie looked up and smiled. In tight black slacks, with the light shining on her hair and her blue eyes sparkling, she looked better than most of the women he'd been dating lately. Maybe the evening wouldn't be so bad after all.

Turn on the boyish Stern charm, Jonah thought, as he walked over to the two women.

"Isn't she a beauty?" Addie said, hugging the cat. "I'm thinking of getting one myself."

"I've convinced her to get a Siamese like Penny here. They're the best—so smart, they're almost human."

Walter smiled. "Janice gives every pet an IQ test before she allows it in the house."

"That's not true. There's the living proof of it." Janice got up and pointed to another cat curled under a corner table. "That's Jurgen, the dumbest animal ever created, and I love him dearly. Male cats are supposed to dominate, but Penny leads him around by the nose. One look from her, and he does *exactly* what she wants."

"That sounds just like our marriage," Walter said. "Must be where the cats picked it up."

"Walter." Janice walked over and linked her arm in his. "You're terrible. What will Jonah think of us?"

"You know what I think—I think Walter's a lucky guy," Jonah paused as Janice beamed at him, then continued, "to have such great cats."

Walter threw back his head and laughed. "You asked for that Janice."

"I guess I did. Oh, Sophie—just in time. They're ganging up on me."

A stout woman in a flowered print dress entered, carrying a tray covered with hors d'oeuvres. She passed it around, then set it on the table in front of the couch.

"Delicious," Addie said, biting into a stuffed mushroom.

"Yes, Sophie's marvelous." Janice helped herself to a pastry puff filled with curried chicken. "She's a real find. Been with us a month now, and we're never going to let her go. Find out what everyone wants to drink, Walter, and let's relax."

By the time Sophie announced dinner, Jonah was glad he'd come. Walter's cocktails had produced a pleasant buzz, and conversation drifted along in an easy stream. Jonah had taken Janice's place next to Addie. He was surprised to find how many things they had in common. They both liked old movies and nouveau jazz. She was one of the few women he'd ever met who actually knew how to play chess, his private passion. If they could just keep the conversation away from astrology, the evening might have possibilities.

But there was little chance of that, not with Janice Turner around. Just as he expected, while Sophie was clearing away the cream of leek soup, Janice brought it up.

"I was wondering, Addie," she said, "if you were given all those charts without any names attached, would you know which was which?"

Addie shook her head. "Probably not. I don't know anyone that well. Of course, Jonah's bios are so complete, I might have a shot at it."

Jonah figured that was a compliment, so he smiled at her.

"There are some I could probably pick out right away," Addie continued. "Ellen Wycliff, for example. And maybe you, Walter."

"Hmm, I don't know if I like that," Walter said, "lumped together with Ellen Wycliff."

"Don't worry—there's no similarity. It's just that certain things are strongly emphasized in both your charts. The one I'd really have trouble with is the vice president."

"What exactly do you see in Simon's chart?" Janice asked, "An empty head with a soul to match?"

"Don't you think you're being a little dramatic?" Jonah said.

"Not at all. I sat next to him at a dinner party once. God— it seemed endless. The man has no emotions, no sense of humor. I tried all night to get a rise out of him, and nothing penetrated that cool armor. There's no subtlety there at all. The simplest things seem to go over his head."

"Well, his love life's certainly a dud," Jonah said. "He's never been involved with anyone that I know of. For a while I thought he was gay, but there's no sign of that either."

"He's probably celibate. He was a minister, after all," Walter said.

Janice shook her head impatiently. "No, celibacy implies a certain amount of choice and restraint. Simon Furst seems to have no feelings, no desire—"

"But that's just it," Addie said. "His chart shows a very warm, empathetic person. Someone who really needs people, who connects with them in a very physical way. In all my years of astrology, I've never seen a chart so different from the actual person. Remember, Jonah, I asked you to double check his birth certificate?"

"Yeah, and I did have the right information. So you see, astrology's not so perfect after all."

"No, astrology is perfect. I'm the one who must be doing something wrong." Addie pressed her lips together in frustration.

Damn, it's happening again, Jonah thought. As soon as the subject comes up, I put my foot in it. He shrugged and turned his attention to Walter. The point of his being here, after all, was to score points with Turner, not with Addie. He looked at Walter and wondered if he'd ever be in that situation: seated at the head of a table, gazing down at a charming wife over an expanse of snowy linen and sparkling crystal.

Jonah sighed with exaggerated weariness. "I really had to pull strings today, to keep that mess out of the papers."

Walter looked up, concerned. "I thought that was all taken care of yesterday."

"Yeah, well it seems Greg Harmon smelled something and he called me. You know what I had to promise the little prick to keep him quiet? A weekend at Camp David. I'll have to spend two days with the guy just to make sure that Hanover's suicide isn't spread all over the *Sentinel*. Believe me, I'm not looking forward to—"

A fork clattered on her plate, as it fell from Addie's hand. "What—what did you say?"

"I was talking about the sacrifices I have to make for this job."

"No—about Bruce Hanover," she choked.

Jonah looked at her. The color had drained from her face and her eyes were twin pools of bewilderment. "Jeez—didn't you know? He committed suicide yesterday. I thought you knew."

Addie swayed in her seat, and Walter jumped up and put his arm around her shoulders. "I don't understand—I don't understand," she kept repeating, looking up at Walter.

"Here, take a sip of this." Walter held her wine glass to her lips. He stood there until some color returned to her face.

"Feeling better?" he asked.

Addie nodded, and he sat down again. "Sorry to make such a scene," she said. "It was such a shock."

"I didn't realize you knew him so well," Janice said.

"No, I—well, you know, he guarded the president whenever I was there. We became—umm—friends."

Jonah felt a twinge of something remarkably like jealousy. Somehow he had regarded Addie as his personal charge at the White House.

"How friendly, Addie?" he heard himself saying.

She stared at him. "Friendly enough to know he couldn't have committed suicide."

"I'm afraid he did, Addie," Janice said. "He shot himself in the head. They found him in his backyard."

"His wife found him," Jonah emphasized the word 'wife.'

Addie ignored him and said to Janice, "Bruce didn't commit suicide. He couldn't have. I know he couldn't have."

"Addie, you're not making any sense," Walter said.

"Oh—what's the difference? I might as well tell you the truth." Her voice broke. "It can't hurt Bruce. Nothing can hurt him any more. He was my client."

Walter looked surprised. "But Addie, we agreed—"

"I know—I know. I wasn't to do any work except for the president. But Bruce had some decisions to make, and he wanted my help. I couldn't see any harm in it. I had the time. Anyway, the point is he didn't have a suicidal chart."

"You can tell that?" Janice asked.

"Not always. Suicide doesn't always show. But you can certainly tell when a chart's not suicidal. But forget about astrology. Bruce had a great new future ahead of him. He had the chance to buy into a resort in Colorado. And he was going to do it. He and his wife were so excited about it." Addie shook her head. "I can't understand it—I just can't."

"Addie, you can't always understand people," Janice said. "Who knows what agony torments a person deep inside, no matter how brave a face he presents to the world."

"Now you're talking like a novelist," Walter said.

"How else should I talk?" Janice smiled at him. "And now I'm talking like a hostess. I insist we change the subject, so we can enjoy Sophie's breast of duck. She worked so hard on it."

While they had been talking, Sophie had removed the salad plates and replaced them with the main course. She did this so quietly and efficiently that Jonah hadn't even realized she was there.

"This is marvelous," he said to Janice, as he chewed on a rare slice of meat. "Best I've ever had."

Janice beamed at him. "Now, aren't you glad you came?" Jonah nodded and looked at Addie. She was eating mechanically, her eyes focused on a spot over his head.

The meal continued with an air of determined gaiety. Everyone exclaimed over Sophie's chocolate soufflé and grinned at Janice's tale of her one and only disastrous soufflé attempt. But afterward, as they sat in the cozy family room sipping cordials, the spirit of Bruce Hanover seemed to hover over them.

Along one side of the family room, a massive tropical fish tank had been recessed to make it appear part of the wall. Brilliant red and green cardinal tetras, silvery angel fish, and iridescent pearl gourami glided by. They sat in silence, eyes fixed on the darting fish. All attempts at conversation circled back to the Secret Service agent.

Jonah stood up and stretched. "Well, I've got to get up early tomorrow. I'm meeting with Bill Sanderson at 8:00." He glanced at Walter to see if he appreciated the dedication shown in giving up his Saturday morning sleep. But Walter's face only reflected relief that the strained evening was ending.

"I'm driving you home, Addie, okay?" Jonah said.

"That will take you so far out of your way. I can call a cab."

Jonah shrugged. It meant driving into Washington and then back to his condo in Falls Church, but he had promised Janice.

"It'll be a breeze. No traffic at this time of night," he said.

They made their way out to Jonah's car and drove in silence through the dark Virginia countryside. As they turned onto the brightly lit highway Jonah glanced at Addie. She was staring straight ahead, and her rigid profile reminded him of a cameo, carved from ivory, that his grandmother used to wear.

He resisted the urge to touch her cheek to see if it was as cool and smooth as the ivory it resembled. Then he noticed a tear etching a path downward. She rubbed her eyes with her fist like a child. Jonah reached down under the dashboard and handed her a tissue.

She smiled weakly. "Don't worry. I'm not going to get all weepy on you. I never cry, really. It's just that Bruce—I'm going to miss him."

"Hey, I'm sorry I sprung the news on you that way. I had no idea you didn't know."

"It's not your fault. I'd feel this way no matter how I heard about it."

She's really shaken up, Jonah thought. He began to plan his moves. When they got to her building, he'd find a place to park and insist on taking her up to her apartment. He'd take charge: go inside with her, make her a drink, lend a sympathetic ear. Who knows what it could lead to. He felt a familiar swelling in his groin and began to hum softly under his breath.

Addie leaned back in her seat and closed her eyes. Then she turned to him. "The terrible thing that I can't get out of my head is I should have seen it coming. I should have been able to help him."

"Don't blame yourself. You don't really know what his personal life was like. He may have had big time problems and in that one moment, he snapped. It happens."

She shook her head. "No. I should have seen something in his chart. Sure, I saw difficulties. I even advised him to wait a few months before he went ahead with the resort deal. But it was all coming from outside—nothing going on within him."

Jonah nodded in what he hoped was a sympathetic manner. If he said what he really felt about things showing in a chart, he'd only put his foot in it again.

"I even saw the violence," Addie continued, "but not from him. Oh, how could I have been so stupid, so wrong."

Tears welled up in her eyes again and Jonah fished for another tissue. He concentrated on the road as she dabbed her eyes. After she gained control, she turned to him.

"Another thing, Jonah. I feel terrible about tonight."

"What do you mean?"

"This dinner that Janice concocted to throw you and me together. I swear I thought there would be other people there—that it was a real dinner party."

"It was a real dinner party. That was a marvelous meal."

"You know what I mean."

"Yeah, but I had a good time, Addie."

"No, you didn't. You had an awful time. And on top of it, you have to go an hour out of your way to drive me home. Was that Janice's idea too?"

He wanted to lie, but somehow he couldn't, not with her looking at him like that. "Yeah. But it was one of her brainier ideas. I wanted to drive you home."

"You know, Jonah, you're much nicer than you pretend to be."

"How do you know that—from my chart?"

Addie nodded. "But a chart only shows potential. It's your choice, whether or not you use your good qualities."

"And am I using them?"

She smiled at him. "Right now you are."

The lights of Washington shone in the distance across the Potomac.

"It looks so beautiful from here," Addie said. "But when you get closer, it's such a cold and lonely city." She shivered and hugged herself. Jonah put his arm around her and squeezed her shoulders lightly.

"It's not always that way," he said.

"Right now, it seems like forever."

Jonah looked at her. Dammit, she seemed so lost and defenseless. He felt his plans for the night evaporating. He couldn't add a one night stand with Jonah Stern to her other troubles.

When they pulled up in front of her building, he turned to her.

"Will you be okay?" he asked.

She nodded. "I'm fine. Thanks Jonah, for the ride and—and everything."

"Listen, Addie. We got off on the wrong foot, but let's forget about all that. If you need a friend—or anything—well, I want you to know I'm here." He was surprised at how much he meant it.

He leaned over and his lips brushed her cheek. It was cool and smooth, just as he thought it would be. He watched her disappear into the doorway, then started the car and headed back toward the Potomac. What a lousy time to get an attack of conscience. And why was he whistling all the way home?

Chapter Eleven

The sound of screaming ripped through Addie's sleep. She sat up, trembling, reliving the dream that had jolted her awake.

She had been running through a forest, a strange tangle of vines and hanging branches, hurrying towards an unknown destination. Then she saw a man leaning against a tree. He had his back to her, but she recognized him: it was Bruce Hanover. He was alive. With a cry of joy, she rushed over to him. He turned, and she saw that the face on Hanover's body was the president's. It was torn and twisted, with great empty holes where the eyes should be. Blood poured from the holes, making little puddles on the ground. Addie began to scream.

She looked at the clock. The glowing numbers flashed 5:53. No more sleep tonight. Addie was surprised she had slept at all; the thought of Bruce Hanover's suicide kept whirling through her brain like a tornado. Three cups of valerian tea had calmed her a little, and she had finally fallen into a stupor sometime after 2:00.

The apartment seemed strange and spooky in the early morning darkness. She flipped on the light switch in the kitchen and the recessed fixtures came to life with a reassuring glow. She had set the automatic coffee maker for 6:00, and it was beginning to bubble. The rich coffee aroma made the kitchen seem less lonely.

Addie sat down at the table and thought about last night's dinner party. She wondered if the others were sleeping soundly right now. Walter and Janice, in their privileged, private world, unconcerned about Bruce's death. And Jonah—if he were awake and thinking about the suicide at all, it would simply be as an annoyance, another matter to be handled. Jonah. She felt her cheek where his lips had brushed it. In another time, another place, perhaps.... Addie pressed her lips together. She would never give anyone the chance to hurt her again.

The coffee finished bubbling, and Addie poured herself a cup. She brought Bruce Hanover's folder into the kitchen and opened it, staring at his chart. She tried to focus on the symbols, but his smiling face kept intruding.

Addie forced herself to concentrate. She checked the details over and over. Nothing—not one indication of suicide.

She looked up at the zodiac clock on the wall, the clock she had bought on a whimsical impulse three years ago. 7:20. Thank heavens Livonia was an early riser. She would wait until 8:00 and then call her.

When she heard Livonia's familiar voice on the phone, Addie's self-control began to crumble. "I hope I'm not calling too early on a Saturday morning," she said, her voice breaking.

"No, of course not. Every day's the same to me now that I'm retired. But Addie—what's wrong? You sound awful."

"Oh, Livonia. I've done something terrible. I read a chart wrong and I made an awful mistake. And a man's dead because of it. I wish I'd never started this whole business. If only—"

"Hold on, Addie—just hold on. Don't tell me any more, so I won't go off on the wrong track. Give me the birth data and I'll set up this chart and take a good look at it. I want you to come over for lunch today and we'll talk about it."

Addie felt herself starting to relax. "What would I do without you, Livonia?" she said.

"I know, I'm indispensable." Livonia chuckled. "But this is a good excuse for a visit. I haven't seen much of you, since you got so important."

"You know I'd be there every day if I could. Listen, can I give you the vice president's data too? I've got some questions about his chart."

"Sure. Glad to have something to do."

Addie gave Livonia the information for Bruce Hanover and Simon Furst. Then, as an afterthought, she said, "You've got the president's chart. Could you take a quick look at that, too?"

Livonia laughed. "Three for the price of one. For you, Addie, anything. But I'd better get to work right now. See you at 1:00."

Addie arrived at the Watergate fifteen minutes early. Livonia was delighted.

"I'm glad you're early," she said. "We'll have a quick lunch and get to work."

Addie followed her through the cluttered living room into the dining area. The glass-topped table was covered with books and papers that had been pushed to one side. Livonia had set out brightly colored place mats on which tropical birds flew through an eternally blue sky. A crystal bowl of chef's salad stood in the center of the table.

Livonia disappeared into the kitchen and returned carrying a plate heaped high with warm rolls. "Sit down," she said, as she plugged a silver coffee urn into the wall.

Addie settled into a cane-backed chair, savoring the cozy security she always felt around her old teacher. How typical of Livonia to have that chaotic jumble: crystal and silver mixed with books and papers.

Livonia put a heaping portion of salad on Addie's plate and filled her own. Addie, who had been unable to choke down food in the morning, ate with enjoyment. The salad was delicious. The dressing was one of Livonia's closely guarded secrets and usually appeared in one form or another at all the meals Addie had eaten there.

When they had finished their second portion, and Livonia had refilled their coffee cups, she smiled at Addie.

"Now that we're nice and mellow, I think we can start talking about your man here." She hunted through the pile of papers and picked out the chart she had done for Bruce Hanover. Addie looked at it quickly, to be sure the numbers matched her own. She was beginning to doubt even her computer.

"Now that I'm familiar with the chart," Livonia said. "Tell me about this mistake you think you made."

Addie looked at Livonia. "First, give me your impression of the chart. What kind of person do you think he is?"

"A very friendly, open sort of individual. Not terribly complex. Idealistic, sincere, strong sense of reality. But he may not always see his own worth and need a little shot of self-confidence now and then."

"Would you say he's subject to fits of depression or despair?"

"Mr. X? Not a chance. Why?"

"Because he committed suicide three days ago."

"What? Impossible!"

Addie shook her head. "They found him shot in the head in his own backyard."

Livonia thought for a moment. "Are they sure it's suicide?"

"Well, I guess so. He was a Secret Service agent. They'd know the difference between suicide and—and—" She looked at Livonia. "You're saying it could have been murder?"

"I don't know. Look at his chart. Look what Uranus is doing to his seventh house. This is a time when he could attract violence."

Addie nodded. "I saw that. He was about to sign a business deal. I told him to wait a few months."

"You told him...I don't understand. I thought you were only doing work for the president."

"Oh, I got friendly with this agent, and he asked me to do some work for him as a special favor. God—what a favor!" Addie shuddered and rubbed her eyes.

Livonia looked at her quizzically. "You're so upset over this. You look like you didn't get any sleep last night. Tell old Livonia—was there something going on between the two of you?"

Addie shook her head. "I've told you before, Livonia. All that's over for me. That part of me died a long time ago."

"Nonsense. You're only thirty-seven years old. You've got your best years ahead of you."

Addie shrugged. "That's the way it is. I'd choose peace over passion any day."

"Well," Livonia said, "sometimes it's not our choice. I took a quick look at your chart this morning, too. You know you have a very interesting Venus progression."

"I know all about it. Venus means money as well as romance, remember. They're paying me more than I expected. And maybe I'll get some inside tip that will make me a millionaire."

"You're not convincing me. But let's get back to Mr. X. When did you say he died?"

"Three days ago. They found him about 9:30 in the morning."

Livonia picked up her ephemeris and searched for the planets' positions on that day. "Here," she said triumphantly. "Mars square the ascendant—if that isn't classic for attracting violence. And he has natal Mars in the seventh house—violence from others."

Addie was getting excited. "There's some other stuff like that. Here, let me show you."

She opened her briefcase and took out Bruce Hanover's folder. A piece of paper fell out of the folder onto the table in front of her. It was the paper on which she had written the name Karl Salazar. Addie shivered. At that moment, she had the feeling that Bruce was in the room with them.

She picked up the paper. "Did you ever hear the name Karl Salazar?"

"I don't know. It sounds vaguely familiar. Why?"

"The last time I saw Bruce—that's Mr. X—he asked me if I ever heard of this Salazar. Said he was checking on a tip, something weird. We joked about it. I said I'd check with some 'weird' friends. God." Addie buried her face in her hands.

"Enough!" Livonia put her arm around her. "No more brooding. We've got work to do." She wrote down Salazar's name and handed the paper back to Addie. "I'll see if I can remember where I heard that name."

"Livonia," Addie said, "do you really think someone killed Bruce Hanover?"

"Yes I do. And I'd guess the Secret Service knows all about it. They must have their own reasons to call it suicide."

"But if someone killed him...?"

"The Secret Service will take care of it," Livonia said. That's their business. We're astrologers, not detectives. So put it out of your mind."

"Well, I'd feel much better, if I knew it was a fact. I wouldn't think it was my fault—that I let him down."

"It *is* a fact." Livonia pointed to the chart. "This doesn't lie, even though the Secret Service might."

Addie smiled. "What would I do without—"

"I know—you said that already. Come on, before I start calling myself Saint Livonia. Give me your notes on Mr. X and let's take a look at Simon Furst."

Livonia put the vice president's chart on the table, and they both studied it. "You know," said Livonia, "I would never have guessed how tall and handsome he is from his chart. I would have thought him a chubby, cuddly type."

Addie nodded. "What do you think about his relationships?"

"I think they're as necessary to him as breathing. He's got to have someone to share things with. Lucky for him he's so good looking. He'll never have any trouble finding someone."

"But that's just it, Livonia. I found out he has never had any close relationships. Not with women—not with men. He's social, but on a very superficial level. I've only seen him once, but you can sense his aloofness."

Livonia pressed her lips together and shook her head. "What's with these charts anyway? One is a happy, well-adjusted man who supposedly commits suicide. The other is a warm, loving person, who turns out to be a cold fish."

"I don't know, Livonia. My head is spinning from it. Obviously a man didn't commit suicide just to prove I'm a bad astrologer, but....Oh God, I just don't understand it."

"Let's look at this logically," Livonia said. "Bruce was probably killed, and the Secret Service wants to have it look like suicide for the moment, so that explains that chart. And the chart you have for the vice president is obviously incorrect."

"That's what I thought. But the man who gave me the birth data insists it's right."

"Tell you what. Simon Furst was born in Santa Fe. I've got a contact there. I'll call him today and get a copy of the birth certificate, just to be sure you've got the right one."

"Oh, would you? Thanks." Livonia had contacts all over the country who furnished her with birth records. She guarded their anonymity fiercely. She also, Addie suspected, rewarded them handsomely for their efforts.

"Let's not waste any more time on this. It's the wrong chart." Livonia crumpled Furst's chart and threw it on the floor. "That leaves us with the president."

"You know," she continued, "He's having a pretty rough time right now. But I didn't see anything really alarming. Until just now, when we looked at Bruce's chart. That Mars stuff is very similar to what's coming up in the president's chart.

"Livonia, do you think the president's going to be in physical danger?"

"Well, I certainly think he should be careful. Look what happened to your friend."

"I have a meeting at the White House in a couple of days. Do you think it can wait till then?"

"Of course. Those transits aren't active yet. My advice to you right now is take a day off. Think about yourself for a change. Go shopping. Go to a movie."

Addie shook her head. "No, I have too much to do. But you've made me feel so much better, Livonia. You've taken a mountain of guilt off my shoulders."

"Only a mountain? I must be slipping."

Addie laughed. "I'm so lucky to have you. What would I—?"

"Now don't start that again. You'd better go, before we both get sloppy and sentimental. I'm feeling a little tired anyway. Lately, by the middle of the afternoon..."

Livonia's voice trailed off. Addie leaned forward and grasped her hand. "Are you sure you're all right?"

"Quite sure." She smiled. "Nature's finally telling me to slow down, that's all. Now run along and enjoy the rest of your day, secure in the knowledge that you did not make any mistake."

"Ah—beautiful words."

"You Virgos," Livonia shook her head. "So terrified of making a mistake. While the rest of us muddle through, you've got to be perfect. I swear, I think half your bitterness about your husband—"

"My *ex*-husband."

"Your *ex*-husband—pardon me. Half your bitterness is due to the fact you made a mistake choosing him."

"Even if you're right—which I'm not admitting for a minute—then if I avoid the situation, I can't make the same mistake again. Either way, I come out ahead."

"If you call being alone the rest of your life 'being ahead.'"

"I refuse to be drawn into a debate with you, darling Livonia. I know I always lose. So, I'll be on my way."

Livonia smiled. "I'll call you as soon as I hear from my man in Santa Fe."

When Addie left Livonia's apartment, she felt so full of energy that she decided to walk up as far as the university. The air was clear and crisp, surprisingly cool for the end of May. She breathed deeply as she walked and felt her tension vanishing. When she reached the university, she stopped in at a little bookstore tucked into a side street.

It was almost empty, except for a few students clustered around a coffee machine. Addie browsed happily. A large paperback, *Science Trivia,* caught her eye. It overflowed with all sorts of odd facts, and there were pages of challenging trivia tests. She thought Jonah would like it and decided to get it for him as a 'thank you' present for driving her home from the Turners. She bought herself a present too, Janice's latest novel.

With her purchases tucked under her arm, Addie walked to the monorail station three blocks away. During the entire ride home, she did not think once about the president or Bruce Hanover.

CHAPTER TWELVE

Le Champignon was buried on a side street, far from the eyes of tourists and attention-seeking natives, a place designed for discreet meetings. When Addie stepped out of the cab, she had to search for the black and gold sign that marked the restaurant's entrance.

This morning, when Addie had answered her phone and heard the smooth, velvety voice, her heart had begun racing.

"Miss Pryce, this is Senator Granit. We met at a White House reception. Do you remember?"

"Oh yes—yes, of course," Addie stammered.

"Would I be lucky enough to find you free for lunch today? I have some things to discuss with you—interesting things."

"Today—umm—I think so. Let me check my calendar."

Addie's thoughts raced, as she stared at the telephone. Of course she was free, but should she do this. She knew the safe thing was to refuse and call Walter Turner immediately. But a stronger part of her wanted to meet this notorious man, this Andrew Granit.

She took a deep breath. "Yes, I'm free," she said.

"Good. Will 1:00 at Le Champignon be convenient?"

"I'm afraid I don't know that restaurant."

"Of course," Granit said. "It's very small and out of the way, but it's one of my favorites. I think you'll like it." He gave her the address. "I'll see you then. I warn you, I'm always on time."

Before Addie could answer, he had hung up. She had very subtly been dismissed.

As she walked down the dimly lit hallway into the restaurant, she smiled to herself. As usual she was following Livonia's orders: she was taking a day off, after all. A maitre d' materialized behind her. His assured, tuxedo-clad presence made Addie feel awkward. She smoothed her hair, as his eyes swept over her black linen suit and gray silk blouse.

"I'm here to meet Senator Granit," she said.

"Yes, he's already here. Follow me, please."

The maitre d' led her to the back of the room where Andrew Granit was seated at a table tucked into an alcove. He rose as she approached. Addie had forgotten how tall he was—easily six-foot-four. His presence dominated the space around them.

"I'm delighted to see you again, Miss Pryce," he said, sitting down, as the maitre d' pulled out her chair.

"I took the liberty of ordering wine for us." Granit pointed to a bottle sitting in a cooler next to the table. "I hope you like Chablis. I'm afraid I'm one glass ahead of you."

He beckoned to a nearby waiter, who picked up the bottle and filled Addie's glass. Granit watched her as she sipped the wine. It was a very good Chablis, and she smiled in appreciation.

"This is good," she said.

"I'm fond of it." Granit leaned forward. "I'd like us to be friends, Addie. May I call you Addie?"

She nodded.

"And you must call me Andrew. Is that comfortable for you?"

"It does take a little getting used to, but I think I can manage it."

He smiled. "I'm sure you can manage a great deal more than you want the world to think."

"Well—you're very perceptive." Addie tried hard to sound nonchalant. The waiter arrived with two large, gold-tasseled menus. The items, all in French, were handwritten in exquisite calligraphy.

As Addie studied the menu, she felt Granit's eyes on her. She closed the menu, deciding honesty was safest. "I'm afraid my French isn't very good," she said. "What would you suggest? I don't want to think I'm ordering veal and end up eating mutton stew."

He laughed. "I'm having their filet of sole. They do it nicely with shallots and mushrooms in a wine sauce. And a Caesar salad."

"That sounds fine."

After he ordered, he motioned to the waiter to refill their glasses. The wine, combined with the warm glow from the shaded lamp on the table, began to blur the edges of the sounds around them. Addie relaxed.

Andrew Granit pressed his lips together, as if coming to a decision. He leaned forward and placed his hand on hers.

"Addie," he said. "I don't believe in playing games. I'm too old for that. You've probably noticed—I'm very attracted to you."

"Me?" Addie was thunderstruck.

He smiled. At least his lips and that part of his face around them smiled. His eyes remained separate, intense and piercing.

Addie shook her head. "I don't understand. You hardly know me. There are so many available women floating around Washington—why me?"

"Addie—don't you know you have eyes the color of the sky—eyes a man can drown in?"

He gazed into her eyes, as if trying to peer into her soul. She looked down self-consciously. "I—I don't know what to say."

"Don't say anything. Just don't look away like that." He seemed to be enjoying her discomfort.

The waiter arrived with their salads. Granit attacked his with relish, while Addie picked at hers. He really likes to see people off balance, she thought. Well, I won't give him that pleasure. She took a large drink of wine for courage.

"Andrew, you said you don't like to play games. Well, I think that's exactly what you're doing with me."

"Is that what you think, Addie? Bravo. You're right, but I only like playing games when I make the rules. Now, exactly what kind of game am I playing?"

"I have no idea. But I do know the extent of my charms, and they're certainly not enough to overwhelm a powerful United States senator."

He laughed. "Oh Addie—don't underestimate yourself. But you're right, of course. It's not just you. It's everything that comes with you."

"I hadn't thought of myself as some sort of package."

His hand pressed her knee under the table and began caressing it gently. She found herself unable to move away.

"We're all packages of one sort or another," he said. "You're a particularly interesting little bundle; you and your astrology and the information you're giving our esteemed president."

Addie stared at him, wide eyed. "You do know," she said.

"Of course, I know. I know everything about you. Would you like me to tell you the exact day that Turner and Stern came to see you? How about a list of your meetings with Henry at the White House?"

"So that's why I'm here. You want to find out—"

His grip tightened on her knee. "Don't be a fool Addie. I know everything I need to know." His hand began to move up her thigh.

"I just want us to be close Addie, very close."

Addie was finding it difficult to breath. She inhaled deeply. "Andrew, take your hand away."

"And if I don't choose to?

"Then I'll have to leave."

He placed both hands on the table, palms up, and smiled. "Round one—won by Addie."

"I don't think I like this game. I don't know the rules at all."

"They'll get more familiar as we go along." He leaned over, picked up the wine bottle and refilled her glass.

Addie shook her head. "I've had too much already."

"It would be a shame to waste this fine Chablis." He drank deeply from his own glass.

The waiter arrived with their food and placed the elegant plates before them.

"Sparring suspended," Granit said. "We want to enjoy our fish."

"Which rule is that?"

He laughed. "Right now, it's rule one." He took a large mouthful of fish and smacked his lips appreciatively. For a man of sixty-five who so obviously enjoyed his food and wine, Andrew Granit was remarkably lean and muscular. He must exercise a great deal.

They ate in silence. Addie glanced up occasionally, but Granit seemed to be absorbed in his food. Was this part of the game, too?

"I see you enjoyed the fish as much as I did," he said finally, looking at her empty plate.

"It was delicious. I understand why you like this restaurant." Addie was surprised to see she had finished her third glass of wine, as well as her food. Following her gaze, Granit reached over to refill her glass again.

"No, no more. I'm starting to feel a little dizzy from the wine already."

He cupped her chin with his hand and studied her warm, flushed face. "Eyes like yours change color, don't they? They're almost violet now from the wine. Tell me, Addie, what color are they when you cry?"

"Why?"

"Just wondering."

Addie shivered. Was there a veiled threat hidden in his words?

As if reading her thoughts, he shook his head. "I shouldn't have said that. It's just—I remembered something...." His voice trailed off.

"Andrew, I don't believe you ever say anything you haven't planned very carefully." Her words were beginning to flow as freely as the wine.

"You sound very sure of that."

"I am. I do have your chart, you know."

"Ah yes, your astrology." He steepled his fingers. "And what does it tell you about me?"

"That you're a very complex person. Frankly, that's the reason I came today—your chart fascinates me. I wanted to meet the person behind the chart."

"And I thought it was my magnetic appeal."

Addie smiled. "That, too. You know, your chart is loaded with personal magnetism. That doesn't hurt a politician."

"My dear, I consider myself a statesman, not a politician."

She shrugged. "Perhaps a little of each. You have a tremendous power drive, Andrew. Nothing gets in your way."

He leaned forward with interest. "Exactly how do you see that?"

"It's a Pluto thing. Pluto dominates your chart, and it's all about power and control. You need to control everything around you."

"And how do I control everything?"

"Well, you have this fantastic mastery of detail. You foresee every possibility—and you don't take action until everything is covered."

"Go on."

"You can also take a large scale view of things. Detail and large scale—now that's a combination very few people have. So, you plan the whole scenario, and we lesser people just fall into step."

"Couldn't you call that leadership?"

She shook her head. "No, it's more than that. Leadership implies that people follow voluntarily. You try to set it up so they have no alternatives."

"Hmm—I don't sound very pleasant, do I?"

"Well, I'd say complex, fascinating—pleasant is far too tame a word for you." She put a hand to her mouth. "I'm talking too much."

"No, I'm enjoying this. Go on."

"All right—there is something else. This need for control—it applies to yourself, too. You have this incredible self-discipline. But it's at the expense of your own feelings." She hesitated. His face had become rigid. "You're so out of touch with them that—"

"I've heard enough," Granit said, motioning to the waiter who was hovering nearby. I've hit a nerve, Addie thought.

"Would you like dessert?"

She shook her head. "No—but coffee would be fine."

He ordered two coffees. When the waiter left, Addie said, "I offended you, Andrew. I'm sorry."

"Not at all. I just got bored with the whole business."

She stared at him. "You never lose your composure, do you?"

"Not in public. Certainly not at a luncheon table." He smiled. "But if you want to see me lose my composure in private—why, that can be arranged."

He took her hand and began tracing the pattern of veins in her wrist with his fingertips.

"Addie," he said, "I don't want to see you hurt. You've wandered onto a battlefield and you're roaming around like some poor innocent. You do want to be on the winning side, don't you?"

"That depends."

"It's where you belong."

The waiter arrived with their coffee, filling their cups from a gleaming silver pot, which he left on the table. Granit sipped his appreciatively. "Perfect," he said.

"What is it you really want, Andrew?" Addie said. "What can a 'poor innocent' like me possibly give you?"

He narrowed his eyes appraisingly. "A great deal of pleasure, I suspect. And—of course—when people are close, they share their secrets. I want to know exactly what you're telling our glorious president at your meetings."

That's it, Addie thought. That's what this is really all about. "How can that help you?" she asked.

"Details, Addie, details. As you said, I depend on details. If Henry takes what you tell him seriously, then I want to know exactly what you're telling him."

She shook her head. "Do you think I'd betray a trust? That I'd—"

"You see everything as so black and white. I'm not asking you to betray anything. Just what your astrology says about Henry, that's all—an interesting discussion between friends."

Granit looked at his watch. "I'm afraid we have to end our lunch. I told my driver to pick me up at 3:00—I have to get back to the Hill. We'll drop you off on the way."

Addie watched as he pressed his fingertips on the credit card pad, the new fingerprint verification system that had replaced signatures. Everything had been planned and timed, the bombshell saved until the end. He slipped her arm through his, as they walked to the door.

"You know where I live?" Addie asked.

Granit seemed annoyed. "I told you I know everything about you. I even know what time you turn your lights off." He pressed his lips together as though trying to take back the words.

She looked up at him. "My lights—?" A sudden memory struck her: the man standing at the corner, looking up—that feeling of being followed.

"It was you," she said. "*You* had me followed. And all the time, I thought—" She shivered. "Why, Andrew, why?"

He shrugged. "I have to take care of every detail. You never know where one might lead. Besides, you weren't bothered long. My man stopped following you when I had all the details I needed. Right when the Secret Service started sniffing around."

Addie pulled away from him. Her voice shook. "I think I'll—I'll pass on the ride. I have some things to do—it's the other direction."

He stared at her. "You're frightened, Addie. You're frightened of me. You have no reason to be."

She stood still, wide-eyed, her gaze fixed on his face.

"Come on, Addie, don't look at me like that. What do you think I'm going to do—pounce on you in the car? In front of my driver?"

Addie shook her head. She felt foolish and naive. They left the restaurant, and she got into the limousine that was waiting in front. Andrew Granit climbed in after her and closed the door. As the car eased into traffic, Addie slid over to the end of the seat. He moved after her, until she was pressed against the door.

"Andrew, you said—"

"You shouldn't believe anything I say." He laughed and put his arms around her. His lips pressed against hers, hard, forcing them open. He thrust his tongue inside her mouth, tentatively at first, and then deeply, searchingly. She felt a sudden surge of desire and pressed her body against his. His arms tightened around her.

Instantly, panic overcame desire, and Addie began to struggle. Granit loosened his grip and she pulled away, trembling.

"Don't be afraid. I'm not going to force myself on you." He looked at her searchingly, those intense eyes boring into her.

"I've misjudged you, Addie. You're not afraid of me at all. It's yourself you're afraid of."

"I think you've misjudged me from the beginning. I'm not looking for an affair with anyone. And if I were, I'm not so needy that I'd want one where I have to trade information for affection."

"Don't make it sound like some sort of business deal. I really am attracted to you, you know. I do want you." He cupped her face in his hands and brushed her eyelids with his lips.

She put her head back against the seat and closed her eyes, thinking about his nearness, wondering if he was watching her. They rode in silence for a few moments. Then Addie turned and looked at him.

"Andrew, I can't do what you want me to. I can't deceive people like that."

"You don't owe that gang anything. You think the Turners care about you? They're using you. If things turned sour, they'd toss you to the wolves without a moment's hesitation."

"And you?"

"At least I'm offering something in return. I'd protect you. But I can't, unless I have your complete loyalty."

"Oh, if it were only as simple as that."

"It is. Stop thinking about right and wrong. Let me worry about the details."

"I can't, Andrew—I just can't."

He opened his wallet, pulled out a card and dropped it into her purse. "Here's a private number, Addie. You can reach me there, if you change your mind."

They rode in silence, until the car pulled up in front of her building. She turned to him.

"Goodbye Andrew. I—it's been memorable."

He put his hand on her arm. "One more thing, Addie. Not a word about this to anyone. This is private—between us. Understand?" His tone had changed. It had become clearly menacing.

Addie nodded. She got out of the car and watched it speed away. When she opened the door of her apartment, its familiar serenity seemed unreal; Andrew Granit's presence still surrounded her.

She sank into a chair and pictured herself leaning on someone strong and powerful. No decisions—no worries—no wrestling with right and wrong. Just the mindless ease of following. She thought, too, about Andrew's lean, hard body and the feelings it had stirred up. There would be no worries about betrayal there, because there would be no trust, right from the beginning.

Addie sat for a long time in the slowly darkening room. Then she sighed, picked up the phone, and called Janice Turner.

Andrew Granit watched the late afternoon sunlight glinting off the windows of passing cars as his limousine inched its way through the traffic of downtown Washington. A police helicopter hovered overhead, monitoring the ebb and flow.

Too bad about Addie. She would have made an interesting plaything. He had expected the lunch to be a boring business, but she'd turned out to be more clever than he thought. And those eyes—they had an aphrodisiac effect.

Getting her input would have been helpful. If Henry really took that stuff seriously, then knowing what Addie was telling him would have put him one step ahead. There was another angle, too. He could have told Addie things to say, things to make Henry play right into his hands. Granit shrugged. He hadn't really counted on her help, but it would have hastened things along.

Well, he had given Addie her chance, but her benighted ideas of loyalty had gotten in the way. She'd be the loser for it. She was unimportant after all, and not worth more than the few hours he had spent on her. He couldn't waste any more time. Too bad though. He would have enjoyed making her change her mind.

He wondered whether she was actually giving Henry an edge with her counselling. He had little confidence in astrology, still he admitted every possibility. She had been right on target about him. Power had always dominated his life; hadn't he traded away his happiness for it? He gazed out at the Capitol building, looming in the distance. The power he would soon have was the sort other men only dreamed about.

Second only to the power was the sheer pleasure of destroying Henry Wycliff. Soon—very soon—Henry would be all through: a spent flower pressed into the pages of history. And Walter Turner, that sanctimonious son of a bitch, would go down with him. He would personally see to that. Perhaps after Walter became a nonentity, he would try his luck with Janice. He had always found her appealing.

Granit stared down at his hands clenched tightly together in his lap. Wycliff's damn speech had scuttled his hearings and pushed him further along the path to violence. He had to decide soon. Time was working against him. And if Addie started blabbing...Granit leaned forward and switched on the car phone. Simon would still be in his office. He had little else to do; the president had seen to that. Well, things would be different soon. Granit punched the button coded for the vice president's private number.

Simon Furst's handsome face appeared instantly on the screen above the phone. Granit smiled. There weren't many cars equipped with the new mobile teleview phones.

"How goes it, Simon?" he said.

"The usual—nothing accomplished, nothing lost. No, wait—I got a call from Cissy Henderson today. Something important she wants to discuss."

"You're moving up. A call from 'deep pockets' Henderson. My, my. I wonder what she wants."

"I know what she wants." Furst laughed. "What all of them want. What none of them ever get."

"Be very pleasant to her, Simon. I can smell campaign contribution."

"Don't worry. I know what to do. How was your day?"

Granit frowned. "A total waste. I took our lady of the stars out for lunch."

"And —?"

"And she didn't buy the proposition. The bitch thinks she'd be disloyal—that she'd be committing high treason."

Furst laughed. "Well, the old Granit charm failed. No wonder you sound in a bad mood."

"Do I? I guess I am. I'm not used to losing. And she did appeal to me. I could have gotten some pleasure out of it."

"You sound frustrated, Andrew."

Granit grimaced. "Frustrated and horny. It's not a good combination."

"Your compudex has half the available women in Washington. Call one of them and take it out on her tonight."

"No, I have other plans. That's why I'm calling. I'm on my way to the Hill now for a meeting. That's probably going to go on until seven something. I'll meet you for dinner afterward— say Peter's Pub at 8:00."

"Can't—I've got plans for tonight."

"Change them. I want to talk to you."

Furst sighed. "It's going to be hard. Jim and Dinah Scully are giving a dinner. I accepted two weeks ago."

"Dammit. I said I have to talk to you—tonight."

"What's so important that can't wait until tomorrow?"

"We need a contingency plan. If Addie keeps her mouth shut about today, we can continue as planned. If not, we're going to have to move ahead quickly. I'm not leaving anything to chance."

"I still think it can wait until—"

"I'll do the thinking, Simon—I said tonight." A hard edge crept into Granit's voice.

"All right—sure. 8:00 tonight at Peter's. See you then."

Andrew Granit replaced the phone, leaned back in his seat, and shook his head. It was a sad state of affairs that Simon Furst was the only one with whom he could be completely himself. What had Addie said about being in touch with his own feelings? Dammit, Addie again. He clenched his jaw. When this whole business was finally over, he just might teach the bitch a lesson.

CHAPTER THIRTEEN

Walter fumbled with his key in the darkness. Janice had neglected to turn on the outdoor light, probably annoyed that he was coming home late again tonight. Finally he found the lock, but before he could turn it, the door swung open. Janice stood in the hall.

"Waiting for me?" Walter asked

"I heard your car. Thought I'd give you the deluxe door lady treatment."

"I'm honored." Walter threw his attaché case on a chair and turned to her. "Sorry I'm so late, sweetheart. Something came up, and I couldn't—"

"That's all right. You're home now." Her eyes were twinkling and her voice bubbled with excitement.

"You look like you're bursting. Better spill it, before you explode."

"Am I that transparent?" Janice smiled. "Come, sit down and make yourself comfortable. I *do* have something to tell you."

Walter put his arm around her and they walked into the living room, settling into the circular couch. His fingers played absently with her hair. "Okay," he said, "let's have it."

"You'll never guess what happened today. Addie had lunch with Andrew Granit."

"What? How did *that* happen?"

"He called and invited her, that's how."

"And she accepted?"

Janice nodded. "Evidently the idea of having lunch with the notorious senator overcame any qualms she might have had."

Walter shook his head. "What a damn fool thing for her to do. Did she do any damage?"

"You know, you're not giving her credit for any sense."

"Come on, Janice. Look who she was up against. Andrew Granit, for God's sake. He can pry information out of a clam. What chance does someone like Addie have."

"You know, you sound as paranoid as Henry."

"I'm beginning to think Henry may be right. If Granit bothers to bend down and pick up every crumb himself—"

"Addie's no crumb."

"Well, she's hardly a main course, is she? It's hard to believe that Andrew spent hours of his time just to find out that Henry's using an astrologer. He's got flunkies to do that."

Janice smiled smugly. "Ah, the great Walter Turner has Andrew Granit's motives all figured out. Except there's more to it than that."

Walter began to lose patience. Janice had this annoying habit of turning every situation into a complicated plot. He sighed. "All right, what else is there?"

"Apparently Andrew made a pass at Addie." She smiled triumphantly at the stunned expression on Walter's face.

"At Addie? I don't believe it."

"Why not? Addie's quite pretty, you know, with that ivory complexion and those fabulous blue eyes. Or hadn't you noticed?"

"No, I can't say I have. But that's not the point. Andrew Granit—my God. You're sure Addie wasn't imagining it?"

"Quite sure. I don't know why you're so amazed. After all, with that mousy wife of his stashed away in Albuquerque, Andrew's practically a free man. He hardly leads a monastic life. That's pretty well documented."

"Yeah, I know. But Addie—she's not exactly Granit's type. And he's nearly twice her age."

"You're thirteen years older than me, remember? That hasn't been a problem." She planted a light kiss on his lips. "Age and sex—there's not much of a correlation after a certain point. Some men are still active in their nineties, you know. Somehow I think that's how Andrew will be."

"Jesus, Andrew Granit—a sex symbol." Walter shook his head. "I can't believe I'm hearing this. Tell me, do *you* find him appealing?"

"Well—he does project an aura of power and self-confidence. That can be pretty sexy. Andrew's a charmer in a sort of old-fashioned way. He's courtly and—"

"I know what Andrew Granit is," Walter exploded. "He's a son of a bitch who doesn't care about anyone—who destroys anything in his way. I hate to shatter your romantic illusions, but the only reason Andrew would deign to notice Addie is because she figures in some plan to get to Henry."

"'Deign to notice.' Really, Walter, you're beginning to divide the whole world into big people and little people. You never used to be that way."

"This isn't the time for a lecture on my social conscience. Tell me, does Andrew know about Addie?"

"Oh, he knows everything. He told her that. He even told her the date of her first White House visit, things like that."

"I thought so. I knew there was more to it. I knew he wanted more than to just get Addie to spread her legs for him."

Janice grimaced. "You have such a delicate way with a phrase, Walter."

"Come on—bottom line. What did the bastard want from Addie?"

"All right. He wanted her to tell him all about her meetings with the president—the details—everything."

Walter jumped up and began pacing around the room. "Jesus Christ, we might as well publish a timetable and mail it to Granit. Addie says this is a good time to do something, so that's when Henry does it—and Andrew Granit's standing there waiting for us."

"Walter, calm down. Addie's not going to do it. She told Andrew 'no.' There's no problem. Why are you getting so excited?"

"You know why. The thought of Andrew Granit knowing everything we're doing..." Walter shook his head as if to clear it. "Are you sure Addie isn't going along with this?"

"She called me, didn't she?"

"Yeah, but maybe that's part of his plan. Maybe he wanted her to call you to throw us off guard."

"Oh Walter," Janice started to laugh. "I couldn't write anything as convoluted as that."

"I guess you're right. But the humor escapes me. I don't think it will strike Henry so funny either."

"No," Janice said, "You can't tell Henry about it."

"What? Why the hell not?"

"Because Andrew warned Addie not to tell anyone. She was even scared to call me, but she wanted us to know about it. She made me promise not to tell anyone."

"You're telling me."

"I'm sure she didn't mean you. At least I don't think so. But it can't go any further. If Andrew found out—you know how vicious he can be. Walter, swear to me you won't mention it to Henry—or anyone. Swear it."

He came back, sat down beside her and put his arms around her. "I promise. My lips are sealed. No, you seal them for me."

She kissed him lightly. "Will that do?"

"No way." He pressed his lips against hers, hard, and they fell back against the couch. A noise in the hall made Walter stiffen. He jumped up, embarrassed. Sophie had been heading toward the kitchen and had dropped a tray she was carrying.

"Excuse me," Sophie said, peering into the living room. "I'm so clumsy." She stood there, ill at ease, clutching the offending tray.

"It's all right, Sophie. You didn't interrupt anything important." Janice flashed Walter a mischievous smile. He glared at her.

"Oh, I think Mr. Turner disagrees," Janice continued. "Well, no harm done."

Sophie nodded and walked out. As she disappeared, Walter whispered to Janice, "Do we really need a live-in housekeeper? She's always underfoot."

"It's the only way we can hold on to her. And she's such a gem."

Walter shrugged. "I guess it's better to have Sophie underfoot than to eat your cooking."

"Oh Walter." Janice tapped him lightly on the head and then ran her finger back and forth across his lips. "Remember—I've sealed your lips. Not a word about this to anyone."

CHAPTER FOURTEEN

B ruce Hanover's replacement met Addie at the North Portico entrance. He was a square, solidly built man, with eyes in perpetual motion.

"Miss Pryce?" he asked. Addie nodded.

"I'm John Velandro. I'm to take you up to the second floor."

"I know the way," Addie said.

"Sure, but—see—they don't like to have people wandering around above the ground floor."

They walked down the hall toward the elevator through a buzz of excitement. People stood in little knots, whispering. Several held copies of the *Sentinel*. Addie glanced at the Secret Service agent, but he continued on impassively.

The door to the president's den was closed, and Velandro knocked softly. Walter opened it and took Addie to one side.

"We tried to call you Addie—to stop you from coming. There was no answer at your place, and we couldn't get you on the radiophone." He glanced pointedly at her bare wrist.

"Oh, I didn't wear it today, because I knew I was coming here. I'm sorry. I should have put it on. What's the matter?"

Walter pointed to the couch. "Sit down. You'll hear all about it." He turned to Velandro. "Please wait outside. Don't let anyone in." He closed the door.

Addie walked over to the couch and sat down next to Jonah, delighted to see him there. There were two unfamiliar people in the room. A tall woman, with close-cropped salt-and-pepper hair, stood talking to the president, who was slumped over in one of the turquoise chairs. A bulky man, so heavy that his expensive suit strained at the seams, stared out the window.

"Addie," Walter said, "You haven't met Eve Kontos, the president's chief of staff, and Martin Shaw, his press secretary."

Eve Kontos stopped her conversation with the president, looked at Addie, and nodded. Martin Shaw did not bother to turn around and acknowledge her.

"Bastard," Jonah muttered under his breath.

"It's just as well you're here, Addie," Walter said. "I gather you haven't seen the *Sentinel* this morning."

Addie shook her head.

Jonah handed her the copy he was holding, open to the "Front Page Rumors" column. "Greg Harmon dropped a bombshell today."

"Take it home and read it," Walter said. "It's a half page of innuendoes about the president—his health, his habits, and, I'm afraid, his consultations with an astrologer."

"And my sanity in general," the president added.

"Does it mention my name?" Addie asked.

Walter shook his head. "No, but it's just a matter of time 'til the newshounds track you down. We're going to have to stop your sessions with the president, of course. But we need to do more."

"It's not just the astrology," Eve Kontos said, looking at Addie. "It's the whole rotten picture this cretin painted. He's made the president into a drunkard, a weakling, a halfwit, a madman—someone you don't want running the country."

"Eve, you always sum things up so nicely," the president said with a wry smile. "It's a positive gift."

"Well, maybe I'm exaggerating a little, but we do need major damage control here."

"Okay," Walter said. "I think I've got a handle on it. Operation disappearance. Addie vanishes, the president makes a foreign trip—and the whole business runs out of steam."

Addie looked at him. "I don't understand, Walter. How do I vanish?"

"Well Addie, I'm afraid you're going to have to leave town for a while."

"What? I don't want to leave town. This is where I live. Where would I go? What would I do? Jonah," she turned to him, "they can't make me leave, can they?"

Jonah gazed at her sadly. "I don't know, Addie."

Martin Shaw turned and looked at Addie with sudden interest. He walked over to the couch and sat down next to her.

"Jonah," he said, "the lady's asking for your sage advice and counsel. Let's hear it."

"Cut it out, Marty," Jonah said through clenched teeth.

"Oh, run out of bright ideas?" Shaw looked at Addie, his little pig eyes buried in deep folds of flesh. "Now if you want my advice, I'll be glad to help. Take advantage of all this. A nice, long vacation. Enjoy it. Find someone to—"

"Okay Marty, that's enough." Walter walked over to Addie and stood gazing down at her. "Of course we can't force you to do anything, Addie. But if you're here, the press will hound you and make your life miserable. And then, there's the president's welfare to think of."

"I don't want to leave Washington, Walter. Everything I have is here."

"It won't be forever, Addie. We'll keep your apartment here—pay the rent—see that everything's okay. And, of course, we'll take care of all the expenses wherever you go."

"How long do you think..."

"Six months. Maybe a little longer. It should all blow over by then."

The president looked up and spoke softly. "I'd be most grateful, Addie."

"I don't really have a choice, do I?"

"There's always a choice," Walter said. "It's making the right one that matters. And I think you—"

A commotion outside interrupted him.

The door flew open, and the first lady, holding a copy of the *Sentinel*, burst into the room, followed by John Velandro.

"I knew I'd find you here," Ellen Wycliff said to the president. "This—this creature," she pointed to Velandro, "tried to keep me out."

"He was acting on my instructions," the president said. "I didn't want to be disturbed."

"I do not consider myself a disturbance, darlin'. Do any of you?" She looked around the room and stiffened when she caught sight of Addie.

"What is that woman doing here?" she shrieked. "Hasn't she done us enough damage?" She waved the paper in the air.

"'The president is lost in the stars,' it says. She is making us the laughing stock of Washington.'"

Addie shrank back against the couch, the color draining from her face. She looked at Jonah. He was staring straight ahead, fists clenched tightly.

The president jumped up and put his arm around his wife. He squeezed just hard enough to make her wince.

"Ellen," he said, "I think we've heard enough on the subject. I am familiar with your ideas and I thank you for your input."

"Don't you dare patronize me!"

"Mrs. Wycliff," Eve Kontos moved respectfully in front of the first lady. "I was going to call you later. Could you spare me a few moments in private now. It's important. I've got some ideas I'd like to run by you. Things I think only you could do to help defuse this mess."

"Well now, Eve—I'd surely like to hear what you think I can do. Let's walk over to my office. Thank God for *your* sanity."

"Will you excuse me, sir?" Kontos asked the president.

"Go with my blessing. And thank you, Eve," he whispered.

An embarrassed silence hung in the air following the two women's departure.

The president sank back into his chair and buried his face in his hands.

"Well, that was worth the price of admission," Martin Shaw murmured, rubbing his hands together in delight. Addie stared at his fingers; they were like overstuffed sausages, sporting a diamond pinkie ring and a wide gold wedding band.

He turned to Addie. "Are you still in one piece? Or did the wicked witch destroy poor little Dorothy?"

"I'll survive."

"Addie, it's been a rough morning for you." Walter looked at her. "Why don't you go home and start thinking about—I know, give Janice a call. She'll have some ideas for you."

"There's something else," Addie said. "You said something about the president taking a trip."

"Yes, I've been thinking about that Asian trip. This would be a good time for it. Take him far away."

"No, it's a terrible time. Some things are coming up I don't like—things very much like Bruce Hanover had in his chart."

Walter looked annoyed. "The president is not going to commit suicide, Addie."

"No, and neither did Bruce."

"Let's not start *that* again. This isn't the place for it."

"I think it would be dangerous for the president to take a trip right now—especially one that far away," Addie said.

The president looked up. "Walter, if Addie thinks—"

"Sir," Walter said firmly. "We're finished with what Addie thinks. Forget about the stars. They haven't done you much good so far, have they?"

Addie shrugged. Suddenly she no longer cared what happened to any of them, including the president. Concentrate on herself—that's what she had to do.

"May I leave now?" she asked, getting up.

President Wycliff walked over and took her hand. "I'm sorry, Addie—truly sorry."

Addie looked at him. She didn't trust herself to speak.

Jonah jumped up. "I'll take Addie downstairs. You don't need me any more and I've got a mountain of calls to make."

Walter nodded. As they left the room, Shaw called after them. "Don't fool around with your girlfriend too long, Jonah. Get started on those calls."

"You and your boss don't like each other very much," Addie said, as they walked towards the elevator.

"I hate his guts. He loves to humiliate people—makes him look big."

"He doesn't have to try hard to do that."

Jonah laughed. "Yeah, he is a fat slob, isn't he. Funny thing—he fancies himself a lover boy. He chases after every female reporter in the White House press corps. Dangles exclusives in front of them, but they have to sleep with him to get them. You know what they used to call lady reporters way back in the thirties?"

"I have no idea," Addie said.

"Sob sisters. Funny, huh? I tell you they've got a lot to sob about after a night with Marty Shaw." Jonah grimaced. "Sometimes I have to pimp for him, too."

"Oh, Jonah."

"What the hell—it's a job." Jonah shook his head "I don't know why I'm dumping all this on you, Addie. You've got your own troubles. Say, how about stopping in at my office for a minute. You've never seen it."

"I'd like to."

They left the elevator and walked down the ground floor corridor.

"Here we are," Jonah said, taking her arm and leading her into one of the rooms lining the hall. He closed the door behind them, and Addie looked around the small room. The office seemed an extension of Jonah: rumpled, cluttered, and very comfortable.

He looked embarrassed. "It's a mess. I've been so busy, I haven't..." He moved some books off an arm chair and motioned her toward it, then perched on the edge of the desk.

"You know, Addie, I feel really awful about what happened up there. That goddamn Ellen Wycliff. I wanted to punch her—hard—right in her aristocratic nose."

Addie smiled for the first time that morning. "I'm awfully glad you didn't."

"Yeah. It would have been the end of my so-called career."

"Oh Jonah," Addie suddenly remembered the book. "I almost forgot. I have a present for you."

"For me? Why?"

"Oh, for being so nice and driving me home that night." The dinner seemed light years away. She rummaged through her briefcase and pulled out a gift-wrapped package.

"Here," she said. "I hope you like it."

He grinned and tore off the wrappings like a little boy opening a Christmas present.

"*Science Trivia*—hey Addie, I love it. How'd you know I like these trivia things?"

"Oh, a lucky guess. You're an Aries, after all, and you love the challenge of tests. You always have to make sure you're number one."

Jonah frowned. Addie bit her lip. "I'm sorry. There I go again, annoying you with my astrology."

"No, you're reading me wrong, Addie. What I was thinking was that I'm gonna miss it."

Addie's eyes misted and she looked down. She made an elaborate show of closing her briefcase. Jonah walked over and rested his hand on the back of the chair.

"You got a really rotten deal, Addie. You gave it everything you had, and that's the thanks you get. Kicked out." He shook his head. "The king, sending you into exile."

"I'm getting used to the idea. Maybe it won't be so bad. I think I'll go back to Cincinnati for a while. You know, that's where I come from—where my family lives. I'll visit there and decide what to do next."

Addie stood up and held out her hand. "Well, I'd better be going now. I guess we'll have to postpone our chess game."

He took her hand and shook it solemnly.

"Listen, the press may start hounding you. Take my advice—don't pick up your phone. Let the answering unit screen all your calls. And if there's anything at all I can do to help, you call me, okay?"

"Thanks, Jonah." He opened the door for her, and she walked away, down the familiar ground floor corridor to the north exit.

As Addie opened the door to her apartment, the green panel just above the lock began to glow, indicating telephone messages. She checked her answering machine. It was a little after 11:00 and there were already almost a dozen calls waiting for her.

The first, at 8:15, was from Livonia. She must have called right after Addie left for the White House. Livonia's voice sounded excited. "Addie," she said. "Call me as soon as you get in. I've got some news from my source in Santa Fe. There's something really fishy about that birth certificate. And I've got information about that Salazar character, too. Call me right away."

A bunch of messages from the media followed. Reporters, columnists, TV people, all asking her to call back. Did they know she was the president's astrologer, or were they calling every astrologer in Washington? She decided to ignore them all.

The last message was from Andrew Granit. "I'm very angry with you, Addie," he said. "You betrayed me. I warned you not to tell anyone. Did you really think you could trust the Turners? You made a very bad choice." Without Andrew's face in front of her, Addie could hear the menace in that smooth, silken voice very clearly.

She shivered and looked around her apartment, the safe world she had built so painstakingly. It was crumbling around her. She took Andrew Granit's card out of her purse and turned it over in her hand. He had been right all along. They had tossed her out like yesterday's dirty laundry. And now Andrew was her enemy too.

It was all Janice Turner's fault. She had pretended to be her friend, and Addie had trusted her. Janice had repeated everything she had told her about Andrew Granit. Who knew about it now? Walter? The president? Jonah? Oh God, not Jonah. She wanted to confront Janice, but she'd call Livonia first. Not that she cared any more about the vice president's birth certificate, but Livonia would tell her what to do.

Addie punched Livonia's number. There was no answer, just an endless ringing. Strange—she never went out these days. Addie was one of the few who knew Livonia's secret, her crippling fear of the outside world. Livonia must be in the shower or sleeping. She'd try again later.

Addie felt as if she'd choke on her own rage if she didn't call Janice Turner. Sophie answered and when she relayed the message, Janice picked up the phone immediately.

"Addie," she said. "Did you see the *Sentinel* this morning?"

"I was at the White House. I saw it there. Then your husband told me I have to leave Washington."

"Walter—why would he do that?"

"I seem to have become an embarrassment."

"Addie, you sound so strange. What can I do to help?"

"You've helped enough already," Addie said coldly.

"What do you mean?"

"I told you about Andrew Granit in confidence. You swore you wouldn't tell anyone."

"I only told—" Janice stopped.

"Yes. Who did you only tell?"

"Walter, that's all. Surely you didn't mean for me not to tell him."

"Especially not him. He must have run right back to the White House with the story, and somehow Andrew found out. He left a message on my answering unit. He's furious and I'm terrified, and—and—I wish I'd listened to him. He was right about you two. I don't want to talk to you any more—ever. You've done enough harm."

Addie slammed down the phone, her fury swirling around her like a living thing. It was the culmination of the whole awful morning. She tried Livonia again, but there was still no answer. Addie went into the kitchen to make some tea. She stared out the window while she waited for the kettle to boil. She had never felt so alone.

Martin Shaw was drawing up a list of reporters to take on the Asia trip when Eve Kontos poked her head inside the door.

"Meeting still going on?" she asked.

Walter nodded. "Just winding down, Eve. Come on in."

She sat down on the couch next to Shaw, running her hand through her hair.

"Well, I gave the first lady a few people to call," she said. "When she gets through with them, I bet they'll be on the side of the angels."

The president looked at her. "You know, you're one of the few people who can really handle my wife. God bless you."

"May I speak frankly, sir?"

The president nodded.

"I think you misunderstand her—all of you. I believe she's really trying to protect you, sir, and she's doing it the only way she knows how—with a combination of Southern charm and Washington acid."

"You sincerely think that, Eve?"

"I do. Maybe it's because I'm a woman and see it from her point of view."

"Woman's intuition," Martin Shaw murmured and rolled his eyes at the ceiling.

"We all know your opinion of women, Marty," she said. "I often wonder how you think you arrived on this planet. Don't you think a woman had something to do with it?"

"Oh, women are good for some things. Would you like a list of them, dear?"

"Easy, easy," Walter said. "We don't need this now." He sank down on the couch next to Eve Kontos, stretching out his long legs.

"I think the president's Asian trip is becoming a fact." Walter turned to the chief of staff. "How long do you think it'll take to get it rolling?"

"A matter of days."

"The sooner the better."

The president looked at Walter. "You're certain it's a good idea?"

"I think it's the only option we've got right now. Rumors have a habit of losing steam when the fuel's gone. You come back with a few good agreements under your belt, and we can hang Harmon and his damn column out to dry and watch him twist in the wind."

"Especially with the right crew along to send back good press reports," Shaw said.

"Agreed. Get the press list finalized and on my desk this afternoon," Eve Kontos said crisply, all business now.

"I'll get on it immediately, madam." Shaw heaved his bulk up from the couch. "Anything else before I leave, sir?"

The president shook his head. "Nothing now. I don't think I need you any more either, Eve. I'm sure you've got a lot to do."

Walter watched the two leave, chatting amiably. He marveled at Eve Kontos' ability to handle people, accepting barbs and praise with equal composure. She refused to be cowed, but never stayed angry. She was a first-rate chief of staff.

When the door closed, the president stood up and bolted to the bar. He poured some bourbon into a glass, adding a large quantity of ice.

"We're alone now," Walter said. "I have to talk straight. You've got to ease up on that stuff."

"I know, I know. You're right, Walter. And I'm going to. I won't touch a drop on the trip. That will be a beginning."

Walter shook his head. "Everyone'll be drinking up a storm. How will you manage?"

"I'll be drinking Diet Coke—with lots of lemon. I've done it before. You know that."

"Yeah, but you've never had this kind of pressure. I hope—"

The desk phone buzzed.

"Damn, I told them no interruptions," Walter said. He picked up the receiver. "Yes," he snapped.

It was Lorna, the president's secretary. "Your wife's on the phone, Mr. Turner. I told her you weren't to be disturbed, but she insisted." Lorna hesitated. "She sounds very angry."

"Okay, Lorna. Thanks. Put her through."

"Walter, are you alone?" Janice asked.

"No, I'm with the president."

"Don't answer then, just listen."

"This better be good, Janice!"

"Oh, it's good, all right. I'm ready to leave you over this, Walter."

"What? Okay—I'm listening."

"I just got a call from Addie. She had a message from Andrew Granit—a very angry message. He knows that she told me all about their lunch. How many people did you blab to, Walter? The entire White House staff? You swore not to tell. I—I sealed your lips, remember? But that didn't mean anything to you, did it."

"Janice, I—"

"Don't talk. Just listen. Addie hung up on me. She was angry and terrified and sounded so alone. God, how could you do that to her? How could you do that to me?"

"Janice, listen to me. I swear I didn't say a word to anyone. I swear by all that's holy to both of us. You've got to believe me."

"Then how did he—"

"I'll figure it out. I'll call you back as soon as I can. I love you—very much." He replaced the receiver with shaking hands and smiled weakly at the president.

"A little domestic problem," he said. "Janice thinks I've betrayed her trust."

"You don't have to explain. I don't like to see you upset, Walter, but it's reassuring to know that you and Janice have problems just like everyone else."

"Nothing's made in heaven, I'm afraid." Walter rubbed his forehead. "I've got a splitting headache, Henry. I don't think there's anything more to do right now. If it's okay with you, I'm going to hunt up some aspirin."

"Sure, go ahead. I've got to get going and face the world anyway. Send Velandro in when you leave."

Walter nodded and bolted for the door. His headache was genuine, but the aspirin could wait. He wanted to get to a phone, away from the White House, where he could talk to Janice privately. The words "leave you" had struck a terror in his soul that he had never known before.

He left the White House and walked quickly down New York Avenue to 14th Street. There was a coffee shop he knew about that had some phone booths buried in the rear. He headed for the shop and breathed a sigh of relief when he was finally seated in one of the booths. He pushed his phone card into the slot and punched in his home number. Janice answered at the first ring. She must have been sitting there, waiting.

"Okay sweetheart. I can talk now. I'm in a phone booth away from the White House."

"Walter, I'm sitting here, trying so hard to believe you, but—"

"You've got to believe me Janice. I've never lied to you. I never would, no matter what."

"You swear you didn't tell Henry?"

"On my life, Janice. On your sweet, precious life. I swear it."

"Then how could Andrew Granit—?"

"I've been thinking about it. He must have a tap on Addie's phone—that's the only way. But for the life of me, I don't know how. The Secret Service secured her phone."

"Then he couldn't have."

"Or maybe he was just guessing. He probably figured Addie would tell you."

"I don't think so. Addie said he was so angry. He knew."

"Right now I don't give a damn how he knew. Just don't blame me, Janice. I didn't do anything. You do believe me now, don't you?"

"I—I guess I do. Oh Walter, I feel so badly for Addie. She was so upset. She said something—that you were making her leave Washington."

"Not 'making her leave,' just 'suggesting.' It's for her own good, Janice. She'll be ripped apart in the press if she stays here. And now with this Granit thing, she's got another reason to get away."

Janice sighed. "I wish there was something I could do."

"I think the best thing is to leave her alone. At least right now. But there is something you can do for me."

"What's that?"

"Promise you'll never say those words to me again."

"What words?"

"You know—'leave you.' I couldn't bear losing you, Janice."

"If I can't trust you, Walter, I can't stay with you. I mean that."

"But you do trust me now, don't you? Say it."

There was silence on the line.

"I have to hear it. Say it."

"I—I trust you, Walter."

"You don't sound like you mean it. Say it like you mean it."

Janice laughed. The sound sang over the wires like a Vivaldi concerto. "Walter, you're acting like a little boy. I do trust you. There. Now, prove you're worth it by getting home early tonight.

"6:00. Date?"

"I'll be waiting."

"Goodbye, sweetheart."

Walter hung up and sighed. His throbbing head matched the pounding of his heart. Goddamn you Andrew Granit, he thought, you almost destroyed my marriage. I won't let anyone do that.

CHAPTER FIFTEEN

Jonah looked at his green marble desk clock. 4:22. Except for two quick trips to the john and a sandwich at his desk, he had worked nonstop since Addie left this morning, not taking any calls, even on his direct line. He leafed through the bunch of messages his secretary had just handed him. Most would have to wait until tomorrow.

He stopped at one message; it was from Addie. He had her number in memory and punched the button. After three rings, her answering machine switched on. Good. She had listened to him.

"This is Jonah," he said. "If you're home, pick up."

"Jonah, thanks for calling back." Addie's voice sounded strained.

"What's wrong?"

"I'm so worried. You remember I told you about Livonia Matthews? My teacher and my—my best friend? She left a message on my unit this morning when I was at the White

House. Said to call back right away. I've been trying to reach her all day. There's no answer."

"She's probably out someplace."

"No, Livonia has agoraphobia. That's a fear of going outside and—"

"I know what it is. She never goes out?"

"Never. It's been getting worse. She won't leave her apartment—not for anything."

"Gee, Addie, I don't know what—"

"That's not the worst of it, Jonah. I called the building manager—Livonia lives in the Watergate. I told him I was worried that something happened to her. He said she called him about ten this morning. Told him she was going away—she'd be back in a week, to hold her mail."

"Well, that explains it then." Jonah began to glance at the clock.

"You don't understand. Livonia would never go away without telling me. And her message said to call back. She expected to be there."

"Well, something came up suddenly." Jonah had a sudden inspiration. "Hey, maybe that's what she wanted—to tell you she was going away."

"No. You don't know how bad her agoraphobia is. She'd never be able to go away for a vacation. I told the manager that. I begged him to go up to her apartment and check. But he wouldn't. Said he couldn't just go into tenants' apartments when they're away. I kept insisting and then—then he hung up on me."

I don't blame him, Jonah thought.

"I know something awful happened. She hasn't been too well lately. Maybe she fell or had a stroke."

"Look Addie—be logical. You think Livonia called the building manager, told him a lie about going on vacation and then proceeded to have a stroke? It doesn't make sense."

Addie's voice broke. "Jonah, you told me to call if I needed help. Well, I need help. I don't know what to do. I've got to find out what happened to Livonia."

Jonah ran his hands through his hair. The kind of help he'd meant was carrying a suitcase or making some phone calls. Still, he enjoyed a challenge. He prided himself on being able to handle any situation. He could get that damn building manager to do whatever he wanted.

"Look," he said, "You want me to go down with you to the Watergate? I can get that guy to let us into the apartment."

"Oh Jonah—would you? I'll never forget it."

"I'll do it, Addie." He sighed. "But I tell you, we're gonna have a lot of explaining to do when we find an empty apartment." He looked at the clock. "I'll pick you up in front of your building in about an hour. Okay?"

"I'll be waiting. I don't know how to thank you."

"We'll figure out a way." He hung up the phone and shook his head. A perfect ending to a typical Jonah Stern day—playing cops and robbers with Addie Pryce.

Jonah parked his car in the Watergate garage, and he and Addie headed for the building manager's office. She had filled him in about Livonia's message—the birth certificate, the Salazar guy—but it didn't justify what they were about to do. He felt queasier with every step.

"Come in," the building manager called in answer to their knock. A thin man in a pencil-striped suit, with slicked back dark hair and a skinny mustache rose from behind the desk and greeted them.

"I'm James Capra. What can I do for you?" he said.

"More than you've done so far," Jonah pointed to Addie. "This lady called you this afternoon about Livonia Matthews."

"Yes, and I told her Miss Matthews is gone. She left for a vacation today."

"We've got reason to think she didn't. We want to check her apartment."

"I'm afraid I can't do that. I can't start—"

"Look," Jonah said, "I don't think you catch my drift. The White House is interested in Miss Matthews." He pulled out a Secret Service badge and thrust it in front of Capra.

"Well, she didn't tell me that," Capra said, pointing a finger at Addie.

"She couldn't. You hung up on her. Now, let's get going up to that apartment. If anything happened—" He shook his head.

Capra nodded and led them to the elevator. Jonah winked at Addie and fingered the badge in his pocket. He tried not to think about the penalty for impersonating a Secret Service agent.

The passkey stuck in the lock for a moment, then turned and the door swung open. Capra walked in first and stopped short with a stifled scream.

"Oh my God, oh my God," he moaned.

Jonah pushed past him and stopped at the entrance to the living room. Papers, books, and magazines were strewn everywhere. At one end of the room Livonia Matthew's body lay on the floor, staring sightlessly at the ceiling. It seemed incredible that her body could have contained the quantity of blood puddling around her, staining her silver hair and beige blouse a lurid red.

Jonah turned to stop Addie, but she was right behind him. She saw Livonia, gasped and swayed forward on crumpling legs. Jonah caught her and half carried, half dragged her onto the couch. He put her head down between her knees and knelt beside her, whispering in her ear.

"Addie, hold on, hold on. I know this is awful, but just hold on. We've got a mess here. I've got to get rid of this clown. Keep your head down and take deep slow breaths. For God's sake, don't go to pieces. Just hold on."

He got up and rushed back to Capra, who was still moaning and wringing his hands.

"You're in big trouble, buddy," Jonah said.

Capra looked at him. "How could this happen? How could they get by security? We don't have robberies here."

"You're in big trouble," Jonah repeated. "We asked you to check hours ago. This woman might have been saved. When the White House finds out—she was valuable to us."

"You mean this might not be a robbery?"

"I'm not saying and you're not guessing—understand. You don't want to know about this. Do you want to get off the hook?"

Capra nodded.

"Okay. Do exactly what I say."

Capra nodded again. "Anything, anything."

"Go back downstairs. Nothing happened—you never saw us. You give us one hour to get what we want and get out of here. Then you call your security guy and say you just got a call about the Matthews apartment—an anonymous call. You come up here, find it just like it is and call the police. That's it. We're not involved—you're not involved. Understand?"

"Right. One hour, then I come up. Then I call the police."

"After that it's police business. A robbery, whatever. But if you ever open your mouth about the White House..."

"I understand. Can I go?"

Jonah nodded. As soon as Capra closed the door, he rushed back to Addie. She was turning greyish white and her eyes looked at him blankly. Her skin was clammy, and her forehead was beaded with perspiration. Jeez, she's going into shock.

He laid Addie gently on the couch, raising her feet up on a pile of books. Then he took off his jacket and wrapped it around her and began rubbing her arms and hands briskly. All the while, his eyes darted around the room.

This was no robbery. The room was full of valuable art pieces, all undisturbed, while papers were strewn everywhere. Someone had been searching for something.

Addie began to stir and moan softly.

"Can you sit up?" he asked.

"Yes, I—oh, Jonah." She caught sight of Livonia's body.

"Don't look over there." He put his arms around her. "You've got to be strong now, for your friend's sake. It's the only way you can help her now."

"I'm all right. I really am." She was calm and breathing evenly. It was a temporary calm, he knew, but it might just get her through this.

She stared at him. "Why—why would anyone want to kill Livonia?"

"I want you to concentrate, Addie. Can you think of anything your friend had that someone might be looking for."

She shook her head. "She had so many things."

"Jeez, it's a needle in a—"

"Oh my God, she knew." Addie clapped her hands to her face. "Livonia saw this coming. She knew she was going to die."

"Addie, come on."

"No, Jonah. It's not easy to see death in a chart, but Livonia did. She just made a new will. She told me about it. She was leaving me her library—it's full of rare astrology books."

"That doesn't prove anything. Lots of people make wills."

"No, listen—she said something funny—said there was one special book, *The Bowl of Heaven*. She kept insisting that I make sure I get that book. She talked like she knew it was going to happen."

"What's so special about that book?" Jonah asked.

"I don't know. It's an autobiography of Evangeline Adams, an astrologer who was famous a hundred years ago. It's out of print, but it's not that valuable. I told her that, and she said, 'No, it's the most valuable book I own. Be sure you get it when I'm gone.' Jonah, what do you think?"

"I think we'd better find that book." He looked at his watch. "We've got to be out of here in half an hour. Where could it be?"

"She said she kept it by her bed, so she'd always know where it was."

"Okay, can you stand up?"

She nodded and stood up, shivering, keeping her eyes away from Livonia's body.

"Put my jacket on," Jonah said. "It'll keep you warm. You have to stay warm."

She put it on mechanically and waited to be told what to do next. He looked at her and shook his head. She's numb, he thought.

"Come on—let's find that book." He took her hand and led her into the bedroom. The same chaos greeted them there.

Books, papers, and clothing covered the floor. The bed was stripped down to the mattress. Drawers were pulled out of the dresser and overturned.

Jonah led Addie to a pile of books near the bed. "You go through these. I'll look over there."

"Wait," he shouted as a thought struck him. "Don't touch anything yet." He pulled out his handkerchief and a small pocket knife, cutting the cloth into two pieces. He handed one piece to Addie. "Hold everything you touch with this. We don't want to leave any fingerprints."

Addie wrapped the cloth around her hand obediently and began fumbling through the pile of books. Jonah had gotten halfway through the books tossed near the window, when Addie shouted, "I've got it!"

He rushed over and found her holding a worn blue book, its spine bent and torn. She handed it to him.

He opened it and shook it hard. Nothing fell out. He flipped through the pages. They were filled with margin notes and highlighting; maybe that meant something. Then he turned to the back of the book. There was a double flyleaf, and the pages were filled with names, organized by states and cities, all in a tiny, meticulous script.

"What's this, Addie?" He handed her the book, opened to the flyleaf.

She stared at it. "Oh, this must be her list of sources—you know, for birth records. It was so precious to her. She guarded that with—oh, Jonah, she left it to me."

Her eyes filled and her face began to crumple. No, Jonah thought, no grief 'til we're out of here.

"Addie, hold on now. We're almost home free. We've just got to go down in the elevator like nothing happened and get to the car. Okay?"

She nodded and walked toward the door, a dazed expression on her face. He looked at her with admiration. He didn't think he'd be able to hang in there like that. He picked up Addie's purse, looked around to make sure they hadn't left anything, and helped her out of Livonia's apartment.

In the car, Addie sat as if in a trance, hugging the book to her chest. Jonah kept glancing at her, praying the protective numbness would last until he could get her safely home.

When they opened the door to her apartment, Jonah felt relief so intense that it swept through him like an avalanche. He leaned against the wall until his head cleared.

"You're home safe and sound," he said. "We'll get you something hot to drink and get you to bed."

"I'm all right, Jonah. I can take care of myself." She sat down in a chair, staring straight ahead.

"Well, I'll stay here a while."

"I'd really rather you go. I want to be alone—to think."

"I don't want to go, Addie."

"Whatever you say. Please turn out the light. I want it to be dark."

He turned out all the lights, except one small lamp in the living room, and sat down in a chair opposite her. The only sound was the soft whirring of the refrigerator in the kitchen.

Jonah couldn't understand what was happening to him. He only knew that the most important thing in the world right now was to be near Addie—to help her get through her pain. God, he'd rather take the pain himself. That was a feeling he'd never had before and it stunned him.

Suddenly Addie sighed, a sigh so huge it seemed to start in the depths of her soul.

"Livonia's gone," she said. "She was all I had in the world—all I cared about. She's gone, gone, gone."

Addie slipped to the floor, buried her head in the chair and began to sob. Jonah had never heard such sobs. They were like waves pounding the beach, each one racking her body. It was as though a dam had burst, opening floodgates to years of grief. Jonah stood there helplessly, watching her. Then he sank down on the floor beside her. He held her tightly, rocking slowly back and forth.

"It's going to be all right, Addie," he repeated over and over. "It's going to be all right." At that moment, he would have given up everything he had to make it so.

CHAPTER SIXTEEN

The alarm jolted Jonah awake. He had set it an hour and a half earlier than usual so he'd have time to go over and check on Addie before work. He padded into the kitchen, cursing under his breath. He had been so tired after leaving Addie last night that he had forgotten to set the automatic coffee maker. It would have to be instant this morning.

Jonah took his cup with him to the telephone. First thing he had to do was call Walter Turner. Livonia's murder would be all over the morning papers and Jonah wanted to speak to him before he read about it. Who knew what the manager might have told the police about the White House.

Walter answered the phone, his voice crackling with the annoyance of being torn out of a sound sleep.

"Yes?"

"Walter, this is Jonah."

"I know—I see you on the screen. What the hell do you want? It's—dammit, it's only 6:30."

"Sorry about that. I had to get you before you left the house."

"Hell, you could have waited an hour. You woke up Janice, too. Scared her. She thought something awful happened."

"Well, something pretty bad did happen."

"What—what is it?" Walter became alert.

Jonah told him the whole story, starting with Addie's phone call and ending with their flight from Livonia's apartment. When he mentioned the Secret Service business, Walter exploded.

"You asshole. What a damn stupid thing to do. To involve the White House in something like that."

"It was the only way I could get that prick of a manager to go up to the apartment. Jeez, that woman's body could have been there a week before anyone found it. Anyway, I figured we owed Addie that much."

"Listen, Jonah. Get this straight once and for all. We don't owe Addie anything. We paid her for everything she did and we'll take care of all her expenses now."

Jonah swallowed hard. "Well, see—Addie was so upset, so worried that—"

"Christ, I'm sick of hearing about Addie. I get it from you. I get it from the president. I even get it from my wife. I'm glad that whole business is finished. Oh goddammit. Now Janice is glaring at me."

"Look," Jonah said, "I don't want to start any trouble. I just wanted you to know about it before you read the papers. And don't worry about that building manager. He won't mention the White House. I scared him shitless."

"I hope so. We've got enough troubles. The last thing we need is to get involved in some cockamamie burglary."

"I'm not so sure it's a burglary, Walter. You should have seen that place. Stuff all over. They were looking for something. And another thing—that business about her telling the manager she was going away. I don't know what that was all about."

"Neither do I, and I don't want to know. That's a matter for the D.C. police. Like I said, we've got enough troubles right now. If the manager keeps his mouth shut, we're okay. If not— I've gotta warn you, Jonah, you're in deep shit."

Jonah rubbed the tense muscles in the back of his neck. "Understood. I'll see you later."

"No, you won't. I'm at my office today. I do have a law practice, you know. I think you guys oughta be able to hold the goddamn fort without me for one day."

"Sure. Sorry I woke you, Walter."

Jonah heard the phone slam down, and he pictured Walter storming around his bathroom, which was no doubt equipped with a marble tub and built-in Jacuzzi, standard for houses in his part of McLean. Jonah cracked his knuckles slowly, one by one, and grimaced. I sure didn't score points with that call.

So, ten minutes later when his own phone rang, he was surprised to see Walter's face back on the screen.

"Jonah," he said, "I didn't realize you were so tight with Addie."

"What's that supposed to mean?"

"Nothing. That's your business. It's just that—well—I think her phone may be tapped. Better be careful what you say."

"How the hell could that be? It was swept and came up clean. Why do you think that?"

"It's just an idea I have. Take my word for it. Even if it's clean, her message unit may be monitored. Anyone who owns an XG570 scanner can tune in to her remote. So watch the messages you leave there."

"Will do."

"No need to alarm Addie about it. Just be careful."

"But don't you think—"

"So long, Jonah." This time the phone was replaced more gently. His ratings had definitely gone up.

Jonah stopped for a dozen doughnuts and copies of all the Washington newspapers. He found a parking spot near Addie's building and leafed through them. The story of the astrologer's murder made all the front pages.

He rang Addie's downstairs buzzer and heard pleasure as well as surprise in her voice when she saw him on the security screen.

"Jonah—what are you doing here?"

He waved the box of doughnuts at the camera. "I thought I'd bring you a little breakfast."

"Come on up."

Addie was waiting at the door in a bathrobe made of some fluffy pink material. Her eyes were red and swollen from all that crying. He wanted to put his arms around her and tell her he wouldn't let anything hurt her ever again. Instead, he thrust the box of doughnuts into her hands.

"Here. If you make some coffee, we'll have a feast. The best thing to cheer you up is to gorge on doughnuts."

She managed a weak smile. "My favorite junk food. How did you know?"

He tapped his head. "Intuition. That's my business. Communication is ninety percent intuition, you know."

They ate and talked, even laughed a little. When they finished, Addie leaned back and looked at him.

"Jonah, I don't know how to say this. I'll never be able to thank you enough for what you did yesterday. I don't think I could have survived it without you."

He shrugged. "Sure you could. You're a strong lady."

"Sometimes. But not yesterday. I'm sorry you had to see me like that. It embarrasses me to think about it. But I'm so grateful you were there."

She looked at him. Even red and swollen, those eyes sent lightning bolts into his heart. He looked away and took a deep breath.

"I'm glad I was there too," he said.

"I didn't sleep much last night. I had lots of time to think and I decided something." Addie walked into the living room and brought back *The Bowl of Heaven*. She opened it to the back and pointed to one of the entries on the flyleaf.

"Here. See this? James McInney—that's the name of Livonia's contact in Santa Fe. The one she mentioned in her message. I decided since I have to leave Washington anyway, I'm going to Santa Fe. I'm going to see this man and find out just what's so strange about Simon Furst's birth certificate."

"Addie—you can't do that."

"Why not?" She shrugged. "I have to go away someplace, don't I? New Mexico is supposed to be beautiful."

"It could be dangerous."

"Do you really think that birth certificate had anything to do with Livonia's being—with her death?"

"It might have."

"Then it was my fault." Addie put her hand on Jonah's. "Don't you see? I got Livonia into it. I have to find out. I have to go."

Jonah thought about Addie's answering unit being monitored. Could Livonia's message have led to her murder?

"What exactly did Livonia say in her message?" he asked, trying to be casual.

"I listened to it over and over when I couldn't reach her. I have it memorized. She said 'I've got news from my source in Santa Fe. There's something fishy about that birth certificate.' Then she said she had information about a man called Karl Salazar. He's someone Bruce Hanover mentioned to me."

Hanover—God, another death. "You can't go down there," he said. "It's too—"

"I knew you wouldn't like the idea. But I'm going, Jonah. I've made up my mind. It's funny. I'm seeing things so clearly today. After last night, it's—I'm like a different person. You know what the Greeks said about catharsis. Well, that's what happened to me. A lot of what cluttered up my head is gone."

"Listen, Addie. All I ask is that you don't do anything without telling me. Give me time to think. You owe me that."

"I owe you lots more than that."

"Okay. You're not gonna do anything—I mean anything—until tonight. You're not gonna mention Santa Fe or New Mexico to anyone. Wipe it out of your mind—you're gonna only think Cincinnati until tonight. Promise?"

"I promise." Addie laughed. "What's going to happen tonight?"

"We're going out to dinner. We'll talk about it then. But until then, Santa Fe doesn't exist."

"I never heard of it," Addie said.

"Good. Now what you have to do today is lie down and rest—listen to some music—try to get some sleep."

"I have to go out, Jonah. Livonia's lawyer called me this morning, just before you got here. He has firm instructions about her death. She wanted to be cremated immediately. Said she didn't want her body lying around for anyone to poke at. So they're having a memorial service at the Surfside Chapel at 2:00 this afternoon. I have to be there."

"All right. But come right back home and rest afterward. Those are orders."

"Yes sir," she said, with a sad little smile that melted his heart.

As Jonah drove to the White House, an idea began forming. By the time he got to his office, it had a shape and existence all its own. But he needed Walter Turner's support.

He punched in Turner's law office number and, after arguing with his secretary, finally got through.

"What is it, Jonah?" Walter said with exaggerated patience. "I'm very busy."

"I've got to see you—today."

"Impossible."

"I've got to. It's important. Just fifteen minutes."

"Does it deal directly with the president?"

"No, but it's—"

"I said it's impossible. I've got meetings all day. I'll see you tomorrow at the White House."

"Tomorrow's too late."

"Goodbye, Jonah." The phone clicked off.

"Bastard, prick, asshole." Jonah stormed around his office. Suddenly he bolted for the door.

"I'll be back in an hour," he told his secretary and he headed for Walter Turner's office.

Everything in the reception area of Turner, Fowling, and Harper was blond: the wood-paneled walls, the coffee tables covered with magazines, even the pretty receptionist behind the glass-topped desk. She smiled sweetly at Jonah, but didn't give him much encouragement when he asked to see Mr. Turner.

"Do you have an appointment?"

Jonah shook his head.

"He's not seeing anyone without an appointment."

"Just call and tell him I'm here."

The receptionist pursed her lips. "I can't do that. He's in a meeting. I can't disturb him."

"Sure you can." Jonah tried his boyish grin. "He'll see me if he knows I'm here."

"I'm sorry. He's got Mr. Fowling and Mr. Harper in his office and—"

"I don't care if he's got God in his office," Jonah said, "I'm gonna see him."

He bolted through the double doors and down the carpeted hallway to Walter's large corner office. He knew the way; he'd been here a couple of times. He had to move fast. If he stopped to think, he'd never have the nerve to continue.

Jonah opened the door to Walter's office and stood there, breathing hard. Walter and his partners stopped talking and stared at him as though he were some strange species, dropped from another planet.

"I had to see you," he said in a shaking voice. "I'm sorry."

A towering figure loomed behind him and Jonah wheeled around. The man was well over six feet tall, with the barrel chest of a wrestler and the hamlike fists of a boxer. He glared at Jonah.

"You want me to throw this clown out, Mr. Turner?" he said.

"Not now, Timothy," Walter said. "You come back in fifteen minutes. If he's still here, he's all yours."

The security guard nodded and left. Walter turned to his partners. "Gentlemen, will you excuse us for fifteen minutes. This—this individual seems to have some pressing matter to discuss."

The two men walked out of the office, glancing back over their shoulders. When they were gone, Walter slammed his fist down on the desk.

"Jonah, are you out of your mind? Or are you trying to drive me out of mine? You wake me up at 6:30 to regale me with your adventures as a Secret Service agent. Then you harass me on the phone. Now you burst into a partner's meeting. You're like a bad dream that never ends."

"It's Addie, Walter. She's made up her mind—"

"Fine, perfect. Now we're back to Addie again. Goddammit, I can't take this." Walter clutched his head. "I'm starting to get my daily headache."

"Just let me finish. I think that astrologer was killed because she found out something about Simon Furst's birth certificate."

"Oh sure, that's a great reason to kill someone—because she doesn't like your birth certificate."

"I know it sounds crazy, but we found the name of someone in Santa Fe who might know something about it and Addie's made up her mind to go down there."

"Great. That will get her out of town and keep her busy. Good idea. That's what you came bursting in here to tell me?"

"No—I came to tell you that I'm going with her." The idea had become fact and with it came the calm of an irrevocable decision.

"What? Impossible. Now I know you've lost your mind. We're in the middle of a crisis at the White House. You're needed here. You can't go waltzing off—"

"I can do whatever I damn please. And that's what I damn please—to go to Santa Fe. I'm not letting Addie go down there alone and get herself killed like her friend."

"It's your ass if you do it, Jonah. I warn you. Why'd you come to me anyway? I'm not your boss."

"Who would I go to? Marty Shaw? Eve Kontos?" Jonah shook his head. "I thought you might understand. You know, Walter, I always looked up to you. You were my role model—the person I'd most like to be. I thought you had it all."

Walter looked down. "You don't want to be like me," he said. "I'm no role model."

Jonah nodded. "Yeah, I'm beginning to think so. The way you won't face what we're doing to Addie. My God, what we've done to that woman. She was working at something she loved. We came along and took her whole business away just to satisfy some whim of the president's. Then when that went sour, we threw her out like some disposable piece of junk—told her to get lost. Now the only person she cares about is killed—probably because of us—and she's brave enough to try to find out why. And *she'll* probably get killed. And you say, 'Great idea—it'll get rid of her.'"

"Jonah," Walter's voice was very soft. "Is that how it looks to you?"

"Yeah, it sure does."

Walter sighed. "That's how it looks to me, too."

"I'm going down there with her," Jonah declared. "That's it. I've made up my mind."

Walter stared at him. "By God, you're doing it, Jonah. You're saying 'Dammit, I won't be a background character any more.'"

"I don't understand."

"It's a private thing between Janice and me. Has to do with taking charge of your own soul. Someday I'll explain." Walter shook his head. "You're putting yourself on the line. God, I envy you."

"You envy *me*. That's a laugh."

"No, I do. You go for it, Jonah. I'll cover for you. I'll tell Eve Kontos that I sent you there to sniff out public opinion in Furst's home state. If Marty doesn't like it, it'll be his ass, not yours."

Jonah swallowed hard and kept still. He was afraid that anything he said might change Walter's mind.

"By the way, did Addie say anything to you about Andrew Granit?" Walter asked.

"No, why?"

"Just wondering. I've got a hunch he's mixed up in all of this."

"But why would Addie—"

"Oh—she pointed out some things about him—about his chart. Maybe she's got the same hunch."

Walter stood up. He was all business now. "I don't want anyone to know where you and Addie are going, so keep it quiet. Get the tickets, and when you're ready to leave, I'll drive you to the airport myself."

Jonah grinned. "Cloak and dagger stuff, huh?"

"Don't get carried away." Walter looked at his watch. "Now get out of here, before Timothy comes back and makes chopped liver out of you."

"Thanks, Walter."

Walter pointed to the door. "Out—now."

Jonah was gone before he could say another word.

CHAPTER SEVENTEEN

I n spite of its nautical name, the Surfside Chapel was nowhere within sight or sound of the sea. Rather, it was squeezed in between a shoe boutique and a grocery store. A funeral home that had seen better days, it consisted of a small chapel and two reception rooms. Addie arrived just before 2:00. Several astrologers she knew were seated up front. They turned around when she entered. She nodded to them and sat down alone in one of the rear pews.

The urn containing Livonia's ashes rested on an altar near the pulpit. A minister in a dark blue suit stood behind the lectern, shuffling papers and glancing at his watch. Addie noticed a man standing at the rear of the chapel, scanning the mourners. She stiffened as he walked to her pew and slid along the seat until he was beside her. He was extremely short, with a beaked nose and a meticulously trimmed beard. It was the columnist Gregory Harmon.

Addie jumped up and moved forward to a more crowded pew, squeezing in between two strangers. The minister began to speak and Addie concentrated on his words. It was a pompous eulogy, full of florid phrases extolling Livonia. Addie knew the sound of it would have sent Livonia into peals of laughter. Perhaps she could hear it and was chuckling away on some heavenly plane. Addie closed her eyes, imagining an ethereal Livonia, doubled up with celestial laughter. She was glad the eulogy was so pretentious. This way she could keep her feelings under control and leave the chapel dry-eyed.

Addie turned around and glanced back at where she'd been sitting. Harmon was still there, watching her. She turned back and concentrated on the eulogy. When it finally ended, the spectators began filing slowly down the center aisle.

Addie looked at the urn on the altar. "Goodbye, Livonia," she whispered and headed for the exit, pushing past the slowly moving crowd. She walked quickly down the street, away from the chapel, and heard footsteps racing behind her.

"Miss Pryce, Miss Pryce, please slow down—for the sake of my poor, pounding heart." Gregory Harmon was beside her, his short legs pumping furiously to keep up with her. His head barely reached her shoulder, and when he looked up at her, she noticed one eye twitching as though it had a life apart from the rest of his face.

He grabbed hold of her arm. "Let's go someplace where we can talk."

"I've got nothing to say to you," Addie said, trying to pull her arm free.

"Oh, but you do. I've heard you're a splendid astrologer. Wouldn't you like some free publicity?"

Addie looked down at him and shook her head. "I have more business than I can handle, thank you. I don't need—"

"Yes, I understand you even advise heads of state. A certain senator, a mutual friend, told me how good you are. He said you might even be counseling the president."

He clung tightly to her arm like a leech that could not be dislodged. She saw an empty taxi heading toward them and she pushed him hard. Harmon almost lost his balance, and Addie broke free. She raced toward the cab. It stopped and she jumped inside, slamming the door before he could reach it. She looked back as the taxi sped away, and saw the bearded gnome standing on the sidewalk in his elegantly styled three-piece suit, shaking his fist at her.

The dinner had turned into a dismal affair. Addie tried hard to be cheerful, but the vision of Livonia's body, lying on the floor surrounded by books and papers, haunted her. She felt sorry for Jonah. His determined attempts at conversation had become a monologue. Addie looked at the other diners, laughing and chattering, their spirits as lively as the bright red tablecloths and the noisy clattering of dishes. She toyed with the spaghetti piled on her plate, twisting it in little bundles around her fork.

"Not very hungry, huh?" Jonah said, buttering a piece of Italian bread. "The food's good here. Try to eat something."

"It is good, Jonah. It's just—I don't feel much like eating."

"Okay," he said, putting down his bread. "I was saving the big news for dessert, but maybe it'll make you feel better. Then again, maybe it won't."

"What news?"

"You know your trip to Santa Fe? You're gonna have a traveling companion."

"I am? Who?"

Barbara Shafferman

Jonah studied his plate. "Well—umm—me."

"You! You're going to Santa Fe? Why?"

"I think that's obvious. To see that you don't get yourself into too much trouble."

"I can't let you do that, Jonah. What about your job?"

"I'm getting time off for good behavior."

"Wait a minute." Addie narrowed her eyes and looked at him. "This is something cooked up by Walter Turner, isn't it? I'm some kind of loose cannon, and you're the watchdog to make sure I don't do too much damage."

"Jeez, Addie. How can you think that?" Jonah's hurt showed in his face.

Addie couldn't stop herself. "Well, it's awfully strange that you can just take off like that. They must need you here with everything that's happening—all those rumors about the president."

"Look. The president will be away on his Asian trip. The press won't—hell, I don't have to explain myself this way to you! Either you believe me or you don't."

Addie shook her head. "I thought I learned my lesson a long time ago. But it seems I have to have it drummed into me over and over again. Never trust anyone." She gave a bitter laugh. "Especially anyone who works at the White House."

"Don't do this, Addie." He looked at her pleadingly.

She traced the pattern of the tablecloth with her finger and remained silent.

Jonah shoved his plate away.

"Okay, fine. Think whatever you want. It was a bad idea anyway. Listen, I've lost my appetite too. Let's get out of here."

He beckoned to the waiter, and they walked out of the restaurant to the car in silence. Addie stared straight ahead as they drove through the dark Washington streets. They pulled up in front of her building, and Jonah leaned across her to open the door.

"So long," he said.

A feeling of desolation swept over Addie, almost as strong as the loss of Livonia. "Do you want to come up?" she asked, her voice barely audible.

Jonah shook his head and began fiddling with the wheel.

"Jonah, please—come upstairs—just for a minute. I need to talk to you."

He looked at her. "I don't think it's a good idea. I might have some secret White House agenda—maybe I'm out to steal some of your goddamn charts."

Her eyes filled. "I know I deserve that. You've been so wonderful and I—I'm so sorry, Jonah. Please forgive me. See, I felt so happy when you said that about going with me that I got scared. I'm afraid I'm depending on you too much. And everyone I ever depend on is taken away from me." She buried her face in her hands and began to sob.

He put his arm around her and waited till the sobs subsided. "Come on," he said, "Let's find a place to park the car."

They were silent in the elevator, but as soon as they entered her apartment, Addie turned and looked searchingly at Jonah. "You are still going to Santa Fe, aren't you?"

"Try to stop me."

"Never again—I promise."

They settled onto the couch and began making plans.

"I'll need all day tomorrow to get things in order," Jonah said. "I'll get airline tickets for early Sunday morning—very early, if it's okay with you."

"The sooner the better. I can't wait to get out of Washington. And I can use tomorrow to do some shopping. I feel like I'm going away on vacation."

"That's exactly what it will be. We'll do a little snooping and then we're gonna have a great holiday. We'll sightsee, and stuff ourselves on New Mexican food, and—"

"Oh Jonah," Addie touched his cheek lightly. "I'm so glad you're coming."

"Not as glad as I am."

He leaned forward and kissed her forehead. Then his lips moved down to meet hers, gently at first, then harder, more insistent. She put her arms around him and held him close.

His hands moved down to her breasts, caressing them gently. He began unbuttoning her blouse, and suddenly the panic started. All her desire disappeared, leaving only the need to escape, to protect herself from the feelings flooding her, feelings that could only lead to pain. She struggled to get free and jumped up from the couch. Jonah remained sitting, staring at her and breathing hard.

"Oh God," Addie said, "Oh, Jonah—I'm so sorry. It's nothing to do with you. It's me. It's just—I'm not ready yet. We have to go slow. I'm—"

"Stop apologizing." Jonah stood up and put his arm around her shoulders. "Look—let's get this straight right now. You don't have to be ready for anything—ever. I'm not in this business for a quick lay, and it demeans me to have you think that."

"I don't, Jonah. I'd never think that."

"Well, I want this out once and for all. I'm doing this because I care about what happens to you. You don't owe me anything—especially not—" His voice trailed off.

She took his hand and raised it to her lips. "Thank you, Jonah—for being you."

CHAPTER EIGHTEEN

The pilot's voice crackled over the loudspeaker: the plane would be landing in Albuquerque in five minutes. Andrew Granit fastened his seat belt and gazed out the window at the clouds. He was in no hurry to arrive.

He thought about the family dinner awaiting him that night with Alicia, his dull daughters, and their even duller husbands. At least he'd have a chance to see Robbie. Amazing that the only worthwhile thing produced by forty-three years of marriage had been that one grandchild. Robbie, with his wiry red hair, deepset darting eyes, and mind that skirted the edges of genius, could have been his twin. It was like looking backward through a time tunnel at himself, the young Andrew, before all the bad choices.

Robbie would celebrate his ninth birthday soon. He'd have to start spending more time with the boy, give him sage, grandfatherly advice. For starters, he'd warn him never to marry a dull, drab girl you despise, even if her father does own half of

New Mexico. Alicia hadn't made such a bad bargain, though. He was hardly ever around to bother her, and she did have the title of Mrs. Senator Granit. That went far in Albuquerque society.

The plane broke through the clouds and began its descent. Tomorrow, another plane carrying Addie and Stern would be landing here. He knew all about their plans, and his people would be waiting for them. He wondered if Stern was fucking Addie. Well, it's what she deserved: a low-level, second-rate flunky.

The wheels touched the ground, and the plane taxied toward the terminal, past the deserted army buildings. What a waste of good land. Those buildings should have been torn down years ago. With Republicans in the state house, that's exactly what would have happened.

The plane stopped and the passengers began filing out. Granit remained in his seat; he detested waiting in line for anything. The flight attendant glanced at him and smiled. He was glad that a female flight attendant had been assigned to first class. It had given him something pleasant to look at during the boring half flight.

She squeezed past the passengers toward him.

"Did you enjoy your flight, Senator Granit?" she asked.

"Only when you were serving me," he said.

She gave him a flustered smile and stretched to check the overhead rack. He watched the way her breasts strained at her tight blouse and thought about pursuing it further. He shrugged. It wasn't worth the effort. The aisles had cleared, so Granit stood up, rolled down his shirt sleeves and put on his gray worsted suit jacket. He picked up his carry-on bag and left the plane.

His driver hurried toward him, took the bag, and led him out to the empty limousine that was waiting in a no-parking zone. Granit was delighted that no one else had come. He wanted to make one stop before going to his Albuquerque office. During the flight he'd gotten a sudden inspiration and he wanted to call Washington right away, but the call had to be made from a secure phone.

He gave the driver an address and they began moving through the Albuquerque traffic, down Lomas, past the University and the Fairgrounds, turning onto Tramway, heading for the Sandia mountains. They entered the foothills, where winding roads led to spacious houses with terraces jutting out for spectacular views.

"Stop here and wait for me," Granit told the driver, as they came to a rambling redwood house with white trim. He walked up the driveway, noticing the green convertible parked there. Damn, Stella's home.

He took out his key and opened the door. A woman peered out of the kitchen. Her face, with the high cheekbones and slanting brown eyes that hinted of Indian heritage, registered alarm, surprise, and then delight.

"Andrew—I didn't know—you didn't tell me."

"I thought I'd surprise you."

She came running toward him, arms outstretched. He turned away. "Not now. Tonight. What you have to do now is get in your car and take a ride. I've got to make a phone call and I don't want you around. Don't come back until I'm gone. I'll be back tonight—about 10:30."

She turned without speaking, picked up her purse from a hall table and went out to her car. Granit watched her go, enjoying the easy swing of her wide hips. Stella knew exactly what she had to do to live in a fashionable house like this, perched at the base of the mountains. It cost a great deal, but what the hell—it was Alicia's money, after all.

He punched in a Washington number, and a face appeared on the screen: his top legislative aide, Stephen Humphrey.

"Are you alone?" Granit asked.

"Yeah. I didn't expect you to call so soon. How was the flight?"

Granit frowned. "I didn't call to talk about my travels. Now listen to me very carefully. I just had a brainstorm. I think we've got a way to get Henry out—safer than we thought. It might take longer, but we won't have to use Marius.

"You know when that fool, Stern, called Turner yesterday?"

"The call that Sophie heard—about finding the body?"

"Of course—what other call would I mean. There was one thing I didn't tell you about. It slipped my mind until an hour ago. Stern used a Secret Service badge to get into the apartment."

"I don't see—"

"No—I didn't expect you to." Granit drummed his fingers on the marble telephone table. "This ties the White House in with that old astrologer's death. And if the White House is involved, what would be the next logical assumption?"

"I'm starting to see the light. That the dead woman was the president's astrologer."

"Exactly. Then wouldn't it follow that the White House might be involved in her death?"

"Yeah. I think you've really got something there. A thing like that could force the president's resignation."

"But we've got to go slowly and carefully. What I want you to do is go see Greg Harmon. Give him this item. But tell him he can't use it until you give him the go ahead. Make sure about that. Then you find out which building manager was on duty that day—they've got a few of them over there at the Watergate."

"That's easy enough."

"He's key to the White House tie in. Just watch him to be sure he stays around. If there's a congressional investigation— and I'll make sure there is—he'll be the noose around the president's neck."

"This is brilliant, Andrew. I love it." Humphrey's voice expressed awed admiration. "Only one thing—won't they produce the real astrologer?"

"That's not your worry. If it comes to that, there won't be any astrologer to produce." Granit frowned. He preferred not to think about that.

"Can you imagine that idiot Stern saying he's Secret Service?" Granit continued. "He's giving us the president's head on a silver platter. And tomorrow he and the astrologer are coming to Santa Fe."

"How did you learn that?"

"Sophie called my private number. She heard Turner telling his wife about it." Granit chuckled. "As long as Turner's calling the shots, I've got a direct pipeline."

"How are you going to handle it?"

"They've got to rent a car when they land at Albuquerque. There's only one database for all the rentals, and I've got someone keying into that. As soon as they rent, we have the license number and we can find them wherever they go."

"What do you think they'll do?" Humphrey asked.

"My guess is they'll head for Santa Fe right away. And one way or another, they'll lead us to the one we want."

"Wonderful."

Granit pursed his lips. He didn't need to listen to praise from an underling. "Is Simon in his office?" he asked.

"No. I think he's on the floor of the Senate today."

"Damn. Tell him to call me first chance he gets."

"Will do. Anything else?"

"Nothing. I'll call you if I need you."

Andrew Granit hung up the phone. He hurried out of the house, down the flagstone steps to his car. As they sped away, he saw Stella in her green car parked down the block, waiting patiently for him to leave. He felt a sudden surge of affection. She was so loyal and uncomplicated, so obedient. He began to look forward to tonight.

Chapter Nineteen

Addie had been waiting in front of her building for ten minutes when a grey Mercedes with a transparent roof appeared. Jonah jumped out and began to put her luggage in the trunk, while she peered inside to see who was driving. Her heart sank at the sight of Walter Turner. The White House *was* involved.

Walter leaned over. "Sit in front with me, Addie," he said. "I want to talk to you. Jonah can sit in back."

She got in, but refused to look at him, staring ahead at the instrument panel.

"You know, you're wrong about Janice," Walter said. "And you're wrong about me. We never—"

"Save your breath. I don't believe you. And you'll forgive me for wondering—why take the time to drive us to the airport? What's *your* stake in this?"

"I do have a stake, but it's not what you think. Maybe Jonah can explain it to you, though I doubt it. God knows, I don't understand it myself."

"What's going on?" Jonah climbed into the back seat. "I heard my name mentioned. What're you saying about me?"

As the car pulled out into the brilliant June sunlight, the roof darkened automatically. Addie turned around and looked at Jonah. "I was wondering how Walter could spare the time to drive us to the airport. Unless, of course, the White House—"

"Jeez, Addie. Don't start that again. We're too far along now." Jonah sighed. "You're gonna have to trust me—all the way. Otherwise—"

"Oh, I trust you, Jonah. I'd trust you with my life. It's other people." She stared at Walter.

"Look Addie," Walter said. "I'm telling you again you're wrong about that matter. And I'm driving you to the airport because for some strange reason, I care about what happens to the two of you."

He turned and looked at Addie. "Now you can believe that or not—but it's the truth."

She looked away without answering and remained silent all through the ride to the airport and Walter's strained goodbyes. Before they entered the terminal, Addie burrowed in her purse for the identity card that had replaced her social security card four years ago. The green plastic square had her photo on top and a computerized code below, containing all her vital statistics.

The frosted glass doors of the terminal swung open, and Addie and Jonah made their way through the crowd to the check-in counter, where a mechanical ticket taker extended a slotted fist. Jonah inserted one ticket and his identity card into the slot. After they were scanned and recorded, the robot arm returned the card and a boarding pass. The metal arm gleamed in the overhead lights as the process was repeated for Addie.

When they were settled in their seats, Jonah looked at his watch.

"It was worth getting up early," he said. "It's 8:15 now. This new super jet is so fast we'll probably be in Albuquerque by 8:00 Mountain Time."

"Why are the tickets for Albuquerque? Why don't we go right to Santa Fe?"

"By parachute? There's no airport at Santa Fe, that's why. I've got a rental car waiting for us, and I understand it's only an hour drive to Santa Fe. We'll have the whole day ahead of us."

The whirring of jets began to fill the cabin. Jonah stiffened, and Addie noticed his hands gripping the arms of his seat.

"Don't tell me you're a white knuckles flyer, Jonah. I wouldn't have believed it."

"Nah—but I don't exactly love it either. I belong on the ground—good old terra firma for me. Don't you mind it at all?"

"Sometimes, but not today." Addie hesitated. "You're not going to believe this, I know, but I—umm—have a very lucky influence right now."

"Influence? You mean something with astrology?"

She nodded. "The planet Jupiter is making a really good aspect to my chart. That's a very lucky, protective thing. I can't imagine anything very bad happening with that Jupiter there, and if—"

"Okay, Addie, it's nice to know the stars are on our side. But, if you don't mind, I'll still buckle my seatbelt and keep my head inside the plane."

Addie laughed. "Just squeeze my hand hard if you get too scared."

When they picked up their rental car at the Albuquerque airport, Jonah was like a child with a new toy. He could hardly wait to get it out on the open road.

"I splurged and ordered a car with the newest Computrol Navigation System. It practically steers itself. Look at this." He pointed to a panel on the dashboard with an illuminated map. As they moved away from the airport onto Yale Boulevard, the map began to change, showing the streets around them. Jonah pulled over to the curb and punched in their destination: 2538 Cerillos Road, Santa Fe. Immediately a well-modulated female voice began issuing instructions.

"She'll keep that up all the way to Santa Fe," Jonah said. "Every time I make a wrong turn, she'll be on my back, letting me know."

"She'll never replace a good jazz combo, but it beats getting lost."

"We'll switch her off for a while when we get on the highway. Turn on the radio." He looked over at Addie. She was staring out the window, absorbed in the sights outside. Jonah smiled and began to whistle. The excitement of a new place and unexpected possibilities swept over him.

The first thing Jonah did when they arrived at the Coyote Court was to leave a message on Walter Turner's voice mail, telling him they were in Santa Fe. They had adjoining rooms, and they separated to unpack, shower, and change. An hour later Addie knocked on his door. She looked fresh and glowing in a white sundress dotted with turquoise and beige flowers. A matching turquoise jacket hung over her arm. Her damp black hair hung loosely to her shoulders. Jonah found it hard to stop looking at her.

"Pretty dress," Jonah said.

She smiled. "It's new. I bought it especially for the trip."

He pointed to the guide books strewn on the bed. "I thought we'd ride around Santa Fe for a while—get the feel of the place. Find someplace nice for lunch. Then we could take a ride up to Española. Scenery's supposed to be beautiful around there. When it's too dark to see anything, we can have dinner. I've got the names of a few good places. Did a little research before we came."

"Sounds wonderful. Today's Sunday. We can't do anything until tomorrow anyway, so we might as well enjoy ourselves. I'll call Mr. McInney first thing tomorrow morning."

It was almost 11:00 when they headed back to the motel. They were enchanted by the beauty of New Mexico: its vivid cloudless skies, its panoramic vistas, its towering timeworn cliffs. Their palates ached from the fierce chili-pepper laden food they had devoured. They had ended up at one of the gambling casinos that dotted the road; each Indian nation seemed to be running one. Jonah had lost at roulette, but when Addie stopped at the slot machines, she won a jackpot on the third try.

As they shoveled the coins into a bucket, Addie looked up at Jonah with an awed expression.

"There's more than $400 here. I told you I had a lucky thing going. Now do you believe me?"

"I believe you—I believe you. Let's not waste this luck. How about some more roulette?"

Addie shook her head. "You don't understand. A little Jupiter goes a long way. I've had my luck for the night. If I push it, I'll just lose what I won."

Jonah sighed. "Okay, it's your call. But I'm gonna see that you get yourself some nice jewelry with this."

"And I'm going to buy you a great meal tomorrow. And some good wine."

"Madam—you're trying to turn a poor innocent young man's head with expensive gifts. They warned me about girls like you."

They both began to laugh, and their high spirits continued all the way to their rooms. Addie slipped her keycard into its slot and opened the door. She gasped. The room was a disaster: clothes strewn around, jewelry and toiletries scattered all over, shoes lying on the bed at crazy angles.

She sat down on the bed, shaking. Jonah looked around, speechless.

"Well," he said finally, "Somebody sure knows we're here."

"You don't think it's burglars?"

"Don't know. Check and see if anything's missing."

Addie attacked the mess, putting the jewelry back into a traveling case and sorting through papers and cards.

"It looks like everything's here. I had my credit cards with me in my purse. But I left some phone cards and a checkbook in the room. They're still here."

"Yeah, I had a hunch it wasn't a robbery. Whoever did this is looking for something." A thought struck him. "Where's that book—you know, *Bowl of Heaven*?"

"You don't think I'd carry it around with me, do you? I wouldn't even leave it in my apartment while I'm away. It's in my safe deposit vault."

"Good. How about that guy, McInney. The one we're gonna see about the birth certificate. Did you write his name down anywhere?"

"I had it with me in my pocketbook."

"That might've been what they were looking for."

Addie looked around the room and shivered. "Look at all my things. The thought of someone pawing through them..."

"Come on, Addie, it's just a little mess. Be glad you weren't here when they came."

"You're right. But messes really bother me. See—I'm a Virgo."

"I know that."

"You do?"

"Sure. I know your birthday and I did my research. Let's see, you're a Virgo and," he counted off on his fingers, "you're intelligent, loyal, analytical—a perfectionist, a worrier, and a workaholic. Right?"

Addie nodded.

"And," he continued, "you have high standards and you're very critical, so sometimes you can be a royal pain in the ass."

Addie laughed. "You're amazing," she said. "You have the whole thing down perfectly—even to the pain in the neck."

"I didn't say pain in the neck. I said pain in the ass. That's another thing. You're prim and proper. You don't like to talk dirty."

"That's right too." Addie looked down, embarrassed, and spied something in the mess.

She knelt down to pick up a small wooden carving of three monkeys and cradled it in her hand.

"I could have lost this."

"What is it?"

"It's something Bruce Hanover gave me. You know—'see no evil, hear no evil, speak no evil.' It was a little joke we had. I— I brought it along for luck."

Damn! There *was* something between her and that Hanover guy. "You really cared about him, huh, Addie?"

She nodded. "He was a friend. You know how sometimes you meet people and it seems like you always knew them? You're comfortable right away. That's how it was. Not a romantic thing, just—nice."

Well, as long as it wasn't romantic, he could settle for nice. Jonah pulled out his keycard. "I'd better take a look at my room. Bet our friends paid a visit there too."

His room looked a little better than Addie's. Not that the clowns hadn't done their job; he just had less things to toss around. He ran a mental inventory of what he had brought. Nothing was missing.

By the time he got back to Addie, she had her room looking like something out of a motel brochure. She looked at him, and the little worry lines in her forehead deepened.

"I'm frightened," she said, "Do you think they'll come back?"

He shook his head. "They don't want to mess with us. They waited 'til we left to break in, didn't they?"

"You're right, but still—do you think they're the ones who—who killed Livonia?"

"Who knows? No sense thinking that way. You'll just scare yourself."

"Oh, I've done a good job of that already." Addie hugged herself. "I feel like a sitting duck."

Jonah looked at her. "You know, you're not gonna get any sleep. You'll be sitting up all night, watching for spooks. I'm gonna sleep in here with you."

"I—I don't know—"

"Come on, Addie. Don't be an idiot. There are two beds, and I don't walk in my sleep."

She smiled. "Well, I *would* feel safer."

"Okay. I'll be back in half an hour." He laughed. "Don't look so worried. I'll get some potato chips and soda from the machines. We'll watch old movies 'til we can't keep our eyes open. It'll be fun—like a sleepover when you were a kid."

Jonah picked up the chips, soda, and ice, then went back to his room and changed into pajamas. He threw some things into his denim flight bag: a comb, a toothbrush, a book—and a .38 revolver he had brought, just in case.

He knocked on Addie's door and she opened it immediately. She was wearing that same pink, fluffy robe. He wondered what she had on underneath.

Addie looked at him and began to laugh. Her shoulders shook helplessly and she doubled up, pointing at his pajamas.

"What—what?"

"You—you have," She could barely get the words out. "You have—bunny pajamas."

He looked down. When he had packed, he had thrown in whatever clean pajamas were around. These had Peter Rabbit and friends cavorting in the vegetable garden. He could hardly tell Addie the pajamas had been a present from last year's girl-friend, an inside joke about his cuddlier sleeping habits.

She was laughing even harder now. He knew it was laughter close to hysteria, an outlet for all her tension. Still, he felt annoyed and embarrassed.

"Cut it out," he said.

She gasped for breath. "Do you—do you have—bunny slip-pers to match?" She fell back on the bed, roaring with laughter.

"I said, cut it out." He picked up a pillow and heaved it at her.

"Oh, you want to fight." She threw the pillow back, hitting him in the chest.

He started to laugh and then ducked as another pillow came flying at him. The pillows sailed back and forth, until they both collapsed, breathing hard and exhausted.

Jonah sat down on the bed next to Addie and put his arm around her.

"Feeling better?"

"Mmmhmm." She closed her eyes and leaned against him. The moment seemed so fragile and precious, he didn't want to do anything to spoil it. He brushed her forehead lightly with his lips, enjoying the scent of her hair. If he had to settle for warm and comfortable instead of romantic, then that's how it would be. He just wanted to share her life, maybe be another Hanover. He winked at the three monkeys, sitting on the dresser.

"Okay," he said finally, "It's movie time. Do you want some refreshments?"

She shook her head. "I'm stuffed."

"Yeah, me too. You get into bed, and I'll see what we've got here." He walked over to the TV to get the movie listings and saw his flight bag.

"Hey, I haven't unpacked yet." He took out the revolver and put it on the night table.

Addie looked at it with alarm. "A gun? Do you know how to use it?"

"Sure. You have to for a permit. I'm a good shot."

"But you said they wouldn't come back."

"Look, I'm right ninety-nine percent of the time. This is insurance for the other one percent. I'm not gonna let anything happen to you."

"Isn't it dangerous, having it around like that?"

He looked at her. "You know, I'm beginning to think there is something to this Virgo stuff. You worry too much."

She smiled. "And you're such an Aries. You rush right in and don't worry enough."

"Then we're a good balance. Now let's see what we're gonna watch. Here's an old movie that just started. About how the earth's covered with water and everyone's looking for land. How does that sound?"

"Perfect."

"Yeah—let's watch it."

He got into bed, picked up the remote and flicked on the TV. They watched in silence, and Jonah became absorbed in the story. At a break in the action he turned and looked at Addie. Her eyes were closed and she was breathing regularly. She slept so quietly, she reminded him of the Sleeping Beauty he had seen in a cartoon when he was a child. A handsome prince had awakened Beauty with a kiss and they lived happily ever after.

Unfortunately, he was no Prince Charming. He knew exactly what he was: Jonah Stern, a bright, ambitious, not-so-young man clawing his way up, always on the lookout for an opportunity, yearning to be on the A-list, but happy if he made the B's. No prize package there.

Jonah flipped off the TV and turned out the light. He tried to sleep, but kept thinking about Addie in the next bed. Suppose he just got in there with her. He played the scenario over in his head. She'd wake up, startled. Then she'd smile and put her arms around his neck and rub up against him. And he'd hold her tight and start kissing her and never stop and...In a pig's eye that would happen.

No, what would really happen is that she'd wake up scared, maybe even screaming. Then she'd jump out of bed and tell him to get out—that she'd never trust him again. Jeez, maybe she'd even shoot him with the gun in her panic. Well, he'd never find out, because even if he had an ironclad guarantee that things would work out the first way, he wouldn't do it. He was here to see that no one bothered her, least of all him.

Well, no one could stop him from dreaming. He put his hands behind his head, stared at the ceiling and started picturing a third scenario. He'd wake up to find Addie creeping into his bed. She was frightened or lonely or whatever. He'd comfort her and then the kissing would start in earnest. He'd get out of those damn pajamas, and she'd feel him against her and pull up her nightgown. He could feel her flesh pressing against his, smell the scent of her hair. Jonah fell asleep smiling.

CHAPTER TWENTY

Andrew Granit opened his eyes slowly. For a moment he couldn't remember what day it was or even whose bed he was in. He looked over and saw Stella sleeping next to him.

He sat up suddenly. It was Sunday, and he had promised to take Robbie to the museum at ten o'clock. He stared at Stella. She slept like a cat, completely relaxed, with her head at a crazy angle. She had a half smile on her face, probably dreaming about one of the young men who visited her when he was away. His lips tightened and he took a handful of her thick black hair. He pulled hard, harder then necessary to wake her up. Her eyes popped open, wide with alarm. They were pools of blackness, so dark it was hard to see where the iris ended and the pupil began.

"You frightened me, Andrew. See. Feel my heart." She put his hand under her breast, and he could feel the rapid beating. She began to move his hand slowly downward.

"I don't have time for that." He kissed the top of her head. "You have to get up and make me breakfast now. I'm taking my grandson out this morning."

She stretched and curled herself around him. "Ooh, such a good grandpa. I wish he was as good to Stella."

"And what would Stella like?"

"To stay in bed a little longer—you know."

He shook her loose. "You're a lazy slut. Do you know that?"

"You like it. You know you do."

"Not today I don't. Out of bed and into the kitchen—pronto." He hurried her along with his foot.

"You're a cruel man, Andrew—to kick your Stella out of bed." She laughed, wrapped herself in her red and gold bathrobe and hurried down to the kitchen. Granit eased himself out of bed and stretched. He'd have time for a shower and a leisurely breakfast.

The twin odors of bacon and coffee greeted him as he walked down the stairs. Stella had prepared everything he liked, even managing to whip up biscuits, which he slathered with his favorite guava marmalade. When he finished eating, he pulled her down on his lap.

"You cook as good as you fuck," he said.

"Now you appreciate me. Last night you were so mean. You frightened me."

"Mean? Because I don't like young men coming here—to *my* house—and fucking you? Because I don't want you acting like a whore in *my* house?"

"It's not true. I don't know who's been telling you stories about me."

Granit sighed. "It's true, Stella. I heard about it yesterday. I should kick you out. Let one of the young men take you in. But I happen to need you right now."

She threw her arms around him. "I'm sorry, Andrew—don't make me leave. You'll never hear bad stories about me again. I promise."

He held her away from him and gave her a piercing stare.

"Andrew, you're frightening me again," she whispered.

A discreet horn sounded outside; his driver had arrived. Granit frowned.

"Listen to me, Stella. If you need to have young men, I can understand that. But don't ever—ever—bring them into this house again."

"Never—I swear it. On the memory of my blessed mother, I swear it."

She knelt down beside him and began fumbling with the zipper of his fly. He pushed her away and stood up.

"You're such a simpleton. You think everything can be solved with that." He laughed. "Maybe you're right—who knows. I have to go now. Can't keep my grandson waiting."

"Will you be back tonight?"

He shook his head. "I doubt it. I have to go up to Santa Fe for a few days. I'll probably leave tonight or tomorrow morning. But you wait for me tonight, just in case."

"Oh yes. And Andrew, no more bad stories—I promise."

As he settled into the limousine's soft upholstery, he turned and looked through the rear window. Stella stood in the doorway, waving. Poor Stella. Her days in the house were numbered anyway. Soon he'd have other things on his mind. When he had Simon safely installed in the White House, he'd have no time to worry about a poor, dumb slut in Albuquerque.

In fact, he'd have no time to spare for the whole state of New Mexico. Andrew Granit wasted no love on his home state, a barren, water-poor wasteland, with a polyglot population skimping along at the poverty level. He could never understand the fanatical devotion of all the artists who came to visit and never left, or the awestruck wonder of the perennial tourists, gaping at mesa-dotted vistas and cloudless skies.

Even the name, New Mexico, was all wrong—the only state with the name of another country. He shook his head, remembering the phone call his office had once gotten, from a Senate office worker who should have known better, for Christ's sake. She wanted to know if the banks in Albuquerque could change her American money into New Mexico currency. That's what people thought about the state he represented.

He spent as little time there as he could, shuttling between Santa Fe and Albuquerque and the house, hidden away up north, in Las Trampas. Washington had been his center since the day he arrived, a fledgling congressman. One whiff of the power and strength that stalked the halls of Congress, and he was hooked forever. When Simon Furst became president of the United States, Andrew Granit would never leave Washington. Somehow he'd get Robbie there and then he'd say goodbye, no regrets, to the whole godforsaken state.

The car pulled up in front of his daughter's home, a large, rambling one-story house on two acres, across the Rio Grande, just outside of Albuquerque. A barn with a few horses in back and split-rail fencing all around gave the property the cachet of a neo-ranch. Robbie was waiting for him, the sun glinting on his auburn hair. Good, he wouldn't have to go inside.

"Tell your mother you're leaving," Granit said, and Robbie skipped back into the house. He was glad he could squeeze in the time to give the boy this treat. The New Mexico Museum of Natural History had one of the most imaginative collections in the country. Responding to a sudden spurt of interest in dinosaurs, the museum had completely revamped its famous prehistoric exhibit. Robbie was dying to see it, but the new collection hadn't opened to the public yet. Granit had prevailed on the curator to give them a private preview.

Robbie came running out and bounced into the limousine. "Let's go," he said. Granit nodded to the driver, and the car pulled away.

Robbie looked up at him, his intense brown eyes sparkling. "I've decided what I want to be when I grow up, Grampa." He paused dramatically. "A herpetologist."

Granit smiled. Robbie changed his ambitions every six months. He'd become smitten with reptiles two months ago.

"I started a collection—with cages in back by the barn. I'm catching them myself. I got a collared lizard and..."

"Be careful, Robbie." Granit was alarmed. "Stay away from the poisonous ones—the rattler and the coral snake—the Gila monster. Can you recognize them?"

"Of course, Grampa. Don't you think I know that? I've got pictures of them and I've seen them at the museum. The rattler's a pit viper and it's got those hollows on the side of its head. And you can't miss the coral snake—all red and yellow and black. I'll be careful."

"I know you will. It's just that I don't want anything to happen to you."

Robbie looked at him. "What did you want to be when you were my age, Grampa?"

"I can't remember. Maybe a herpetologist."

"Really. Oh, you're kidding me."

Granit laughed. "Well, maybe not that, but probably something to do with science."

"I love science too. What made you change to politics?

"I don't know. It seemed the thing to do."

"I'd never do that. I hate politics."

"You do? Well, perhaps it's just as well. Politics changes people—in a lot of ways."

"You know why I hate politics, Grampa? Because it makes you stay away from us all the time. I miss you!"

"I miss you too, Robbie." Granit smiled at him. "Remember when I took you to Washington last year? Did you really like it?"

"I loved it. The Smithsonian and the FBI Building and—"

"How'd you like to live there—with me?"

"Oh Grampa, could I? Oh boy, I'd love it. Nah—they'd never let me."

"Who—your mother and father?"

Robbie nodded.

"Leave it to me." Granit narrowed his eyes. "You wouldn't miss them—your mother and father and Ginny?"

"Sure I would, but I'd rather live in Washington with you. Boy, that'd be great. We could go anywhere, right? 'Cause you're a senator. Like here—getting to see the dinosaurs before anyone else."

"You'd get to do a lot of things like that." Granit looked out the car window. They were entering Albuquerque's Old Town.

"We're almost at the museum," he said. "One thing, Robbie. If you want to come to Washington to live with me, let's keep it our secret for now. Don't tell anyone, understand?"

Robbie nodded solemnly. "I promise. I want to come so bad. Even if they tortured me, I wouldn't tell."

Granit smiled. Robbie was his. He could handle the family.

They had just begun the tour when the radiophone on Andrew Granit's wrist buzzed. He moved to one side, pressed a button and put it to his ear.

"It's Smitty here. I got the news you're waiting for."

"Where are you?"

"At Sullivan's office in Santa Fe."

"I'll call right back." Granit walked over to Phillipson, the curator.

"I have to make an important call. Is there a phone I can use?"

"In my office. Make yourself at home, senator. Joe will take you there." He beckoned to a guard. "Take Senator Granit to my office, Joe."

"Go on with the tour. Don't wait for me. I'll join you when I'm through. Take good care of my grandson."

"You bet, Senator. We'll go slow so you won't miss too much."

Granit nodded and followed the guard to the elevator and then down the winding halls to the curator's office.

"I'll find my way back. Don't wait for me," he said.

He waited until the guard left, then closed the door and punched in Sullivan's number.

Smitty answered. When he heard Granit's voice, he said, "Is it okay to talk, senator?"

"Go ahead."

"Everything's under control. The pigeons landed about 8:00 this morning."

Granit pressed his lips together. The men working for him were the last remnants of a local militia outfit that had dissolved about five years ago, after the Supreme Court bombing. When the explosion that killed three of the judges had been traced back to a loose federation of militia groups, the outrage of the American public had spelled the end of the movement. Little pockets of so-called "minute men" remained scattered across the country.

Andrew Granit had ferreted out eight ex-militia members to form his own private army of men who knew how to use a threat and a gun. They all bore traces of paranoia, seeing spies everywhere and talking in crazy code, but he needed them. They were fiercely loyal and would obey unquestioningly every command. Only three—Smitty, Duke, and Barney— knew what was really going on.

"They picked up a car, and Patrick radioed the license number to us," Smitty continued. We were waiting in Santa Fe. Figured the pigeons would fly right up there and—"

"They're people, not birds," Granit snapped. "Try to remember that."

"Sure, senator. Just figured maybe someone's listening—you know."

"Do you know where they are now?"

"You bet. About 9:00 we started hunting. A couple guys went down to the Plaza. Joe and me, we went up to Cerillos Road—you know that strip where all the motels are. We went in and out of parking lots, and in the fourth one—bingo."

"You found the car?"

"Right. They're at the Coyote Court on Cerillos. We got the room numbers too. Right now the pigeons—I mean the people—are out. Joe's tailing them, and Duke and me—we're gonna go through their rooms soon as I'm off the phone. We'll get what you want."

"Good work, Smitty. I didn't expect you to find them that quickly."

Smitty grunted with pleasure at the unexpected praise.

"I want you to tail them everywhere," Granit continued, "and I mean everywhere. I want to know what they're doing and who they're seeing—especially who they're seeing—and I want everything written down. I don't want any slip-ups."

"Right, senator."

"Oh, one more thing. Who's with Salazar?"

"Barney's up there."

"Good. He handles him best. I'm coming up to Santa Fe tonight—tomorrow at the latest. After we finish the business there, we'll go on to Las Trampas. I'll see you tomorrow."

Granit hung up the phone and headed down the winding halls to the elevator. The guard met him and took him back to Phillipson and Robbie.

The boy was flushed with excitement. "Grampa, this is super," he said.

Andrew Granit smiled. "Did I miss much?"

"We'll backtrack," Phillipson said. "I don't think Robbie'll mind seeing it again—right, son?"

"You bet I won't. Take a look at this guy, Grampa. Look at that tail. It's gotta be ten feet long."

Robbie's enthusiasm was contagious. Seeing the exhibits through his eyes stimulated Granit's interest and he was sorry when the tour ended. Afterward he took Robbie to lunch at a restaurant in Old Town that was off the beaten track, away from the hordes of tourists.

On the way home, Robbie was very quiet. Granit smiled at him, but he turned his face away and stared out the window.

"What's wrong, Robbie?" Granit asked.

"I wish you could stay here. When're you going back to Washington?"

"In a few days. I have to go up to Santa Fe first."

"Could I come with you to Santa Fe? Please, grampa."

"You've got school, Robbie. Anyway, I've got boring business in Santa Fe. I couldn't spend any time with you."

"Yeah—but I'm gonna miss you."

"Whenever you miss me, remember our secret. You're coming to live with me in Washington—I promise you."

"But when?"

"How does six months sound?"

"Really—you mean it?"

"I don't say anything unless I mean it. I've got some business to take care of—something very important. In six months it should all be over, and I'll be able to do whatever I want."

"And what you want is for me to come and stay with you, right?"

"That's what I want."

"Okay, I can wait."

The limousine pulled up in front of the house, and Robbie put his arms around Granit's neck and kissed him.

"Thanks for a great day, Grampa."

"Remember our secret. Not a word to anyone."

Robbie nodded solemnly and walked toward the house.

The limousine swung onto I-40, heading east. As Albuquerque's population grew, neighborhoods pressed in on one another, and the wealthy fled outward. Five years ago, Alicia had moved to the newly fashionable area up Route 14. Land values had skyrocketed as far up the Turquoise Trail as Madrid.

They turned onto Route 14, and then down a long side road that led to the Granit estate. Aspen and ponderosa pine flanked the long winding driveway. The artfully landscaped grounds boasted thirty varieties of cactus and, of course, the ever-present yucca. The house, built of pink and white stucco, combined modern and Spanish influences in what Granit regarded as an architectural monstrosity. It had been Alicia's choice, not his, but it was built with her money and she was the one who had to live there.

Wind chimes sounded as he opened the door—another of Alicia's annoying fancies. He knew where to find her: in the dining room or kitchen, fussing over the details of the big dinner party tonight. He decided to wait until they finished their business before telling her he wouldn't be there.

As he neared the kitchen, he heard her voice telling the cook how to handle the rissole potatoes. He stopped in the doorway and watched. Bland was the word that best described Alicia. She had the kind of face one could never quite recall, round with regular, rather squat features and a perpetually amazed expression. Her blond hair was thinning, probably from so many years of bleaching, and she wore it heavily teased.

She felt his stare and turned. "Andrew, I'm glad you got home early."

"We have some business to take care of. I want to get it done, before you immerse yourself totally in this dinner."

Alicia looked at the cook. She didn't like to air personal matters in front of the help.

"Let's go into the office and discuss it there."

She led the way to the den that she called the office in the rear of the house. It was a cozy family room; the only business-like touch was a tooled leather-topped desk with a computer, phonefax, and copier.

"I need you to make a transfer," Granit said.

Alicia sighed. "How much?"

"Oh, 125—no, let's make it an even $150,000."

"So much?"

"Stop complaining. You know the expenses. Or would you rather have me give up the senate because I have a penny-pinching wife?"

She stared at him.

"Answer me—is that what you want?"

"You know I don't."

"Anyway, it'll all come back in the timber subsidy and the mining grant. Those things don't happen by themselves, you know."

Alicia walked over to the computer and flipped it on, pressing the communication button. Granit watched her as she keyed in her code and the necessary information for the transfer. She refused to give up control of her money. It had been one of her few smart moves. If they had joint accounts, he would have cleaned them out and left her long ago. Of course, he had his own fortune, tucked away safely in the Caymans and Switzerland, but he preferred using her money.

When the transfer was finished, Andrew Granit walked over to the small corner bar and poured himself a glass of sherry.

"Want anything?" he asked.

She shook her head. "No, I'll save my drinking for tonight."

"Oh, about tonight—I'm afraid you'll have to manage without me. I have to leave for Santa Fe in about an hour."

"Andrew—how tiresome. I'm having the Simmons and the Drews—that whole country club crowd. I was counting on your being there."

"You flatter me. I won't be missed."

"No, you will be. Jerry Simmons wanted to talk to you about some newspaper thing. And Faye Muralla's coming. She never goes anywhere—it's just because you'll be there. Oh God, I don't know what to do."

Granit finished his sherry and walked over to her. He began to massage her shoulders, smiling as he felt her stiffen beneath his fingers. "I'll tell you what, Alicia. We'll leave it up to you—your choice. I'll stay for your dinner and go up to Santa Fe first thing tomorrow. But, I'm in a lonely mood—I can't sleep alone tonight. There are some new things I want to show you."

She stared at him, and for an instant her eyes blazed. Then she turned away. "I'll make your excuses," she said.

"It's your decision." He smiled again. *Poor Alicia—she isn't even a worthy sparring partner.* He hummed softly under his breath as he went upstairs to pack his bag for Santa Fe.

Chapter Twenty-One

The Department of Birth and Death Records was housed on the first floor of a rambling two-story building near the park separating the government complex from downtown Santa Fe. As they neared the building, Addie's high spirits began to disappear. She had been floating on a cloud, buoyed by the excitement of new surroundings and the nearness of Jonah. Now the reality of Livonia's death and the task ahead settled on her like a heavy weight.

They had spent the morning strolling through the narrow streets of Santa Fe, wandering in and out of art galleries and boutiques and drinking in the beauty of the earth-toned adobe buildings. Unlike most state capitols, Santa Fe retained its old world flavor. Strict ordinances preserved the past, with its blend of Native American, Spanish, and Anglo cultures.

At lunch time they stopped at a charming sidewalk cafe on the Old Santa Fe Trail. As tourists streamed by, they devoured a basket full of warm, homemade breads, along with their Southwestern salads. After a second cup of strong, black coffee, Jonah looked at his watch.

"Almost time for our appointment with McInney," he said. Reluctantly they left the restaurant.

At Birth and Death Records, they found themselves in a large, white-walled room with a high wooden counter in front. Addie and Jonah waited; the workers behind the divider seemed oblivious to their presence. A heavyset man who had come in right after them stood to one side, leaning against the counter. His bulbous red nose and close-set squinty eyes looked familiar. Addie remembered seeing him in the cafe.

She was about to point him out to Jonah, when a woman noticed them and rose slowly.

"What can I do for you?" she asked.

"We have an appointment with James McInney," Jonah said. Addie noticed the man with the swollen nose turning away and writing something on a piece of paper.

The woman pointed to a hallway. "Through there—second door on the right."

"Did you notice that man out there?" Addie asked Jonah, as they walked down the hall.

He shook his head. "Why?"

"I think he's following us. I saw him at the restaurant while we were eating."

"Are you sure?"

Addie nodded. "And he wrote something down when you asked for McInney."

"Damn. If they wanted that name, now they've got it. Well, let's find out what's so important." He knocked on McInney's door.

"Come in." A ruddy-faced man in his sixties, wearing a checked shirt and tan, fringed vest, rose from behind his desk. He walked toward them, hand extended.

"I'm Addie Pryce, Livonia's associate," Addie said, shaking his hand, "and this is—"

"Jonah Smith," Jonah said quickly. "Thanks for seeing us, Mr. McInney."

"Sure," McInney said, "Sit down. Make yourselves comfortable. How's Livonia?"

Addie swallowed hard. "She's doing fine," Jonah said.

"She is one nice lady. I've had dealings with her for a long time. Say, are you both astrologers too?"

Addie nodded.

"Well, that must be very interesting. Now what can I do for you?"

"We've been doing some research on Simon Furst's chart," Addie said. "Livonia spoke to you about his birth certificate. You know how important accurate birth data is."

"Yep—like I said, Livonia and me—we've had many dealings."

"Well, you said there was something—unusual—about the vice president's birth certificate," Addie said, "And Livonia asked us to stop in and find out about it."

"Didn't she tell you what I said? I told her everything I know."

"She was a little confused," Jonah said, "She figured as long as we were down here anyway, we could hear it right from you. Get the whole business straight."

McInney nodded. "See, we're a little behind here—only been computerized for ten years. Before we got computerized, all our birth certificates were on paper."

"We still have all the paper," he continued, "stacks and stacks of file boxes in the storeroom in back. Only old-timers like me ever bother going in there."

"How long have you been working here?" Addie asked

"Forty-two years, this February. I've seen a lotta changes, I can tell you. Anyway, when Livonia asked me about the vice president's birth certificate, I went back and looked at the paper in the files. And you know—it's the damnedest thing. There's something funny there."

"Funny in what way?" Jonah asked.

"Well, back then we numbered every certificate as we issued it—by a machine stamper. The numbers moved ahead automatically. Never made a mistake. But when I pulled out Furst's birth certificate, I happened to look at the one right next to it—and damned if they didn't both have the same number."

"What could that mean?" Addie asked.

"Don't know. At first I thought: well, the machine did make a mistake. Nothing's infallible. Then I looked at Mr. Furst's birth certificate very carefully. The number looked different from the others. I think—no, I'm sure—it was made by another stamper."

"So, what's your guess, Mr. McInney?" Jonah said. "If anyone would have an idea about it, it would be you."

McInney smiled and puffed out his chest. "You want to know what I think? I think the records were shuffled around a little."

Addie leaned forward. "But why? Why would anyone do that?"

"Oh, I guess there's lots of reasons. Say the vice president wanted to be a few years younger. Someone who worked here could issue a new certificate with a later birth date. But the one thing they couldn't do is get the number sequence right. They'd have to use the same number as the one before or after."

"Is that what you think happened?" Jonah asked. "That Simon Furst wanted to change his age?"

"Don't know. I was only giving you a for instance."

Jonah narrowed his eyes. "If someone wanted to take on another identity, they could do the same thing—right?"

"You suggesting that the vice president—"

"No, no. I was only talking theoretically. But I bet it's done by people."

"Never saw it. But, yes—it's possible."

"So what you're saying is that the certificate on file isn't Simon Furst's real birth certificate?" Addie looked triumphant.

"That'd be my guess."

"See Jonah—I told you he was nothing like—"

"Well," Jonah broke in. "This changes our research. Lucky we stopped by to see you. I'd like to see that birth certificate and get a copy of it."

"Well, I'm afraid I can't help you out on that. I can tell you about the birth certificate, off the record, like I explained to Livonia—so you won't use it. But if I went any further, I might get into trouble. And I'd appreciate it if you didn't mention this to anyone. If the vice president wants his birth certificate this way—" He shrugged.

"Sure," Jonah said. "It's none of our business. We just don't want to waste time on research that's not accurate."

He stood up and stretched. "Well, thanks for your time, Mr. McInney. We appreciate it."

"It was a pleasure meeting you folks. Give my regards to Livonia."

When they got back to the big, white-walled reception room, Addie looked around for the man with the red nose and beady eyes. He was gone. But when they got outside, she spotted him, lounging in a doorway across the street.

She nudged Jonah. "There—across the street—that's the man."

They turned and walked back toward the Plaza in the center of town. She glanced over her shoulder. "He's following us. I was right."

"Okay. Nothing we can do about it. Let's just get back to the car."

They walked quickly until they reached the parking lot where they had left the car. As they headed back to the motel, Jonah glanced at the rearview mirror.

"Shit," he said. "There's a car tailing us. Those clowns must have been following us around all the time. Jeez I feel stupid. I was having such a good time, I never noticed."

"What should we do?"

Jonah shrugged. "Nothing. They're not bothering us. If they want to play games—let them."

"Just ignore them?"

"Yep. We'll stay on our guard, but we won't let it stop us enjoying ourselves."

Addie looked down at her hands clasped in her lap. "Jonah, I wondered. Why did you give McInney a phony name?"

"Oh, I just thought it was the right thing to do at the time."

Addie shook her head. "That's not why. You were ashamed. Ashamed to have that man think you had anything to do with astrology."

"Don't analyze my feelings, Addie. I'm entitled to them, aren't I? Besides, that was before we found out about the birth certificate. I gotta admit you were right—that it didn't match Furst. I guess there's gotta be something to it."

She smiled. "That's a start. What do you think the phony birth certificate means?"

"Know what I think? I think Simon Furst's a world class con-man. 'The posturing preacher' the president calls him. Well, that's the first anyone ever heard of him—when he was on TV doing his 'come to the lord' stuff. It's like he didn't have any real history before that."

"What do you mean?"

"Well, Jeez—look at his bio. Sounds phony to me. Born in Santa Fe. Whisked off to Africa before he was a year old by his parents, who were missionaries for some godforsaken sect with a membership of maybe just the two of them. He grows up there, and his folks die of some creepy virus. He comes back to the states at thirty-two with the light of God in his eyes."

"You think it's all made up?"

Jonah nodded. "Yeah. I think he's a con-man from way back. Probably born in some little town with a population of a hundred, so no one remembers him. Knocked around the country until he found this preaching racket. And then Andrew Granit spotted him."

"So you do think Andrew Granit is mixed up in all this?"

"I'm sure of it. What I think happened is Granit sees him and thinks 'this guy's a natural.' Best of all, he's no great brain, so Granit knows he can control him. But he's gotta have some kind of decent history. So Granit gets this fake birth certificate stuck in there—he'd have no problem with that—and makes up a phony bio for him. The only thing they have to worry about is someone popping up from the past."

Addie frowned. "Jonah, if what you're saying is true, then Andrew Granit has a lot invested in Furst. Do you think he'd do anything like...do you think he had anything to do with Livonia's death?"

"I don't know if I'd go that far. I can't stand Granit, but the guy's a senator, not a murderer. Listen, we don't even know for sure if Livonia's death is connected to any of this. For all we know, she could have been killed by some nut case."

"But the people following us. Our rooms broken into. It all seems connected."

Jonah looked in the rearview mirror and clenched his jaw. "The damn guy's still on our tail."

Addie realized he was more concerned than he wanted her to know. "Do you think we're in any danger, Jonah?"

"Nah. Whoever's in back of this knows there's a limit to how many things can happen before someone starts connecting the dots. And don't forget—we're White House staff. Anything happens to us, they bring out the Secret Service, the F.B.I.— the works."

"They didn't do that for Bruce Hanover."

"Yeah, but we're not gonna commit suicide."

"Bruce didn't commit—"

"I know—I know. Look, the Secret Service is just what the name says—*secret*. For all we know, they're investigating Hanover's death. Or they may have their own reasons to call it a suicide." Jonah frowned. "Do you really think Hanover's connected to all this?"

"Well, see, he mentioned the name Karl Salazar to me. That's the same man Livonia talked about in her message. She said 'I've got some information about Salazar.'"

"Yeah, I know. But you never told me that Hanover—exactly what did he say about Salazar?"

"Just that he had some kind of weird tip about Salazar. Thought I might have heard of him. Salazar had some sort of New Age involvement, and Bruce thought everyone in that world knew one another."

"Well, evidently Livonia had heard of him."

"She didn't at first. But then on her message—now we'll never know." Addie stared into space. "Jonah, I just remembered something else Bruce said. He said the tip came from his brother-in-law in Colorado. Colorado's just north of New Mexico. Do you think Salazar might be here?"

Jonah slapped the steering wheel in excitement. "I think he might be the thing that ties it all together. We've gotta find out about this guy, Addie."

The motel loomed just ahead and they pulled into the parking lot. Jonah stopped in front of the office and watched the entrance. The ancient blue Plymouth that had been following them drove by.

"Wanna bet he U-turns a few blocks down and comes back here?"

They waited. Sure enough, the car returned, heading in the direction of their rooms.

Jonah clenched his fists. "Bastard," he said. "I'd like to shoot out his tires."

"You said to ignore them, remember?"

"Yeah, I know. Listen, Addie. I can't leave you alone while that jerk's out there. I'm giving up my room and moving into yours permanently. Okay?"

Addie nodded.

"And then," Jonah said, "After we move all my stuff, let's go out and have a great dinner someplace. That clown can cool his heels in a parking lot while we enjoy ourselves."

Addie looked away. "I'm sort of glad he's following us," she murmured.

"What—oh, you mean—yeah, you'll have the pleasure of my company all the time." He grinned. "But you'll have to share the bathroom."

"Just don't make a mess."

Jonah looked at her.

"I'm only kidding," she said. "I'm not really that bad."

"Good. We don't need any 'odd couple' routine. Come on, let's get started. It's moving day."

A ddie and Jonah sat at a table in La Casa Sonora, finishing their T-bone steaks and seasoned fries. The odor of broiling meat hung in the air. Waiters scurried back and forth between the tables and the open kitchen, partially hidden by a terra-cotta brick wall.

The blue Plymouth had followed them to the restaurant. The thought of its driver waiting outside in the parking lot emphasized the warmth of the dining room. They felt festive and relaxed: Addie in a red and white silk dress, with a new silver and turquoise pendant around her neck; Jonah in a crisp, long-sleeved blue shirt and spotless chinos.

"They sure know how to make a steak here," Jonah said. "I needed nourishment after all that heavy moving."

Addie laughed. "Poor Jonah. Your four shirts weighed a ton. And then that shaving stuff. I don't know how you carried it all."

"Hey, so I travel light. Don't knock it."

It had taken less than half an hour to move Jonah's stuff into Addie's room. Afterward, they discussed the best way to find out about the mysterious Karl Salazar. Jonah remembered an old newspaper friend, Don DiAngelo, who worked on the *Santa Fe Examiner*. He called him, and after some catching-up talk, made an appointment to see him the next morning. Don had never heard of Salazar, but suggested they tap into the paper's database and see what they could come up with.

Jonah was excited. "If we get a handle on this Salazar guy," he said, "I think we'll have an idea of what's going on." His buoyant mood had continued all the way to the restaurant.

They had just ordered dessert when Addie stiffened, staring at a group approaching a table in back of Jonah.

"Don't turn around," she said. "You won't believe who just came in."

"Who, who?" he asked. "Salazar, with a big name tag on his chest?"

"No," Addie laughed. "Andrew Granit."

"What? You're right. I don't believe it. What's he doing here?"

"This is his home state. I guess he's got a right to be here."

"Yeah, he's gotta show his face to his constituents every now and then."

Addie twisted her napkin. "God, Jonah—he's coming over here."

"Here! Why would he—"

"Addie, Stern—what brings you to New Mexico?" Andrew Granit stood in front of them, towering over the table.

"We're here on vacation, Senator," Jonah said. "Wanted to find out if all the PR about your state is true."

"And does it live up to its reputation?"

"Goes way beyond."

"I'm glad to hear that. We're very honest down here. We wouldn't want to mislead anyone."

Granit turned and gazed directly at Addie. "You're looking very well, Addie. Vacation agrees with you."

Addie's mouth was dry and her heart pounded. "Thank you," she whispered.

"You looked so tired and tense the last time I saw you. Remember—I told you that you needed a change. You didn't like my suggestions, as I recall."

Jonah looked from Granit to Addie in bewilderment. "I don't think I'm following this."

Granit flashed a cold smile. "Oh, didn't Addie tell you about our lunch?" He stared at Addie, his eyes twin daggers. "Strange. She seems to have told every one else in Washington. Well, I just wanted to welcome you to our fair state. Enjoy yourselves." He turned and went back to his table.

"What the hell was that all about?" Jonah said. "When did you and Granit—?"

"I'll tell you all about it when we get back to the room. He's looking at us, and I don't want to give him the satisfaction of knowing we're talking about him."

"Are you crazy? He can't hear us. Do you think he can read lips?"

"I—I just don't want to talk about it here. Please Jonah."

The waiter brought their desserts and coffee. Andrew Granit's presence had chilled the warmth around them, and they ate silently, anxious to leave.

"What's he doing now?" Jonah asked.

"He keeps staring. He knows we're not here on vacation. Those people following us. I bet they're reporting back to him. He—he had me followed in Washington."

"What? What are you talking about?"

"I'll tell you later. Not now." She began to shiver and clasped her hands together tightly. "I don't want to let him see I'm upset."

Jonah sighed. "Okay, Addie—tell me later. Who's he with? Do you recognize anyone?"

Addie shook her head. "He's with two men and a woman. They don't look familiar."

"I don't want to turn around. Tell you what. I have to use the john anyway. When I walk out, I'll be able to look them over and see if I know them. Just calm down."

Jonah rose and walked toward the restrooms, turning to examine the people at Andrew Granit's table. Addie smiled. He looked so comical, like one of those amateur spies in a film who manage to complicate plots instead of solving them. Then her smile faded. As Jonah disappeared, Andrew Granit got up and headed toward her.

He sat down in Jonah's chair.

"I don't recall inviting you to sit down," she said.

"I don't recall asking permission." His gimlet eyes bored into her. "I'm disappointed in your choice of traveling companions, Addie. It doesn't do you justice."

"Really. I can't see where it's any of your concern."

"I don't like to see you demeaning yourself. You can do better than someone like Stern."

Addie flushed with fury. "And who would you suggest? You? Jonah's half your age and twice the man you are."

He pressed his lips together. "You're developing a mean mouth, Addie. It's not becoming."

"I wish you'd leave."

"When I'm ready. And don't flatter yourself about me. I made my offer when you had something to give in return."

"Then what are you doing here? What exactly do you want, Andrew?"

"Do you know—I'm not sure." He leaned forward and placed his hand over hers. "But I know what I don't want. I don't want to see you get hurt. Stop mixing in things that don't concern you. I don't want to see you end up like—"

"Like who?" she whispered.

Their eyes locked, and at that moment Addie knew, with sickening certainty, that he was responsible for Livonia's death. She pulled her hand away. It felt like it had been seared by a hot iron.

"Don't you dare touch me."

He stared at her. His eyes had become daggers again. Addie saw Jonah approaching, a look of bewilderment on his face.

"You seem to be sitting in *my* chair, Senator," he said.

"You sound remarkably like papa bear, Stern. Or was it baby bear? I can't recall." He continued to stare at Addie.

Jonah balled his hands into fists. "I'm not up on New Mexico law, Granit. What's the penalty for beating up an aging senator?"

Granit turned and looked at Jonah. "The penalty's rather harsh, Stern. And I don't think you'd care for our penal accommodations."

Addie jumped up and slipped her arm through Jonah's. "Let's go, Jonah. We're finished here." Jonah's body was rigid and she tugged at him. "Jonah, please."

Granit stood up. "By all means, listen to the lady. You wouldn't be much good to her behind bars, now would you?"

He made a mock bow in Addie's direction. "I hope I haven't spoiled your evening, Addie." He walked slowly back to his table.

Driving back to the motel, Jonah sat stiffly, staring at the road ahead. Addie kept her head turned away, gazing out the window. The blue Plymouth trailed after them.

When the door of the motel room closed, Jonah wheeled around. "All right. We're back in the room—satisfied? Now, tell me about your hot affair with Andrew Granit—which you didn't think important enough to even mention."

"It—it was nothing. One stupid lunch. And the reason I didn't tell you—I was ashamed to. I cared too much about your opinion of me. I didn't want you to think I was such a stupid fool. Especially after you warned me about him."

"Okay, tell me now."

Addie told him everything, including the kiss in the limousine and Granit's admission that he had her followed.

"You see, I wasn't imagining that," she said. "Even though you didn't believe me."

"Anything else?" Jonah asked.

"Just that he warned me not to say anything, and I made the mistake of telling Janice Turner about it. She told Walter, and he passed the word on to the White House. Somehow Andrew found out and left a threatening message on my unit. That's what he meant when he said I told everyone in Washington."

"Andrew—you call him Andrew?"

"He made a pass, Jonah. It's hard to call someone senator, when he's making a pass."

"Christ," Jonah said and slammed his fist down on the bed.

"It was nothing—truly."

"Maybe it was nothing to you, Addie. But the thought of that sleazeball pawing you."

"It's over. I don't understand why you're so upset."

Jonah looked at her. "Can't you see that I'm crazy in love with you? There. I've said it. I tried hard to keep my feelings to myself, but the hell with it. I'm crazy about you."

Addie moved in front of him and looked into his eyes. "Do you really mean that?"

"Jeez—I trailed after you halfway across the country. I almost lost my job. Now I'm being followed by a bunch of lunatics. Do you think I'd do all that if I didn't mean it?"

Addie felt the tremors of an earthquake deep within: glaciers melting, brick walls crumbling. She looked down and whispered, "I'm the luckiest person in the world—that someone I'm so crazy about is crazy about me."

Jonah's eyes widened. "Did you really say what I just heard?"

"I never thought I'd be able to tell you."

He threw his arms around her and began to kiss her wildly, everywhere at once, as if to make up for lost time. Her lips found his ear and she whispered, "We don't have to go slow—anymore."

The bunny pajamas lay unused on the empty bed all night.

CHAPTER TWENTY-TWO

Walter Turner crouched on his hands and knees, peering under the bed. Janice stood in the doorway, laughing.

"What a picture," she said. "The dignified Walter Turner with his rear end sticking up in the air. That would make a nice shot for *Washington Insider.*"

"I'm trying to find my cuff link. The damn thing rolled under the bed."

"I'd help you look, but I can't bend in this dress."

Walter looked up at her. She was a vision in a long, jade brocade gown. The single strand of pearls he had given her two years ago clung to her still slender neck, and matching pearl earrings peered out through a halo of chestnut hair.

He continued hunting. "I've got it," he shouted, stretching one long arm under the bed.

"Here," she perched on the edge of the bed, "let me do it for you."

He sat down next to her and put his wrist in her lap, watching her as she worked the onyx link through his shirt cuff. He hated the thought of going out tonight to the Kennedy Center. The party honoring the new president of Ecuador would be a deadly affair, where two hundred people would be jammed together, fighting to see and be seen.

He heard voices downstairs. Sophie called up from the landing. "Your driver's here, Mr. Turner."

"Tell him we'll be ready in ten minutes."

He took his dinner jacket out of the closet. Janice, still sitting on the bed, watched him.

"Why is it," she said, "that in all the films, the man is waiting for the woman to get dressed? Whenever we go anywhere, I'm always waiting for you."

"That's because you're a perfect person, darling. A goddess come down from Olympus to grace the lives of poor mortals like me."

She stuck out her tongue. "You don't know how lucky you are. We goddesses are very choosy."

"Which goddess are you tonight? I know—Hera, the queen of them all."

"God no—never Hera. Zeus was always fooling around, and I wouldn't stand for that. No. I think I'm Athena."

"Ahh—the goddess of wisdom. I'll buy that. Oh, wait a minute, Athena was the gray-eyed goddess. Your eyes, my darling, are very definitely brown."

"Well, goddesses wear contact lenses you know. If I took mine out, you'd see the gray eyes."

Walter laughed. "Keep them in. I love my brown-eyed goddess, just the way she is."

He took her hands and pulled her up from the bed.

"Don't muss me. I've got to be the perfect trophy wife tonight."

He kissed her lightly on the forehead. "Now I've got another reason to hate tonight—look, but don't touch."

Laughing, they went downstairs to the waiting car.

The Kennedy Center was showing its age, Walter thought, as they walked through the lobby. Flags of all nations still waved bravely and the crystal chandeliers still sparkled, but everything had a slightly worn look. The elevator whisked them upstairs, where the rooftop terrace and glassed-in cafe gave a spectacular view of the city, aglow with light. From one side you could see the Capitol and all the monuments. Looking the other way, Georgetown provided a glittering show.

The restaurant was filled with people. Waiters with trays of hors d'oeuvres and wine inched their way through the crowd. Walter plucked two glasses off a tray, and they plunged into the melee.

"Walter, darling. Janice, my sweet." It was Libby Tyler, the television anchor, her nose twitching for a story.

"Libby, angel, you're looking lovely," Janice said.

Libby smiled and turned to Walter, all business now. "I see that the president left this morning for China and points East. Sudden, wasn't it?"

"Not really, Lib. He's been planning this trip for months."

"Well, the press people only got two days notice. Sam told me he just had time to board his cats and get his dry cleaning back. I don't know what you call it. I call that sudden."

Walter cleared his throat. "I think there was some kind of scheduling conflict. The president had to be in three places at once. Afraid I can't tell you any more, Lib. I'm not up to speed on this."

"Any time you're not up to speed on something, the country's in trouble." She narrowed her eyes. "Come on, Walter. Did this trip have anything to do with the president's—umm—problems? A little long distance drying out, maybe?"

"Like I said, I can't help you out on this. Why don't you check with the White House press office?"

Libby Tyler frowned. "Thanks, Walter. I'll do you a favor someday." She waved to someone across the room and left.

"Bitch," Walter said. "It's people like that..."

"Don't let it spoil your evening," Janice said.

"My evening was spoiled before we even got here."

"Well, don't let it show. Look, there's Simon Furst over there, alone for once. Let's go over and try to make him miserable."

Walter laughed. "I'm game."

Furst smiled as he saw them approaching—the same smile that had won the hearts and votes of women across the country. There was something so practiced about that grin. It was always the same, no matter who the recipient. Walter pictured him rehearsing the smile in the mirror, timing it with a stopwatch to be sure it would always last the same fifteen seconds.

"Janice, you look pretty as a picture." Furst shook his head. "No—elegant is the only word to describe you tonight."

"Thank you, Mr. Vice President," Janice said, making a half curtsy.

"What happened, Simon? You don't seem to have your usual harem around you," Walter said.

The smile flashed again. "The ladies appear to be giving their husbands a break tonight. And it gives me a chance to chat with old friends."

"Seriously, Walter," he continued, "I'm glad we have a chance to talk. I was going to call your office tomorrow. With the president away, I'll have to be much more involved. You know everything that's going on. I hope I can count on you for some of your wise counsel."

"Oh, you know the government runs itself, Simon. There's nothing you have to be concerned about. But, of course, anything I can do..."

"Thanks Walter." Furst frowned. "I knew I could depend on you."

Walter looked around the room. "Speaking of wise counsel, I don't see your pal, Andrew Granit, around. If he misses this shindig, that would be wisdom of the first order."

"He's missing it all right. Andrew's in New Mexico."

Walter's eyebrows shot up. "With the debate on the minimum wage bill coming up, I would have thought—"

"Yes, well, he should be back in time for the vote. He had some kind of family emergency. It seems every now and then Alicia realizes she has a husband."

Janice shot a quick glance at Walter, then looked back at Furst. "I hope it's nothing serious."

"Oh no—just some domestic matters to take care of." He smiled. "That's the advantage of being a bachelor. No one makes demands."

Mrs. Gideon Grey, one of the party's organizers, bore down on them like an express train sweeping the locals out of its way. "Mr. Vice President," she said, "may I borrow you for a few moments? We need to talk about your speech."

"Excuse me," Furst said. "I'm afraid there are still some demands made." He left in Mrs. Grey's wake.

"He's so transparent," Janice said. "I wonder what Andrew's really doing in New Mexico."

"I've got a bad feeling about it." Walter frowned. "I don't like it. Not with Jonah and Addie there."

"You think it might—"

"Don't say any more now." He looked around. "Let's not talk about it until we get home."

Walter and Janice tried to leave the party early, but did not get home until long after midnight. Walter took off his jacket and headed into the kitchen for a cold drink, while Janice kicked off her shoes and flopped down on the couch.

"I'm exhausted," she said. "My mouth aches from smiling and my feet just ache."

Walter returned with a glass of diet cola and sank down into his favorite armchair. "Want some of this?" he asked, holding out the glass.

Janice shook her head. "I'm too tired to swallow."

He took a huge gulp and smacked his lips. "Best thing I had all night. I was thirsty."

He stared at the liquid in the glass. "I don't know, Janice. I keep wondering why Andrew Granit raced down to New Mexico all of a sudden. He never cared about Alicia's problems before."

"Do you think it could have anything to do with Addie and Jonah? That seems crazy."

"I know. Still I'd better call Jonah and tell him about it." Walter looked at his watch. "It's almost eleven o'clock there. It can wait until tomorrow."

"Do you have Jonah's number?"

Walter nodded. "He gave it to me when he called yesterday. I've got it upstairs."

"I wonder how they're doing. I wonder if they—"

"I know just what you're thinking, and it's none of our business." Walter suddenly stiffened. He put his finger to his lips and got up quietly, tiptoeing into the hallway. There, in the darkness, he could just make out a figure. He switched on the hall light and saw Sophie, with her ear pressed against the wall.

She stared at him, frozen with fear, and in one quick movement Walter grabbed her and twisted her arm behind her back.

"You were spying on us," he roared.

Janice came running into the hall. "What is it—what happened?"

"This—this creature—was spying on us." He twisted Sophie's arm hard.

She screamed in pain. "My arm—my arm—you're hurting me!"

"I'll break your goddamned fucking arm if you don't tell me what the hell you're doing." He twisted it harder and Sophie screamed again.

"Walter, are you crazy? Stop it," Janice cried.

He turned and glared at her. "Shut up, Janice. Just shut up." Janice backed up against the wall, her hand over her mouth.

Sophie began to sob and he twisted again. He could feel the bones beneath his fingers and he knew they were ready to snap. "Talk," he said, "or I'll break this one and start to work on the other."

"Anything—I'll do anything," Sophie sobbed, "only stop hurting me."

"You came into my home. You spied on me. Why?"

Sophie stared at him, her mouth moving wordlessly.

"Answer me," Walter shouted.

"I—I didn't want to. He made me."

"Who?"

"Senator Granit. He knew something—" She began to sob again.

"Andrew Granit—goddammit—you were telling *him* about things going on in this house?.."

Sophie nodded. Walter turned to Janice, who stood frozen in her spot against the wall. "Satisfied? *That's* how he knew what Addie told you. Sophie listened to us and ran back to Granit. And you blamed *me*."

He looked back at Sophie, who was hugging herself while tears ran down her face, and he shook his fist in fury.

"Walter, stop." Janice put her arms around him. "She's telling you what you want. Don't hurt her any more."

"She violated our home, Janice." He began to shake violently.

"Please, Walter, please—get hold of yourself." Janice was close to tears. "I don't want something awful to happen."

"Something awful *has* happened." He stared at Sophie. "What else did you tell Granit? Did you tell him about our friends going to New Mexico?"

"Yes," Sophie whispered.

"So that *is* why Andrew went there. I'll have to call Jonah first thing in the morning." He glared at Sophie. "Anything else? Tell me, or I'll choke the truth out of you."

"I told him about Mr. Stern and that dead astrologer—how he said he was Secret Service," Sophie whispered.

"Oh my God. What a mess. Granit'll use that if he can. We've got to get them both back to Washington. Now what are we going to do with her?"

He stared at Sophie for a minute, thinking. "Watch her Janice," he said and bolted up the stairs to the bedroom. He came back carrying Janice's diamond pin.

"Remember how you've been looking all over for your pin, Janice? Guess where I just found it. In Sophie's room. She's a thief, as well as a spy."

Sophie sagged against the wall. "That's not so. I never—"

"Well, I guess it's our word against yours, Sophie. Now who do you think they'll believe? A respected lawyer and his wife. Or their housekeeper, a liar and a spy. Who do you think, Sophie?"

"I don't want to go to jail!"

"Then you'll do exactly as I say. Now who do you contact with your filthy information?"

"Sometimes Senator Granit—sometimes a man in his office, Stephen Humphrey."

Walter shook his head. "Humphrey—another beauty. All right, you're calling Humphrey now. You'll leave this message on his voice mail: we let you go—decided we didn't need a housekeeper. Gave you two weeks pay and sent you on your way. We don't know anything about your spying—understand. Then tell him you're going to visit your daughter in—in Seattle. Someplace far away. And you go there and stay there."

Sophie nodded. "Is it all right if I go to Tulsa? I've got family there."

"I don't care *where* the hell you go—as long as it's far away from Washington, and I never have to see you again." Walter picked up the phone and handed it to Sophie. "Make that call right now."

They watched in silence as Sophie made the call, following Walter's instructions exactly.

"Now, I want you to pack your things and get the hell out of here." He shoved her toward the spare bedroom off the kitchen. "We'll call a cab. And if I hear of any surreptitious calls to Humphrey or Granit—any more of your dirty spy-ing—I file charges against you for stealing my wife's diamond pin. I'll see you rot in jail."

Sophie began to sob again. I'll do everything just like you said. I swear I will." She turned to Janice. "Mrs. Turner, I'm—I'm sorry."

Janice stared at her coldly and walked into the living room. She sat on the couch with her hands folded in her lap, while Walter called a cab service. Then he came into the living room and sat down beside her.

"Thank you for not forgiving her," he said. "That was impor-tant to me."

"I know. I hate her too—not so much for the spying, but for what she turned you into back there. I never saw you act like that. I hope I never see it again."

He put his arm around her, and they sat quietly until they heard the cab's horn outside. Sophie scuttled out of the kitchen, pulling a large suitcase on wheels and carrying a smaller one. Walter opened the front door and watched the driver pile Sophie's belongings into the trunk and get back behind the wheel. Breathing heavily, Walter remained very still until the cab disappeared down the long driveway.

It was after 9:30 when Walter and Janice finally came down to the kitchen for breakfast. They were exhausted from the night before and had turned off the alarm and gone back to sleep.

Walter picked up the phone and called his office to tell them he'd be late, while Janice wandered around the kitchen, looking for coffee. The can in the refrigerator was almost empty. She was trying to find where Sophie kept the extras.

"Here it is," she said, reaching up to the top shelf. She measured out the amount for the instant brewer. "It'll be ready in a few minutes."

Janice poured some juice into two glasses. "Now let's see. What will we have? It won't be one of Sophie's spectacular breakfasts, but—"

"Toast will be fine. Just make plenty of coffee. Where's the paper?"

"Oh, Sophie always brought it in."

"Look, let's made a deal. We will not mention Sophie's name until after breakfast. Okay? I'll get the paper."

Walter went outside and walked down the winding path to the black *Sentinel* box. He took out the newspaper and came back to the kitchen, enjoying the coffee aroma that had begun to fill the room. He sat down and spread out the paper on the table.

"Here's a story about Henry's trip." he said, "It made the front page." He began to read while Janice set out toast, butter, marmalade, and jelly. She brought the coffee pot to the table, poured two cups, and sat down.

"Not bad coverage," Walter said, looking up. "They list the itinerary and some of the events—a little personal stuff about who's going along—nothing that makes it sound like it was a sudden thing."

Janice sighed. "Henry's away. There's nothing you can do about the trip. Let's not think about the president—at least for one morning."

"Mmmhmm," Walter said, chewing absently on a piece of toast, while he flipped the pages of the newspaper. He spotted the "Front Page Rumors" column. "Let's see what venom Gregory Harmon is spewing today."

"Goddammit" He slammed his hand down on the table, spilling the coffee. "Goddammit—Goddammit—" he kept repeating, as Janice ran for a sponge and began wiping up the mess.

"Listen to this." He began to read, oblivious of Janice on her hands and knees sponging up the dripping coffee. 'Up to now, the identity of the president's astrologer has been classified information, as closely guarded as any state secret. This column has it on reliable authority that the astrologer found murdered in the Watergate last week had close ties with the White House. Before the police were called, a mysterious Secret Service agent arrived on the scene and threatened the manager. Was the murdered lady the president's astrologer? Was this an ordinary burglary, or will this develop into another Watergate presidential scandal? Watch this column for new developments.'"

"Oh my God," Janice said. "How did he ever get hold of that?"

"Don't you remember? Sophie said she told Granit about it. That goddamn bastard—he leaked it. Do you realize what this could do? Henry's got enough problems without this murder being brought to his doorstep."

Janice poured Walter another cup of coffee. "Here. Don't spill this one. I don't think it's as bad as you're making it. After all, that murdered woman *wasn't* Henry's astrologer—Addie was. Once that's made public, he won't be involved."

Walter shook his head. "No. It's not that easy. We still have that Secret Service business to explain. Shit. Why did Jonah have to do such a damn fool thing?"

"He did it for Addie. I think it was kind of noble. Anyway, we're as much to blame. If we hadn't talked about it in front of Sophie—"

"Come on, Janice. This is our home. We can't expect spies to be lurking in every corner." He rubbed his forehead. "I need some aspirin."

"Walter, I'm worried—this constant tension. You're getting headaches all the time. God knows what's happening inside you. You've got to get away from all this."

He looked at her. "Remember, I told you I'd think about it? Well, I have. And you're right. I've got no stomach for it any more. As soon as this mess is straightened out, we're going to take a long vacation—just the two of us. And while we're away, we'll think through everything."

"Do you mean it, Walter—really?"

He nodded. "But right now, we've got to deal with this. First thing I have to do is call Jonah." Walter looked at the wall clock. "It's a little after 8:00 in Santa Fe. I've got his number upstairs. I'll go up and get some aspirin and call him from there."

He went upstairs, swallowed three aspirin, and sat down on the bed to call Jonah. While the motel desk rang the room, Walter looked at his bed. It was so inviting. He just wanted to lie down, close his eyes and sleep all day. Christ, he thought, I'm sixty-one and I feel like I'm a hundred. He rubbed his head. When the aching stopped, he'd be able to think more clearly.

"I'm sorry. That extension doesn't answer," the desk clerk said.

Walter chewed his lip. Would anything go right? "I want to leave a message," he said. The clerk switched on the recorder.

"Jonah, this is Walter. Call me right away. It's urgent. I'll be at my office until 5:30 Washington time. Then I'll be home."

He hung up and went back downstairs. Janice was straightening up the kitchen.

"What did he say?" she asked.

"He wasn't there. They must have gotten up early. I left a message to call back right away, said it was very important. But they could be gone all day." He grimaced. "Well, I've got to get going now."

"How's your head?"

"I'll live. I'll be home early."

"I'm going to cook something special for you tonight."

"Oh yes, your cooking—that's another thing. Sure you don't want to go out to eat?"

"Come on. I broil a mean steak—you know that."

Walter made a face. "It'll be fine, as long as you don't set the house on fire." He ducked as she punched him in the arm.

"Oh, and if anyone calls and asks you about Harmon's column, its 'no comment.' That's to everyone, including friends. Until we decide what line to take, we're not saying anything, understand?"

Janice nodded. "Seal my lips."

She raised her face and he kissed her. "I hate to leave you. I wish it were tonight." He shrugged. "Well, off to the minefields."

CHAPTER TWENTY-THREE

Halfway across the continent, Andrew Granit picked at a huge breakfast that Senator Mendoza's cook had set before him. He often stayed at the state senator's home when he was in Santa Fe. Frank Mendoza was an old friend and political ally.

Granit had been up since dawn and had come down for breakfast long before his host's family was stirring. He was grateful for that. In his present mood, he had no desire to make conversation. He looked at the bacon, sausage, pancakes, and grits with distaste. After a sleepless night, all he wanted were some of Stella's biscuits and strong, black coffee.

Things were sliding out of control, and it made him uneasy. Details, details—Addie had said he was preoccupied with details. Well, the devil is in the details. One thing goes wrong and the whole fabric falls apart. Look at what was happening, all because of that damn birth certificate.

He stared out the window. In the distance he could see the Sangre de Cristo mountains. Tomorrow he'd be in Las Trampas, in the heart of those mountains. Sangre de Cristo—the blood of Christ. Andrew Granit shook his head. There'd been too much blood spilled already.

Now, because of Addie's foolish prying, Henry's blood would have to be added. He had really wanted to avoid it, hoping that the rumors, leaks, and innuendoes would be enough to force the president out. The scandal of the astrologer's murder could have been the final nail in the coffin. But he had lost the luxury of time. Simon Furst had to be safely installed as president before annoying questions about his birth certificate and his past could damage him.

So it was back to Marius, the option he had hoped never to use. And it would have to be done quickly. The president's Asian trip might be the best opportunity; it would be easier to get close to him there. The situation had a kind of twisted irony. Addie and Stern, with their pathetic bumbling, had sealed Henry's fate.

Granit clenched his jaw. He had to get hold of himself. That business at La Casa Sonora last night, for instance. It had been a mistake going there. He had planned to intimidate Addie and Stern with his presence, but the situation had gotten out of hand. He replayed the scene in his mind: Addie's eyes—the hatred in them. Addie had been wrong about him. He was in touch with his feelings, but he would never allow them to rule him. They had lost their power over him long ago. Doubt, regret, longing—those were the pitfalls of the weak and the enemies of the strong.

He attacked his breakfast, pouring syrup on the pancakes and spearing a sausage. He felt his appetite returning. Granit had just poured a second cup of coffee from the carafe when the maid brought in a portable phone.

"There's a call for you, Senator Granit. It's your office in Albuquerque."

Granit picked up the phone. It was Lorenzo, an aide whose primary job was to get in hours before anyone else and man the Netputer, searching the online newspapers for important stories. This was how his Albuquerque office kept abreast of what was going on around the world. Lorenzo was very good at his job and would often pick up items ahead of the Washington office. He had been instructed to watch for any story detrimental to the president.

"I just found something I thought you'd be interested in senator," Lorenzo said. "It's very hot and I knew I could catch you at Senator Mendoza's."

"This better be good," Granit said. "I don't appreciate having my breakfast interrupted."

"Yes, well, you said anything about the president—"

"Go on. What is it?"

"It's that 'Front Page Rumors' column in the *Washington Sentinel*. You know, Gregory Harmon—"

"I'm well acquainted with it," Granit said wearily. "Get on with it."

"You know that astrologer who was murdered in Washington last week?"

Granit stiffened. "Go on."

"Well, Harmon's saying that the White House may be involved in this. Some Secret Service business."

"Did he say she was the president's astrologer?"

"Yeah, something like that. Do you want me to read it to you?"

"That won't be necessary. I'll get a copy later. Thank you Lorenzo, that was good work."

Andrew Granit hung up the phone. For a few seconds, he found it difficult to breath. Rage welled up inside, choking him. That inept fool, Humphrey, and that malevolent devil, Harmon. They had gone ahead, without his permission. They'd pay—both of them. He shook his head to clear it. First he had to get control of the situation. He'd have plenty of time to deal with them later.

He looked at his watch: 8:00. It would be 10:00 in Washington. He had to call Humphrey as soon as possible, before he did something else. But he didn't want to call from here.

He picked up the phone and called his Santa Fe office. Someone should be in by now. After seven rings, an aide answered.

"This is Senator Granit," he said. "I'm at Senator Mendoza's house. I want a car and driver here in twenty minutes."

"I don't know if I can get one that quickly, senator."

"I said twenty minutes." He slammed down the phone.

When the car pulled up, he was waiting at the door. They moved quickly through the downtown traffic and he reached his office sooner than he had hoped. He closed the door, picked up the private phone and punched in his Washington number.

"I need to talk to Stephen Humphrey right away," he said.

In less than a minute, Humphrey was on the phone.

"Andrew. Have you seen Greg Harmon's column?"

"I was just told about it." Granit spoke very slowly and deliberately.

"I want you to know this isn't my fault. I did exactly what you told me to."

"I'm very upset over this, Stephen. I specifically told you that Harmon wasn't to release this until we were ready."

"Andrew—I—it's Greg Harmon we have to go after. That little bastard went ahead—"

"Not we, Stephen. You're out of this matter. You've handled it very badly and I don't want you involved in it any more. You understand. Stay out of it! Not a word to Harmon—not a word to anyone."

"Sure, whatever you say. But I don't think you should blame me for this."

"Are you telling me how to think, Stephen?" Granit's voice dripped ice.

"No, no. Of course not. It's just—Christ, you know how Harmon is."

"*You* were supposed to know how Harmon is. *You* were supposed to handle him. I don't think you did. Do you?"

"I—I guess not. I'm sorry, Andrew."

"I never accept apologies. An apology implies that you made a mistake. I allow no room for errors."

"Jesus, Andrew. What do you want me to do?"

"At the moment—nothing. Forget you ever spoke to Harmon. Deny it, if he contacts you. I'll deal with him myself—later."

"Sure. I understand."

"Do you? Right now I place your ability to understand somewhere below that of the average chimpanzee."

Humphrey was silent, and Granit could hear him breathing heavily.

"Stephen," he continued. "Do you know the position you and Gregory Harmon have put me in? You've forced my hand. I'm going to have to do something I don't want to do—

something very difficult, very unpleasant. I don't like it. I won't forget this."

He hung up. For a moment he enjoyed the picture of Humphrey squirming and sweating as he stared at the dead phone. But Humphrey knew too much and was too important to alienate right now. Later, when everything was done, he'd dispose of him.

Andrew Granit rested his chin on his hands and stared into space. He had to think through this situation. It might work out well, after all. A scandal hanging over the president would defuse any questions raised about Simon and that damn birth certificate. The media would zero in on the White House like big game hunters, overlooking any smaller prey.

Granit rubbed his eyes. He'd have to face the one detail that kept gnawing at him, that had been festering ever since Lorenzo's telephone call. To make this work, there could be no president's astrologer for the White House to produce. He would have to do something about Addie. He sighed, flipped the dial of the radiophone on his watch and set the frequency for Smitty.

Chapter Twenty-Four

Jonah and Addie left their room and walked arm in arm through an early morning haze. For the first time, clouds covered the sky, blotting out the sun. If they had been listening, they might have heard the telephone ringing. But they were too busy talking.

They continued talking all through breakfast and in the car heading for the *Santa Fe Examiner.* They had reached the stage where they needed to know everything about each other, to fill in all the empty blanks.

"Do you have any photos of when you were little?" Jonah asked. "I picture you with long hair—maybe down to your waist—and a skinny little face with huge blue eyes."

"Actually, I had my hair short most of the time. And I was pretty fat 'til I got to be a teenager."

"Fat!" Jonah's eyes swept over her. "I'm glad I know you now. Well anyway, I bet you were quiet and shy—kind of an old fashioned little girl."

Addie nodded. "There you're right. I was very shy. I think it all started with my name. How I hated it. Everyone else was Crystal or Heather. I was the only Addie."

"I love it. It makes you special."

"You know what the kids used to call me? 'Adelaide Marmalade.' I can still hear it. Maybe that's why I can't stand marmalade to this day."

Jonah laughed. "I know what you mean. Do you know how many whale jokes I used to hear? But it never bothered me. I was a street-smart New York kid, and I always had a wise guy answer."

"Well, you certainly don't have your namesake's patience."

"No, you're mixing me up with someone else in the Bible. That was Job. Anyway, I'm an Aries, so I'm allowed to be impatient."

Addie smiled. "You really boned up on astrology didn't you—just to make me feel good. You must have spent a lot of time—"

"Nah. Just one little paperback. I'm a quick study."

"Also very modest. Typical Aries. But seriously, Jonah—you don't have to do this. You don't have to talk astrology to please me. I understand the way you feel. Just understand me, too."

Jonah pulled the car over to an empty space at the curb and turned off the ignition. "Come here," he said. "I need a kiss—badly."

She leaned across the console and kissed him hard. Jonah ran his tongue over his lips. He loved the taste of her.

"Did you really mean what you said last night? That this was the first time—since your husband?"

Addie nodded. "I didn't think I'd ever care for anyone again—that way, I mean. But Livonia said I would. She was right."

"Livonia was a smart lady. I'm sorry I didn't know her."

"You would have liked her." Addie looked around. A gray Ford had pulled over to the curb about half a block behind them, with the motor still running.

"Look, Jonah. There's our escort. The Plymouth must have broken down."

Jonah turned. He could just make out the shapes of two men in the car and shook his head in disgust.

"Those clowns never give up, do they?" He smiled and stretched out his arms. "Let's give them a good show. Something to report back to Granit about."

"No, Jonah. Not with them watching."

He laughed. "I'm just teasing you. Okay, if you won't let me have my way with you, let's go."

He sped away, grinning as he heard the Ford's motor gunning up in the distance.

They were only five minutes late when they pulled up in front of the newspaper building. It was a small, three-story structure with a sign in black letters over the entrance: *Santa Fe Examiner.*

Don DiAngelo had a tiny office on the third floor, on one side of a room filled with desks, computers, and fax-copiers. People scurried about and phones buzzed constantly.

"Jonah," Don shouted, jumping up when he caught sight of them. He was a short, round man, with a thick handlebar mustache that compensated for the thinning hair on his head. He pumped Jonah's hand and turned to Addie.

"You're Jonah's girlfriend, right?"

Jonah put his arm around her. "This is Addie Pryce, a very special girlfriend. And this is Don DiAngelo, a very special old pal."

"Good, good," Don said. "Now we know each other. After we finish here, I'm taking you both out to lunch and we'll catch up on old times."

"Great." Jonah smiled. "I warn you. We both have big appetites."

"You can't scare me," Don said. "Yesterday was payday. Now tell me. What's this all about?"

"We're trying to get a handle on this Salazar guy. I've got an idea he's down here somewhere."

"If he's done anything at all—good or bad—he'll be in our own database or in the network. It won't take long to track him down. There's only one problem."

"What's that?" Jonah asked.

"Well, see—we have our dedicated computers and our film library in the building across the street. It's special stuff, and there's limited access. I can go over there any time I want. But it's hard to get anybody else in. I can sneak you in, Jonah, but two people—" He shook his head. "I'd really be sticking my neck out for that."

"That's all right," Addie said. "I can wait here."

"Sure you won't mind?" Jonah asked.

"It'll be fine." She looked at Don. "Where can I wait?"

"Right here in my office. But, tell you what. We've got a cafeteria on the ground floor. Why don't you go down and have something—cup of coffee maybe. We won't be gone more than an hour, tops."

Addie nodded. "That sounds good. Go on, Jonah. I'll be fine. The important thing is to find out about Salazar."

Jonah kissed her and walked away with Don. He looked back once, smiled, and waved. The two men hurried down the stairs, out the building and across the street. Jonah wanted to get the business over as quickly as possible, so he looked straight ahead, walking rapidly. Otherwise he might have noticed the man leaning against the building—a man with a swollen red nose and squinty eyes.

I t took some digging, but they found information on Karl Salazar in both the *Examiner* database and the newspaper network. They sent the data to the printer as fast as it came up on the screen. Jonah summarized it as they watched.

"Karl Salazar, born May 15, 1956 in Newark NJ. Doctorate from MIT in 1979. Stayed at MIT, working in the Artificial Intelligence Lab with William Daniel Hillis. Wow, that's big time. Hillis is one of the fathers of the connection machine theory."

"What's that?" Don asked.

"Thousands of simple parallel processors working together, rather than a single linear CPU. Gives a more literal simulation of the human brain."

Don looked at him. "You know all that? Oh, I forgot. You used to do the science stories."

Jonah glanced back at the screen. "Salazar was an avid connectionist. Wrote a brilliant paper on the Bolzmann machine theory."

"And what's that?"

"Basically the same thing. Hey, look at this. He coauthored a breakthrough paper with Isaac Templeton, a biogenetic engineer—it's called 'The Android Ingredients: Artificial Intelligence and Recombinant DNA.' This guy's a real heavyweight!"

"In 1985 he became a visiting scientist at James Farmer's Center for Non-Linear Studies in Los Alamos—specializing in artificial life." Jonah punched the air triumphantly. "I had a feeling he was tied in with New Mexico. Sure—see—in 1986, he took a permanent position as external faculty member at the Santa Fe Institute."

"What's that?"

"It's a think tank. Dabbles in things like the origin of life, creation of lifelike organisms—things like that." Jonah peered at the screen. "While he was there, Salazar did advanced work on the Genetic Algorithm."

"And what the hell would that be?"

"I'm not sure. We'll search for that when we're finished with Salazar."

"I think we're just about finished with the gentleman now," Don said, pointing to the screen. The row of asterisks that signaled the end of a topic flashed below the words, "1989—Karl Salazar left Santa Fe Institute on medical furlough: nervous collapse."

"Damn—that's seventeen years unaccounted for. Let's search for that Genetic Algorithm. Maybe he'll pop up again under that."

They called up the data and the screen snapped into life. Jonah stared at it. "It's the brainchild of John Holland from the University of Michigan. Look—he was at the Santa Fe Institute the same time as Salazar. Let's see now. The Genetic Algorithm applies the principles of genetic evolution to computer optimization."

"Clear as mud."

"Take my word, it's very significant. It's a way of improving computer programs through the natural methods of genetic evolution. It's complicated stuff and this Salazar guy was fooling around with it."

"Well, there's nothing else about Salazar here," Don said. "I can print out abstracts of the papers he wrote from our science library. Want that?"

"Sure. Why not. Addie won't mind waiting a little longer."

While the printer churned out its material, Don and Jonah sat at a nearby table and waited.

"What do you make of it, Jonah?"

"I don't know yet. This Salazar guy is brilliant—a regular M.I.T. whiz kid. Obviously interested in artificial life. Also, a bit unstrung. But what's he been doing for the last seventeen years? That's what I have to find out."

"You think he's still in this part of the country?"

Jonah nodded. "He's tied in with what I'm looking for—how, I don't know, but I'm sure he is."

"Want to tell me more about it?"

"I can't, Don. It's hot stuff. You understand."

"Sure." Don looked over at the printer. "The thing's finished. We'd better get back."

Don gathered up all the papers, stuffed them into a large envelope and handed it to Jonah. He tucked it under his arm and they left the building, heading back to Don's office. They walked through the crowded main room and stopped short. The office was empty.

"Wonder where Addie went," Jonah said. "She's not the wandering type."

"Probably down in the cafeteria. Let's pick her up there and go out for lunch. It's a little early, but we'll have more time to talk. I just have to take care of a couple of things."

Jonah nodded and waited while Don finished. They went down the stairs to the ground floor and walked to the back of the building. Although it had begun filling with people, the cafeteria was still half empty. Jonah scanned the tables. Addie was nowhere around.

"Jeez, where could she be?" Jonah said uneasily.

"Let's see if she came down here at all." Don walked over to the counter and spoke to a woman who was lining up glasses of iced tea and lemonade. He turned and came back to Jonah.

"Leona remembers seeing her about half an hour ago. She ordered some iced tea. Leona doesn't know how long she stayed. Bet she took the elevator back up. We must have just missed her."

Jonah wheeled around and raced back to the lobby and up the stairs, Don trailing behind him. When they reached the office, he kicked the door in frustration. There was no sign of Addie.

"Where the hell can she be?" he said.

"Listen—take it easy. Sit down. I'll ask around and see if anyone knows anything." Don shrugged. "Maybe she's in the bathroom. I'll ask one of the gals to take a look."

Jonah sat still for a moment. Then he jumped up and stared out the tiny window. A few people were strolling on the street, probably on their way to lunch. He stretched his neck to see their car parked outside. It was empty. He began pacing up and down, keeping his eyes fixed on the door, hoping to see Addie suddenly materialize.

Instead Don came back into the office. Jonah didn't like the look on his face.

"You couldn't find her," he said.

Don shook his head. "She asked someone where the cafeteria was—that was the last anyone remembers seeing her. That was almost an hour ago—right after we left."

"Hey, how about the ladies' room at the cafeteria. Maybe she got sick or something."

"One of the gals went down there to check. She'll be back any minute." Don cleared his throat. "Umm—did you and Addie—umm—have a fight or anything before you got here? Maybe she got fed up with waiting and took off. If she was sore about something—you know."

Jonah shook his head. "You saw her. Did she look like she was angry? We had such a great thing going. She wouldn't have left if—"

He stopped and clapped his hand to his head. "Holy shit—it must have been those guys following us. They did something—"

"Following you? Who's following you?"

"We've had creeps following us ever since we got to Santa Fe. I figured they were harmless jerks who were keeping tabs on us. But I was carrying this, just in case." He held up a pen-shaped rod, designed to shoot paralyzing pellets. "This baby could stun an elephant. Only works at short range, though. It's the latest Secret Service issue."

"Wow," Don said wide-eyed. "How'd you get hold of that?"

"You don't want to know. Those goddamn bastards. Why didn't I use this on them when I had the chance. They were after Addie all the time. Just waiting 'til I wasn't there. Shit—why did I leave her alone?"

Jonah began pacing back and forth, pounding the wall with his fists. "Jeez, if I could only get my hands on one of them now. I'd find out what happened."

"Sit down for a minute," Don said. "Let's think this through. Why would anyone want to get Addie?"

"Oh, I know who's behind it." Jonah sank into a chair. "But try to prove it. And I don't know why he'd single out Addie. See, there's this stuff we found out. I can't go into it now. But I know just as much as Addie does. Why her?"

"Who is it, Jonah? Who?"

Jonah looked at him. "You wouldn't believe me if I told you, so what's the use. This guy's got influence here, big time. If the story got out, I don't know what would happen to Addie."

He jumped up. "What am I gonna do, Don? I don't know what's happening to her right now. I gotta do something—I gotta get the police on this. Do you know anybody important in the department?"

Don thought for a moment. "A couple of people—no one major."

"Come down to the station with me now. If I go by myself—some guy from out of town—they'll just laugh at me. I know what they'll figure. Lovers' spat. Sweetie takes off. Guy goes bananas. Even you said that."

"No, no—I didn't mean that. Just asked if it was possible. Sure, I'll go with you. Let's just give it a half hour more. Make sure she doesn't turn up."

I t was after 3:00 when Jonah got back to the Coyote Court. He and Don had spent two hours at the police station: arguing, cajoling, pleading. Finally the police issued a missing person's bulletin, statewide. But the way they looked at Jonah, he knew they would sit on their hands on this one. He couldn't even blame them when he thought of how it sounded. Addie disappearing into thin air from a crowded building, sinister guys following them, a mystery man he couldn't even name in back of the whole thing. Jeez, if it weren't happening to him, he'd be laughing his head off about it.

He opened the door of their room, praying Addie would somehow be there waiting for him. Nothing had ever felt so empty. Jonah spotted the message light above the phone right away. He raced over to it; maybe it was Addie. His shoulders sagged, when he heard the recorded message. It was from Walter Turner—something urgent. Jonah's lips tightened. Whatever it was, he had something much more urgent to tell Walter.

He tried Walter's office first, but he was gone. Then he called his home and spoke to Janice. He didn't mention Addie. He couldn't go through the story twice. Just told her he'd wait by the phone for Walter's call.

Jonah sank down on the bed and looked around the room. Addie's pink robe lay on the other bed, her slippers stood neatly under the night table, and the three little monkeys sat on the dresser. He buried his face in his hands. When he finally looked up, his eyes were wet.

The phone rang and he swallowed hard to get himself under control. He was glad to hear the sound of Walter's voice. It felt like a pipeline to reality.

"Jonah," Walter said. "Where the hell have you been all day?"

"Something awful happened. Addie's disappeared." He told Walter everything in detail. When he finished, there was silence on the other end. He could almost feel Walter's thoughts crackling across the wires. Finally, he spoke.

"I've got some ideas on this, Jonah, but I've got to think it through. I'll get back to you in about an hour, okay?"

"Walter, I'm going out of my mind just sitting here. I've gotta do something."

"We'll do something, together. Just give me some time."

"Do I have a choice? What were you calling about?"

"Can you handle some more bad news?"

"Sure. I don't give a damn about anything else."

"Harmon's got an item in his column about that murdered astrologer. Says there's a White House connection. That a Secret Service agent was snooping around. He even hints that this Livonia was the president's astrologer."

"Jeez." Jonah took a deep breath. "That's serious stuff. Ties the president in with the murder. When they find out I was the Secret Service guy, there goes my job."

"Don't jump ahead, Jonah."

"How do you think Harmon got hold of that?"

"I know how—Andrew Granit. The bastard found out and leaked it."

"Granit's behind Addie's disappearance too. I'm sure of it. Do you think there's a connection to that article?"

"I hope not, but that's what I'm thinking."

"Holy shit." Jonah's voice grew shrill. "If Addie's out of the way, it'll be hard to prove Livonia wasn't the president's astrologer. God, Walter, that's what this is all about. Those bastards are gonna kill her, if they haven't already. I've gotta do something."

"I've got to think clearly, Jonah. I'll get back to you as soon as I can. Just hold yourself together."

The phone clicked and Walter's voice was gone. Jonah threw himself on the bed and buried his face in the pillow.

CHAPTER TWENTY-FIVE

Walter hung up the phone and turned to Janice. He hesitated, trying to think of the right words.

"What is it?" Janice said. "Your face. You look like—"

"Something's happened. It's Addie—she disappeared."

"Disappeared. I don't understand. How could she disappear?"

"Let's sit down." Walter put his arm around her and they sat down on the couch, while he told Jonah's story.

Janice shook her head, bewildered. "I don't see how Addie could just disappear in the middle of a newspaper office."

"I'm just telling you what Jonah said. The fact is she's gone, and I—I'm afraid she's in a lot of danger."

Janice's eyes widened. "What do you mean?"

"Think about it. Remember what you said this morning, about Harmon's column? You said there was no problem— that Addie is really Henry's astrologer, and once that's made public—"

"My God, Walter. If there's no Addie, then what? Do you think someone would really try to—to do away with her?"

Walter frowned. "I don't think Andrew Granit would stop at anything to get Henry."

"Andrew," Janice gasped. "I know he's power mad, but murder..."

"I don't know what to think any more. That astrologer killed in the Watergate. Hanover's suicide. Now Addie's disappearance. Jonah thinks Granit is behind everything."

They stared at each other in silence. The antique grandfather clock chimed the hour, shattering the stillness.

Walter stood up suddenly. "Well, I do know one thing. I'm not going to just sit around and wonder. I'm getting down there as fast as I can. And I'm taking Timothy with me."

"Timothy. You mean the security guard at your office?"

"Do we know any other Timothy? Of course that's who I mean. You get on the phone and order two tickets for the first flight to Albuquerque tomorrow morning. I'll call Timothy on the cell phone."

Janice put her hand on his arm. "Three tickets, Walter. I'm going too."

"Out of the question. It's too dangerous."

"If you think I'm going to sit here and worry about you, you're—"

"I said no! I won't hear of it."

"All right, Walter. Here's your choice." Janice folded her arms and stood in front of him. "Either I go to New Mexico with you and Timothy—that way you'll know where I am and what I'm doing. Or I go by myself after you leave."

"Janice, you wouldn't."

"Wouldn't I! Don't you know me by now? Let's see—the first thing I'll do when I get there is call Andrew. I'm sure I'll be able to reach him at one of his offices. Maybe I'll meet him somewhere. I'll let him know he can't get away with this. I'll tell him if he dares to harm one hair on Addie's head, I'll personally—"

"Okay Janice—you win." Walter sighed. "Get three tickets. But you're just adding to my load, giving me one more thing to worry about."

By the time Walter called Jonah back, all the arrangments had been made and Janice was upstairs packing. Jonah picked up the phone at the first ring.

"How're you doing?" Walter asked.

"Lousy, if you really want to know."

"Feeling sorry for yourself won't help things, Jonah. You've got to hang tough."

"Sure—sure. I know."

"Listen to me carefully," Walter said. "I'm coming down to Santa Fe."

"What? You—I don't understand. Why?"

"You're not the only hero around." Walter smiled grimly. "Besides—with the president away, I've got nothing better to do. Figure Janice and I deserve a vacation."

"Janice! She's coming too?"

"She twisted my arm a little. Oh, and I'm bringing Timothy."

"Who?"

"You met him last time you were at my office."

"You mean that gorilla who wanted to throw me out. Yeah, he'd be a handy guy to have around. Jeez, I don't believe all this. When will you—"

"We'll be in Albuquerque about 9:00 tomorrow morning—your time. Then we'll pick up a private shuttle plane that takes us to Santa Fe."

"You want me to meet you?" Jonah asked.

"No, you stay where you are, just in case someone tries to reach you. We'll get a cab. But we need a place to stay. How's that Coyote Court?"

"It's not what you're used to, Walter. Just a run of the mill motel on a tourist strip."

"Well, I have to be near you. Is it clean at least?"

"Oh sure."

"Okay—get us two rooms. As close to you as possible. We should get there sometime after 9:00."

"I'll be waiting. And Walter—thanks."

"Not necessary. I told you—this is a vacation. That's what I told Eve Kontos. That you stumbled onto something interesting about Furst, and I had to get down to Santa Fe to check it out myself. Janice insisted on making a vacation trip out of it."

Walter rubbed his aching forehead and shifted the phone to his other hand. "By the way, Timothy says he's looking forward to seeing you again."

Jonah laughed. "I bet he is. Glad he's on my side this time."

"See you soon." Walter hung up the phone. It was good to hear Jonah laugh.

Bringing Timothy had been a brainstorm. The giant guard had been with the firm five years, but Walter had known him longer, much longer. Timothy's father had been his barber, and Walter had put in a good word for Timothy when he applied to the Virginia state police. He'd been a good officer too, building a reputation as a tough and feared cop. Until all that drug business started.

On probation, with his career shattered, Timothy had come to Walter for help. He had hired him over his partners' strong objections and never regretted it. Timothy's hulking presence created a feeling of security in a business where a disgruntled client could be lurking around every corner. His gratitude matched his size. He had developed a fierce loyalty to the firm, and to Walter in particular. It would be good to have Timothy with them in Santa Fe, especially with Janice around to worry about.

When the cab pulled up in front of the motel office, Walter saw Jonah waiting. He ran over and opened the door, before the driver could turn off the motor.

"I can't believe this," Jonah said, as they climbed out of the cab. "You're really here. Janice—you're a beautiful sight."

"Too bad it takes an emergency to have you appreciate me," she said kissing him on the cheek. She squeezed his hand. "I'm glad we're here, Jonah."

He turned away, but not before Walter saw his eyes filling up. He looked at Janice and she shook her head. They waited until Jonah regained his composure.

"Sorry," he said. "I've got rooms for you a few doors down from me. Soon as you check in, I'll help you get settled."

Timothy stood awkwardly, looking from one to the other. "You remember Jonah Stern, don't you, Timothy?" Walter said.

"Sure—good to see you again, Mr. Stern."

"Hey, I'm Jonah." He stuck out his hand and it disappeared in Timothy's huge paw. He gazed up at the hulking giant and grinned. "You look even better than Janice."

"Let's get this over with," Walter said and disappeared into the office, emerging a few minutes later with their keycards. In half an hour, they had unpacked and gathered in Jonah's room to plan their strategy.

"Here's what I think we ought to do first." Walter felt more alive than he'd been in years. "I want to talk to the police myself. Get an idea of just how hard they're trying on this. Then I want to get over to that newspaper office. Speak to a couple of people. Jonah, you'd better come with me."

Jonah nodded.

"You want me to come too, Mr. Turner?"

Walter looked at Timothy. "I told you on the plane, Timothy. While we're here, we're going to be working very closely. Mr. and Mrs. is out. It's Walter and Janice for now. When we get back to the real world, you can do whatever's comfortable for you."

"Sure. Anything you say, Mr. Turner." He grinned. "I mean, Walter."

"That's better. No, I don't need you to come with us. I want you to go out and rent a car—under your name. They know Jonah's car, but they won't know this one. Oh, and while you're out, pick up two cell phones. I brought two with me, but I want us each to have one. Put everything on your card and I'll reimburse you."

Timothy nodded. "Then what do I do? Come back here?"

"Right." Walter handed Janice one of the two cell phones he had in his lap. "Here, you keep this one. You're going to be our communications center. You stay here in case Addie—or anyone with her—tries to reach us. Oh, and get hold of all the local papers and read them cover to cover. There may be something that—"

"I don't want to just sit around here, Walter. That's not what I—"

"Janice," Walter pointed a finger at her. "You blackmailed me into coming down here. Now you're going to do exactly what you're told."

"Who made you the leader? I don't remember any elections." They glared at each other, while Jonah and Timothy looked away, embarrassed.

"Anybody want a vote?" Walter said finally.

Jonah shook his head. "You're running the show, Walter." Timothy's head bobbed up and down in agreement. Janice looked from one to the other, then smiled sweetly.

"Aye aye, skipper. Your orders will be carried out to the letter." She gave a mock salute and winked at him. Even in defeat, she managed to be utterly charming. Walter wondered how he'd handle it, if she were the one missing. He didn't think he'd survive.

"Here's something else you can do," he said. "I want you to call Andrew's office here in Santa Fe. Make believe you're someone from a news magazine looking for an interview. Find out his schedule."

"What good is that gonna do?" Jonah asked.

"Not much, but right now, he's our only connection to Addie. It's time for us to be following him. Speaking of that, has anyone been shadowing you since Addie disappeared?"

Jonah shook his head. "Nah, they weren't interested in me—just Addie. I wish to hell one of those assholes *would* show up. I'd beat it out of him—where Addie is. Then I'd rearrange his face, just for the fun of it."

"I didn't know you were so physical," Janice said.

"Lots of things you don't know about me. I was top middleweight on the boxing team when I was in college. It's like riding a bike or a horse—once you're a fighter, you never forget how."

"That explains it," Walter said. "I notice whenever you get angry, you make fists."

"Gee, I didn't know I was that obvious. I've gotta watch that. You know, I threatened to beat up Andrew Granit in that restaurant. Jeez, I wish I had."

"That wouldn't have helped matters. You'd be in jail for battery, and Addie would still be missing." Walter frowned. "Do you think it was an accident—his being there?"

"That's what I thought at the time. Now I'm sure he had the whole thing planned."

"Well boss, can I make a suggestion?" Janice smiled at Walter. "Let's get something to eat. I'm starving."

After lunch at a nearby taco place, they split up to carry out their assignments. By the time Walter and Jonah returned to the motel, afternoon shadows were deepening. Timothy had gone to the pool for a swim, and Janice was inside, sitting at the desk, reading a newspaper. She jumped up when they entered the room.

"What happened? Any news of Addie?"

Walter shook his head and Jonah sat down on the bed, staring straight ahead.

Walter looked at Janice. "Did you call Andrew's office?"

She nodded. "He's not there. I spoke to an aide. She told me he's away for a few days—up in the Taos area—and can't be reached. I asked her when he'd be back in Santa Fe. She said he's not coming back—he's going directly to Washington. Said I should call him there next week."

"Taos," Jonah said. "Why would he go there? Nothing there but lots of scenery."

"Maybe he wanted a few days off to relax," Janice said.

"With Harmon's story breaking—not likely. Not Andrew." Walter narrowed his eyes. "He should be on his way back to Washington already. Unless..."

"You think it has something to do with Addie, right?" Jonah said.

Walter nodded. "And maybe something else we don't know about."

"You think maybe Addie's in Taos? I'm calling Detective Gonzales."

"Not a good idea." Walter frowned. "I don't like what's going on here with the police. I've got a bad feeling about it. I know missing persons, especially out-of-towners, isn't top priority, but it's more than that. I think there's someone higher up, saying 'sit on this one.'"

"You think Andrew got to someone?" Janice asked.

Walter shrugged. "That wouldn't come as a shock to me. If I *did* find out anything, I wouldn't let the police in on it. No, I think we're all alone on this. We may have to call in help from Washington."

Jonah looked at him. "FBI?"

"Or Secret Service. I have to think it through. With Henry—umm, the president—out of the country I may have trouble throwing my weight around. Besides, we don't have much to go on. The Taos area—Christ, it's like a needle in a haystack."

"We've gotta do *something*."

"We will. First thing tomorrow, we'll go up there—with or without help."

"I want to show you something I found in the paper." Janice had a strained expression on her face. "Jonah, what was the name of the man you saw at the Records Department?"

"James McInney. Why?"

"I was afraid of that." She handed Jonah the newspaper, folded to page 7.

Jonah scanned the article and looked up at them. "Jeez—I don't believe this. Walter, his house burned down last night. He and his wife were killed in the fire."

"When I read that he was from Birth and Death Records, I wondered if he was the same one," Janice said.

"Listen to this." Jonah read from the article. "'Officials say the fire was not of suspicious origin. It started in the downstairs family room, when Mr. McInney apparently fell asleep while smoking.' Not suspicious, my ass. It's too damn convenient. Now no one knows about that birth certificate."

"*We* know, Jonah."

"Yeah, for all the good it's gonna do. Poor McInney. He was a nice guy—just trying to do his job. Goddammit. Granit doesn't stop at anything. And now he's got Addie." Jonah buried his face in his hands.

Walter walked over and put a hand on his shoulder. "It's possible the fire is a coincidence. These things happen."

Jonah looked up. "No, it was Granit. I'd bet my life on it. If I could only get my hands on him."

"We'll get him," Walter said quietly. "I promise you, Jonah."

Chapter Twenty-Six

It had happened so quickly. Whenever Addie thought about it, the pictures in her mind ran together—like fast forwarding a tape while the visual was on. She shook her head to clear it. She still felt dazed and groggy.

She had been sitting in the cafeteria, sipping iced tea, when a man walked in and looked around the room. He spotted her and came over to the table.

"Are you Addie Pryce?" he asked.

Addie looked at him and nodded. He wore a bright Hawaiian print shirt that hung loosely over his khaki pants, and his hair was oiled back over his ears in an old-fashioned ducktail. He looked out of place in the newspaper cafeteria.

"Mr. Stern needs ya across the street. He sent me to find ya."

"But I thought I couldn't go there."

The man shrugged. "They said to getcha, so I guess it's okay."

Addie gulped down the rest of her tea and followed the man out of the cafeteria, through the lobby, to the front of the

building. He looked outside, both ways, before holding the
door open for her. They walked out and as they stepped down
from the curb, he took her arm. A gray Ford pulled up in front
of them, blocking their way. The man yanked open the back
door, pushed Addie inside and jumped in. With a screeching
of tires, the car sped away.

Addie began to scream and the man clamped his hand over
her mouth. She twisted her face and bit down hard, feeling
the fleshy part of his hand give between her teeth. He
squealed in pain.

"Goddamn bitch bit me!" he shouted.

He grabbed Addie's neck and pressed her face into the seat
cushion. A sour smell—a mixture of damp clothing, stale
smoke, and musty body odors—assaulted her and she began
to choke. He pressed her face down harder.

"You want to breathe," he hissed, "then behave. No screaming. No biting."

Addie tried to nod, and he released her slowly. She sat up,
gagging, tears streaming down her face. He put his hand back
on her neck, ready to push her down again. They stopped for
a light, and the driver turned around. Addie recognized him at
once: the man from the Records Bureau, the man with the bulbous red nose.

"Take it easy," he warned. "The boss don't want her hurt."

"Can it, Smitty—you try sitting in back, see what you do. I
don't give a shit what the boss wants. I don't want no more
trouble from her." The man glared at Addie.

The light changed. Smitty shrugged and turned his eyes
back to the road. Addie sat very still and silent, and the man
finally removed his hand. At the next red light, she sprang into
action. She rammed her knee into the man's groin. He doubled

up and she lunged for the door handle. She twisted it frantically, but it was locked. The man leaned over and yanked her
back by her hair. Her screams echoed through the car.

"Dammit Smitty, I can't fight this bitch all the way up to the
house," he said.

Smitty nodded and reached into the glove compartment. He
took out a handkerchief and handed it to him. "Be careful," he
said. "Don't use it too long."

The man pressed the handkerchief against Addie's nose and
mouth. A sweet, sticky smell stung her nostrils. Chloroform!
She struggled harder.

"She's a tough cookie," the man said. "I'd like to knock her
out my own way."

"You do that, and it's your ass that'll be..."

The voices grew fainter and fainter. The next thing Addie
knew, she found herself lying on a bed. She was nauseated and
weak and stayed very still, replaying the pictures in her mind.
Finally, she felt strong enough to sit up on the edge of the bed.

Now, as her head cleared, she looked around the room. It
was small, about ten feet square, painted a light green with a
white plastered ceiling. There was a bed, a pine night table and
matching dresser, and next to the window a straight-backed
chair with a white cushion.

The window! Addie ran over to it and looked outside. She
was on the second floor of a house. Dry bleached land, with
clumps of green vegetation scattered about, stretched in all
directions. Mountains loomed in the distance. Addie tugged at
the window, but it was sealed shut. She took off her shoe and
slammed the window with it as hard as she could. The blow
bounced off with a hollow thud, not even making a dent in the
unbreakable plastiglass.

Addie turned back to the room. There was a door across from the window. She turned the handle and pushed, but the door refused to move. It was bolted from the outside. She began to bang on it with both fists.

"Let me out—let me out—let me out of here!" she screamed. Tears of frustration poured down her face, and her shouts dissolved into choking gasps. Exhausted, she sank down into the chair and stared out the window. The sun was low in the sky. It must be late afternoon.

Addie looked around the room again. She had to get hold of herself, keep her mind sharp and use whatever was around to best advantage. She took several deep breaths and got up to explore the room again. There was another door, opposite the bed, opening onto a tiny bathroom with a sink and toilet. Some towels hung on a rack. Soap, a glass, a toothbrush, toothpaste, and even a little can of powder were lined up on a small shelf over the sink. Addie sighed. All the amenities for a happy stay. The perfect guest room from hell.

The dresser was next to the bathroom, and Addie went through the drawers, looking for some clue to reveal where she was. They were empty, except for some flannel shirts and a pair of pajamas. She looked over at the night table and saw her pocketbook sitting on top of it, next to a small lamp. When she opened her purse, she saw they had left everything intact, even her wallet with her money and credit cards. She checked the glassine folders with her identification, medicard, and a few photos. How she wished she had a picture of Jonah.

Jonah—what must he be thinking? What had he done when he came back and found her gone? He must be frantic with worry. She pictured him with his hands balled into fists, pacing and cursing. If only she could tell him she was alive.

She looked down at her dress. She had wanted to look pretty for Jonah's friend, so she had worn the white print sundress he liked so much. It was wrinkled and smudged with dirt. Her bare shoulders emphasized her vulnerability. Addie shivered. The room was air conditioned, and she was very cold. She remembered the flannel shirts in the drawer, and she took one out and draped it around her shoulders.

Addie returned to the chair and gazed out the window at the slowly darkening mountains. Her ankle ached. She must have twisted it while fighting. She looked down at her useless white sandals. If only she had worn pants and sneakers.

Addie closed her eyes and visualized her astrological chart, focusing on the twelfth house, the area that shows confinement. She fumbled in her purse for her pocket ephemeris to find the current positions of the planets. Her fingers moved slowly across the page, and she nodded as she read. Whatever indications of her captivity she could find seemed very brief, only a few days at most. What did that mean? Would she escape? Or would it end in death?

Addie heard a fumbling of the bolt at the door. She jumped up, flattening herself against the wall. The door opened and Smitty walked into the room, carrying a tray.

"I brought you something to eat. Some chili, a sandwich, an apple, and a thermos of coffee." He pointed to the items on the tray.

Addie decided to be pleasant. Maybe she could find out something. "I'm not very hungry. But thanks."

Smitty shrugged. "I'll leave it. The boss said to make you comfortable. I left pajamas in the drawer and a coupla shirts. I see you got one on. They're big, but they're clean."

He turned to go. "Wait," Addie said. "Tell me—where am I?"

"You're in a house. That's all you need to know."

"Smitty—that's your name, isn't it?"

"That's what they call me."

"Umm—who's this boss you talk about?"

He stared at her. "Anything you need? I gotta go."

"Yes—could you get me something to read? I don't have anything to do and—"

"I don't know what we got. You wouldn't want what I read."

"How do you know?"

"You like girlie magazines—porno stuff?"

She shook her head. "I'd like a newspaper." A paper would tell her where she was.

"I'll see what I can find. Anything else?"

"Yes, my head aches so. Could I have some aspirin?"

"Yeah, that stuff'll do it to you. I'll get you something."

"Thanks." She smiled at him, but he gazed back stonily, turned and left.

Addie began to pick at the chili and was surprised at how good it tasted. Of course—she hadn't eaten since breakfast that morning. She devoured the chili and decided to save the sandwich and coffee for later. Sinking back into the chair at the window, she watched the mountains disappear into the darkness.

Addie heard the fumbling of the latch again, but this time Smitty knocked before opening the door. He tossed a newspaper, two copies of *Current Gossip* and a bottle of aspirin on the bed. She handed him the empty bowl of chili.

"Did you make this yourself?" she said. "It's very good."

"Listen—get this straight. It's not gonna do you any good to chat me up. I don't like this playing nursemaid. I'm only doing what the boss tells me to do."

"Oh, Senator Granit told you to—"

"How'd you know he's—?" He stopped and glared at her. "You're a real smartass, ain't you? Think you can trick me. Well—no more talking. You tell me what you need. I bring you stuff. That's it."

He picked up the empty chili dish and walked out, slamming the door. Addie heard the bolt slip into place. She rushed over to the bed and picked up the newspaper. It was a weekly, *Las Trampas Observer*. She smiled in triumph. Smitty was so dumb. It was a small victory, but at least she knew where she was.

Addie read the newspaper while she ate the sandwich and drank the coffee. The words began to dance in front of her. She rubbed her eyes, trying to concentrate. The remains of the chloroform combined with the aspirin to create a numbing fogginess. She yawned and stretched. There was no use fighting it. She had to sleep to keep her mind sharp.

Addie took out the pajamas. They were men's pajamas, large, but clean, just as Smitty had said. She went into the bathroom, washed, and changed into them. Then she rinsed out her underwear and spread it on top of the dresser to dry. She sighed, amazed at the resiliency of the human mind. Even here, in this awful place, she was doing all the little normal things.

When she pulled down the spread, the bed looked soft and inviting. Her body ached with fatigue. Addie lay very still, closing her eyes and beginning to relax. She sat up suddenly. Suppose someone came in at night—Smitty or the man from the back seat. She pictured their sweaty hands grabbing her and she shivered.

Addie jumped up and pulled the chair across the room, shoving it in front of the door. It wouldn't stop anyone; the door opened outward. But at least the noise of its moving would wake her and she'd be ready to fight.

She got back into bed and stared into the darkness. Thoughts swirled through her head, weaving a mosaic of questions. Why was she here? What was going to happen to her? What did Andrew Granit want? She fell into a deep sleep without finding any answers.

Addie's sleep was shattered by scraping noises. She sat up, heart racing, and through the sunlight streaming into the room, saw Smitty in the doorway kicking the chair. He held her breakfast tray in both hands and booted the chair out of the way. Smirking, he turned to her.

"You didn't need no chair." His eyes flicked over her. "You're nothing special. Nobody'd break in to get at you. You don't look bad in bed though—kinda cute in those pajamas."

She shrank back against the pillows, as he approached with the tray. He set it down on the bed and leaned over, so close she could smell his sour breath.

"Here you are. Room service deluxe. Don't I get a tip?" He laughed at his wit and the terror in her eyes. "What—no talking today? Guess you used up all your smarts."

He turned and left. Addie began to breathe again. She picked at the breakfast, but finished all the strong, black coffee. Afraid that Smitty would come back for the tray while she was still in pajamas, she dressed quickly. After an hour had passed, Addie decided she was rid of him until lunch.

She settled into her familiar spot by the window and began to visualize charts, focusing this time on Andrew Granit. She narrowed her eyes and gazed up at the ceiling, picturing the connections between their charts. His Saturn afflicted her Moon closely, showing emotional and spiritual restriction; she was quite literally his prisoner. Yet, there was a tight, favorable connection between her Mercury, the planet of communication, and the Pluto that dominated his chart. A tiny tremor of hope began to flicker within her. Perhaps she would be able to reach him, to reason with him, to win her freedom.

A small black spider made his way across the ceiling, toward a network of cracks in the corner. Addie loathed all crawling things, especially spiders. But she knew that the cracks toward which he was heading meant his escape from the room. This time she was rooting for the spider. Addie watched him inch toward the corner and pictured herself, suddenly tiny and pliant, following him into the cracks to freedom. She barely heard the rattling of the bolt. Two men she had never seen before entered and closed the door quietly behind them.

Addie jumped up and backed away in terror. Were these her executioners? She opened her mouth to scream, but the shorter of the two put his finger to his lips and motioned her back to the chair. The two men sat down on the bed, facing her.

The shorter man, who seemed to be in charge, was bone thin. Horn-rimmed glasses rested on a large, curved nose, and behind them a pair of bulging eyes peered out at her. His movements were kinetic, as though fueled by a barely controllable nervous energy. The man next to him was tall and husky, with even features, a placid expression, and gray eyes that seemed to stare past her. He reminded Addie of someone; she couldn't quite remember who.

"Allow me to introduce us," the shorter man began. "I'm Karl Salazar. And this is my friend and bodyguard, Marius."

Addie gasped. She was face to face with the elusive Karl Salazar. She had pictured him as someone pale and shadowy, cloaked in mystery. In the flesh, he seemed quite ordinary. She looked at Marius, who nodded to her.

"I heard there was an astrologer—umm—visiting here," Salazar said. "Although, I'm afraid you're not exactly a voluntary guest."

"A prisoner's more like it. I've been locked up in this room since yesterday."

"My status isn't much better. I had a brief respite a few weeks ago, though, an adventure just over the Colorado border, in Trinidad." His leg began to shake and he put a hand on it to steady it.

"But today we have a little more freedom than usual, don't we, Marius? Our keeper is, shall we say, distracted. And we took advantage of it to visit you. I'm most anxious to talk to you. I'm afraid I don't know your name."

"Addie Pryce. How did you know I was an astrologer?"

"I heard Smitty tell Barney."

"I wouldn't think Smitty even knows what an astrologer is."

"Well, he used the word, so I decided to take a chance."

"I'm glad you did. I haven't seen or spoken to anyone but Smitty since—"

"We've been gone ten minutes," Marius interrupted, tapping his watch.

"Thank you, Marius." Salazar turned to Addie. "I asked him to keep track of the time, because I tend to go off on tangents—and our time here is quite limited. You're probably wondering why I'm so anxious to talk to you."

Addie nodded.

"I'm a very rare bird. A scientist who's interested in the occult. I analyze everything and break the physical world down into its tiniest particles. Yet I'm drawn to what can never be documented. I am truly a split personality." He added, as if to drive home his point, "I am also a diagnosed schizophrenic."

Alarmed, Addie stood up and edged toward the door, which she suddenly realized was unlocked. They had opened the bolt when they came in. She could make a dash for freedom.

Salazar smiled at her. "Don't worry. I'm only a threat to myself, and not even that, if I take my medication. I've been very good about that lately."

He motioned to Marius, who got up and stood leaning against the door, blocking her way. Addie's shoulders sagged and she sat down in the chair again, staring at the floor. They were part of the enemy too.

"It wouldn't do you any good," Salazar said. "The downstairs door is locked. You couldn't get out. And if they found you running around, I'd be in trouble. So you see, Marius can't let you leave. You understand?"

Addie nodded. It would do no good to antagonize them. She'd have to play along.

"I'm a deeply troubled man, Addie—may I call you Addie?" She nodded, and he pulled a crumpled piece of paper from his pocket. "Here's my chart. Take a look and tell me what you think."

"It takes time to—"

"No, no, no. I don't want you to analyze it. I can do that myself. I'm quite informed, really. I want to confirm something. Tell me what you think is happening—right now."

Addie studied it, trying to keep her hands from shaking, and checked several times with her pocket ephemeris. Finally she looked up. "I'd say you have a major change coming."

"Exactly what I thought! With Uranus opposing the mid-heaven and Neptune conjoining Mars."

"I think it's going to be positive," Addie said. "Pluto trines its natal place and Jupiter crosses your ascendant later this year."

"Fine, fine," Salazar jumped up and began to pace excitedly. "That's what I wanted to hear. The numbers say the same thing." He stopped in front of her. "Do you know numerology, Addie?"

"Just a little."

"You must study it. That's where the answers are—in the numbers. All the way back to the Kabbalah—a primary source of occult knowledge."

"I think there are some things we're not meant to know," Addie said, "things that are hidden because—"

"Nonsense—that's an excuse for the timid. To survive in this universe, we must know everything—the occult as well as the scientific. It takes a special kind of courage to pursue knowledge."

He began pacing again. "That change—I don't know if I can wait. My burdens are crushing me—things are closing in."

Marius walked over to Salazar and put an arm around his shoulders. "Steady. We're gone twenty minutes now. Better start getting back."

Salazar shook him off. "No—let them look for us. I need to talk to this lady. I need to talk to her now."

He leaned against the window sill, staring into Addie's eyes.

"I've been choking on my thoughts for so long. I believe you were sent here by providence."

He began to pound his hand with his fist. "The horror of it. Do you know the horror of it? Trapped in an inexorable lock-step. You go on and on—always forced on by your own greed for knowledge—and all the time you know what you're doing is destroying you."

Addie was rigid with fear. Salazar's words made no sense. If she said the wrong thing, he might lose all control. She took a deep breath.

"I don't understand. Perhaps if you started at the beginning—"

"Of course, how could you understand. Let's see—the beginning. I suppose it all started at MIT. I was one of the shining lights there—in the Artificial Intelligence Lab. My specialty was parallel processors to simulate human neural networks. All theoretical of course. Do you have any science background?"

Addie shook her head.

"I'll keep it simple then. I met a man named Dr. Isaac Templeton. We were two halves looking for a whole. He was a biogenetic engineer—a DNA specialist. I was a computer scientist trying to duplicate the human brain. We had one common goal: to create a fully autonomous robot."

"A robot?"

Salazar nodded. "Self-contained, with its own systems—binaural hearing, binocular vision—everything to mimic the human machine. But I used the wrong term. I shouldn't have said robot. Our goal was to create an autonomous android."

"What's the difference?"

"An android is a robot in a human form. That was Dr. Templeton's challenge. I created the systems. He created the form."

Addie leaned forward, fascinated in spite of her fear. "You said *created*. Were you successful?"

"At first it was all theoretical. Then I joined the Santa Fe Institute and Templeton followed me as a visiting lecturer at the University of New Mexico. We spent every spare moment in secret on our project." His eyes stared into the distance. "Yes, we were successful. In 1988, we created a man. He could think. He could mimic emotional responses. He had perfect speech synthesis. I felt like God. Then I had my first nervous collapse."

"It's understandable. The strain—the moral questions..."

"No, it was schizophrenia—voices, hallucinations, everything. It has been laying in wait for me all my life. I've always been nervous, hyperactive, could never maintain a relationship. But I had it under control until then."

"How long were you hospitalized?"

"About three months. They found the right medications for me. But the Institute didn't want me back. They put me on medical furlough. That's when I met Andrew Granit."

"Andrew Granit! How does he fit into this?"

"I was at loose ends and he tied them together neatly. He had a foundation to fund our research. His wife is a very wealthy woman, you know, and she put up the money. Templeton left the University and we worked full time on our android. Everything was top secret. Only Granit and the two of us knew the whole story.

"By 1991, we had our man—just the way we wanted him. He was perfect. We even gave him a rudimentary digestive system, so he could eat like a human. We stopped at reproduction, though. That was too much for us."

Salazar began to pace around the room again, waving his hands in the air.

"Yes, we had our man all right. We were so arrogant. Do you know what we made him? A preacher. As if to throw the whole thing right in God's face. A great cosmic joke. And he became wildly successful. In two years, he was on local television, preaching to the faithful. Imagine. The flock being led by an android. And then I had my second breakdown. When I got out of the hospital—that's when I started studying the occult. I believe it saved my life."

Addie stared at him, wide-eyed.

"You're ahead of me now, aren't you, Addie?"

"Did—did this preacher become a senator?" she whispered.

He nodded. "And a vice president. Now you're starting to understand my burden. But that's only part of it. He beckoned to Marius. "Would you like to meet an android, Addie?"

"I already have. I met the vice president."

"No I mean now—right now. Marius, shake hands with the lady."

Addie drew back, as Marius approached, hand extended.

"Go ahead, shake his hand. See if it feels different."

Addie took his hand. The texture, the warmth, the muscle tone—everything felt human. She looked at Salazar in disbelief. The story was too bizarre—the ravings of a madman.

"You don't believe me, do you?"

"I don't know," Addie said. He does remind me of Simon Furst. There's something about his eyes. But..."

"Roll up your sleeve, Marius, and give me your pocket knife." Salazar walked over, took the knife and stuck it into the fleshy part of Marius's arm. The android's face was expressionless.

"You see, Addie. No pain—no blood—no feelings."

"And Simon Furst is like that too?"

"Yes, but Furst is much more complex. You see, Marius is a simple, dedicated android. He was created for a single purpose."

"What purpose?"

"When I tell you, you'll understand the depths of my torment. Marius is an assassin. He was created to kill the president."

CHAPTER TWENTY-SEVEN

Addie's brain burned. It was too much to absorb all at once. Here she was, face to face with the man who only an hour ago had been an elusive phantom. Now he was assaulting her with stories of androids and assassins. She clutched her forehead.

"I don't understand. Kill the president! How? Why?"

Salazar sat on the edge of the bed and leaned forward. "To make room for the vice president, of course. That's been Andrew's grand plan, ever since he got Simon Furst elected to the Senate. Do you realize the power he would have—a man who controlled the president."

"But through assassination! Even someone like Andrew Granit would—"

"Some men lack a conscience—totally. Andrew Granit is one of them."

Addie stared at him. "And how about you? You created these—these creatures."

"I have a conscience, Addie, I do. And it's destroying me."

"You knew about Andrew's plan." Addie's voice grew shrill. "You went ahead and engineered this killer for him."

Salazar removed his glasses and rubbed his eyes. "I'm weak—I'm sick—I'm obsessed with this quest for knowledge. Can a man be condemned for that?"

He began to wring his hands and nod his head up and down in a jerky motion. Realizing she had gone too far, Addie changed her tone.

"I don't understand the need for assassination. Why couldn't Granit just groom Furst to run for president?"

Salazar breathed deeply until he got himself under control. "That would take too long. Andrew's old. He doesn't have the time. And even if he could wait, Simon could never be elected president. He's not clever enough. His brain stores massive amounts of data, but he lacks spontaneity, wit, subtlety. With his good looks and pleasant disposition, he's an asset to any ticket as vice president. But to head it—never."

Addie nodded. "Yes, he's not what you'd call a mental heavyweight."

"Exactly." Salazar replaced his glasses and looked at Addie. "No, the only way Simon Furst can ever become president is by elimination."

"How—how is Marius going to do it—kill the president?"

Salazar stiffened. "I think I've told you too much already."

"What difference does it make." Addie's shoulders sagged and her eyes filled. "I don't think I'm leaving here alive."

"No, no. Don't think that way. That's not going to happen." He seemed genuinely concerned about her. As if to distract her, he continued.

"Let's see, you wanted to know about Marius. He has a bomb built into his body, where his gonads should be. A subtle touch, don't you think?"

Addie stared at him.

"No, I can see you don't appreciate that. No matter. Marius can detonate the bomb by pressing a button that's buried in his wrist, where his pulse should be."

"Isn't that awfully dangerous—having him walking around like that?"

Salazar smiled. "Not at all. Marius would never do it, unless he was specifically instructed to. Besides, there's a built-in safety device. I'm the only one who knows the formula to release it. If the time ever comes, then I'll give the formula to Marius."

"What happens to him?"

"Oh, he's disposable, aren't you, Marius?"

Marius nodded. "Quite disposable. There won't be any need for me afterward."

Addie's lips trembled. "That's awful. Don't you have any feelings toward him?"

"He's not human, Addie. He has no emotions, no soul. He's only a machine. Now we, on the other hand—" Salazar closed his eyes for a moment, then opened them and looked at her. "Tell me—what does astrology teach you about death?"

"You're not supposed to look for death in a chart. That's sort of an unspoken rule. But some people can see it."

"Can you?"

She shook her head. "I don't want to. Not for anyone."

"What do you think it's like, Addie?"

"I think the spirit survives. And continues on in a different form."

"Reincarnation?"

Addie nodded.

Salazar stood up and began to pace back and forth. "I believe that also. I don't see how any rational person can believe anything else. But how about punishment—retribution for your sins? What do you think about that?"

"Well—there is karma. I suppose you could consider that a form of punishment."

"How do *you* define karma?"

Addie chose her words carefully. "I believe that your actions provoke reactions. Sometimes it's here, in this life. Sometimes you can spend many lifetimes working out the bad karma you've built up."

"That's it—that's exactly it." Salazar's pacing grew more agitated. "That's what terrifies me so. I've done so many evil things, flown in the face of nature. What will happen to me? How many lifetimes of torture do I face?"

"Perhaps what you're suffering right now is a form of karma. And I believe we all have the chance to reverse things—as long as we're alive."

"Do you really believe that?" Salazar began wringing his hands. "No, it's too late for me. How can I ever atone for what I've done? I'm doomed, doomed to—"

The door flew open, and a barrel-chested man charged into the room. He stopped and stood still, on legs that seemed too short for his stocky body, while his eyes shifted from one to the other.

"Dr. Salazar," he said. "I've been looking everywhere for you. I didn't expect to find you here. I don't think the senator's going to appreciate this."

Salazar's prominent Adam's apple bobbed up and down, as he gulped air in a visible effort to calm himself. "Barney," he said finally. "You've come to fetch me. Have you met Miss Pryce yet?"

Barney looked at Addie, expressionless. Then he took Salazar's arm. "Come on Dr. Salazar, Marius, we've got to get back. Excuse us, Miss Pryce."

Salazar kept his eyes fixed on Addie. "Goodbye. I enjoyed our talk a great deal. I hope I haven't upset you too much."

"Goodbye," Addie whispered. They were gone, and she was alone again.

Addie stared out the window. She had been gazing at the mountains ever since Salazar's visit, drowning in their shadowy vastness. She pictured herself there, surrounded by space, far away from this room with the walls that were closing in on her. It felt so real. Entranced, she failed to hear the door opening. The floorboards creaked, and she wheeled around. Andrew Granit stood in front of her.

At the sight of him, all the rage and frustration that had been building swept over her. "You bastard," she screamed and flew at him, fists beating against his chest. He gripped her shoulders and held her away from him, while she flailed helplessly. His fingers pressed into her flesh like a hawk's talons, and she winced in pain.

"If you don't stop, I'll have to hurt you," he said. "It's your choice."

She stood still, breathing heavily, and he slowly released his grasp.

"That's better." Granit raised his eyebrows. "I didn't expect that kind of greeting."

"What *did* you expect?"

"Certainly nothing this physical. Possibly recriminations, hysterics. Not an attack."

"Do you really think I'm that passive? If I could, I'd kill you without a second thought."

"Oh Addie, I think not."

"Don't underestimate me. Give me a weapon and see."

He frowned. "No games today. It's not my pleasure. I understand you had visitors."

"So that's it—that's why you're here. You want to find out what Salazar told me. I'm afraid I can't help you." She pressed her lips together, turned away, and stared out the window. He moved in front of her, blocking her view.

"I know exactly what he told you. The fool was so terrified, he blurted out the whole thing. I want to find out *how* he told you. I want to know his state of mind."

"Oh, he was very calm, very self-possessed. He's a very stable person."

"Damn you. I said no games." He glared at her.

Addie shrugged. What difference did it make? It wasn't worth enraging him.

"All right. He's upset, he's conscience stricken, he's tormented. Satisfied?"

"Did he seem—unstable?"

"If you mean do I think he's on the verge of another breakdown—yes, it's very possible."

His voice softened. "Thank you, Addie. His state of mind is very important to me right now. You deal with a lot of different people. I value your opinion. I certainly can't depend on the fools here."

Addie stared at him. "I don't believe this. You—you kidnapped me and now you're keeping me shut up in this little room. I have no idea why. And you expect me to have a consultation with you about some psychotic's behavior. You're incredible, Andrew."

"You know, Addie, this whole business—this bringing you here—circumstances gave me no choice. You had to disappear."

"Why? Why are you doing this to me?"

"You really don't know, do you? I thought your clever little mind would have figured it out. I guess you haven't seen Harmon's column. That astrologer who died in the Watergate—"

"You mean the astrologer you murdered."

"Is that what you think?"

"It's what I *know*. You killed her."

Granit shrugged. "Think what you want. At any rate, Harmon hinted that she had a connection with the White House."

"Oh my God—Jonah." The color drained from Addie's face.

"Yes, your traveling companion seems to have messed that up too. The idiot. Pretending to be Secret Service."

"How do you know about that?"

"I've told you before, Addie. I know all about you."

Her shoulders sagged. "What does Livonia's death....What does that have to do with me?"

"Don't you see? Stern couldn't have been more helpful if he were working for us. The public will think your friend, Livonia, was the president's astrologer. Then the questions will start—about what the White House had to do with the murder. It could well mean the end of the president."

Addie's hand flew to her throat. "If I'm not around, then no one can prove that I was his astrologer, not Livonia."

"Exactly. Now you see why I had to do this."

Hatred and terror swept over Addie. She found it difficult to breathe. "You're despicable—you lying, murdering, loathsome—"

He frowned. "I told you I had no choice. I'm not enjoying any of this."

Her voice grew shrill. "Do you think I care about your enjoyment?"

"Well, I want you to understand how I feel—"

"How you *feel!* You don't have any feelings—none at all! Her eyes blazed. "You know, the first time I met you, Jonah compared you to a hooded cobra. He was right. There is something reptilian about you."

"Some people find reptiles fascinating. My grandson is in love with them."

"I'm not surprised. It must be something in the genes. I'm sorry for your grandson, poor thing. Destined to grow up into a coldblooded monster like you."

"Easy, Addie."

She knew she should stop, but the need to wound him overwhelmed her. "I know you, Andrew. I have your chart, remember? And I've had lots of time to think about it, sitting alone in this room. I know your weakness. You can't feel like other people do. You can't imagine happiness or love. Oh, you pretend, but you—"

"Don't analyze *me,* Addie. I warn you."

"You did it to yourself too—that's the saddest part. You put your emotions in a straitjacket for so long that they disappeared altogether. I pity you. You don't have any more feelings than your robots."

His hand flew up and he slapped her across the face, so hard that she staggered backward and almost fell. The pain and shock made her eyes fill. She turned away, so he couldn't see the tears rolling down her cheeks. All her fury vanished, leaving only terror.

He stepped in front of her, took her chin in his hand, and gazed into her eyes. "All right, Addie," he said. "We're even now. You've seen me lose my composure and I've seen the color of your eyes when you cry. Just as I thought—pale, purplish blue—the color of Nemophilia, a plant they call baby blue eyes. Have you ever seen it?"

Addie choked back a sob and shook her head.

"Well, that's the color." He wiped her face with his handkerchief. "Do you know why your eyes fascinate me so? They're exactly the eyes of someone I knew a long, long time ago."

He looked at her, but gazed past her through the years. He was in a different place. The muscles of his face relaxed, the lines softened. Addie suddenly remembered that connection between their charts and felt a surge of hope. Maybe, just maybe, she could reach him.

"What was her name?" she asked softly.

"Sarah. The last time I saw her, her eyes were the color of Nemophilia, too. Sweet, innocent Sarah. Can you imagine anyone choosing an Alicia over a Sarah?" He shook his head in wonderment. "Can you imagine anything like that?"

He grew silent. Suddenly his eyes left the far place where they had been and snapped back to the present.

"Strange—when people resemble each other, we think they're alike in other ways. I suppose that's why I've been thinking of you as sweet, innocent Addie. But of course, you're not innocent at all." He smiled coldly. "Running around the country, fucking a wise guy like Stern. You could probably teach *me* some things."

Addie shrank back. He looked at her and narrowed his eyes.

"Don't worry, Addie. You're safe from me. I have neither the time nor the inclination for that." He turned and headed for the door. Addie sank into the chair, trembling.

"Andrew, wait."

"Yes," he turned impatiently.

"What's going to happen to me?"

"I don't know the future. Isn't that your specialty?"

"You're going to kill me, aren't you?" she whispered.

He walked back and looked down at her. "You're trembling."

"I don't want to die."

"None of us do, Addie." Granit extended his hand and stroked her hair, then withdrew it abruptly. He turned back toward the door.

"I really must leave."

"Tell me, Andrew—please—what's going to happen to me?"

"I don't know. I honestly don't know."

He walked out and closed the door softly behind him. Addie heard the bolt slip back into place.

CHAPTER TWENTY-EIGHT

Jonah awoke to the sound of banging, a knocking on his door that began softly and grew in intensity.

"Who's there?" he shouted, jumping out of bed.

"It's Walter."

Had he overslept? Jonah glanced at the clock. It read 6:45; the alarm hadn't gone off yet.

"Just a minute." He padded to the door, running his fingers through his hair. Walter stood in the doorway, holding two containers of coffee. He handed one to Jonah and sat down on the bed.

He pointed to the chair. "Sit down. We've got to talk."

Jonah looked at Walter. His face was drained of color and his eyes were wide with shock.

"Jeez, what's the matter? Oh my God—it's Addie, isn't it. They found her. She's—" His voice broke.

"No," Walter said quickly, "It isn't Addie. It's—there's been a crash. Air Force One."

"What! The president's plane?"

Walter nodded. "It was landing in Tokyo about seven o'clock at night—five in the morning in Washington. I'm not sure what happened. The landing gear locked, a tire blew—" He shook his head. "What's the difference. It crashed."

"How bad?"

"Very bad. The president's unconscious. Head injury, broken leg, I don't know what else. They stabilized him and put him on a supersonic medivac to Washington. He's in the air right now. The first lady is with him, won't leave his side for a minute. Eve Kontos called me at 6:00."

"Why didn't you wake me up right away?"

"There's nothing we can do. You need your sleep."

Jonah looked at him. "Were there any—fatalities?"

Walter nodded. "I told you it was bad. The back of the plane got the worst of it. Some of the press people were killed. And Marty Shaw was riding back there with them."

"Oh God, Marty! He's dead?"

Walter nodded and sighed.

"I can't believe it. I won't pretend I liked the sonofabitch, but Jeez—to be killed like that. In a crazy way, I'm gonna miss him. I got used to his pushing me around."

They were silent for a moment; then a thought struck Jonah. He leaned forward.

"Remember that last meeting with Addie? She was so upset about the president making the trip—said it was a terrible time for it."

"I remember. And I told her to shut up and go home." Walter rubbed his forehead. "One more thing for me to wrestle with."

"Nah, it's probably a coincidence. Still, it makes you wonder."

"We'll never know, will we? But the past is over. No sense dwelling on it." He looked at Jonah. "There's something else we have to talk about."

"God, what else."

"Well, Eve tells me Simon Furst is already making noises. He's waving the twenty-fifth amendment around—saying the president can't fulfill his duties. His chief of staff, Lem Granger, and Granit's main flunky, Stephen Humphrey, are talking about rushing affidavits to the House and Senate. If the president is still unconscious tonight, I'm afraid we're looking at Acting President Furst."

"What a great time to be out of Washington."

Walter smiled grimly. "The thing is—with the president out of the picture and Furst in charge, I don't have any clout at all. We're not going to get any help here. We're on our own."

Jonah jumped up. "We gotta do something fast. If Furst takes over, Andrew Granit will be calling all the shots. We'll never be able to get to him then. And Addie—"

"I know, I know. I've been thinking the same thing. Timothy and I are leaving for Taos now. See what we can find there."

"I gotta get dressed. I'm going with you."

Walter shook his head. "I know how you feel, Jonah. But you can't come with us. The people who have Addie know you. They don't know Timothy or me. We can ask questions, wave a little money around. Maybe find out something. If they spot you—"

"So what the hell am I supposed to do? Just sit here and wait? I'll crack up, Walter."

"I know it's tough, but we've got our cell phones. If we find anything, you can get up there in a couple of hours. Now, tell me anything you can think of about these characters."

Jonah rubbed his eyes. "There's next to nothing to go on. A beat-up blue Plymouth with New Mexico plates, GD755. That's the car that followed us. But they're phony plates. Don DiAngelo checked it out for me. Motor Vehicles told him those numbers don't exist. Then Friday it was a different car, a newer one. A gray Ford. I didn't get that license number, but it was probably phony, too."

"You're right. That isn't much." Walter frowned. "How about the people following you? Did you get a good look at any of them?"

"Only one. A heavy-set guy, almost your height, with a big red nose—looks like someone with rhinophyma."

"What the hell is that?"

"Oh, a swollen red nose—usually you get it from a big drinking problem. The guy's got little shifty eyes too. Not much to look at."

Walter laughed. "Doesn't sound like it." He stood up. "We'd better get going. You and Janice stay around the motel, in case Eve Kontos or anyone else tries to reach us."

"Wait a minute," Jonah said. "Do you have a gun?"

"No, but Timothy does. I don't even know how to use one."

Jonah opened the top drawer of the dresser. "Here, take this." He handed his revolver to Walter. "It makes an impression, even if you don't know how to use it."

Jonah stood in the parking lot and watched the rented black Mercury pull away. He wanted to go along so badly his guts ached with it. He turned and began to jog around the buildings, circling the motel complex three times. Breathing heavily, he walked over to the pool and sat down on a lounge. He stared into the water, watching sunbeams dance across the clear blue surface. He seemed to be gazing into Addie's eyes. Jonah jumped up; he couldn't bear to be alone any longer.

He walked back inside and knocked on the Turner's door.

"Who is it?" Janice's voice sang out.

"It's me, Jonah. Are you decent?"

The door swung open. Janice stood there, barefoot, in bright pink slacks and a pink and white striped shirt.

"Come on in, Jonah." She turned off the radio. "Nothing new about the president. They're repeating the same stuff over and over again. I'm just straightening up Walter's mess. He was so upset this morning, he just threw things around. Sometimes he can be such a trial."

"Listen—your husband—don't knock him. When I grow up, I want to be just like him."

"Walter's hard to equal." She looked at him. "But I think you might make it."

Jonah sat down in a chair. "How about some breakfast when you're finished? I'm buying."

Janice beamed. "Sounds good. I've worked up an appetite."

She threw some clothes into a laundry bag, hung Walter's pajamas in the closet, and stuffed some books and a minicomputer in a drawer. Getting down on her hands and knees, she peered under the bed. "Now if I can just find my sneakers, we're in business."

"Over there." Jonah pointed to pink and white sneakers lying under the desk.

"Thanks, pal." She sat down on the bed and began lacing the sneakers.

"Janice," Jonah traced the floral pattern of the chair's upholstery with one finger. "Do you really think there's anything to astrology?"

"Why?"

"No, I asked you first. Do you?"

"Yes, I do. Maybe not as much as the president does—I wouldn't run my life by it—but I'm sure there's a lot of truth to it. It goes back a long way. You know, Jonah, everything can't pass a reality check—whether you like it or not."

"Sure, sure—I understand. At least I'm starting to."

Janice smiled at him. "Now it's my turn. Why do you want to know?"

"Well—see—Addie said she had this Jupiter thing going on in her chart. She felt nothing really bad could happen to her. And she was so lucky—when we stopped to gamble, she won a jackpot, just like that." He snapped his fingers.

"I'm not surprised. Astrologers say Jupiter's the best thing you can have going for you."

"So you think it really works—that she'll be okay—that this Jupiter thing can protect her?" He looked at Janice, his eyes pleading. She walked over and sat on the arm of his chair.

"Addie is a first rate astrologer. She knows what she's talking about. If she said that, then, yes, I think she'll be all right."

"God, Janice," Jonah said in a choking voice. "You don't know what I'm going through. After all these years of fooling around, I finally found someone—I don't know—when I'm with Addie, all I care about is what she's feeling, not how I feel. You know?"

Janice nodded. "It sounds like the real thing."

"I know it is. I know it. And she feels the same way. She's just scared, because she had a lousy marriage. And just when it all started to come together—"

He looked up at her. "Do you know what we had, Janice? One night—one lousy night. The next day we were so happy.

Everything was a joke, even those assholes following us. And then she was gone."

He buried his face in his hands. "What am I gonna do, Janice? What am I gonna do without her?"

She leaned over and squeezed his hand gently. "We'll get her back, Jonah. We will."

After breakfast they went back to Jonah's room, and Janice called Eve Kontos. She listened quietly for a moment, then looked at Jonah and frowned.

"No Eve," she said, "I don't know where he is. We haven't seen him since yesterday morning. I think Walter sent him out of town—hunting for something."

Janice nodded in response to something the chief of staff said. "Right. I'll have him call you as soon as I hear from him." She hung up and looked at Jonah.

"Eve wants to talk to you. With Marty—ummm—gone, they need you in Washington. You heard what I told her. Did I do the right thing?"

Jonah nodded. "We have to stall. I'm not leaving here without Addie. I'll think of something. Maybe develop a case of food poisoning or desert flu."

Janice smiled. "You do look a little green around the gills. Too much chili pepper."

"Hey," Jonah said, "How about the president?"

"He's back in Washington. They have him in surgery right now at Walter Reed."

"What do they think?"

"Eve sounds pretty hopeful. There's some kind of blood clot. But it's in an easy place to get to."

"They sure didn't waste any time."

"That new medivac plane's a marvel. It's the fastest thing in the air—it only took them six and a half hours from Tokyo. And it's a flying hospital. They can even operate if they have to, using robot telemetry from Walter Reed."

"We better let them know about it." Jonah jumped up and grabbed his cell phone, punching the memory button for Walter.

"Hello." Walter's voice came crackling through the phone.

"Janice just spoke to Eve. The president is already in Washington—on the operating table. Looks good."

Walter sighed with relief. "Keep me posted as soon as you know anything."

"There's something else. They need me back in Washington. I won't go, Walter, not till we find Addie. Janice told Eve she didn't know where I was."

"Good. Just keep away from the phone. I'll speak to Eve later."

Jonah took a deep breath. "What's doing up there?"

"Well, we sailed up Route 68. Got to Taos about a half hour ago. We stopped in a few places already, asking around. Not much to ask about though—guy with a red nose, blue Plymouth, gray Ford. My hunch is they're not here anyway. The place is too big and it's crawling with tourists. There are some small towns south of here—on Route 76. We're going to head down that way, when we're finished."

"Okay. We'll hang out in my room—wait for messages." Jonah hung up the phone and shook his head.

"It's hopeless. They're just wandering around Taos. They don't have any leads—nothing."

"Walter's a resourceful guy. You'll see. In the meantime, let's turn on the TV and watch the latest about the president."

Jonah switched on the news channel, and they settled back to watch. After a few minutes, he jumped up and began pacing.

"This waiting around is killing me, Janice."

"I know." Janice looked up at him. "But you've got to be strong, for Addie's sake. Waiting here is the only way we can help her."

Jonah sighed and sat down again. They watched in silence as the news flickered across the screen.

CHAPTER TWENTY-NINE

Smitty was late with her breakfast. She had no watch or clock, but Addie was sure of it. She began to pace back and forth, wringing her hands. Was today her execution day? Did they think feeding her was a waste of time?

She looked out the window, but even the mountains failed to distract her. She twisted her head to see the sun climbing in the eastern sky. It must be between nine and ten o'clock. Andrew's last words yesterday echoed in her mind: "I don't know. I honestly don't know." Oh, he knew all right, the bastard. He couldn't let her live with the information she had.

Addie heard the sound of the bolt opening. She grabbed her hairbrush and waited. If Smitty came in without her breakfast, then she'd know. She'd ram the brush into his groin as hard as she could and run past him, trying somehow to get away. She wouldn't die without a fight.

Instead, Salazar rushed into the room, closing the door behind him.

"We've only got a few minutes," he said, "All hell broke loose this morning. The president's plane crashed in Tokyo and—"

"The president! What happened to him?"

"I don't know. He's alive, I think. No time for questions. The whole place is in an uproar. Andrew had to rush down to Santa Fe. He's coming back tonight and then he leaves for Washington. Marius and I are going with him."

Salazar put his arm around Addie. "I overheard him talking to Smitty before he left. They plan to kill you. Andrew wants it done before he gets back tonight."

Addie began to tremble violently. "I knew it—I knew it—I knew it."

"We've got to stay calm, Addie—both of us. I'm not going to let that happen. Remember how I thought you were sent here by providence? Now I'm sure of it. You're my chance for redemption."

Addie stared at him wide-eyed. The pounding of her heart matched the roaring in her ears.

"Now listen," Salazar continued. "I've devised a plan. Emilio drove Andrew back to Santa Fe. Rico went up to Taos for supplies. Smitty and Barney are the only ones here. I told them I wasn't feeling well—that I was going back to bed."

Addie clenched her fists to control her shivering and began to breath slowly, deliberately.

"They think I'm asleep. They're in the kitchen right now, planning what to do with you. In a few minutes, Marius is going to yell for them to hurry—an emergency. When they get there, he'll say I'm missing, that they did something to me. He's going to go berserk. Marius is very strong, and it'll take both of them a while to subdue him. In the meantime, you're going to follow me down the stairs to the front door. It's unlocked. I'll open the door, and you're going to run as fast as you can."

"What about you?"

"I'll rush back upstairs and come in furious. I'll accuse them of upsetting Marius and threaten to tell Andrew they were bothering him. I'll say I couldn't sleep and was trying to walk off the nausea. Oh, and the best part: we'll bolt your door as we leave, so they'll think you're still here. That should give you time to get away."

"But when they find out I'm gone, they'll know it was you. What will they do to you?"

"Nothing. You see, I'm too valuable. Andrew needs me—to control Simon and Marius. He can't do it without me. But I have no illusions. If the time ever comes when he doesn't need me, he'll dispose of me, as easily as I'm disposing of Marius.

"But why—"

He shook his head. "No more questions. Now listen carefully. This house is isolated down a side road, miles from the main highway. When you get outside, head left. About a mile and a half away, there's another road with some houses."

He looked at his watch and moved next to the door. Addie grabbed her purse and slung it over her shoulder. They stood with their ears to the door, listening. Suddenly they heard Marius shouting, and the sound of running feet coming up the stairs.

The noise of the men running grew fainter and they heard a door opening and closing. "Now," Salazar whispered. They tiptoed out of the room and he closed the bolt behind them. Joy swept over Addie. She was on the other side of that bolted door. She followed Salazar down the stairs, through a hallway to the front door. When he opened it, the smell of the fresh air and the space spreading in all directions made her dizzy. She turned to him.

"Go," he said, pushing her out and closing the door behind her. Addie turned to her left and began to run. She stopped once and looked back at the house that had been her prison. It appeared quite ordinary, a two-story white stucco building with a rambling wing tacked onto one side. Nothing to hint at the terrible things happening inside.

The mountains formed a wall to her right. Cactus, sage, and scrubby green bushes that looked like pine dotted the parched, tan earth beneath her feet. The sun beat down on her as she ran, but she welcomed its fierce warmth after the days of confinement. Her throat began to burn with thirst. Her sandals dug into her feet, and the straps forged bands of pain. Her sore ankle began to throb. Addie slowed her pace, limping, but continued to push blindly forward.

After a while, the terrain began to change, growing less wild. A road appeared in the distance. This must be where the houses were. Addie kept far from the road in case they were already looking for her, but she followed its curving contour. Then, like an oasis, a house appeared. Her aching eyes drank in its beauty: a one-story adobe building, white with earth-colored trim. A curved stone wall formed a half circle around a carefully tended garden, filled with bright flowers.

She ran around to the front and grabbed a brass door knocker shaped like an artist's palette, banging it over and over.

"Take it easy. Take it easy. I'm coming." She heard a voice and footsteps growing nearer.

The door swung open. A middle-aged man in paint-stained jeans and an oversized denim shirt stood there gaping at Addie.

"Help me. Please help me." She started toward him, swayed and almost fell.

He grabbed her arm and helped her inside, leading her to a wicker chair with orange-flowered cushions. She sank into it and he knelt down beside her.

"Grace," he hollered. "Come quick! My wife," he said, shaking his head. "When she's working, she doesn't hear anything."

Addie nodded. "Thank you for letting me in." She spoke so softly through her parched throat that he had to lean forward to hear her.

"You in some kind of trouble?" he asked.

Addie's eyes filled and she swallowed hard. "Could I have a glass of water, please. My throat's so dry, it's hard to talk."

"Grace," he shouted again. "Will you get in here for Christ's sake. And bring a glass of water."

"I've been kidnapped—held for two, three days," Addie whispered. "What day is it?"

"Thursday."

"Yes, Thursday. This would be the third day then. So hard to keep things straight."

"What's the big hurry, Teddy?" A woman in a long green smock, her gray-streaked hair tied back with a striped bandanna, came into the room. She stopped at the sight of Addie, then rushed over to her, handing her the glass of water she was carrying.

"Here," she said. "Drink this slowly."

Addie took the glass, noticing the smears of plaster on the woman's hand. She sipped the water gratefully.

The woman followed Addie's eyes. She held up her hands and smiled. "I'm not usually such a mess. I was working when

Teddy called. I'm a sculptor and he's a painter. We're Grace and Ted Palmer. We came here two years ago from—"

"Stop rattling on." Ted looked at Addie. "This girl's in trouble. Says she was kidnapped."

"Kidnapped! I thought she might have been lost, but kidnapped! Who kidnapped you?"

"Oh, I can't—some men. They had me in a house in Las Trampas. Am I still in Las Trampas?"

Grace nodded, and Addie jumped up in panic. "They could be looking for me already. They could come here. I've got to make a phone call. Right away."

Ted narrowed his eyes and looked at Grace. Addie caught his glance and began wringing her hands.

"You think I'm crazy," she said. "I can see it. Please—let me make this phone call. Then you'll know it's true. Please."

"Sure," Grace said. "Who do you want to call?"

"Jonah Stern at the Coyote Court in Santa Fe."

Grace picked up the phone and started the Instasearch. In seconds, the Coyote Court's number appeared on the screen. She punched in the number and when the office answered, asked for Jonah. Addie clenched her hands tightly, praying Jonah would be there. Chances were slim, she knew. He might be out, searching for her. Or maybe he had given up hope and gone back to Washington. When she heard his voice and saw his face on the speaker-screen, she began to sob.

"Are you Jonah Stern?" Grace asked.

"Yes, who's this?"

"We've got someone here, says she was kidnapped. Don't even know her name..."

"Addie—you've found Addie." Jonah shouted. "Put her on—now."

Grace handed the phone to Addie. "Oh Jonah," she choked out between sobs. "I can't believe I'm looking at you..."

"Thank God, Addie—you're alive. Are you all right? Where are you? I wish I could see you. There's no screen on this goddamn phone."

"I'm in a place called Las Trampas. Oh Jonah, come and get me—quick. They're going to find me and kill me."

Jonah rubbed his eyes. Even on the screen, you could see the moisture welling in them. He took a deep breath. "Addie, calm down. Is Las Trampas near Taos?"

"Yes, yes it is."

"Good, Walter's in Taos right now. He'll be there in—"

"Walter! Walter Turner's in New Mexico?"

"Yeah, and Janice too. They came down to help look for you."

"For me. They came here for me." Addie began to sob again.

"Listen Addie. Put someone else on. I've got to get directions. We'll get you—I promise."

Ted grabbed the phone from Addie's shaking hand. "She's okay—just shook up. We'll take care of her until your friend gets here. But he better hurry. She says some guys are after her."

"Listen—be careful. They're rough customers. Exactly where are you?"

"We're right off Route 76—that's the High Road to Taos. If your friend's coming from Taos, he takes 518 south to 75. That hooks up to 76. Then once he's in Las Trampas, he looks for the turnoff called La Cienega. It's on the right. We're number 110 La Cienega."

"What's your phone number?"

"325-7422. Same area code."

"I'll get right back to you. Soon as I get hold of Walter."

Jonah's face disappeared from the screen. Ted hung up the phone and turned to Addie, smiling.

"Well now—everything will be fine, you'll see. You know, we don't even know your name. Your boyfriend called you Addie."

"Addie Pryce. I'll never be able to thank you enough for what you're—"

"Glad to help," Grace said. "Say, are you hungry? You look kind of starved."

"I haven't eaten since last night."

"How about some scrambled eggs and coffee?"

"Wonderful. Could I could just wash up a little first? I haven't—"

They all jumped at the sound of the ringing phone. Addie picked it up and Jonah's face appeared on the screen again.

"Okay. Walter and Timothy are on their way. They were just leaving Taos heading south when I called, so they should get to you in less than an hour. You won't be able to reach me for a while. Walter wants us out of here pronto. He's right. Some of those creeps might come here, trying to find out where you are. Janice and I are moving downtown right away. We're going to La Fonda and if we can't get in there, we'll try the St. Francis. We're leaving the car and our stuff at the motel, so it'll look like we're still here."

"Are you taking anything with you?"

"Just a change of clothes. I'll take something for you."

"Jonah, would you bring my three monkeys?"

"Sure. Listen, we gotta go. Every minute counts. Oh, get a pencil. Walter's got two cell phones with him, so you can reach him at RPX 32788 and RPX 32789. But don't call unless you have to. They could be listening on a tracer channel. Did you get those numbers?"

Ted nodded to Addie.

"We've got them," she said. Then she suddenly remembered. "Jonah, the president. I heard he—"

"We spoke to Eve Kontos. They're operating on him at Walter Reed right now—doing all they can. Let's worry about ourselves, okay?"

"Okay, Jonah. Goodbye. I'll—I'll see you soon."

"Goodbye, Addie. I love you."

The phone clicked off, but Addie could still hear Jonah's last words singing around her, drowning out a little of the terror.

Grace put an arm around Addie. "He sounds like a swell boyfriend—cute looking too. You use the bathroom right through there, and I'll start the food."

When Addie came into the kitchen, she found a plate of eggs and hot biscuits awaiting her. Grace poured the coffee and Ted sat down opposite her as she attacked the food.

He stared at Addie. "What did you mean back there about the president?"

"We—umm—work for the White House."

"Does this kidnapping have any connection with your line of work?"

Addie nodded. "I guess you could say that."

"And what about this operation your boyfriend was talking about. They operating on the president?"

"Haven't you heard about the plane crash? Didn't they have it on the radio?"

"I haven't turned on the radio or TV all day. I'll put it on right now." He started to get up, when they heard the sound of tires crunching on the gravel in the driveway.

"Oh, that must be your friends coming to get you." Grace got up and started for the door.

"Wait a minute," Ted said. "They couldn't have gotten here that fast. Come here, Addie."

He motioned her into the small family room off the kitchen. They stood in front of the window and he pulled the curtain off to one side. Addie saw a car stopping on the driveway. The doors opened, and two men got out. She froze in terror. Smitty and Barney were walking toward the house.

"Those are the men," she gasped. "They found me. Oh please, please—don't let them get me. They're going to kill me."

"Stay calm." Ted looked at Grace. "We'll hide her in the crawl space. They won't find her there."

"But it's so filthy, Teddy."

"It's better than what's out there, isn't it? Get going."

Grace nodded and grabbed Addie's arm. "Come on. Into my studio in back."

The door knocker thumped several times. Ted turned and walked very slowly to the door, while Grace and Addie ran to the back of the house. They entered a room with whitewashed walls and a worn, wooden floor. Piles of clay, blocks of stone and half-finished sculpted pieces lay everywhere. Grace pulled a woven mat aside, revealing a trapdoor. She pulled it open and pointed inside.

"There's just room to squeeze in here, Addie. It's where I keep my supplies. I've got to warn you. There are lots of critters crawling around in there—lizards, spiders, ants. They won't hurt you, but you can't make any noise if you feel them on you."

Addie shuddered. "I can't go in there. I can't." Then she heard the door opening and the sound of Smitty's voice as he entered the house. She squeezed into the crawl space and lay face up, as Grace closed the trap door and pulled the mat back over it. Darkness surrounded her.

As Addie's eyes grew accustomed to the dark, she began to see shapes around her: cans of paint, barrels of plaster, piles of cloth and canvas. The sharp, stinging smell of turpentine and shellac saturated everything. She was lying on some wooden boxes, and their edges began digging into her back. Her head rested on something soft. She felt it with her hand; it was an open box of clay.

She heard muffled voices. As they grew louder, she could hear footsteps as well. They were coming into the room.

"This is my studio." She could hear Grace clearly now. "You're welcome to look at my work, but you're not going to find any woman here."

"Look, we're just trying to do our job." Smitty said. "This crazy lady's dangerous. She killed two people already. We gotta find her, before she hurts anyone else."

"I'd feel a lot better about this if you'd show me some iden- tification. How do I know who you are?" Ted said.

"We don't hafta show you anything. We're special deputies looking for this lunatic. That's all you hafta know."

They were standing directly over Addie now. She wondered if they could hear her heart pounding through the floorboards. Suddenly she felt something slither across her face. It ran down her neck and shoulder onto her arm. She didn't dare move to shake it off. Addie squeezed her eyes shut and bit her lip so hard she tasted blood.

The voices began to recede. They were moving away, out of the room. As they faded into the distance, Addie began to shake with dry, heaving sobs. Things were crawling all over her now, half real, half imagined, horrid, creepy things that live underground in the dark. It was getting harder and harder to breathe. She must be using up all the oxygen in the crawl space. Good. If she passed out, she would escape this torture chamber.

Her head began to swim and she drifted in and out of consciousness. Suddenly she heard footsteps again. They were back, and this time they'd find her. She heard the scraping sound of the mat being pulled away, and daylight flooded her prison. Ted and Grace bent over her, half lifting, half dragging her out of the crawl space. She tried to stand, but her legs collapsed under her. Ted held her up, while Grace brought over a canvas chair. She sank into it, her head drooping onto her chest.

"Are you all right?" Grace asked

Addie nodded. She was too weak to speak.

"Well, they're gone," Grace said. "Imagine, forcing their way in with a story about being special deputies. We had to let them look. I don't know what they would've done to us if we didn't. But we fooled them, didn't we? They're convinced you're not here."

"I'm not so sure," Ted said. "We're the first house on La Cienega. After they go to the other houses, I'm worried they'll be back. I sure hope your friend comes soon."

CHAPTER THIRTY

When he heard Jonah's voice saying Addie was alive, Walter had clutched the cell phone as if it might dissolve in his hand. Relief swept over him. He had never admitted, even to himself, just how responsible he felt for the whole sorry mess. It was he, after all, who had insisted that Addie disappear. He who had stressed the damage her presence would cause. Without him, she would have been safe in Washington, poring over her charts.

As the car raced toward Addie, the knowledge that she was alive filled him with quiet joy. At the same time, a surge of adrenalin shot through him at the thought of what might await him. Walter pressed his lips together and looked down at the map he was holding. Time to watch for 75. Too bad they didn't have a car with Computrol Navigation.

He glanced at Timothy. He was hunched over the wheel, his huge hands gripping it tightly, staring at the road ahead. Whatever Timothy did, he did with total concentration. Another good thing about Timothy was his habitual silence. He spoke only when necessary, and the quiet that surrounded them gave Walter a chance to sort out his thoughts.

"Slow down," Walter said. "I think that's the junction with 75 up ahead."

Timothy nodded. "That's it." He veered west on the new road.

"Don't go too fast. It's only a few minutes 'til we link up with Route 76."

Timothy grunted and focused on the road. Fifteen minutes later, they were in Las Trampas, searching for the turnoff. They were almost past it, when Walter spotted the sign, a weathered wooden post with the words La Cienega barely visible. Timothy slammed on the brakes and turned down the narrow road.

Number 110 was the first house on the right, and they pulled up into the driveway.

"Okay," Walter said, "We're going in. Get your gun out. I don't know who's inside." His hand closed over Jonah's gun in his waistband. He hoped he wouldn't have to use it. As they walked up the driveway, he saw a curtain being lifted in a back window. Someone was watching them.

Walter lifted the brass door knocker. Before he could bring it down, the door opened.

"Come in. Come in. Hurry."

He walked past the man holding the door into a large living room. The walls were covered with unframed paintings and two standing easels held paintings as well. Walter motioned to Timothy to follow. He heard footsteps approaching from the back of the house. A woman appeared in the entrance to the living room, supporting a bedraggled, dazed Addie.

Walter stared at her. Her hair was matted with something that looked like clay. Her feet were spotted with dried blood. Her face was streaked with dirt and tears. She was the most beautiful sight he had ever seen. He held out his arms and she rushed into them.

Her breath came in gasps. "Oh Walter, they came here. I had to hide in a dirty hole full of...they were going to kill me." Her knees buckled and she collapsed against him.

"They were here all right—two tough-looking characters," the man said. "And I think they'll be back. Better get going as fast as you can."

Walter turned to Timothy. "Carry her out to the car. Put her in the back and stay with her. I'll be right out."

Timothy scooped up Addie in his arms and headed for the door, never looking back. Walter watched him go, then turned to the couple.

"Gratitude's a small word to use, but we'll find a proper way to thank you. How would you like a trip to Washington and a meeting with the president at the White House?"

Grace's mouth fell open. "You mean that? Washington? The president?"

Walter smiled. "Consider it done. We'll be in touch. Just be careful if those guys come back. Don't let anything slip. You don't want to get hurt."

"We can handle them," Ted said. "You just get going."

Walter nodded and raced to the door. Timothy was already at the wheel, studying the map, and Addie was slumped in the back seat. Walter jumped in next to her, slammed the door and shouted "Go!" Timothy backed off the driveway, pressed the accelerator to the floor and they sped away.

Walter turned to Addie. "Let's make you comfortable. Can you sit up? Would you feel better lying down?"

"I'm all right, really." She smiled weakly. "Even though I don't look so good. You know what I want, more than anything else in the world? To soak for hours in a hot tub."

"You will. Janice will see to that."

"You know, Walter—you and Janice coming all the way to New Mexico to help me." Her eyes filled. "After the way I acted to both of you."

"I'm not exactly blameless, Addie. It's my fault you're here at all. I was the one who made you leave Washington."

"You didn't make me—"

"I didn't give you much of a choice, did I? And I can understand how you blamed Janice for telling your secret. How could you know we had a spy in our house?"

"A spy?"

"That's right. You don't know about Sophie." Addie listened wide-eyed as he told her about the housekeeper.

"Andrew has spies everywhere," she said. "He even had me followed. I hate him so much. Just thinking about him..." She leaned back against the seat and closed her eyes.

Walter watched her. He should let her rest, but he had to know Granit's game—exactly what was behind all this. And time was so precious.

He cleared his throat. "Addie, I hate to bother you now, but do you feel up to talking? We could save so much time, if you could just tell me everything that happened. Everything. Then afterwards, when we get back, you won't have to talk at all. Just soak in your hot tub till you turn into a wrinkled prune."

"Anything would be an improvement. I'm such a mess."

"Well, I have seen you look a lot better."

Addie laughed. "It feels so good to smile again. I've been doing nothing but worrying and crying for three days."

"Put it behind you. You're safe now."

"Safe—what a beautiful word." She sat up suddenly. "Walter, what about the president? What happened to him? Is he alive?"

"All I know is he's in surgery at Walter Reed. Soon as we get back, I'll check with Eve Kontos. I don't want to use the cell phone unless I have to."

She leaned back again and looked at him. "I'm all right, Walter—really. I can talk."

"Good. Start from the beginning. What happened at the newspaper office?"

Addie began, dredging up every detail she could remember. When she got to the part about Salazar and Marius, she hesitated.

"What is it, Addie?"

"You won't believe me. You'll think I'm crazy."

"Try me."

When she told him, he pressed his lips together and shook his head.

"You're telling me that Simon Furst is a robot?" he said.

"No, not a robot—an android."

"Oh, of course, an android—that makes all the difference."

"See, you don't believe me."

He hesitated and cleared his throat. "Addie, you've got to admit it's a little...look, I know Simon Furst. He's as much a human being as I am."

"Is he? Think about it, Walter. He lives alone. No relationships. Has that strange look in his eyes—that studied smile. And he has a phony birth certificate and his chart doesn't match him at all."

"That doesn't make him a robot, Addie."

"No, but he is—he really is. There's another man who worked with Salazar to create him—a Dr. Isaac Templeton."

"Isaac Templeton! He's involved in this?"

"Do you know him?"

"Of course. He's a prominent doctor in Washington. Has a very limited practice. Spends a lot of time on research." Walter looked at Addie. "He's Simon's personal physician. Furst won't let anyone else near him. I remember once when...my God, could that be the reason why?"

He stared out the window at the winding mountain road. Timothy had slowed down, manuevering carefully around the narrow curves.

Walter turned back to Addie. "This Karl Salazar. You know, Jonah did find out he was involved in artificial life research. It all makes some kind of crazy sense. But still—a robot."

"It's true, Walter. It is. And that's not the worst of it. This Marius—he's a robot too. Salazar stuck a knife in his arm and he didn't feel anything—didn't even bleed. I saw it. Salazar called him a dedicated android."

"What the hell is that?"

"It means he was created for only one purpose. He's an assassin—engineered to kill the president with some kind of built-in bomb."

Walter pressed his hand against his temples. His head was beginning to throb. "You're telling me that Andrew Granit has a robot to kill the president? Addie that just doesn't—"

"They're flying back to Washington tomorrow: Andrew, Salazar and Marius. They were going to kill me this morning. That's what Salazar told me when he helped me escape."

"Salazar helped you escape?"

Addie nodded. "He came to my room this morning and told me about the president's plane crash. And about their going back to Washington. He said they were going to kill me and he wouldn't let that happen."

Addie described her escape and Walter stared at her grimly. When she told him how she hid in the crawl space, afraid to move while she heard the footsteps overhead, he put his arm around her and drew her towards him till her head rested on his shoulder.

"The nightmare's over, Addie. Just relax. I have to think about what to do."

Walter stared out the window at the thickening traffic. They must be nearing Route 84, the main highway back to Santa Fe. He tried to sort out the facts. If Addie's story were true—and he couldn't take the chance of doubting it—then there were two possibilities. If Henry remained unconscious or died, an android under Granit's control would be running the country. If he did survive the operation, then there'd be an assassination attempt—probably right away, because of Addie's escape.

"My God, I know how they'll do it," he declared, thinking out loud. "Templeton's on the staff of Walter Reed. He'll get Marius in there as a medical technician or something. Get him past the Secret Service and into Henry's room, and then he'll set off his goddamn bomb."

Addie raised her head and looked at him. "What can we do?"

"We've got to get Salazar out of there before they leave for Washington. Without him, I don't think they can do much of anything. He'll probably cooperate. He did help you escape. Sounds like a very sick man who would jump at the chance to escape the whole mess."

Addie nodded. "I think so. He's been searching for answers everywhere. I told you he sneaked in to see me because I'm an astrologer. But how can you get him out?"

"We'll do it. How many are there in that house?"

"I don't know. There's Smitty and Barney. Those are the two who came looking for me." Addie thought for a moment. "Salazar mentioned someone called Rico, who went up to Taos. Then he said that Emilio had driven Andrew to Santa Fe this morning."

"Andrew's in Santa Fe?"

"He's coming back to the house tonight." Addie's lip trembled. "He told them to—to kill me, before he got back."

"That goddamn bastard." Walter's arm tightened around Addie. "He'll get what's coming to him. I only hope we—"

"We're coming to 84," Timothy said, as they neared a cluster of signs.

"Good." Walter looked out the window. "Soon as we're on it, I'll be able to use the cell phone without too much chance of being monitored. We've got to find out where Jonah and Janice went. We'll try La Fonda first."

He stared at Timothy's broad back. "Were you able to hear everything, Timothy?"

"I think so. Sure got the drift anyway."

"Fine. Then I only have to repeat this once, to Jonah and Janice."

As they headed south on 84, Walter got the number of La Fonda and punched it in. "Jonah Stern, please," he said and heaved a sigh of relief as the call was transferred.

"Yes, who is this?" Walter smiled. Jonah was being cautious.

"It's Walter. We've got Addie, safe and sound. We're less than a half hour away."

"Why the hell didn't you call before?" Jonah exploded. "We've been going crazy here waiting. Janice has had you killed five different ways."

"Take it easy. I couldn't use the cell phone until we got on a crowded highway. Those clowns were out looking for Addie and I didn't want them to pick up any signal."

"Okay, sorry. It's just—how's Addie? How's she doing? What's she saying?"

"Here. Talk to her yourself." He handed the phone to Addie.

"Oh, Jonah," Addie said, "I missed you so much."

She smiled at what she heard, and Walter smiled too, imagining Jonah's response. He let them talk for a minute, then gently took the phone from her hand.

"Have to cut this off, Jonah. I don't want to press our luck. Have you heard anything more about the president?"

"Only what's on TV. They say he's holding his own."

"Okay. I'll call Eve as soon as we get to the hotel. Tell Janice she's got a big kiss coming for worrying about me. See you soon."

He hung up the phone and turned to Addie. "Next stop, Santa Fe."

CHAPTER THIRTY-ONE

Jonah sank into the ergometric contour chair and felt it grip him, as the chair molded itself to the shape of his body. He stared at the diamond patterns in the hotel carpet.

"Jeez—what's taking them so long?" he said.

He jumped up and opened the door, looked up and down the long corridor, then slammed it shut.

"That won't make them come any faster," Janice said.

"Yeah, it's just—I can't wait to see Addie. She sounded so shook up on the phone."

"I'm sure she is. She must have gone through a lot."

Jonah clenched his fists. "That goddamn Granit. If I could just get my hands on him."

"Listen, Jonah—try to be calm when they get here. Addie may be in a very delicate emotional state and you don't want to—"

They both froze at a knock on the door. Jonah raced over and put his hand on the knob.

"Who is it?"

"Open up. It's Walter."

Jonah flung open the door and Walter walked in with his arm around a bedraggled Addie. Timothy followed, looked behind him and closed the door.

Janice clapped a hand to her mouth. "Addie, look at you. What did they do to you?"

Jonah frowned at Janice, whispering in her ear, "Take your own advice, sweetie." He hurried over to Addie and put his arms around her.

"You look great," he said. "Beautiful, wonderful. Never saw you look better." He kissed her gently, but tightened his arms around her.

"You're such a liar," she said. "I frightened myself when I looked in the car mirror."

"All right, lovebirds," Walter said, picking up the phone. "I'll give you five minutes while I call Eve Kontos and find out about the president. Then we've got to get down to business. Can't waste any time."

Jonah sat on the bed, pulling Addie down on his lap. She leaned against him, while he stroked her matted hair and caressed her neck lightly with his lips. The room was silent, as they all watched Walter talking on the phone. He spoke so softly and rapidly that Jonah had to strain to hear anything, but one word, assassination, hung loudly in the air.

Walter put down the phone with a sigh of relief. "Okay," he said. "Here's the story. The president's going to be all right. They used a new laser technique that zapped the clot with no side effects. He's conscious and talking—already asking when he can get out of there. So, we don't have to worry about Simon Furst taking over." He looked at Jonah. "And I told her she has a whole press office to write those damn releases—that I need you here. She agreed. Now I'm going to tell you exactly what Addie told me and I don't want any interruptions. Understand?"

Jonah and Janice nodded, and Walter repeated Addie's story. When he finished, Janice stared at him in disbelief, while Jonah looked thoughtful.

"It's fantastic," Jonah said, "But you know, it is possible. The work that Salazar was doing put him miles ahead of anyone else. And Templeton's supposed to be brilliant."

"We have to go on the assumption that it's possible," Walter said. "We can't take any chances. We've got to get Salazar away from Granit. And we've only got a few hours."

"I can't believe it." Janice's eyes were wide. "Simon Furst, a robot. Impossible. He's a human being. I've talked to him, touched him."

"Exactly where have you touched him?" Walter asked.

"Oh, don't be silly—his hand, his arm. He felt just like anyone else. I wish I'd known, though." She smiled. "I could have checked out other parts."

Jonah laughed. "Robots don't make love, Janice. And that could explain why someone as good looking as Furst never got involved with anyone."

Addie spoke for the first time. "He's not a robot. He's an android. Robots don't look like us—androids do."

Walter nodded. "But Simon Furst isn't our problem right now. It's that other android, Marius. Salazar told Addie he's programmed to kill the president. I didn't go into any details with Eve Kontos. I could never have convinced her about robots. All I told her was that we stumbled onto a possible assassination plot and we need help."

"What did she say?" Jonah asked.

"She's going to get two or three Secret Service agents into Albuquerque tonight. It's the best she can do." Walter looked at his watch. "But that's too late to help us. We've got to get up there before Granit gets back."

Jonah jumped up. "Let's go."

"Take it easy. We have to eat. We have to make plans. Janice, call room service and order a bunch of sandwiches. We'll take them with us so we won't waste any time. And get some extra sandwiches for you and Addie for tonight. Once we leave, I don't want the two of you to open the door for anyone. Understand?"

Janice nodded. "Then I'd better get some things I need. Our room is just across the hall and Timothy is next to us."

"Call room service first. Tell them to hurry."

Janice handed Timothy his keycard and picked up the phone. As she ordered, Walter tapped impatiently on his watch. "We'll meet back here in fifteen minutes," he said. "I want to be on the road by 2:00."

As soon as they left, Addie headed for the shower. Jonah lay on the bed, listening to the splash of the water, letting the knowledge that she was really there sink in. The despair of her absence and the joy of her return had swept away any doubts. He knew that he wanted to spend the rest of his life with her. Sure, there were adjustments he'd have to make: his feelings about her work, his ingrained pattern of bed-hopping, his fear of forever. But he could handle all that. Addie emerged in ten minutes, glowing, with a towel around her head and her pink bathrobe wrapped around her. Jonah was glad he had remembered to bring it.

"I feel wonderful." she said. "That was the first shower I had in three days. And I managed to get that gook out of my hair."

Jonah stared at her. She reminded him of a pink and white birthday cake, with her eyes the blue candles. He wanted to sweep her into bed and stroke away all the bad memories. If only they could be alone for a few hours.

He held out his arms. "Come here and let's have a proper reunion."

A knock on the door stopped her halfway toward him. Walter's voice outside announced the end of their private time. Jonah opened the door, and the others trooped in. Janice and Timothy settled into the two club chairs, while Addie and Jonah perched close together on the edge of the bed. Walter paced back and forth between them.

Jonah put his arm around Addie. "I owe this Salazar guy big time."

"You'll have plenty of time to thank him." Walter said. "After we get him out of there."

"Do you know exactly where this house is?" Jonah asked.

"We've got a pretty good idea," Walter said. "From what Addie tells us, it's about a mile past the turnoff where we found her. She thinks it's the only house on the road, so if we can find where that road cuts into 76, we won't have any trouble."

Timothy looked at Walter thoughtfully. "How many guys do you figure will be there?"

"If we get there before Granit comes back, I think only two or three. Most of them should be out looking for Addie. Don't forget—they think she's still out there someplace. That's why we have to move quickly."

Addie nodded. "Even Smitty and Barney were out looking for me this morning. They're the ones who came to the house—where I hid in the crawl space."

"Well, by now they've had time to call in extra people." Walter said. "But I think most of them will be out searching."

Timothy shrugged. "Then I don't see any problem. We've got two guns and three sets of fists. And they don't know we're coming."

"Yes," Walter said, "That's important. We've got the element of surprise on our side."

Jonah stood up. "The thing is to get going as fast as we can. While it's daylight and they're still out looking."

They all started at a noise outside the door.

"Room Service," a voice announced. Walter put on the latch-chain and peered out. When he saw the cart loaded with food, he opened the door. As soon as the waiter left, Timothy took two of the plastic bags that the hotel provided for laundry, filled one with sandwiches and the other with cans of diet cola, and walked over to the door.

"I guess we're ready to go," Walter said. He hugged Janice. "Don't miss us too much."

"Miss you." Janice laughed. "We'll have so much to talk about, we won't even notice you're gone."

"Take good care of Addie," he said. And don't forget. Don't open that door for anyone. Even if they say they're from the police."

"I won't—I promise." She frowned. "Please be careful, Walter. I don't know what I'd do if—"

"Nothing's going to happen to us. You heard Timothy. He doesn't see any problem and he knows about these things. We'll keep in touch on the cell phone."

Jonah leaned over and kissed Addie. "Don't you worry either. We're tough guys. We know how to handle ourselves." He made a tough guy face, and they all laughed.

"Okay, tough guy—let's go." Walter walked out the door, followed by Timothy. Jonah winked at Addie and closed the door behind them.

Janice stared at the door for a moment, then squared her shoulders, smiled at Addie, and began to set out the food on a small round table in the corner of the room.

Addie sat down and attacked a ham and cheese sandwich. When she had finished half of it, she looked across the table at Janice, who was nibbling on hers.

"This is the first food I've had since last night—except for a few forkfuls of scrambled eggs," she said. "I didn't realize I was so hungry."

"Didn't they feed you?" Janice asked.

"Yes, except for this morning. I guess they figured if they were going to kill me, why waste good food." She devoured the rest of the sandwich and drained her glass of cola. Janice watched her, beaming with satisfaction.

"I'm going to straighten up this room a little, and then we'll have dessert—our own private tea party." Janice pointed to the cake and coffee on the cart. "And you can tell me everything that happened—all the exciting details."

Addie smiled. She felt safe and cozy, wrapped in her bathrobe, watching Janice bustle around the room. Whatever Janice did she managed to turn into something blithe and special, an expression of her happy-go-lucky Sagittarius nature. Janice was indeed a free soul, and she swept those around her into her own exciting world.

"I envy you," Addie said, "You're so independent, so sure of yourself."

"Why? You're a very independent person."

Addie shook her head. "No, I'm solitary. There's a difference."

Janice laughed. "You don't seem very solitary to me. You and Jonah—I don't think I've ever seen two people any closer."

"Did—did Jonah say anything about me to you?"

"He never stopped. He's in love with you, Addie. If you don't watch your step, you're going to be stuck with him for the rest of your life."

"Oh Janice, I'm so confused. I'm very happy and very frightened—all at the same time."

Janice stared at her. "You can't go around hiding out, being afraid of life. You miss too much that way. And whatever you're most afraid of will find you in the end anyway."

"I suppose. But I don't ever want to really depend on anyone again. It hurts too much, when it's snatched away."

"I agree you've got to have your own life. That's essential. But, Addie—leave a little room for someone to share it."

"You're right, Janice. I know it. But my head is swimming right now—and I still don't feel clean. All I want to do is just soak in a tub for a long time. Wash away all the mess of the last few days and get my thoughts in order."

"And so you shall. I'll run a nice hot bath for you. I think I even saw some bubble bath on the shelf inside. But first, we're going to have our coffee and talk."

Janice brought over a platter of little pastries from the cart and poured steaming coffee from the thermo-carafe into two china cups. Addie dove into the pastries, as though the sweets would begin erasing the bad memories.

"Tell me," Janice said, stirring her coffee, "Were you shut up in that one little room for the whole time?

Addie nodded.

"How did you stand it? I would have gone stir crazy, like an animal penned up in a cage."

Addie pictured Janice pacing back and forth like a lion, tossing her great mane of hair. It would be hard for a Sagittarius like Janice to be trapped anywhere.

"That part wasn't too bad. I had some magazines and a newspaper to read. And I kept busy picturing charts in my mind. Mostly I looked out the window at the mountains. The worst thing was that I was so frightened. I didn't know what was going to happen to me."

"It's hard to picture Andrew Granit involved in something like this. I mean he is a senator, after all. Did you see him there?"

"Only once."

Janice put down her coffee and leaned forward. "Tell me what happened."

"Oh, it was very strange. We argued and he slapped me. I started to cry and he changed completely. Told me I reminded him of someone he knew a long time ago, some girl. He was almost tender then and I thought—oh, I don't know what I thought."

"And then what?" Janice leaned forward expectantly.

"And then he turned back into the old Andrew. I begged him to tell me what was going to happen to me, but he wouldn't."

"Did he try to do anything—you know..."

"No, not at all." Addie narrowed her eyes and stared at Janice. "But you know something. I think I almost wanted him to. I was so scared and lonely. A few more days there—"

She grabbed Janice's hand. "Please, don't ever tell Jonah about that. Promise me you won't."

"Of course I won't. And I won't tell Walter, either. Scout's honor. I learned my lesson. I don't want you to get angry at me again."

Addie's voice shook. "I haven't even apologized to you about that. Walter told me all about Sophie. I'm so sorry. I was awful to you, and you came all the way to New Mexico to help me. "

"Nonsense." Janice got up and put her arm around Addie. "I've always wanted to see New Mexico. Now, I think it's time for that long soak in a hot tub, don't you?"

Addie nodded and tried to smile. "Janice, I—"

Janice put her finger to her lips. "Sshhh…not another word. I'm going to get a bath ready for you and let you have some quiet time, all by yourself." She disappeared into the bathroom.

Addie gazed after her, filled with a quiet happiness. She had lost Livonia. Perhaps she had found Janice Turner.

Chapter Thirty-Two

Timothy kept a steady speed all the way to Las Trampas, staring at the road ahead in silence. Occasionally he nodded, as if in agreement with a plan taking shape in his head.

Jonah sat next to Walter in the back, giving him a crash course in guns with Timothy's empty .45. Walter screwed up his eyes in concentration. Just before they turned off onto 76, Jonah reloaded the gun, put on the safety, and handed it back to Timothy. He fingered his own gun, which was hooked onto his belt. Then he took out the slender pen-rod from his pocket and gave it to Walter, showing him how to eject the pellets.

"This can put someone out of commission for a while. It only works at close range, but it's better than nothing."

The car slowed to a crawl after they passed the turnoff marked La Cienega.

"Better start looking. That road should come up in half a mile," Timothy said.

They turned their heads to the left, searching for some break in the scrubby landscape, dotted with sage and soapweed, that bordered the road.

"Up ahead," Jonah shouted. "Just ahead." He pointed to a dusty patch of road, unmarked, not much wider than a driveway. They were almost past it before Timothy could turn, and the car skidded across some underbrush until its wheels found the road.

"Let's see where this takes us," Timothy said. They started down the dirt road, bouncing as the tires hit rocks and deep ruts.

Jonah frowned. "Shit—this looks like the road to nowhere."

"We'll give it another mile or so," Walter said. "If this is the road they use, it must chew the hell out of their tires. Still, if they want privacy, they—"

"Look. Up ahead to your right." Timothy slowed the car. A building appeared in the distance: a two-story house with a one-story wing on the side, all in white stucco, just as Addie had described.

"That's it, goddammit, that's it." Jonah slammed his hand against the seat. "We found it."

"End of the line." Timothy said, slamming his foot on the brake. He began backing the car down the narrow road. "We can't take a chance driving near the house."

Walter and Jonah nodded. A subtle change had taken place. Timothy was now clearly the one in charge. As he backed up slowly, Timothy swiveled his head in all directions until he spotted a clump of stunted pines set far back from the road.

"Hold on. This is gonna be bumpy," he said, as he eased the car off the road and drove across the barren terrain toward the trees. When he neared the pines, he gave a sigh of relief. "Perfect. They'll never see our car here."

They got out and examined the cover from all angles. When they were satisfied that the car was hidden, they headed back toward the house on foot, keeping the sparse vegetation between them and the road. As they neared the house, Timothy pointed to a battered blue Plymouth parked in front.

"That's the car that was following us," Jonah whispered. "We've got the right house for sure."

Timothy waved them around the rear, keeping a distance of about forty feet between them and the house. They bent low and moved rapidly. Without any cover of foliage, they were visible from the back windows.

Jonah glanced at the house. It loomed large in a land where most of the homes were one-story ranches that hugged the ground. Otherwise it seemed quite ordinary, with its white stuccoed exterior and windows shuttered against the late afternoon sun. As they neared the wing, its appearance changed. The one-story addition seemed to have been tacked on as a storage facility. It had no windows or doors, just some air conditioning vents.

Jonah smiled. "Guess they don't want anyone looking in. But that works both ways. They can't see us coming either."

They straightened and stretched, moving closer and rounding the side of the wing, where they found a small door. Timothy tried the handle, but the door was locked.

"I didn't expect a welcome sign," Walter said, "but this looks too damned secure."

Timothy examined the lock carefully. "No problem," he said, digging in his pocket and holding up what looked like a miniature corkscrew.

"This little sucker can take care of locks like that in a jiffy."

Jonah stared at it. "I've never seen anything like that."

Timothy shrugged. "Tool of the trade." He inserted the tip of the gadget into the keyhole, moving it in and out and twisting it gently. A faint click announced that the lock was open.

"Okay." Timothy turned to Walter and Jonah. "Now, if there's no alarm, we're in. Ready?"

They nodded, and Timothy took out his gun. Jonah pulled out his .38 and moved next to Timothy, who shook his head.

"No, let Walter follow me. He doesn't have a gun. You stay in back—cover our asses. Stay that way until we see what's going on."

Timothy opened the door slowly, and they were hit with a blast of cold air. "Like a fucking freezer," he muttered and stepped inside, his head turning in all directions to spot any telltale wires.

"Looks good," he said and motioned them inside. They moved down a narrow hallway, lit with fluorescent light and flanked by closed doors on either side.

"I shouldn't do this," Walter whispered, "but we've got to know what's going on here." He stopped, listened at one of the doors, then opened it carefully.

Jonah glanced into the room and whistled softly. "I've never seen a computer setup like this." Monitors lined one wall, with 3-D images passing from one to the other in an intricately programmed pattern. The side of another wall had more monitors with numbers flashing too rapidly for the eye to follow. A large machine that looked like a dozen computers piggy-backed on each other dominated the room from its perch on a heavy stone table. Several minicomputers were laying on top of a desk in the center of the room.

"No wonder they keep it so cold," Jonah whispered. "Heat would murder a setup like this. I wonder what's in *there*." He pointed to the door across the hall, and Timothy pulled it open.

"My God," Walter gasped. "It's really true." A gleaming white table, about ten feet long, filled the room. Glass fronted cabinets lined the walls, their contents clearly visible from the doorway. What looked like legs and hands—even a few partly shaped heads—lay on the shelves. Other cabinets were filled with medical instruments.

Jonah shook his head. "A human body shop. Spare parts for Simon Furst. I don't think I believe what I'm seeing."

"We've gotta keep moving." Timothy frowned. "We don't know what's waiting for us. Time to look around later."

"Right, right," Walter said. They turned and followed Timothy down the long hallway to a door at the end.

"Bet this leads into the main house," he said, turning the knob lightly. He looked at Walter. "It's not locked. You want to go in now?"

Walter nodded and followed Timothy through the door. Jonah gripped his gun and trailed after them. For the first time he felt really frightened. What kind of crazy thing had he gotten himself into. Look at them—a beefy bodyguard, an aging lawyer, and a smartass press guy—trying to take on a gang of God knows what.

They found themselves in another hallway, this one dimly lit, with a bathroom on one side and what looked like a storage closet on the other. Up ahead was a room that Jonah figured was the kitchen. Light and voices spilled out through the half-open door.

"Hold it—freeze. Move a muscle and you're dead." Jonah felt the hard nozzle of a pistol pressed into the small of his back, while up ahead he saw a short, skinny figure pointing a gun at Timothy.

"Throw your guns on the floor. Now!" The man barking orders dug his gun harder into Jonah's back, as they tossed their weapons on the ground. "Now march."

They walked single file toward the kitchen, while the skinny man in front picked up their guns, waving them on like a drill sergeant. As they entered the kitchen, three people sitting at a large round table looked up at them in amazement.

"Over there—against the wall," the man ordered, giving Jonah a shove as he withdrew the gun from his back. Jonah looked at him and recognized him instantly. The beady-eyed guy with the swollen red nose.

"Good hunting, Smitty." The heavyset man at the table grinned.

"Yeah, Barney. I told you I heard something out there." He nodded to the other man, who was swaggering in front of them.

"Rico, get their guns. Put them on the table. Now we gotta find out who these jokers are."

He stared at Jonah. "Hey, I know him. He's the bitch's boyfriend. I tailed the two of them long enough."

He sneered at Jonah. "Did you miss your sweetie? She's hot stuff, huh?"

Jonah clenched his fists and glared at him. His arms ached with the need to batter that smirking face into a shapeless mush.

Smitty stiffened. "Wait a minute. If he's here, she must have made it. Told him where to come. That's it, ain't it?" He slammed Jonah against the wall.

"Answer me, asshole. That's it, ain't it?"

Jonah nodded. "She's safe from you, you fucking bastard. Now you're the one who's in deep shit."

"I'll show you deep shit." He swung and punched Jonah in the face, just missing his eye. Jonah's knees buckled and he sank to the ground. Smitty stood over him, jeering.

"Look at the big hero with the glass jaw. One punch does him."

He turned away, and Jonah looked up at Timothy, winking imperceptibly. He hoped he got the message. Jonah had learned how to take a lot of punishment during his college boxing days. He'd also learned how to fake a fall. If they thought one of them was out of commission, they might get a little careless.

"Watch them, Rico," Smitty said. Rico puffed out his hollow cheeks and stood in front of them, brandishing his gun. He looked down at Jonah and kicked him with one bony leg. Jonah's only response was a glassy stare.

Smitty walked over to the table. Barney had gotten up and was glaring down at a small, thin man, whose eyes bulged behind horn-rimmed glasses. Jonah realized he must be looking at the mysterious Karl Salazar.

"Well doc, I hope you're satisfied," Barney said. "She got away."

"I told you I had nothing to do with it."

"Sure, she vanished through a solid door."

"Maybe Smitty let her out."

"Yeah, and maybe pigs fly."

Salazar edged closer to the man next to him, who put a protective arm around the back of his chair. The android, Marius, Jonah thought, staring in wonder.

"We'll let the boss figure it out," Smitty said, looking at his watch. "He should be here in an hour."

Barney shook his head. "He's gonna hit the ceiling when he hears she got away safe."

"Yeah, it'll be our asses. Maybe it won't go so bad though, when he sees the prizes we got here." Smitty smirked at the three of them.

"Hey," Barney said. "We better get on the transceiver and call off the hunt. Get the guys back here."

Smitty nodded and walked over to a radio phone hanging on the wall. Jonah looked up at Timothy, flashing a silent message. They had to make their move now. If more people came, they'd never have a chance.

Timothy nodded and sprang into action. In one swift motion he had his huge arms around Rico, knocking the gun from his hands, lifting him above his head and hurling him across the room. Rico lay still in a crumpled heap. At the same instant, Jonah sprang from the floor and raced toward Smitty, tackling him before he reached the phone. The two men rolled over and over, grunting and cursing, until Jonah had Smitty pinned to the ground.

Barney headed for the gun that Rico dropped. As his hand closed around it, Timothy stepped on it and ground his heel down. There was a crunching sound of bones snapping, and howls of pain echoed through the room. Barney dropped the gun and sank to the floor clutching his broken hand. Timothy picked up the gun and looked around.

Walter had run over to the table and grabbed Timothy's .45. He was waving it at Salazar and Marius with one hand while he clutched the pen-rod in the other. Timothy raced over and took the gun out of his hand.

"Easy, Walter, before it goes off." He handed him Rico's gun. Take this—it's a lot smaller." Timothy frowned at Salazar and Marius. "You guys gonna give us any trouble?"

Salazar shook his head. "We're neutral observers."

"Keep it that way." Timothy looked at Jonah who was sitting astride a dazed Smitty, with his hands around his throat. "Get his gun."

Jonah pressed down hard on Smitty's throat with one hand, while he felt in his pockets with the other. He pulled out the gun and tossed it to Timothy. Then he yanked Smitty up, leaning him against the wall.

Jonah drew back one fist. "This is for Addie," he said, as he smashed it into Smitty's nose. Blood started to trickle down his face. "This is for me," Jonah said, as he hit him again, directly in the jaw. Smitty moaned and sank to the ground. Jonah pulled him up again. "And this is for the whole, goddamned fucking world." He punched with all his strength, glorying in the feel of his knuckles against the other man's flesh and the sound of cracking bones. Smitty fell unconscious on the floor, his face a pulpy mass..

Before Jonah could pull him up again, he felt Timothy's hands gripping his shoulders.

"Stop it," he said. "You don't want to kill the bastard."

"Oh, don't I," Jonah said, struggling to get free of Timothy. "He was gonna kill Addie."

"Come on, Jonah. Sit down and cool off." Timothy dragged him away from the prostrate Smitty and pushed him into the chair opposite Salazar. Jonah put his head in his hands, breathing heavily.

"Okay, let's get this together," Timothy said. "You," he waved his .45 at Barney, who sat frozen on the floor, holding his hand. "Over there next to your friend." Barney rose slowly and moved towards Smitty.

Across the room, Rico began to stir. "Get up," Timothy barked. "On your feet. Get over there with your buddies." Rico shook his head and stared with a dazed expression at Smitty and Barney. Then he stumbled over to them.

Timothy turned to Walter. "Okay, I'll watch these jokers. See if I can wake up sleeping beauty. I think the guys *you* want are over there." He pointed to Salazar and Marius.

"We'll take care of them." Walter said. "Are you all right, Jonah?"

Jonah looked up. "Yeah, fine. Got myself under control now. Sorry."

Walter sat down next to Jonah and looked at the man across the table. "You're Karl Salazar?"

"Guilty as charged. And you are...?"

"I'm Walter Turner."

"Yes, I've heard that name."

"I work in Washington. Sometimes my name gets in the papers. And this is Jonah Stern. He works for the president."

Jonah held out his hand. "Pleased to meet you. I owe you for what you did for Addie."

Salazar smiled faintly. "Is she really all right?"

"She's fine, thanks to you." Jonah looked at the man next to Salazar.

"Oh, forgive me," Salazar said. This is Marius, my—umm—companion."

"Yes, we've heard about Marius," Walter said. "And we've heard about the vice president, too."

"Then there's no need to go through it again."

Jonah stared at the android, fascinated. He stuck out his hand and Marius grasped it in a firm handshake. It was smooth and warm, and Jonah could feel bones underneath the skin.

"I guess I should thank you, too," Jonah said.

"I only do what I'm told."

"I do, too—most of the time anyway." Jonah grinned.

"I do it all the time," Marius said without any change of expression.

"Humor's lost on Marius," Salazar said. "It wasn't necessary to program that factor. Now, I'd like to know exactly why you're here."

"Of course." Walter leaned forward. "We came to get you out of here—you and Marius—and take you back to Washington with us."

"Go with *you*?" Salazar began to chew on his lip. "I don't know who you are, where you'd take me."

"I told you who we were," Walter said, "I'll be more specific. I'm the president's legal counsel, his friend and adviser. Jonah's a deputy press secretary."

Salazar's voice became shrill. "I don't believe you. How do I know you're not Secret Service—out to eliminate me. Oh, I know how you people work."

Jonah fished in his pocket and threw cards on the table. "Here," he said, trying to keep his voice even. "Here's my I.D. card, my press badge, my White House pass, my driver's license. Everything. Besides, you know we're friends of Addie's. We'd never hurt you."

"I don't know—I don't know." Salazar jumped up and began to pace back and forth.

Walter got up and put his arm around Salazar's shoulders. "Dr. Salazar—we want to help you. We know about everything that's going on here. You're involved very deeply, but you can get out now. The president will be very grateful for your cooperation. I guarantee it."

Salazar shook Walter off and stared at him. "I've done criminal things."

"We'll work it out. You'll see. And we'll get you all the psychiatric help you need. You can make a whole new start."

Salazar pressed both hands against his forehead. "My head's burning. I feel sick." He stumbled back to the table and sank into the seat next to Marius.

Walter followed and leaned over him. "We want to make you well, Dr. Salazar. Trust us. It's your only chance."

He looked up at Walter, his eyes suddenly hopeful. "What about Isaac—Dr. Templeton?"

"When we confront him, I'm sure he'll cooperate and do whatever's necessary. He'll want to get out of this with his reputation intact. This whole matter has to be handled very discreetly. If the public ever knew about the vice president—"

The phone rang. Everyone froze but Timothy, who raced over and disconnected the telescreen. He motioned to Barney.

"Answer it. Remember, I got a .45 pointed right at your cock. You think your hand hurts? You make one wrong move and you'll feel pain you won't believe."

Barney's face twitched with terror. He picked up the phone with his good hand and whispered "Hello" into the instrument. Timothy leaned over and pressed the audio switch. Andrew Granit's voice filled the room.

"Who is this?"

"It's Barney," he said in a shaking voice.

"You sound strange. Are you drinking?"

"No boss, no. I was just—umm—just dozing."

"Well, wake up. Have they found her yet?"

"No—not yet. When the phone rang, I thought—"

"I don't want to hear about your thought processes. I want you to find Addie and take care of her. Do you understand?"

Yeah, sure—sure, boss."

"I'm calling from the car. I should be at the house in half an hour. You'd better have good news waiting for me." The phone clicked off.

At the sound of Granit's voice, Salazar began to shake violently. Now he looked at Walter, his fear-filled eyes bulging behind his glasses. "I can't do this—not to Andrew."

"Do you owe him any loyalty?" Walter asked.

"No, no—I despise him. But you don't know him. You can't imagine what he'll do."

"I do know him. I know what he's capable of. When we're through with him, he won't be able to hurt anyone."

"What are you going to do?" Salazar asked, his voice barely audible.

"We've got Secret Service agents coming into Albuquerque tonight. They should get up here before midnight. We'll hold Granit and the others until they get here. Once they take over, everything will be under control."

"What's going to happen to Andrew?"

"I'm sure he'll plead guilty to any criminal charge we offer him. Better than treason. That carries the death penalty and a dishonor I don't think he'll want to face." Walter shook his head. "No, you won't have to worry about Andrew."

"But now. I can't face him now. When he comes in, he'll—"

"You don't have to see him at all. You can stay in your room."

Salazar began drumming on the table with his fingers. "You make it sound so easy. Oh, if it were only like that."

"It can be. Just trust us."

The two men stared at each other in silence. Jonah held his breath, while Marius gazed straight ahead.

Salazar lowered his eyes. "I believe you," he said in a barely audible voice. "We'll go with you—Marius and I."

"You'll never regret it Dr. Salazar—I promise. Now we've got to get these characters locked up somewhere so we can deal with Granit when he gets here."

Marius stood up and touched Salazar's arm. "The room, the room where they kept Addie."

"Of course. Good thinking, Marius." Salazar smiled. "That new program improved your cognitive powers vastly. I'm delighted."

"Wait a minute," Walter said, as a thought struck him. "We've got one more job for this character." He pointed to Barney, who glanced quickly at Timothy and then fastened his eyes on Walter.

"How many men are out there looking for Addie?" Walter asked.

"Four," Barney muttered in a voice so low they could barely hear him.

"Speak up," Timothy said, waving the .45 at Barney's groin.

"Four," Barney shouted.

"Okay," Walter pointed to the radio phone. "What you're going to do is get on the transceiver and get a message out to your boys. You tell them that the big boss says they have to stay out—all night, if necessary—until they find Addie. The next day too. They can grab a little sleep in their cars, but he doesn't want them coming back empty-handed. And tell them they're not to call in—for any reason—unless they've found her. He doesn't want to hear the sound of their voices unless they get results. Got that?"

Barney nodded and moved toward the phone.

"And speak up loud, so we can hear every word."

Barney glanced over at Timothy and nodded vigorously. He picked up the transceiver and followed Walter's instructions exactly. When he finished, Walter smiled at him.

"Good job. That should keep them away from you. I don't think we have any more use for you or your buddies." Walter turned to Marius. "Could you show us where that room is?"

Marius nodded and walked out of the kitchen to the stairs. Timothy followed, herding the three prisoners in front of him. Taking out his gun, Jonah got up and joined them. Smitty, who was conscious but still dazed, flinched as Jonah came near him. They climbed the stairs, and Marius opened a door at the end of the hall.

Jonah looked inside. This was where they had held Addie prisoner. Two days of her life had been spent in this little room. He raised his arm and shoved Smitty inside with such force that he fell sprawling on the floor. The other two men hurried after him.

"Enjoy your stay, compliments of Addie," Jonah said, as he slammed and bolted the door.

"Now they're the captives in there," Marius said.

"Yeah, it's ironic." Jonah stared, fascinated by Marius. It was incredible. He was talking to a machine. "Good idea you had."

Marius nodded, and the three went downstairs to join the others. Salazar seemed calmer now. He rested his arms on the table and Marius settled into a chair beside him.

"Marius, I think you'd better take Dr. Salazar to his room now," Walter said. "Wait with him until we call you." The two rose and left the kitchen.

"Well," Walter said to Jonah and Timothy, "We might as well try to relax. There's nothing we can do now, but wait—just wait for Andrew Granit to get here."

Chapter Thirty-Three

A ndrew Granit looked at his watch and shook his head. Almost 6:00. He turned to Emilio, who was hunched over the wheel beside him.

"You're crawling," he snapped.

"I'm going ten miles over the limit," Emilio said.

Granit tightened his lips and stared at the road ahead. Addie's escape made the timing more urgent. They had to get back to Washington tonight. He fingered the tickets in his pocket: three seats on a plane out of Farmington at 10:30. He'd just have time to collect Salazar and Marius and head for the airport.

He thought of Addie and frowned. If she had found shelter in one of the few houses in the area, his men would have unearthed her by now. They were masters of intimidation. Anyone foolish enough to hide her would have been bullied into giving her up.

No, she must have headed for the mountains. Probably wandering around now, lost and frightened. If his men didn't find her, a mountain lion or coyote pack probably would. They'd do the job for him. He hoped whatever happened, it wouldn't be too painful.

Poor Addie. Granit's lips tightened. This mess was snow-balling out of control. For one thing, there was the matter of Sarah's eyes. Ever since that scene with Addie, whenever he closed his own eyes, he'd see Sarah's eyes. There they waited, sorrowful and reproaching, just behind his eyelids. If anything happened to Addie, they'd probably haunt him forever.

Granit shrugged. There were more important things to think about right now than Sarah's eyes. Karl Salazar, for example. The sheer idiocy of the man; to put them all in danger, to imperil all their plans, for one moment of benighted heroism. Karl would pay a dear price for that heroism, but not now. For now, Granit had to be calm and understanding. He needed to have Karl as stable as possible for the flight back to Washington.

Then there was Walter Turner, wandering around the state, playing hero. Fool. How far did he think his pitiful power base extended? Outside Washington he was nothing. Fifteen minutes after he had tried to throw his weight around the police station in Santa Fe, Granit knew all about it.

He wondered how long Turner would stay, sniffing a dead trail, especially with the president's health in danger. He'd probably be flying back to Washington today. That was exactly why Granit had decided to leave from Farmington, rather than Albuquerque. An encounter in the airport with Walter Turner did not figure in his plans.

The bumpy road jolted him back to the present. They were nearing the house. As Emilio nosed the car into the parking area, Granit looked around. Only two cars there. That meant the others were still out searching for Addie.

They walked up the path and Granit scowled as Emilio fumbled with the double lock. When he opened the door, Granit strode in and stood in the hallway, looking upstairs. A light glimmered under Salazar's door. He must be in there, waiting for him, cowering in fear. He glanced to the right and saw the kitchen door half open; a light glowed there also. Granit motioned to Emilio, and the two turned and walked into the kitchen.

Emilio gave a startled gasp. Granit stared in disbelief. Turner and Stern sat at the table looking at him, while a hulking giant jumped up and waved a menacing .45 in his face.

"Welcome back, Andrew," Turner said, rising from his seat. Stern also had a gun and he sat, chair tilted back, pointing it at Granit's head with obvious delight.

"See if they have weapons, Timothy," Walter said.

Granit tightened his lips, as the giant patted down both of them, extracting a pistol from Emilio's belt. He tossed it to Stern.

"Okay, they're clean now. Whatta you want me to do with them?"

"Take that one upstairs with the others." Walter nodded at Emilio. "I want to talk to the senator."

Emilio's eyes darted around the room, like a trapped animal looking for some way to escape. Timothy slammed his back with one huge hand, and Emilio hurried toward the stairs.

Andrew Granit stared coldly at Walter. "I don't know what you think you're doing here," he said. "You're armed and trespassing. We have laws against that in New Mexico."

"Save your breath, Andrew. We know all about what's going on here. We've got Addie back, safe and sound, and she's told us everything."

Granit felt a surge of something almost like relief. There, Sarah, he thought. Addie survived. You can stop your infernal staring.

He looked at Walter. "I can't imagine what she told you. Hysterical ravings of an unstable woman. And on the basis of that, you break into my house."

"You goddamn sonofabitch," Jonah said, gripping the table edge until his knuckles turned white. "You keep your mouth shut about Addie. First you kidnap her and then—"

"Kidnap her. Is that what she told you? She came here with me quite willingly, I assure you. Jumped at the chance to get away from *you* for a while." He sneered at Jonah. "She told me I was a damn sight better at fucking than you."

Jonah sprang at him, like a terrier attacking a greyhound, and began hammering him with his fists. Granit staggered back, but managed to get one arm around Jonah's throat and pressed down hard. Walter tried frantically to separate them as Jonah began making strangled, choking sounds.

"Break it up—break it up, goddammit," Timothy was back in the room, slamming Granit's arm with one huge fist. Cursing, Granit released Jonah and clutched his arm. Jonah stumbled and fell to his knees. Timothy put an arm under his shoulders and half lifted, half tossed him into a chair.

"Now stay put," Timothy grinned at Jonah. "Can't leave you alone for a minute, without you starting some kind of trouble."

"All right," Walter said, his voice shaking. "Let's have no more of that. Andrew—for your own sake—sit down and keep quiet."

Granit narrowed his eyes and settled into one of the chairs, resting his injured arm on the table. Jonah glared at him while Timothy positioned himself between them.

Walter sat down next to Granit and began rubbing his forehead. Granit tightened his lips and stared straight ahead. His arm throbbed, but it was a small matter, compared to the rage and frustration seething within him.

"You know, Andrew, you're in no position to go on the offensive," Walter said finally. "Dr. Salazar has agreed to cooperate with us. With his testimony—"

"His testimony! The man's a certified lunatic. He's schizophrenic, been hospitalized several times. He's on heavy medication now, has been for years. How much credibility do you think he'll have?"

"And Isaac Templeton. Do you think he'll have a credibility problem too?"

Granit stared at Walter. He couldn't have called Templeton yet. It would have given Isaac too much warning and a chance to escape from the whole mess. No, Walter would wait until he was back in Washington before he contacted Templeton, Granit was sure of that.

"I think you'll find Templeton a harder nut to crack than poor Karl," he said. "I wouldn't count on any cooperation from him."

"We'll reach him." Walter leaned forward. "I suggest you be as flexible as possible, Andrew. It'll go easier for you in the long run."

"Are you going to have me tried for treason?" Granit smiled grimly. "On whose testimony? A hysterical woman, who practices a rather dubious profession, and a known schizophrenic?"

"We have the physical evidence, remember Simon and Marius, your androids."

"I'm surprised at you, Walter. I never thought you had such an overactive imagination. There are no such things as androids. And even if there were, it would be an easy matter to dispose of them. Accidents can happen to androids too."

Granit's eyes narrowed. "I'm getting tired of this whole business. I'll give you a chance to get out now—you, and your pathetic little sidekick, and your hired goon—or I'm calling the police and having you all picked up for trespassing. I have a great deal of clout around here, you know."

Walter shook his head wearily. "All right, if you want to play hardball, so be it. Secret Service will be here tonight. They'll take care of you. But think it over. I know the president will want to handle this discreetly, and if you cooperate—"

"I've had enough of this." Granit slammed his good hand on the table, jumped up and strode to the telephone. His mind was racing. If he could just buy some time, find a way to disappear, he could spend his remaining years very comfortably in some place where extradition was an unknown word.

Before he could reach the phone, Timothy grabbed him by the shoulders and spun him around.

"Take him upstairs," Walter said.

"Okay, senator. We'll go up and join your friends now."

Timothy's hand was an iron vise on his shoulder, as he propelled him toward the stairs. When they reached the landing, the door on the right opened, and Karl Salazar peered out. Their eyes met: Granit's sharp and piercing, Salazar's wide and terrified. A message flashed between them, and a hard knot of panic that had taken root within Granit began to dissolve. The pathetic weakling would never testify against him.

They turned to the left and walked down the hall, reaching the little room where he had kept Addie captive, where he would now be transformed from jailer to prisoner. Granit shook his head in disbelief.

Timothy took out his gun and opened the door. "Inside, senator." He pushed him into the room and bolted the door behind him.

L ucky they kept a well-stocked refrigerator." Walter took a last swallow of coffee and pushed his plate away. He looked around the table at his odd assortment of dinner companions. Timothy was working on his second hero sandwich, piled high with bologna, cheese, lettuce, and tomatoes. Jonah tapped his fingers against a half empty bowl of chili as he gazed out at the hallway, his mind clearly upstairs with Andrew Granit. Karl Salazar picked at some sort of fish salad, which he washed down with little gulps of selzer. Marius sat beside him, arms folded, staring impassively ahead.

"Nothing we can do now but wait," Walter said.

He had called Janice to assure her they were safe. Addie had been sleeping, the best thing for her right now. Then he had contacted Eve Kontos to bring her up to date. Three Secret Service men were on their way, and Walter had reached them in flight to tell them what to do as soon as they landed at Albuquerque.

Walter considered giving the men upstairs some food. Then he remembered Addie and shook his head. He owed no compassion here. It wasn't worth the risk. He'd keep them safely locked up until the Secret Service arrived.

"How about some cake and coffee?" he said, turning to Salazar, who had pushed his salad aside.

"No—I'm not hungry." Salazar stared straight ahead, mumbling to himself. Then he jumped up, so suddenly that his chair fell backwards.

"No, no. This will not work, it will not work." Salazar began pacing back and forth. Marius turned and watched him.

"Everything's under control, Dr. Salazar," Walter said. "The Secret Service men should be here in a few hours. The president's chief of staff knows the whole story. By now, wheels have started turning, I guarantee it."

"No—no—you don't understand. I saw Andrew upstairs. His eyes..." Salazar shuddered. "He'll find a way out. I know it. He's a devil. And then he'll find me." He continued his frantic pacing.

"Your medication, Dr. Salazar." Marius had taken a bottle from his pocket and approached Salazar with two pills and a glass of water. Salazar swallowed them and walked to the kitchen window. The pills seemed to have a calming effect, for he stood silently, staring outside for a long time.

"How long does that last?" Jonah asked Marius.

The android shrugged. "A few hours. It depends on the degree of agitation he's experiencing."

Salazar continued to stare out the window. Finally he turned and walked over to Walter.

"I just remembered. You must see what's in the shed."

"What is it?"

"No, I have to show you. I can't describe it. It's out in back of the house."

"All right," Walter rose. "We'll be right back."

"No—no—I want everyone to see this." He pointed at Jonah and Timothy. "Everyone."

Walter looked at the others and shrugged. Salazar had grown relatively calm; it would be better to humor him.

"Okay, Dr. Salazar," Jonah said. "We'll all go out and take a look at this shed. Those creeps upstairs can't go anywhere. We don't have to babysit them."

They all trooped outside, even Marius, and followed Salazar to a small structure set far back from the house.

"Just a minute," Salazar said. "The door's locked. Marius knows where the key is hidden."

He moved to one side and spoke to the android in a voice so low no one could hear him. Marius handed him his bottle of pills, turned and began walking quickly toward the house. Walter looked after him, puzzled. Why had Marius given Salazar the pills? Suddenly the knowledge slammed into him like a blow to the gut. Marius was not coming back.

"My God—no," he shouted to Salazar. "Stop him."

Salazar shook his head. "It's too late."

"I'll stop him myself." Walter began running after Marius.

"You can't do anything. You'll just get killed. Come back— come back—somebody make him come back."

Timothy had already started after Walter. He caught up with him just before the door and locked his arms around him in a tight embrace. Walter struggled feebly, then allowed himself to be dragged back to the others in front of the shed. They all watched Marius disappear inside the house.

A ndrew Granit heard the footsteps in the hall. Walter was probably sending food up to them—softhearted fool. It would probably be that giant and Marius, and maybe Stern, come along to gloat. Their hands would be busy with trays. If they took them by surprise, they might overpower them.

He motioned to the three men to position themselves near the door.

The door opened and Marius stood there, alone. The android looked around the room, as though counting heads. He nodded slowly. Granit froze in terror as Marius pressed his fingertips into his wrist.

In the moment before the explosion shattered the room and engulfed the house in flames, Andrew Granit's mind filled with a single thought: he would never live to see Robbie become a man.

CHAPTER THIRTY-FOUR

Simon Furst's body lay in state in the Capitol Rotunda. The line that had been forming since early morning to view the body stretched down the Capitol steps and around the outside of the building. The June sun blazed brightly in contrast to the pall that had settled over Washington at the news of the vice president's fatal heart attack.

Addie walked past the line, made up mostly of women clutching little wads of tissue. She was meeting Jonah, Walter, and Janice to view the body. She presented her pass at the door of the VIP room and looked around for them. She was first. Two men in pin-striped suits and a woman in a burgundy dress more suitable for a cocktail party glanced at her and looked away. Obviously she was no one worth noticing. They would never know the part she had played in bringing Simon Furst to this place in the Rotunda.

Addie found a seat in an inconspicuous corner. Her thoughts flashed back to that moment, close to midnight, when Walter and Jonah had returned from the house in Las Trampas. She pictured their faces as they described Andrew Granit's last moments. Addie shivered. It was hard to imagine Andrew dead. He had occupied her thoughts for so long and had loomed so large in her life.

Early the next morning a helicopter took them to the airport in Albuquerque. A private supersonic jet was waiting for them, and Secret Service men rushed them aboard. Karl Salazar held onto Addie's hand throughout the ninety-five-minute flight. He was taken directly from the plane to a private sanitarium, where he would receive the best psychiatric care.

When they landed in Washington, they learned that Isaac Templeton had already been taken into custody. That same day Walter and Eve Kontos met with him. Templeton broke down immediately. In exchange for a ten-year jail sentence and no public trial, he agreed to turn over all his notes to the Secret Service, deactivate Simon Furst, and sign his death certificate.

The president had returned to the White House under tight medical supervision and had already picked up the reins of government. He had given up alcohol after his close brush with death. Addie thought about Neptune and Saturn, how favorably they would be aspecting the president's chart in the near future. His new sobriety might well prove lasting.

Under the twenty-fifth amendment, Henry Wycliff was now free to choose a proper vice president. After the twin shocks of the presidential plane crash and Simon Furst's death, Congress could be counted on to give his candidate the majority vote necessary for confirmation.

Addie looked around. Some of the women in the VIP room were dabbing at their eyes. If they only knew they were lavishing their grief on a machine. Addie thought of Marius. Gone with Andrew and the others. Marius had helped save her life. He was only a machine, but still—

"Addie—you look a million miles away."

Janice stood before her, smiling. She lit up the room in a creamy linen shift, gathered at the waist by a jeweled belt. Her chestnut curls shimmered around her face. She pulled over a chair and sat down.

Addie smoothed her own hair. "I wonder where Jonah is. He told me he's always early." She laughed. "He's such an Aries."

"My better half's over there with a prospective client," Janice said, pointing to a corner where Walter stood, talking to a ruddy-faced man who kept nodding his head.

"Walter's concentrating on building up his practice now that he's decided to get out of politics. He told the president last night. Once the new vice president's confirmed, he's out—for good." She leaned back and sighed with satisfaction.

"Wonderful, Janice. I know that's what you want."

"More than anything. I hope we never set foot in the White House again."

Addie frowned. "I wish I could say the same. Look at what I got by messenger this morning." She fumbled in her purse and pulled out a square white card with gold lettering and the first lady's distinctive monogram in the corner.

Janice grabbed it out of her hand. "It's an invitation to high tea with Ellen at the White House. I am impressed. No one gets that, except movie stars, astronauts, and the Pope."

"Then why me?"

"I guess it's Ellen's way of saying she's sorry. That she appreciates what you've done and wants to thank you. It's a social coup, Addie. Most of Washington would sell their souls for one of those."

"Well, I wouldn't. I guess I have to go though. You'll tell me what to wear won't you? I don't want to—"

"Sorry I'm late." Jonah rushed over to them. "I had to stop at the White House." He leaned over, kissed Addie, and hugged Janice.

Janice jumped up. "Let's go collect Walter. He made a reservation for the four of us at Giorgio's for lunch. But first we have to view Simon's remains. I wouldn't miss that for the world."

Walter showed his pass to the guard outside the great bronze door, and they were ushered into the huge Rotunda. A woman frowned as she moved back to let them into the line.

The vice president's body lay in a half-open casket of gleaming mahogany lined with white velvet. Overhead spotlights illuminated the coffin. A blanket of red, white, and blue carnations was draped over the casket, and baskets of lilies, roses, and chrysanthemums filled the space around it. Simon Furst's head rested on a white velvet pillow. His hands lay folded on his chest. In repose, his features seemed more perfect then ever.

The line moved slowly around the black velvet rope, separating the viewers from the coffin. Muffled sobs and sighs echoed through the Rotunda.

"Never saw Simon look so good," Jonah whispered to Janice. "Almost intelligent. Kinda deep."

Janice nudged him "Stop or you'll make me laugh. You're not supposed to laugh at a wake."

"This isn't a wake," Jonah said. "It's mass hysteria. Look at all these people, weeping over an android."

Addie watched Walter, who kept his lips pressed tightly together as they circled the coffin. What did he feel, as he viewed the remains of Andrew Granit's puppet? She wondered what the people in the line would do, if they knew they were viewing a broken machine. The president and Eve Kontos had been right to insist on secrecy. It was the only way to handle it.

They moved slowly around the casket and neared the exit of the Rotunda. Addie turned for a last look at the coffin. For a moment Simon Furst's face vanished, replaced by Andrew Granit's craggy features. Addie closed her eyes. Andrew's body had been destroyed by the fire, but a part of his soul would lie buried forever with the android.

They stopped for a moment at the top of the Capitol steps, each lost in his own thoughts. Jonah broke the silence.

"I've got big news and I can't hold it in a minute longer. I guess Walter knows already."

Walter nodded. "I've got champagne waiting for us at the restaurant to celebrate."

"Celebrate what?" Addie asked.

Jonah grinned. "I just found out today when I was at the White House. You're standing next to President Wycliff's new press secretary."

"Oh Jonah, that's wonderful." Addie threw her arms around him and kissed him.

"I'll have to get a promotion every week, if it gets that kind of response," Jonah said. "You know, I'm an important guy with a lot of responsibilities now. Too much for me to handle alone. We're gonna have to do some serious talking about that tonight."

Addie gazed into his eyes. "What about that fear of forever?"

He turned and looked at the buildings in the distance and then back at Addie. "From where I'm standing, forever looks pretty good. I'll take my chances with it."

Janice walked over and hugged them both. "I've got a feeling we're going to be celebrating more than Jonah's new job today."

Jonah grinned. "Janice, if it hadn't been for you—"

"I know," she said. "And here's something else to celebrate. I just started blocking out a new novel in my mind. I never discuss my books till they're finished—it's the only thing I ever keep to myself. Walter will tell you that. But I need your opinion." She looked at Addie. "Especially yours. I've just come up with a working title and I have to know if you approve. I'm calling it *The President's Astrologer*."

Addie's eyes shone as she clasped Jonah's hand tightly. "Better make it a big book," she said. "That story is just beginning."

THE END

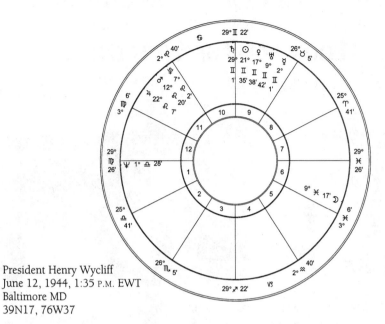

President Henry Wycliff
June 12, 1944, 1:35 P.M. EWT
Baltimore MD
39N17, 76W37

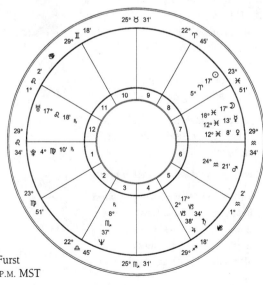

Vice President Simon Furst
March 25, 1960, 3:23 P.M. MST
Santa Fe, NM
35N41, 105W57

COMPUTERIZED ASTROLOGICAL SERVICES

Personality Profile Horoscope

Jargon-free and loaded with insight, this is our most popular reading! Based on the interpretation of your birth chart, this ten-part reading offers a complete look at how the planets help shape who you are and what you do. Learn about your inner self and your outer image. Discover your career strengths and emotional needs. Very reasonable price, too!

Personality Profile Horoscope APS03-503   **$20.00**

Transit Forecasts

Love, money, health—everybody wants to know what lies ahead, and these reports will keep you one-up on your future. Transit Forecasts can be an invaluable aid for seizing opportunities and timing your moves. Reports begin the first day of the month you specify.

3-month Transit Forecast APS03-500   **$12.00**
6-month Transit Forecast APS03-501   **$20.00**
1-year Transit Forecast APS03-502   **$30.00**

Compatibility Profile

Find out if you are really compatible with your lover, spouse, friend, or business partner! This is a great way of getting an in-depth look at your relationship with another person. Find out each person's approach to the relationship. Do you have the same goals and values? How well do you deal with arguments? This service includes planetary placements for both people, so send birth data for both and specify the type of relationship (i.e., friends, lovers, etc.). Order today!

Compatibility Profile APS03-504   **$30.00**

Ultimate Astro-Profile

This report has it all! The Ultimate Astro-Profile is like a consultation with a professional astrologer, but it costs so much less. Receive over 40 pages of fascinating, insightful descriptions of your personal qualities and talents. Explore your inner self, your desires and challenges, and your place in the world. Read about your "burn rate" (thirst for change). Examine the things that make you stand out. The Astro-Profile doesn't repeat what you've already learned from other personality profiles, but delves much deeper into your birth chart to deliver the most complete picture of YOU astrology has to offer!

Ultimate Astro-Profile APS03-505   **$40.00**

To Order, Call 1–800–THE–MOON
Prices subject to change without notice

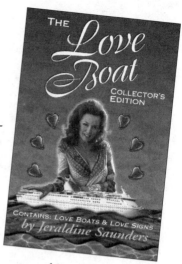

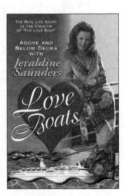